learning
the world

learning the world

a novel of first contact

ken macleod

orbit

www.orbitbooks.co.uk

ORBIT

First published in Great Britain in August 2005 by Orbit

A CIP catalogue record for this book is available from the British
Library.

ISBN 1 84149 343 0

Typeset in Garamond by M Rules
Printed and bound in Great Britain by
Mackays of Chatham plc

Orbit
An imprint of
Time Warner Book Group UK
Brettenham House
Lancaster Place
London WC2E 7EN

www.orbitbooks.co.uk

To James, Jess and Eilidh

acknowledgements

Special thanks are due to Carol for giving flight to my characters; to Charles Stross for handwaving their limbs; to Farah Mendlesohn for helpful comments at various stages of the draft; and to Del Cotter for sending me a paper about world ships.

Some of the ideas and images were inspired by *The Millennial Project*, by Marshall T. Savage, and *Reason in Revolt*, by Ted Grant and Alan Woods.

epigraph

Population will mightily increase, and the earth will be a garden. Governments will be conducted with the quietude and regularity of club committees. The interest which is now felt in politics will be transferred to science; the latest news from the laboratory of the chemist, or the observatory of the astronomer, or the experimenting room of the biologist will be eagerly discussed . . . Disease will be extirpated; the causes of decay will be removed; immortality will be invented. And then, the earth being small, mankind will migrate into space, and will cross the airless Saharas which separate planet from planet, and sun from sun. The earth will become a Holy Land which will be visited by pilgrims from all the quarters of the universe. Finally, men will master the forces of Nature; they will become themselves architects of systems, manufacturers of worlds.

Winwood Reade, *The Martyrdom of Man*, 1872

A note on translation: for convenience, some numbers used by characters who count in an octal system have occasionally been rendered in decimal. Terms derived from a dead scholarly language are rendered as if from Latin. There is an explanation for this.

contents

ONE

THE SHIP GENERATION

LEARNING THE WORLD

14 364:05:12 17:24

The world is four thousand years old. I was eight years old when I found that out for myself. My name is Atomic Discourse Gale and this is the first time I have written something that anyone in the world can read. It is strange and makes me feel a little self-conscious, but I reassure myself that not many people will read it anyway.

14 364:05:13 18:30

That was a joke. I see I have a few readers. J—— wants to know how I found out the age of the world. It was six years ago now but I remember it quite well. I was very young then and didn't under-stand everything that happened, but looking back I can see that it was a significant event in my life. That is why I mentioned it. So this is what happened.

*

'How old is the world?' I asked my care-mother.

'I don't know,' she said. 'Why don't you look it up?'

'I've looked it up,' I said. 'I don't believe it.'

'Why not?'

'Seventeen billion years?' I said. 'That's impossible.'

'Ah,' she said. 'That's the universe. Well . . . everything we can see. The stars and galaxies.'

I went off and formed a more careful query. Nothing came back. I returned to my care-mother.

'This world,' I said. 'I can't find anything about that.'

'All right,' she said. She pointed up to the sky. 'See up there . . . where the sunline enters the wall? Inside there, in the forward cone, you'll find what is called the keel.'

'Like the bottom of a boat?'

'In a way, yes. It's really the base of the engine, and it's the first part of the ship to be put in place. You will find the date of the final assembly there. And from that you can work out the age of the world.'

'You don't know what it is?'

'No,' she said. She frowned, in the way adults have when they're searching. 'It isn't in memory.'

'All right,' I said. 'I'll go and have a look.'

'Good for you,' she said. 'I'll help you pack.'

So thirty minutes later I hitched my little rucksack, heavy with a litre of water and a kilo of sandwiches, on to my shoulders and set off to climb into the sky. I walked out of the estate and after a while I found a ladder at the edge of a dense and ancient clump of trees. The ladder had been familiar to me since I was much smaller, but none of us had ever climbed more than a few score steps on it. It soared into the sky like a kite-string, the kinks of its zig-zag flights smoothing into a pale line and then disappearing. You couldn't easily fall off it – it had close-spaced rings around it, and every thirty metres or so there was a small platform and another flight. The first day I climbed a kilometre, found a big platform, ate my sandwiches and drank my water, and pissed in a far corner like an untrained kitten. I sat and watched the shadow-line creep across the land towards me. It reached me in what seemed a final rush, and the sunline turned black. The land below was dim and beautiful in the farlight from the other side of the world, and within minutes lights pricked on all across that shaded scene. After a while I curled up and went to sleep. When I woke the sun-line was bright again. It seemed as far away as ever, and the ground a long way below. I was just thinking of setting off back down when a crow landed on the platform, carrying a package.

'Breakfast,' said the bird. 'And dinner. Your ma says hi.'

'Tell her thank you,' I said.

'Will do,' said the crow, and flew off. Crows don't have much conversation. I unwrapped the package and found, to my great delight, hot coffee and hot berrybread for breakfast, and a fresh bottle of water and another pack of sandwiches for later. As I ate my breakfast I let my clothes clean me. Normally I would have washed. The clothes did a reasonable job but made my skin feel crawly and tickly. After I had eaten I chewed a tooth-cleaner and gazed around. The estate looked tiny, and I could see a whole sweep of other estates and towns, lakes and hills and plains, along and around. I was almost level with the tops of the slag-heaps piled against the forward wall. Between me and the sunline a few clouds drifted: far away, I could see rain falling from one, on to a town. It was strange to see rain from the outside, as a distinct thing rather than a condition. More interesting was to see aircraft flying high above me, and a few below, taking off or landing. I faced resolutely upward, and continued my climb.

Of course I did not climb all the way. I was a tough and deter-mined person, but it would have taken a month even if the ladder had extended all the way there, which it did not. What happened, about halfway through my second day, was that a small aircraft landed on a large platform a few hundred metres above me, and when I reached it, a man stood waiting for me. He even reached over and took my hand and hauled me up the last few steps, which I thought was unnecessary, but I made no objection.

He then backed away and we looked at each other for a few seconds. He was wearing a loose black suit, and his skin was not a lot lighter. His features might have been carved out of mahogany, with deep lines scored in it around the eyes and mouth.

'My name is Constantine the Oldest Man,' he said.

The name meant nothing to me but seemed suitable.

'Mine is Atomic Discourse Gale,' I said, sitting down on the platform.

'I know,' he said. 'Your care-mother asked me to meet you.' He jerked his head back, indicating the aeroplane. 'I can take you to the keel, if you like.'

I had been determined to reach the keel myself; but I saw the man and the aircraft as part of my adventure, and therefore within my resolution rather than as a weakening or dilution of it. Besides, I now had a much better idea of how long it would take to climb all the way.

'All right,' I said. 'Thank you.'

He stepped over and peered into my eyes. I noticed a tiny shake of his head, as if something that might have been in my eyes wasn't there (a nictitating membrane, I now realise). He led me over to the aircraft, motioned me to sit in the front and lower seat, showed me how to strap up and passed me a set of wraparounds, transparent and tinted. I slipped them on. He climbed in behind me and started the engine. The propeller was behind us both, the wing above. After the engine had built up some power the little machine shook and quivered, then shot to the edge of the platform and dropped off. I may have squealed. It dipped, then soared. My stomach felt tugged about. Wind rushed past my face. The collar of my jacket crept up over the top and sides of my head, and stiffened. I hadn't known it had that capability.

We flew in an irregular spiral, perhaps to avoid stair-ladders and other obstacles invisible to me, but always up. I looked down, at the ground. I could see houses and vehicles, but not people. Other small aircraft buzzed about the sky, at what seemed frighteningly short clearances. The air felt thinner as we climbed. As we levelled out I could feel the sunline hot on my shoulders, bright out of the corners of my eyes. Ahead loomed the forward wall. Featureless from the distances at which I had always seen it, it now looked complex, with gigantic pipes snaking across it and great clusters of machinery clamped to it. Wheels turned and pistons and elevators moved up and down. Rectangular black slots became visible, here and there on the surface, and we flew towards one. As naively as I'd thought I could climb to the sunline, I'd imagined we would fly to it, but we flew into the slot – it was two hundred metres wide by at least thirty high – and landed. Other small aircraft were parked in the artificial cavern. It was in fact a hangar. Constantine helped me out of the seat. My memory may be playing tricks, but I fancy I felt slightly lighter.

'I thought we were going to fly all the way,' I said, trying not to sound querulous.

'The air doesn't go all the way to the sunline,' Constantine told me. 'So we will take the lift.'

I followed him across the broad floor to an inconspicuous door. Behind it was an empty lift, big enough to hold about a dozen people. Its walls were transparent, giving a view of a dark chasm within which gigantic shapes moved vertically, illuminated by occasional random lights. The doors hissed shut and the lift began to ascend. So rapid was its acceleration that my knees buckled. Constantine grasped my shoulder.

'Steady,' he said. 'It doesn't get worse than carrying someone piggy-back.'

Vaguely affronted, I straightened up and stared out. Looking down made me dizzy, so I looked up. The space in which we moved was in fact quite shallow in relation to its size. We were headed for a bright spot above, which I knew to be some manifestation of the sunline. The lift decelerated far more gradually and gently than it had accelerated. As it did so, I found that I was becoming lighter. An experimental downward thrust of the toes sent me a metre into the air. I yelled out, startled and delighted, as I fell back.

Constantine laughed. 'Hold the bar,' he said.

The lift halted, as if hesitating, then shot upward again. We passed through a hatch or hole. For a moment I was pressed against the wall of the lift, then I found myself weightless. Constantine glided over my head, twisting and somersaulting at the same time. I let go of the bar, flailing. The sensation of falling was for a moment terrifying. My stomach heaved, then settled.

'It's all right,' he said. 'We're in the forward cone now.' The teeth of his smile were a vivid white. He caught my elbow and swung me on to his back. I gripped fistfuls of fabric at his shoulders and clung. He grinned sideways at me and kicked off. The door of the lift hissed open. My eardrums clicked. We skimmed above the floor of a long tube. Shafts of light stabbed down from small holes or windows above us; my eyes adjusted quickly to the dimness, not darker, in truth, than indoor lighting. About three metres high by two wide, the tube ran straight into the distance as far as I could see. Within it, as we moved along, I noticed many other corridors branching off. Constantine's foot flicked at a wall and we hurtled into one of these side corridors. There was a smell of earth and ozone, of plant and animal and machine. Rapidly and bewilderingly, we passed through a succession of corridors and chambers, within which I glimpsed machinery and instruments, gardens hanging in mid-air, glowing lights and optical cables, and many people flying or floating or scuttling like monkeys along tubes or flimsy ladders. And what strange people they were, long of limb and lithe of muscle and wild of hair. Naked as the day they were born, lots of them; or looking similar, but in bright-coloured skin-tight suits; others crusted with stiff sculptured garments, like the camouflage of a leaf insect, or swathed in silky balloon sleeves and pants. Their indifference to orientation was for me disorienting; looking at their antics I felt a resurgence of unease in my belly.

I closed my eyes, and when I opened them again we had reached our destination. We floated near the floor of the biggest enclosed space I'd ever been in, apart from the world itself. The floor was smooth, and extended far ahead of us, and curved up on either hand like a smaller version of the curve of the world. Up and down had in a manner been restored. The thing that I craned my neck to look at, from my vantage on Constantine's back, was unmistakably *up*. Above us it vanished into shadows, ahead it stretched and tapered into distance. A thousand or more metres long, hundreds of metres high, it was complex, flanged, fluted and voluted, yet seemed cast from a single block of metal, ancient and pitted as an iron asteroid. There was one piece of metal, however, that shone bright and distinct from the rest: a metre-long rectangle of burnished brass, on which some writing was engraved. We hung in the still, rust-scented air not an arm's length from it. The inscription was as follows:

> *Sunliner* But the Sky, My Lady! The Sky! *Forged this day 6 February 10 358 AG*

Constantine reached around and disengaged me from his back. We drifted for a few minutes, hand in hand.

'I never knew the world had a name,' I said.

'I named it,' said Constantine.

'Why did you call it that?' I asked.

He swung me and caught my other hand, like a dancer, and once again gazed into my face as if looking for something.

'You'll know one day,' he said.

I know now.

Horrocks Mathematical blinked away the girl's biolog. It seemed that like all of the ship generation she was maturing on schedule. He himself had gone through adolescence, five or six years ago now, without any such epiphany. The Mathematicals were tenth-generation crew and Horrocks had never had to suffer a grounded upbringing. Although born in the ship he did not consider himself or his cohort part of the ship generation. They were among the youngest members of the crew, that was all. Through the foliage of the air-tree and the skin of the bubble in which he floated he could see the land twenty-five kilometres below: its parks and copses, rivers and lakes, estates and towns an ideal of savannah and suburbia that was said to be a hard-wired part of the human evolutionary heritage, though only manifested among flatfooters. As a free-flyer, Horrocks felt that his was a more evolved biophilia.

The air-tree, growing from a hydroponic tank, its branches grafted to form an open wickerwork sphere, was about fifty metres in diameter and five years older than he was. Horrocks pushed through the lianas that criss-crossed its interior and thrust himself out into the greater confinement of the bubble. He had work to do. The bubble was one of scores strung on a circular cable around the sunline like beads on a bangle. The cable contra-rotated the ground, putting the bubbles in an approximation of free fall. Only the slight intermittent backward tug of the small jets that countered the effect of the ship's deceleration broke the spell, but that was all they broke.

On the other side of the bubble, making a rocky counterpart to the air-tree, hung a tethered lump of asteroid clinker about a hundred metres across. A thrust of his feet took Horrocks towards it. As he drifted he tugged on his cuffs. The fabric slid over his hands and fingers, to form tough gloves by the time he impacted the rock's side. He worked his way over and around the rock, checking each of the scores of machines he'd spent the past few days bolting to its surface. They jutted out a metre or so; their display and control panels – some of them simple touch-screens, others elaborate but rugged arrangements of knobs, push-buttons and dials, and a few remote brain interfaces – were already filmed or crusted with dust. All in order, however. The tenebrific shade had passed over him many times, and half the morning had passed, before he was satisfied with that.

Ready for the kids to play with. Horrocks tweaked a final bolt and took a deep breath. He pulled his collar up over his head and down over his face until it sealed under his chin, and launched himself towards the bubble's airlock. The scooter on the other side of it took him, on a spiralling trajectory that would have dizzied and sickened a flatfooter, around and along the sunline to the airlock of the forward wall. Once inside, he pulled his hood off his face, gasped a couple of times, and relaxed into his own world, the world of the forward cone.

Immediately the corner of his eye filled with messages. It was not that they were unavailable outside, but that they were easier to ignore. He blinked through them rapidly, discarding most as routine. One from his friend Awlin Halegap, a speculator, urged him to check one of the latest observations of the new system into which the ship was decelerating.

Horrocks smiled – Awlin's speculations were often indeed speculative, and had already cost Horrocks and other acquaintances almost as much credit as they had profited them in the last couple of years – but tuned in to the list anyway. Most of the observations were of the first tranche of asteroids detected, and of the moons of the ringed gas giant and the waterworld that were the most prominent bodies in the system, and a few of the planets. The one Awlin had tagged was of the least immediately usable of the planets: the habitable-zone terrestrial. When he expanded the data he could see nothing of note; its amount and resolution, from a distance of several light-hours, were sparse. He made contact with Awlin.

'What's the big deal?' Horrocks asked.

'Lightning spikes,' replied Awlin.

'Thank you,' said Horrocks. He concentrated on the section of the data on the relevant portion of the electromagnetic spectrum. There it was: a recurring surge of activity that suggested an agitated atmosphere, in which a great deal of interesting stuff was going on. Research claims on the planet were sure to become a lucrative proposition. So Awlin thought, at any rate.

Horrocks considered it for a moment, then patched to his broker and unloaded a hundred in waterworld phytochemicals for a thousand in terrestrials: blue-sky investments. As he worked his way through the capillaries of corridor to the main hollows he checked their progress by the minute. Their rating barely twitched. He sent a copy of the flat wavy line to Awlin, with a querying tic.

'See?' Awlin flashed back. 'You got in ahead of the rush!'

Horrocks tried for a moment to compose a thinkable reply, gave up, and zapped a rude burst of static to the speculator. He hesitated over dropping the terrestrials, looking hard at his portfolio. His claims in mercurials – the tiny planet near the sun might some day be a power-beam construction site – were sound and edging upward. Bids were coming in for time on the training habitat he'd just completed. He could afford to gamble. He kept the claims.

TWO

AERONAUTICAL RESEARCH

Darvin placed his chin on the strap in front of him, and slid his feet into the stirrups behind him. The other straps of the harness pressed across his hips and the lower part of his ribcage. Ropes from all of them converged to a hook in the ceiling. The concrete floor was not far beneath him, but in this position it could be nothing but too close. He forced himself to look straight ahead at the blank concrete wall. The bright lights hurt his eyes. The glare was increased by reflection from the white paper sheets criss-crossed with black ribbon tapes tacked to the wall on his right.

'Comfortable?' Orro asked, from off to his left.

'No!'

'Too bad. Oh well.' The Gevorkian made some minute adjustment to the tripod-mounted kinematographic apparatus over which he stooped. Apparently satisfied, he looked up with an encouraging grin and a thumbs-up. His other thumb was poised over the motor switch.

'Ready?'

Darvin stretched out his wings and folded back his ears.

'Yes.'

Thumbs went down, the switch clicked, clockwork whirred.

'Flap!' shouted Orro.

Darvin beat his wings up and down, imagining himself in level flight, facing into an imagined slipstream.

'Flap harder!'

Darvin realised he'd been subconsciously afraid of his wingtips hitting the floor. They were in fact well clear. He flapped harder, almost rising out of the harness, until a much faster flapping sound told him the reel of film had run out.

'All right, stop,' said Orro. He dismounted the film from the camera, placed it in a round flat can and labelled it before stalking over to help Darvin out of the harness. Orro's toe-claws, as usual overgrown, made scratching sounds on the floor that set Darvin's teeth on edge.

'How did it look?' asked Darvin, folding his wings behind his elbows and flexing his hands.

'A start,' said Orro. 'I can't say it looked terribly realistic, but at least I got half a minute of wingbeats. We may have to try something else.'

Darvin glanced sidelong at the harness. 'As you say,' he said, 'a start.'

He walked out of the test area and into the main part of the lab. The walls, in between shelving, were almost covered with tacked-up pieces of paper scrawled with calculations or sketches of several failed designs. The long table was cluttered with hand tools, among the crumpled wings, smashed noses and cannibalised engines of at least a dozen crashed model chiropters. The smells of wood-glue and solder hung over it like a miasma. In a corner lay the engine nacelle of a dirigible. The propeller was as wide as a human wingspan. Gods knew from where Orro had scrounged that piece of expensive junk. A fugitive thought stirred in Darvin's mind as he gazed at it. Then the insight, whatever it had been, was gone. He shook his head. No doubt it would come back. He had a vague disquiet at the prospect.

'When do I see the result?' he asked.

Orro straightened, thrusting the can into his belt satchel. 'Tomorrow,' he said. 'If I take it straight to the development lab.'

'Oh,' said Darvin. He had forgotten that part of the kinematographic process. 'All right. Give me a bell when you get it back.'

'Of course,' said Orro. His face brightened. 'It is just a start, but it's a *historic* start.'

'I wouldn't want to miss it,' Darvin said, as they left the lab. Orro locked the door. The frosted wired glass bore, in barbed Gevorkian script, the legend: *Department of Aeronautical Research. KEEP OUT*. There was no Department of Aeronautical Research, and Orro had not known that Gevorkian script was, in the cartoons and playbills of Seloh's Reach, a conventional signifier of the at once scientific and sinister. Probably, Darvin reflected, he still didn't. The exile physicist still affected surprise at encountering journals and discourses written in Selohic.

At the end of the corridor the two scientists paused at the ledge.

'See you tomorrow, then,' said Darvin.

Orro nodded. 'Or tonight, perhaps.'

'Perhaps,' said Darvin, with mild surprise. No doubt the usually sombre Gevorkian felt he had something to celebrate. 'After you,' he added.

Orro nodded again and stepped to the edge. He raised his arms and unfolded his wings and dived forward, swooping away down about a hundred feet and banking around and back in to the lower floor where the technical labs were located. Darvin sprang harder from the ledge and with vigorous downbeats lifted himself higher, riding the Physics Building's updraught and soaring over the Modern Languages Tower, on whose flat roof idle students sunned themselves or groomed each other. He climbed higher; the mid-afternoon air was static and hot, caught between the sea and the mountains, from which the morning and evening breezes respectively came. Over the town it was trapped between the beach and the cliffs. Darvin ascended a few hundred feet to clifftop height, catching a cooler current as he gazed across miles of yellow grassland to the deeper ochre of the higher cliffs that marked the broader table-land of the interior. Pylons bearing transport and telephone cables marched across that distance like a single file of giants. Prey herds grazed the grass, great patches of dark like the shadows of absent clouds, clustered around the waterways that meandered across the plain to tumble into the five ravines which gave the town its name.

He wheeled. The blue of the Broad Channel refreshed his sight as much as the high air cooled his skin. Sullied by steamship smoke, spotted by the black of sails, the Channel was still an immense and soothing body of water which even at this height went clear to the horizon. Darvin wondered whether Orro ever climbed high enough – thousands of feet – to see all the way across it to the Realm of Gevork. It struck him as unlikely. Nostalgia, to the best of Darvin's knowledge, was not among his colleague's pains. Glancing upward, to that fancied height, Darvin noted the dark speck of a dirigible of Seloh's Flight, patient in its patrol. An obscure sense that he had trespassed troubled him. It was not a feeling he associated with or wished to have in the sky. He dropped.

From the top of his downward spiral, Five Ravines looked like a freak regular woodland, a vast elaboration of an abandoned enclosure on the grasslands where trees sprouted because their saplings could not be cropped by the prey. Trees lined its streets and filled its parks and gardens: fruit trees for the most part, not so much from deliberate planting as from seeds spat or (in ruder times) shat by people on the wing. Trudges hauled carts along the streets, here and there making way for the noisy, fuming motor-vehicles. The town was divided by the watercourses of the rivers from the ravines, united by its roads and bridges and sky-wires. The ravines converged, the streams diverged; from a sufficient height they showed a pattern like outspread wings. Expensive roosting and offices covered the verdant cliffs of the ravines; cheaper and more recent buildings crowded the riversides to the shore, like wooden gulleys. Among such were the university's faculties and departments; its charter, centuries old, was younger by far than that of the borough.

Darvin's own office was in the Faculty of Impractical Sciences, whose five-floor wooden building was little different from the town roosts on either side of it. Darvin skimmed the topmost branches of one of the street's trees and swooped to the fourth-floor landing platform signboarded: *University of Five Ravines. Department of Astronomy.* Sweating and panting from his exertions and the renewed heat, he strolled to the entranceway's array of wicker baskets and checked his post. A broad and thick package awaited him. He hefted it with satisfaction as he hurried to his room. An eight-nights' worth of photographic plates, dispatched from the observatory in the high desert. Each night usually afforded at least eight plates. Checking them all could take up most of his working time for eight days, and then the next set would arrive by the cable-car post, just as impatiently awaited.

A year's accumulation of such packages and their plates made up a small proportion of the clutter in his room. First things first: he set the pot over the brazier and chewed some leaf while waiting for the tea to brew. The leaf relaxed his muscles and cleared his head, and the tea took away the aftertaste. He gazed absently at the old wall poster of the solar system, given away in a special issue of a children's popular science magazine: the picture that had first inflamed his interest in astronomy.

On the left of the picture was the Sun Himself, the smiling king. A little to His right was the Fiery Jester, so close to the Sun that a solar prominence sometimes smacked him about the head. Then, after a gap, was Ground, the Mother, with Her attendant maids, the two moons. But though Ground was without doubt humanity's Mother, who fed Her children with the milk of Her waters and with a rich variety of fruit and prey, She was not (except in some backward heathen mythologies) the Sun's consort. She was, it was sometimes speculated, His daughter, or (more daringly, in the racy poems of the Dawn age) His illicit lover. It was the third planet, more than twice as far from the Sun as Ground, that was the undisputed Queen of Heaven. Even on the diagram, which was – as the inevitable small-print caption cautioned – Not To Scale, the Queen's diameter was three times that of Ground, and this was no exaggeration. In real life Her blue-green light far outshone anything in the night sky. In the past five centuries telescopic inspection had revealed that the planet was blue with green patches which had at first been thought to be continents, but whose shifting coast-lines and relative positions made more likely to be floating mats of vegetation. By imaginative analogy with floating islands, on which entire complex ecosystems could build up from an initial conglomeration of weeds and logs, the Queen's floating continents had been planted with jungles and populated with all manner of creeping and flying things. How many fanciful tales had been told of the strange beasts and beings of that world! It was as sad as it was certain that they were false. After the telescope had come the spectroscope, and while it had revealed that the Queen was indeed a world of water, it had indicated that the floating mats were little more than thin layers of algal scum.

Far out beyond the Queen was the Warrior. What intuition

the ancient cliff-men had had, in so naming it, neither Darvin no anyone else could guess — perhaps their eyesight had been better than those of the men of this latter day — but the telescope had confirmed that the Warrior had the appearance of being winged, and of clutching two bright weapons. Here on the diagram, this mythical representation was outlined beside the astronomical reality: a ringed gas giant, more than thirty times the diameter of the Queen, and within its ring two glinting, flinty-looking moons. Between the Queen and the Warrior marched a rag-tag army of small worlds. The largest of them, a few hundred miles across, had been discovered not long after the invention of the telescope. It had been given the name of the Exile, and it still held the title of a planet, but was now classed among the many smaller asteroids — the Camp-Followers, to give their poetic name — discovered in its wake.

What planets, if any, roamed the skies beyond the Warrior's octades-long orbital patrol was not known. Darvin had spent the past two years, and was willing to spend many more, in finding out.

He pushed aside the tea-cup, spat the wad of leaf out of the open window, and with his thumb-claw ripped open the package and eased out the contents: sheets of transparent acetate, separated by sheets of thin paper. He lifted the top sheet of acetate and held it up to the light from the window. A number and a date were written in tiny characters along the side. The plate was clear, but spattered with a mass of black dots of varying size and intensity. He turned over all the plates and their protective sheets one by one, double-checking their dates and numbers, and found them in order. Sixty-four altogether, as usual. He arranged sixteen along the side of a table, eight for the first night, eight for the second, in pairs matched by area of sky, and took the first pair to the bulky apparatus that filled a quarter of his room.

The blink comparator looked, in a bad light, like some

absurd, weighty abstract of a human form: two metal-framed translucent white platforms with a black metal crosspiece projecting from the sides like wings, their accompanying adjustment and positioning rods like forearms, and a cluster of knobs, levers and eyepieces on the top of the central pillar like assymetric features on a deformed face. Behind that face was the intelligence of the thing, a mirror that flipped the view through the eyepiece from one platform-mounted plate to the other in rapid succession, over and over. Any change in an object's position, from one night to the next, could be detected by its apparent jump. Such was the principle. In practice the job was difficult – aligning the plates so that the stars didn't all jump at once was a finicky matter, and once that was done many passes were necessary to make sure nothing – among the thousands of separate points of light in each long-exposure plate's field – had been missed. Even then Darvin could not be sure. Any world beyond the Warrior – given that perturbations in the Warrior's orbit were themselves minute and disputed – was certain to be a small one, and its proper motion tiny. So far, everything that had jumped out at him had turned out not to be that distant and hypothetical seventh planet. Eliminating known planets and asteroids should have been routine, but was not – Darvin had rediscovered several known asteroids, whose orbits had long since been calculated but whose current position no one bothered to track, and had added three new ones to the catalogue. His colleagues called them Darvin's Little Bastards.

He clipped the two plates on to their respective platforms and turned on the electric light that illuminated them from behind. The electric motor that flipped the mirror he set to its lowest speed, producing a blink rate of three per second. Then he perched on a stool and kicked off his sandals to grip a crossbar with his toes and clicked the lowest magnification of the monocular lenses into place. Peering through, he aligned the plates, by angle and by vertical and horizontal axes. Then he moved his hands to the paired knobs that shifted the view vertically and horizontally, and began in the top left-hand corner.

By the middle of the afternoon he had finished examining the fourth pair of plates. As he carried the plates back to the table he gazed out of the window, focused on infinity, and noticed the spots that danced in front of his eyes. Time to take a break. At the same moment the half-shaped thought that had struck him when he'd looked at the dirigible engine and propeller came back to his mind, fully formed.

He yelped. He laughed. 'How stupid of us not to have thought of that!' he said aloud.

Darvin wanted to share it at once. He couldn't share it with Orro; the Gevorkian physicist would be lecturing or calculating, and in neither activity would he tolerate interruption, however well intended or urgent. Oh well – Orro might turn up at the drinking den in the evening, as he'd hinted. But still, but still – Darvin couldn't wait. Suppose he were to die at this moment, suppose his heart were to fail or brain to fuse, why then the great insight would be lost to the world! It was intolerable!

With a sort of morbid solemnity, Darvin grabbed a pen and sheet of paper. He sketched out and described the notion, and clipped the note to one of the platforms on the blink comparator. Let fate do its worst now, he thought, this idea wouldn't die with him. Unless a meteor or dirigible were to crash into his office . . . he smiled at his overheated fancies. The impulse to tell someone *right now* didn't go away. He felt as if something would explode out of his chest if he didn't.

He looked at the clock on the wall, and at a timetable. He could tell Kwarive.

Darvin clambered out of the window and threw himself into the air. He flew to the Life Sciences Building and swooped

under the canopy of the Lecture Pit. A cone of light rose out of
the dark; slides illustrating the lecture were projected from
below on to the canopy. He circled outside the cone, looking
down, letting his eyes adjust. The lecturer stood in the middle,
at the bottom; above him rose twenty or so tiers of concentric
wooden rings, scattered with students hanging upside down,
wings enfolding them as though asleep, eyes in most cases
open, ears pricked. Darvin circled until he spotted Kwarive,
hanging on the fourth ring, and dropped in beside her to the
mutters and sideways shuffles of her neighbours. He clamped
his feet around the railing, swung down, grinned apologies to
left and right, and nuzzled Kwarive's shoulder through the
warm skin of her wing.

'Something to tell you,' he said. 'Really exciting.'

She smiled and shushed him. 'I'm listening,' she whispered.
'To the lecture,' she added.

Darvin pulled a disappointed face and settled to listen too.
The illustration in light above him was of a human, all limbs
outspread, matched with the smaller but similar shape of a flitter.

'. . . philosopher Dranker, in the Classical Age of Orkana,
was the first to classify humanity with the chiropterae,' the lecturer said, 'in his great work *De Vita*, which comes up to us in
regrettably fragmentary form. It was only in the Dawn Age
that Nargo, in his *Tabulae Animalia*, took the bolder step of
subsuming man and flitter within the order *Octomana* – the
eight-handed. Why was this bold?'

Because we don't have eight hands, Darvin thought, but
the question was rhetorical.

'This is why.' The slide projector rattled through a dozen or
so pictures, all of them crowded with photographs or engrav-
ings of diverse animals: trudges, various other species of flitter,
cursors, grazers, hunters, swimmers; it settled on a bright and
much-enlarged photograph of a skitter, its beady red eyes star-

ing, its bristles in mid-twitch, its hands clutching a nut and a berry and clinging to the twig on which it crouched. 'This lowly little beast is the third member of that order, and close – as we would now put it – to the ancestral form. The bifurcate distal portion of the anterior and posterior limb—'

Why, Darvin wondered, did lecturers insist on larding their language with Orkanisms?

'—and eight manipulative extremities are in fact the primitive condition, from which those of the chiropterae including ourselves are derived. In the chiropteran arm one hand and forearm has become the wing; in the foot, the two are fused, but the condition is still evident though relict, in our heel-claws. All of the land vertebrates – amphibians, reptiles and mammals – and the sea mammals and reptiles are descended from octomanal ancestors, as can be shown by comparative anatomy—'

More slides.

'—embryology, and teratology.'

'Ugh!' grunted Kwarive, as the slides illustrating the last-mentioned study flashed past.

'In conclusion then: far from being the crown of creation, as our illustrious ancestors fondly imagined, humanity is a minor offshoot of one of the most primitive of the mammalian classes. An outline of human evolution will be the subject of my next lecture, here tomorrow at noon sharp. Suggested readings are given in the handouts. Dismissed.'

With that he leapt into the air, flapped spiralling up the lecture pit, and flew out. The room filled with flapping wings and chattering voices. Darvin's overloaded proximity sense made him see red. He clung to the rail until the air was clearer, then glanced at Kwarive.

'After you,' he said. She launched and he followed her, out of the building and into the nearest of Five Ravines' many small public parks. Kwarive landed on a long bare branch of an

F/1027106

ancient tree and perched upright on it. Darvin perched beside her. They looked at each other for a moment. Kwarive groomed behind Darvin's ear. He stroked her neck, admiring as always the subtle shading of the fur, from red at the ear to pale gold below the jaw. He wanted to enfold her in his wings, but this was too public a place.

'What's your exciting news?' Kwarive asked.

Darvin told her about his experiments with Orro, and she laughed. He went on to tell her of his idea. She clapped her hands and flapped her wings.

'Brilliant!' she said. 'Using the propeller like that is very ingenious.'

'Isn't it indeed,' said Darvin. 'I can't wait to see Orro's face when I tell him.'

Orro's face did not disappoint, when Darvin told him the following morning. He'd gone round as soon as Orro had telephoned him to say that the film was ready.

'How stupid of me not to have thought of that,' Orro said. 'We'll definitely try that next. But let's have a look at the film anyway.'

Orro closed the slat blinds on the windows and started up the film projector. The jerky kinematographic record of Darvin's imitated flight made it all too clear that static flapping was not the same as flying. The film ran out and the tail end of it slapped at the wheel. Orro sighed and turned the projector off.

'So much for that,' he said, opening the blinds again, blinking. 'I'll keep it for comparison purposes, of course.' He strolled to the engine nacelle and stroked the propeller blade. 'I'll rig up something so that we can test your idea,' he went on. Abstracted, he didn't look at Darvin. 'I may be some time.'

'I'll see myself out,' said Darvin.

He wasn't offended. The Gevorkian exile could be a little socially inept sometimes – he was quite unaware, for example, of the effect his glossy black fur and striking white chest-streak had on certain female colleagues and students, and his conversation tended to the intermittent – but once you understood that no disrespect or disdain was intended you could see it as an aspect of his genius. That Orro was a genius Darvin did not doubt. The rest of the faculty and the university regarded the physicist as either a prize catch or a prize nuisance.

Orro had begun his research in Lassir, the capital city of Gevork. The son of an ironmonger, he had shown an early devotion to tinkering. Its first result had been a two-wheeled vehicle, which was of no use to anyone. Casting around for a more practical application of its ingenious pedal-and-gear-chain mechanism, he had, at the age of ten, become obsessed with heavier-than-air flight. Some bold spirit in the Lassir Academy had sponsored the lad. Orro's scholarly career had been brilliant, and he had soared up the military-scientific civil service, but the old sabreurs of the Regnal Air Force had shown no interest in his schemes for chiropters. Dirigibles and sky warriors had been good enough for their fathers and grand-fathers, and were therefore good enough for them. If the gods had meant us to build flying machines, they'd chortled, they wouldn't have given us wings. It was not that the sabreurs were hidebound: much of their military research budgets was dedicated to etheric communication. Command and control was the key to modernising warfare, they believed, but the projects in that new and fascinating area were secret.

Orro had decided to pursue his research in the freer air of Seloh; he had money from the patents of various inventions; he was a fine lecturer in his way; his pure and applied mathematics were beyond reproach; and winning a Gevorkian scientist was a matter of some prestige for a Selohic university. Five Ravines had taken him into its wings. But his persistence in his fruitless pursuit was beginning to give people pause. Aeronautical research was not likely to bring credit to the university, let alone results.

There were times, Darvin admitted to himself as he landed in the Astronomy Department, when he felt dubious about it himself; when he wondered if, perhaps, his childhood fascination with engineering tales had not warped his sense of the possible. The cheap-paper magazines of the genre were heavy on heavier-than-air (there was even a standard abbreviation for it: HTA) and illustrated with garish etchings of gigantic, multi-winged chiropters, carrying passengers across the great channels or dropping bombs on defenceless towns (usually Gevorkian) while dirigibles plunged in flames and entire squadrons of aerial sabreurs fell to deadly blizzards of flechettes.

Darvin walked into his office and made his habitual acquaintance with the leaf-wad and the tea-cup. Then, with a mixture of excitement and resignation, he set up the first pair of plates for the third and fourth nights' observations. He worked his way down and up, across and back. He reached the centre of the plate.

Something jumped. Back and forth, back and forth.

Darvin swallowed his thrill. He leaned back and reached for the well-thumbed ephemeris. It fell open at almost the right page; the region of sky covered by these plates was one of the most thoroughly mapped and examined, containing as it did the most conspicuous constellation of the green-tinged stars known as the Queen of Heaven's Daughters. He ran a finger-claw down columns and along rows of numbers. He checked equations, the data becoming orbits in his mind as he laboured through the calculations. When he'd satisfied himself that the moving speck was not a known planet or asteroid, he rotated higher-magnification lenses into place on the two objectives, and re-applied his eye to the eyepiece.

At ten times higher magnification the speck was a definite streak, though mere hair's-breadths across. The object must be moving quite fast, to show up thus on even a long-exposure photograph. This time it was disappointment that Darvin swallowed. Whatever it was, it wasn't a hitherto undetected outer planet. Nor an asteroid: it was too fast for that, too.

A comet? That might at least make up for the disappointment. Darvin's Comet! It would do him no harm for his name to be blazoned on the skies. He indulged the fantasy for a moment. Then he shook it off, stood up and removed the plates, and carefully fitted the plates for the same region for the next two nights, the fifth and sixth. He focused on the centre of the field. Nothing moved.

His held breath escaped, his finger-claws dug into his palms. His shoulders slumped, his folded wings drooped. A flaw in the photograph, that was all. A flaw. Or maybe . . .

Moving by intuition, he shifted the plates up and to the left; still gazing through the eyepiece, fingers twirling the knurled knobs of the vertical and horizontal axes. Dots streaked past his vision. He stopped moving the plates. The view settled.

And there it was. Larger now, by an eyelash, its jump wider by the width of a claw-tip: Darvin's Comet.

He repeated the process for the seventh and eighth nights, then sat back, wrapping his wings around himself with a shiver of delight. After a minute's indulgence he stood up and telegraphed his discovery to the Observatory. Then he returned to the earlier pair of plates, and resumed his search for the unknown planet that he had already in his own mind named the Wanderer.

'I've found a comet,' he told Orro, a few days later when the discovery had been confirmed.

'So I hear,' said Orro. 'Congratulations.'

'You've heard?'

'A note on the physics wire.'

'Ah. Very good. At least I'll be remembered for something more than Darvin's Little Bastards.'

'It would be better if you find Darvin's Planet,' said Orro.

Darvin wasn't sure if this was a jibe or a kind word. He chose to take it well.

'Still looking, of course,' he said. 'I'll have the current batch finished in a couple of days, and then the next eight-days' worth will come in. So it goes.'

'I'd like a look at these, if I may,' said Orro. 'It might be possible to work out the comet's path, and where it's going.'

'That would be wonderful,' said Darvin. 'Where are *we* going, by the way?'

Orro stopped and looked around as if lost. They had emerged on to a small plaza from an alleyway between the student roosts and the back of the Study of Ancient Times Building. Orro closed his eyes and shook his head.

'I'll just take you there,' he said.

The Gevorkian set off again with confident stride. Darvin hurried after him, though the scratch of his friend's claws made him want to take wing. After crossing the plaza and negotiating another couple of alleys, through which trudges were hauling carts of fresh-killed prey for the refectory, they arrived at a patch of waste ground before the slope to the river bank. The air was heavy, loud with insects and the laughter of students wing-sailing on skiffs on the water. Yells rose when someone fell off.

On the patch of waste ground, surrounded by a sparse crowd of idle students and curious town kits, and watched over by a stern technician, stood a contraption that Darvin recognised as the realisation of his inspiration and his sketch. He spread his arms and wings in exultation.

'Brilliant!' he said.

It was a long cylinder of rough white fabric, about two wingspans in diameter, made rigid by eight rings of bend-wood, and held in place by guy-ropes like a tent. At one of its open ends stood the dirigible engine, mounted on sturdy tres-tles, its propeller facing the entrance to the tube. Halfway along it was a large acetate window, into which peered the kinematographic camera on its tripod.

'Well,' said Orro, 'to work!'

He signalled to the technician, who warned everyone – espe-cially the kits – out of the way, and hauled on the starter. The engine coughed into life with a fart of petroleum smoke. The propeller began to turn, slowly at first, then faster, until it became a deadly flashing disc. The trestles shuddered but remained in position.

Orro stepped to the kinematograph, and Darvin walked around to the end of the tube and faced into the gale that blasted towards him. He threw himself forward, taking to the air, and laboriously flew halfway down the tube, to where a large black cross was marked on the floor and black lines grid-ded the side opposite the window. With some difficulty he managed to make himself fly above the spot, maintaining posi-tion without hovering but as though flying into headwind.

'That's it!' he heard Orro shouting, through the window and above the howl of the engine. 'Hold it there! Flap! Flap!'

THREE

SPECTRAL LINES

14 364:06:18 01:25

I hate Horrocks Mathematical. He's the crewman who runs the training habitat I had the bad luck to pick. Node 52 on the gamma ring. (It says here.) I'm sitting/lying in the branches of an air-tree, in a cocoon that's like a sort of sleeping-bag combined with a hammock. Everybody around me is snoring (or making even more disgusting and distracting noises) and I'm exhausted, my bones and muscles are aching, but I can't sleep. Not yet.

The day started well. I decided long ago that I wasn't going to take my training along with all my friends, or even with people I knew. It's not like I intend to homestead with them, and besides, being with the same people as I've grown up with would not be exactly the Out There Experience.

I got up before sun-on, and walked out in the dimness of farlight to that copse from which I had once tried to climb the sky. The ladder was long since gone, along with all the rest of the left-over scaffolding of the world, its components recycled or perhaps added to the mountains of trash, now much diminished, piled against the forward wall for throwing as reaction mass into the maw of the drive. I found a comfortable enough place to lean my back against, on an ivy-grown cuboid structure that might have been the ladder's base. Bats flitted and chirped among the trees. A few early birds stirred, and some small animal moved in the long grass. It didn't look like anything that could harm me.

My virtuality genes haven't kicked in yet. (This is an admission.) (The other stuff is happening, all right?) So I blinked up the sky option on my contacts. The world disappeared, like it does. The sky took its place. I chose a stable image, one not turning with the world. The Destiny Star is hard to pick out without cheating, but I did it, sighting carefully along where my memory placed the forward cone. It's brighter than the others in its region, that's all. The sight of it works a strange effect on my diaphragm, on what the ancients called the heart. Something between a gasp and a jump; something between *home* and *hope*. It's like – all right, this is childish, but – it's like I've all my life been an exile from some marvellous place, and now I can see it in the distance. I couldn't see its comet-cloud around us, of course, not without magnification, but just burning there it looks haloed with glamour.

I turned carefully, my gaze sweeping along the Bright Road, and faced in the opposite direction, through the rearward cone. The Red Sun is easy to spot, of course, and around it – which is to say, behind it – one by one until they multiply in a haze, the green-tinged stars of the Civil Worlds. I tried to think of the trillions of worlds, some larger than ours, some smaller, that that green glow proclaimed, and the quadrillions of people and indeed of stranger beings that inhabit them. How vast it all was.

And in the whole sky, how small.

14 364:06:19 20:35

I fell asleep writing that. I hope you stayed awake reading it. And I see I have told you nothing that I meant to tell you. Now I have more, and I have to catch up.

So: I walked back out of the copse to the estate, made over my business pro tem to my three-quarter-sister (I'm checking up on you, Magnetic Resonance Gale, don't think I'm not), said goodbye to my care-mother and took the train to the forward wall. Just before it entered the wall it passed through a valley between two trash mountains. Never having looked at them up close, I was surprised (though I shouldn't have been) to find that the trash isn't just raw junk and clinker: you can see ruins in it, pipework, walls and spires, the rubble of cities built when there was less room in the world. Huge machines crawl over it like crabs, breaking the junk down small enough to chuck into the service lifts to the drive. I got out at a long, low-ceilinged station and after checking directions and assignments and a bit of hanging about while the rest of the contingent straggled in, took the lift to the upper levels. It was a much bigger lift than the one Constantine had taken me to, and the journey took about an hour. There were thirty other passengers, all of them booked for the same training habitat as myself. I hadn't wanted to train with people I knew, and in this I've certainly been successful. I didn't know any of them. What I hadn't expected was that no one else I was with would have had the same idea. So the rest all know each other, or rather, they're in two cliques from two estates, New Lamarck and Long Steading, adjacent to each other and distant from mine, Big Foot. (Does that name come from its once having been at the foot of a big ladder? Very likely; back when the estates were construction camps, their naming was quite arbitrary.)

The New Lamarck clique are into somatic hacks, some of them in questionable taste. But I'll take their plumed scalps and cats' eyes and parti-coloured skin any day over the Long Steading crowd's conspicuous conformity. (If any of them are reading this, which I doubt, I make no apologies. I've told you this to your faces.) What they are into is *each other*. Their plan is to train together, homestead together and become a founder population together. There's already at least one *triple* among them. That is just disgusting. It is behaving like old people.

Anyway, none of them talked to me on the way up, or in the scooter. I was first out of the airlock at the habitat. I emerged into the big bubble of air; it contained two roughly spherical objects, the air-tree and the rock. The sunline burned above, the downward view was dizzying, but my childhood experience, brief though it was, of free fall came back to me. I wasn't disoriented. A guide-rope snaked from the airlock to the air-tree. Holding it, waiting to greet us, was Horrocks Mathematical.

He's tall – or rather, long. About two metres from his heels to the top of his head, and a good half-metre more if you were to measure from his toes to the top of his hair. His hands are long too. Like his feet, they protruded bare from his red one-piece coverall. His hair is long and in numerous braids. Brown skin, blue eyes, angular features. It was sorely evident that he's not six years older than most of us.

He waved, smiled, and beckoned us along the rope. I had some idea of how to handle myself, and kept close behind his feet, which waved in front of me like a skin-diver's. The others did a lot of giggling and screaming and fooling around, or so it sounded. I disdained to look back. At the entrance to the tree Horrocks turned around, and shook hands with everyone as they passed him. Then we all followed Horrocks through the branches and into the tree. Its interior space was criss-crossed with llanas and with branches extended and shaped to a clutter of grown furnishings: hoops of wood to put your legs through, flat tables, hand-holds, complex storage spaces, sleeping pods, a few opaque cylindrical chambers that I guessed were privies; and with optical and plastic tubing and modified leaves or nuts that formed translucent skins for great wobbling spheres of water.

Horrocks darted to the centre of the tree's interior space and we all clustered around him, clutching various hand-holds or leg-hoops. It was in a leg-hoop that I sat, my arms hooked over the upper part, my pack looped to my wrist. Horrocks himself just hung there in the air, now and then twisting or somersaulting to vary his address.

'Welcome,' he began, 'and thank you all again for choosing my habitat. We'll be here for a week or so. This tree is a typical first-generation home, nothing too elaborate. It's a lot more comfortable than a free fall construction shack, but we'll get on to that in due course. For now, the main thing you have to learn is how to work in free fall, how to work in vacuum, and how to operate the machines . . .'

He went on for a bit, telling us what we were going to do, and then we suited up and went out and started to do it. We weren't in vacuum, of course – the main reason for the suits was to acquaint us with their use, and secondarily to protect us from the dust thrown off by the machines. There's no point in describing it all; you'll either have done it, in which case it'll be boring, or you haven't, in which case you won't understand. What I want to talk about is why we do it, because, as I huddle here with my muscles aching, I wonder too. Everybody who plans to homestead does basic training. It's customary, yes, but that doesn't explain it. Why are we doing things ourselves that could be done, and that we hope eventually to see done, by automata? Nobody has told me. So I have figured it out. It's like camping. It builds character.

14 364:06:19 22:21

Having thought about it further, I now understand that it has much more to do with how far away we are from anyone else. We are four hundred years from help and four information-years (hence eight or more elapsed years, counting question, turnaround, and answer) from advice. Our automata are the result of generations of iteration: long enough for source code to mutate. The Destiny

Star system will likely contain molecules no one has encountered before. Some of them could burn our machinery. Accidents happen.

So we have to be ready to work, with digging and forging tools, in free fall and raw vacuum, in space suits, just like primitive man. We all have to become like the Moon Cave People, for a while when we are very young, so that in an emergency we can be as tough and self-reliant as they were.

Oh yes. Why I hate Horrocks Mathematical:

We had just come off shift the first night and we were all brewing and cooking, and the others were all talking in their two little cliques, when Horrocks turned up beside me. I offered him tea and he took it.

'I like your biolog,' he said. '"Learning the World".'

My ears burned. 'You read it?'

'Now and again.'

He looked away, squirting the tea-bulb straight into his mouth. I still couldn't do that without scalding.

'Constantine?' he went on. 'You know who he is?'

'No,' I said. I bit some berrybread. Crumbs floated. I tried to avoid inhaling any; scooping them was difficult, like catching flies: they danced away from my fingers. 'It's funny, I never tried looking him up, even in memory. I suppose when you're a child some things seem like a dream.'

'I suppose they do,' said Horrocks, looking amused for no reason I could discern. 'And your care-mother didn't tell you about him?'

'No,' I said. 'What about him?' I resented the tone of querulous suspicion in my voice.

'He's one of your gene-parents,' said Horrocks. 'Your half-father, in fact. That's why he was so solicitous of you.'

I said and did nothing for a minute. I must have squeezed a bulb too hard; tea floated past my face in little hot drops.

'This is not the time or the place,' I said.

'Sorry,' said Horrocks. He looked more baffled than sorry. 'I'd forgotten how flatfooters—'

Then he shut his mouth, shook his head as if at himself, his beaded braids clattering, and with a flick of his foot was away and out of sight like a minnow in a pool.

I have never been so offended in my life.

Synchronic Narrative Storm flashed a note to Horrocks Mathematical, warning him to be more polite to her care-daughter, then summoned a presence of Constantine. He appeared in the garden seconds later. Not many could have bidden so swift a response from the Oldest Man. Synchronic was half smiling at the thought as she straightened from a flowerbed and made herself comfortable in a deckchair. Constantine was sitting, wherever he was; in her eye, in the garden, he seemed to be sitting on nothing. Small children ran oblivious through his presence.

'Hi, Synch,' he said. He looked around. 'Nice place.'

The virtual image of Constantine could not, of course, see, but the real Constantine was no doubt perceiving a point of view built up from the inputs of various eyes scattered around the garden: a camera here, a bird there, an insect somewhere else. In the sunline light his skin looked as black as his suit. The effect was as easily gene-fixed as the trim bulk of his muscles, but was seldom so created – it would have been considered pretentious to appear thus ancient, though some of the ship generation affected it in adolescent bravado. Synchronic herself was happy that her deep tan manifested an age of mere centuries, older than the current voyage but far, far younger than the ship – and the Man.

'Hi yourself,' she said. 'And yes, it is a nice place. But I didn't call you to chit-chat. Take a look at this.'

She flashed him a text version of the 'Learning the World'

biolog. While he was scanning it, Synchronic signalled to one of the children, who walked self-consciously up a few moments later with a tall glass of lime juice on ice.

'Thanks,' she said. The child smiled and ran off.

Constantine focused again on Synchronic. 'I'm flattered that she remembers me,' he said. 'Adventurous little lass, wasn't she?'

'Still is,' said Synchronic. 'But I'm interested in the later entries. She and Horrocks . . .'

Constantine frowned. 'She's too young.'

'For now. But the signs are there.'

'Genome calls to genome, eh?' said Constantine. 'I shall open a future on it.'

'You were always the romantic,' said Synchronic.

'That I was, my lady,' said Constantine. 'That I was.'

Constantine the Oldest Man had told his story to Synchronic Narrative Storm half a millennium earlier, when she had been young and naive. She still believed it. The records were difficult to check, but he had had no manifest reason to lie: he was already in her bed, and they had already speculated profitably on their compatibility. The story he told was this:

Constantine was born a long way and a long time back on the Bright Road, in the Civil Worlds. In his early teens he had acquired some restlessness. In his early twenties he had acted on it. It was like dying. Nobody who had loved him would ever see him again, no matter how long they lived. In those days in the Civil Worlds life expectancy – untested, but actuarial – was ten thousand years and rising. This made no difference. People wept. Constantine left.

'It was too staid,' he'd said, 'and too weird. That sounds paradoxical, I know. But talking to my parents was becoming like SETI. They had grown distant and strange. When I was a kid, my pet animals uplifted. My imaginary friends became virtual and autonomous. My real friends upgraded and diversified. They haunted the walls and sent me presences to converse with and meat puppets to fuck. I couldn't evade the feeling that they were giving me less than their full attention. I lit out for the territories.'

'What's it like,' Synchronic had asked, 'lighting out?'

'Boring,' Constantine had told her. 'Even with time-dilation, it takes months to get anywhere in the long tubes. I worked my passage, stevedoring and whoring.'

'"Passage",' she'd sniggered.

'Tell me about it. Eventually, and I'm talking about years – decades, centuries – subjective, I arrived in a system where there were no electromagnetic acceleration tubes out front. No stars ahead were green. I'd reached the surface of civilisation, from the inside. Everything was raw in the territories, even reality. It sufficed for a while.'

He'd gone off in a dwam, at that point.

'And then what?' she'd prompted.

'And then? I was talking to a woman a thousand years older than I, much as we are now but the other way round, so to speak, when I listened to her for the thousandth time and I heard myself saying, "But the sky, my lady! The sky!"'

'What a romantic.'

Synchronic Narrative Storm was not a romantic. She was very maternal. This proclivity was in her genes. She could have fixed that: many of her cohorts had. She did not choose to do so, and she felt the decision was free. Brides and babies and strong dark men and intellectual and sensual women and the prospect of wide open spaces to populate with humanity had always made her weak at the knees. She regarded that as a strength, knowing that this evaluation too was in her genes. Freedom, she had decided in a vehement childhood, long before the relevant genes had kicked in, was to be what you were. That changing what she was would change what she wanted to be she regarded as an irrelevant curiosity, a philosophical abstraction. (A predisposition to this conclusion, too, was in her genes. She knew it and didn't mind.) She had fallen in love many times, married many times, borne many children and had raised and generated more; sometimes – most times, to be honest – without having met the other gene-parents in the flesh, but never without having fallen in love with all of them. She had no continuously cohabiting lover. Falling in love indicated that your genes were complementary to those of the loved one. It told you nothing about whether your personalities and sexualities were compatibile. Constantine thought it did, about her and others. It was one evidence that he was a hopeless romantic. The world was another.

'I have to leave,' said Constantine the Oldest Man. 'Something has come up.'

'Always the romantic,' said Synchronic Narrative Storm.

The Man sneered and left.

Awlin Halegap, the speculator, seldom let broader considerations override his pursuit of profit. When he saw the pattern in the supposed lightning spikes, right there in the raw data stream, and interpreted them before even the scientists had noticed, he was torn between alerting the relevant authorities and the tempting prospect of swift insider trading. He could have shifted the terrestrials in milliseconds. He sighed and did his duty. To his surprise the prospecting jury didn't send one of its own members.

'Show me it,' said the Oldest Man, manifesting without warning in Halegap's cramped brokerage. His apparent position was behind the speculator's shoulder. Halegap felt the virtual presence more than he saw it. The back of his neck prickled.

Halegap ran the numbers. 'Signal, not noise,' he said.

'I can see that,' said Constantine. His presence flipped, to perch on the edge of Halegap's data table, and made a show of peering into its depths. He fingered his ebon chin. 'Hmm,' he said. 'Troubling.'

Halegap had nothing to fear from Constantine, but he felt the unease of the bearer of bad news to the great nonetheless.

'You think we've been jumped?' he hazarded. Being over-taken by fast probes was a minor but real hazard for travelling worlds. Rare because it was bad form, impolite and not the done thing, but sometimes a scientific enterprise in an origin system would become impatient and, as the expression went, gun the jump.

'Most likely,' said Constantine. 'I'd have expected a priority-jumper to broadcast their claim, though. It's only happened to me twice before, and a long time ago. Customs may have changed, manners coarsened. The youth of today.'

'Oh no!' said Halegap, stung. He had grown up in the system they'd left four centuries earlier. The obscure urge to defend it surprised him. 'The latest information doesn't bear that out. We've drifted apart, of course, but Red Sun is devel-oping into a most polite society.'

'I'm sure it is,' said Constantine. 'They all do, for a while . . . You know, my best heuristics can't make head nor tail of these signals. They must be encrypted. Rather pointless, out here, one would think?'

'Rival establishments?' suggested Halegap. 'There are at least two sources in there, perhaps more.'

Constantine shot him a data-freighted glance. 'Good think-ing,' he said. 'But for more than one scientific society to override its manners, well . . .'

'There is always the possibility of data colonies,' said Halegap, with an uneasy laugh. *Very* uneasy; the prospect dis-quieted him at a level he didn't care to access.

'And if matters had reached such a pass, one might indeed see rivalry,' said Constantine, taking the notion in his stride. He smacked his fist on his palm again and again, a gesture made more disturbing by its lack of sound effects. 'Damn! Damn! To be jumped by some degenerate offshoots just as we're entering orbit, it's most aggravating!'

'There is that,' said Halegap. He was already thinking of worse possibilities, his mind racing ahead of the facts, ahead of the curve, into the worst-case scenario. 'But if Red Sun society were to go into full burn . . . well, I wouldn't want to be four light-years away from it. Not if I were a flatfooter, especially.'

'Rock the flatfooters,' said Constantine. 'They can dig deep and ride it out, like they would a supernova. That's what they're bred for. It's the rest of us who'd take the full blast of the thing.'

Halegap shivered, feeling as vulnerable as some drifting, soft-skinned sea creature before a landslide. Full burn was rare, far rarer even than data colonies, but data colonies were among its first stigmata. A society undergoing exponential evolution was unstable; no persistent examples were on record. All that was left were dark spots in the green haze of the Civil Worlds: ashes of the full burn. In the fifteenth millennium of the space age, the bulk of humanity with all its hacks and tweaks remained close to its terrestrial ancestral form, and the bulk of thinking machinery around or below the human level; there seemed to be an upper bound on the complexity a society or an individual could sustain.

Constantine's presence refocused itself, brightening. 'Let's not run away with ourselves,' he said. 'The most we have real evidence for is a couple of probes. If they're data colonies, we'll know soon enough. Either way, I suggest you release the news.' He chuckled. 'Expect a momentary panic, then a boom in ter-restrials.'

*

14 364:06:20 06:30

I'm scared. I've never seen a world slump before. The one last night lasted for *hours*. Down below I could see lights going out all over the place; it was as if people had lost the will to live. Today, things are picking up. Confidence returns, every newsline says, a bit too urgently. I don't feel confident at all. I'm watching the Long Steading crowd waking up, stirring, red-eyed. I think some of them were crying last night; I'm sure I heard them.

I'm not going to do that myself. I'm not. I'm sure the signals, if that's what they are – and as you can see *here* there are doubts about that – are just from fast probes from Red Sun, and not any of the nasty things some people say they could be. But to think that the system that we thought was all fresh and empty and untouched, waiting for us, our future, already has somebody else's grubby fingerprints on it just makes me sad and sick.

And angry.

14 364:06:20 21:24

What a day. On the one hand, it's been totally absorbing, tremendous fun. At least when I was totally absorbed in the work, which was most of the time. I excavated a small cavern, lined it and sealed it, and began work on its externals – the airlock's machinery and such – with some metals I'd mined out yesterday. Only a small amount, of course, a few grammes of iron and trace elements, but for the refining and casting I got to use my first machine with a brain interface. Unlike an adult, I had to use a headband kit – trodes and goggles – but it was exciting all the same. It makes a sort of tickle in your head – you know, like when you've solved a problem, made a new connection, but more intense.

'You're feeling the dendrites growing,' Horrocks said, when I mentioned it. I'm not sure whether or not he was joking.

Which brings me to the other hand. Throughout the day

Horrocks tried to cheer people up, and at first I thought this was him being kind. But then I realised that he really was cheerful himself. After we came off work and cleaned up and had dinner I asked him why.

He was a few metres away, sitting in a loop. A lot of us were listening. He looked around and grinned.

'I made a fortune today,' he said. 'I have lots of claims on the terrestrial planet.' He laughed. 'I should just leave you all to get on with it. I've made far more from these claims than I'm ever likely to from this place.'

'The value of the claims will go down,' said one of the New Lamarck girls, her quills bristling. 'You wait.'

'Maybe they will,' said Horrocks. 'But they might go right out the hatch. What if what's down there is . . .' He dropped his voice to a low and hollow tone, like someone telling a scary story: '. . . *aliens*?'

Everybody laughed and felt better, except me. I felt patronised, treated like a child who is first scared then reassured by a story about frightening things that everybody knows don't exist, like gods or ghosts or hideaways or, well, aliens. Aliens! I ask you.

I hate Horrocks Mathematical.

FOUR

A MOVING POINT OF LIGHT

Third Finger Street was the axis of night life in Five Ravines. Stumblefruit groves and laughterburn grottoes lined it. Trudge-drawn cabs jostled motor-vehicles in its metalled way; unsteady walkers thronged the pavements. Cable seats whizzed overhead, carrying the elderly or pregnant above this louche promenade, and those already too intoxicated to safely fly away from it. To look up was to risk a headache-inducing fireworks display of proximity-sense overload. To fly above it was to risk worse, and plenty did. Flitters, small and deft, dodged between the lumbering flights of humans.

Darvin and Kwarive walked along the pavement, heading for the Bard's Bad Behaviour, a popular copse. Kwarive, as usual, teased Darvin about his refusal to take a cab.

'Too tight-fisted for a fare,' she said. 'You don't know how to impress a lady.'

'It isn't that,' Darvin said. 'I think it's cruel.'

'Now you're just being sentimental.'

It was a joke between them. Darvin was tiring of it. Needled, he needled back.

'And I wouldn't be if I cut up animals?'

'Instead of looking at stars? Sure you wouldn't.'

'I eat prey,' he pointed out.

'Oh, *that*,' said Kwarive. 'Everybody *eats prey*. It's dissection that makes you understand.'

Darvin resisted the urge to quibble that not everyone ate prey; he intuited that calling mystics from the South to the witness perch would not help his case.

'Understand *what*?' he asked. 'That the beasts have bones like ours, blood like ours, nerves like ours, and who is to say they don't have feelings like ours? Doesn't a flitter squeal when you flay it?'

Dissecting flitters was a cheap and moral way of learning human anatomy, he had gathered.

'We kill or anaesthetise them first,' Kwarive said.

'Ah-hah!' said Darvin. 'So you admit they feel pain? That not anaesthetising them would be inhumane?'

'No,' said Kwarive. 'It would be difficult, because they would struggle and might bite, and their physiology would be that of an animal in pain. Which is not what we want to examine.'

'So most of what we know of physiology is based on that of drugged animals? Interesting.'

'You have a point there,' Kwarive said. 'But what I've learned from dissections and other studies is that humans really are different from other animals. Brain size, speech, self-awareness, use of tools . . .'

'Trudges use tools,' Darvin said, 'and they can speak. That's why what we do to them is cruel, and that's why I won't—'

'Take a cab?' Kwarive snorted. 'You make my point for me. Trudges can be trained to hammer or hoe, but they don't *invent*—'

'Oh, it's inventing now?'

'—don't invent new uses, and they can utter a few simple phrases and understand a few dozen more, but they don't converse. They don't even use human speech to talk amongst themselves. They use their own grunts and cries. What they have is signals, not speech.'

'A fine distinction!'

'One that makes all the difference in the world,' said Kwarive.

They had stopped at a crossroads. Traffic was tangled up; a street warden swooped and circled overhead, screaming imprecations and instructions at drivers and trudges. Darvin glanced sidelong at Kwarive. Her face was stern and earnest. This was not their usual banter.

'All right,' he said. He jutted his chin at a brace of cab-hauling trudges who stood panting at the junction. Their hands clutched the T-bar of the cab's yoke; their feet, claws trimmed, were shod in thick rubber; their wings, the webs slashed in kithood from joint to trailing edge, hung atrophied and useless at their sides. Their arms and legs seemed by human standards grossly overmuscled, with tendons like cables. Their jaws champed leaf and their lips dribbled saliva. Their eyes, glazed by the drug, rolled, their gaze darting hither and thither. Behind them and the driver, in the two-seater cab, a couple held hands and giggled over a smouldering bunch of laughterburn. With one wing the boy enfolded and hooded the girl, with the other he wafted the smoke into the tent thus created. The driver, perched in front of the cab, paid this unseemly display no attention.

'Do you think,' said Darvin, 'that the trudges really don't suffer? That they don't miss using their wings?'

'They wouldn't be trudges if they could fly.'

There was something maddening in the unassailable logic of this missed point.

'Forget flying, there's enfolding to consider too.'

Kwarive shrugged. 'Doesn't seem to stop them pairing and breeding.'

'Those we don't geld or spay, at any rate.'

'Exactly. So I don't think they miss their wings.'

The traffic became unsnarled. The warden swooped, and hooted an order. The cab-driver flicked his whip across the shoulders of the two trudges. They trotted off.

'See?' said Kwarive. 'They didn't even wince.'

'It was the leaf,' said Darvin, plodding across the road.

'No,' said Kwarive. 'They are less sensitive to pain than we are. Their skin is thicker, and has fewer nerve-endings.'

'How do you know that?'

She looked at him. 'Dissection.'

At the Bard's Bad Behaviour every tree-branch and other perch was crowded. Electric lights blazed from cables strung across the tree-tops. Pulleys drew cables bearing fruit-laden or empty baskets. Darvin squelched to the stall across a floor littered with discarded stumblefruit rinds and laughterburn ash and bought a double wingful of fruit. Kwarive joined him halfway back and relieved him of half the burden. As they gazed around and up looking for a perch or for anyone they knew a cry came from above.

'Up here!' shouted Orro.

'Not likely!' Darvin yelled back. 'We're loaded! Come on down!'

Grumbled assent was followed by Orro's arrival, crashing and swinging one-handed, a half-used fruit in his free hand. He dropped in front of them and straightened, swaying. His white chest fur was yellow and sticky-looking with juice. He slapped Darvin's shoulder and, with the exaggerated gallantry of the drunk, touched his nose to the crook of Kwarive's wing.

'To the wall!' he said. 'Only perch left in this dive.'

The three made their way through the crowd and hopped up on to one of the few remaining available spaces on the top of

the wall around the grove. By unspoken agreement, Darvin
and Kwarive let the unsteady Orro sit between them. Sitting
cross-legged, they could hold the fruits in their laps, freeing
their folded wings for balancing and their hands for holding.
Darvin passed a fresh fruit to Orro, lifted his own with both
hands and bit in. He spat away the first chunk of rind and
tipped the fruit to let the flow of fermented juice flood into his
mouth. His belly warmed and the world became more cheerful. Orro scooped the last of the pulp from his almost empty
fruit, stuffed it in his mouth and threw away the husk. With
hardly a pause to chew and swallow he tore into the new fruit.

'Hmm,' he said, juices trickling down his chin, 'good.
Thanks, Darvin. You're a pal, you are. And a colleague.'

'Think nothing of it,' said Darvin, hoping Kwarive, to
whom he'd praised Orro's genius many times, wasn't utterly
disillusioned by the physicist's unwonted excess. He looked at
her over the back of Orro's hunched shoulders and waggled his
ears and rolled his eyes. She grinned back.

'Didn't expect to find you so, ah . . .'

'Drunk?' Orro guffawed and sat up straighter. 'Not drunk.
Seriously. Just badly behaved. Place for it, yes?'

'I suppose so,' said Darvin.

'I have a reason,' said Orro, staring up into the night sky.
The two moons hung like curved blades. The priests of the
cults would be scrying the angles and sharpening their sickles
for the bi-lunar sacrifices of green herbs to the blue-green
Queen.

'You always have a reason for doing things,' said Darvin. 'So
what is it?'

'Take your little student here,' said Orro.

'Ye-es,' said Darvin, no longer relaxed. The word came out
like a half-drawn blade.

'Nothing to worry about, has she? Have you, young lady?'

'Nothing you need know about,' said Kwarive.

'Ah. Indeed. No offence meant. Still. For a student, life is simple. Study. Make love. Eat and drink. Learn. And what you learn, Kwarive, you and your cohorts, is what is *known*.'

'We learn what is known,' said Kwarive. 'Now, there's a surprise.'

'What I said is not empty,' said Orro. 'Unlike this fruit.'

He cast away the rind. Darvin passed him another drink.

'Thanks,' Orro mumbled, munching in. 'Hmm. Right. Now for us scientists, on the other wing, life is not quite so simple. Because we learn the *unknown*. Unlike, hah-hah, our esteemed friends the philosophers, who learn the unknowable.' He waved skyward, almost losing his balance. 'The great flapping unknowable, like the wings of God.'

There had been a charming legend that night was the result of the Sun's enfolding Ground with His wing. So charming was it that even today a disrespectful allusion to it could cause offence. Of all the sciences, astronomy was the one the superstitious liked least.

'Leave the unknowable alone,' said Darvin.

'Sound advice. Well, my friends, imagine my discomfiture to discover, this very day, that by investigating the unknown I had diminished the known. That, in short, I did not know all I had thought I knew. That, to make it even shorter, I did not know how to calculate correctly. That I do not. That I can't count. I am pitiable.'

'Don't be silly,' said Kwarive. 'Everybody makes mistakes.'

'I do not make mistakes,' said Orro. 'Not in arithmetic. Not in measurement. Not in calculation.'

'Did you use a calculating machine?' asked Darvin.

'Of course,' said Orro.

'There you are,' said Darvin. 'A bug. They're everywhere this time of year.'

Orro looked at him morosely. 'I thought of that. I sprayed insecticide. I cleaned the gears. I oiled. I ran test calculations.

All was well. And when I turned to my own calculations, I could not make them come out right.'

'What were they?' asked Kwarive.

'Ah!' said Orro. 'That is where your friend and my colleague here drops into the clearing, so to speak. I was trying to calculate the orbit of his comet.'

Darvin felt a rush of relief as potent as the first spurt from a stumblefruit.

'That's all right,' he said. 'You're a physicist, not an astronomer. There are always disturbances in the paths of comets. You can't expect some perfect trajectory, you know.'

'I know that,' said Orro. He had dropped his husk, and not so much as hinted at wanting another fruit. Agitated, he began licking his hands and the juice-matted fur of his arms. 'I do not expect a perfect trajectory. But nor do I expect to find every equation I try for the path disproven by the next night's plates.'

He stopped, stared upward again for a moment, then sighed and reached a hand sideways. Without demur, Darvin passed him the last fruit in his lap.

'So that's why you find me here,' said Orro. 'Badly behaved, in the Bard's Bad Behaviour. Trying to jolt my brain loose from whatever stupid misconception is giving me this stupid anomaly in my results.'

'What anomaly?' asked Darvin.

'A comet slowing down,' said Orro.

They took him home.

The following morning, Darvin sat in his office and waited for the chewed leaf and the tea to dispel his stumblefruit headache, and mulled over a deeper unease. He hadn't given the comet much thought in the weeks since its discovery, having persisted in the quest for the unknown outer planet, and he'd assumed that Orro was concentrating likewise on his own major research. The photographs from the wind-tube kinematography had provided a plausible intuitive basis for a rigorous mathematical account of wing-flapping flight. Orro had talked about little else for days after the film had been processed. It was disquieting to discover that he was wasting time and passion in hunting down what he himself had called a stupid anomaly. It was unworthy of the man.

Darvin sighed. Perhaps not. The very rigour that made Orro's work so promising was doubtless the reason why he couldn't let this problem go unsolved. Darvin berated himself for letting Orro investigate the comet's orbit in the first place, without giving him any help or advice. No doubt some assumption or premise, second nature to an experienced astronomer, had been overlooked by the physicist.

He stood up and dived out of the window and flew to the Physics Building. There was no response when he knocked on Orro's office door, not to his surprise. He tested the door, found it unlocked, and let himself in. At first glance the place looked reassuring: long strips of film tacked to the walls, showing moment-by-moment frames of himself in flight; a complex, incomplete model of a chiropter, the fine paper of its wings still undoped; sheets of scribbled reckoning on the tables. A second look revealed that these sheets had been brushed aside, and a space cleared for a rack of Darvin's night-sky images, in between an electric lamp and an apparatus of mounted lenses: he guessed it was Orro's jury-rigged approximation to a blink comparator. Beside these devices lay a current ephemeris and a closed notebook bound in black grazer leather. Darvin opened it, and found page upon page of crabbed, jagged Gevorkian script. Equations and formulae, arithmetic, results from . . . ah yes, there was the calculating machine, behind the swivel perch on which Orro would have sat.

Darvin sat down himself, the heels of his hands against his

temples, and began to work his way through the notebook, trying to see where his colleague had gone astray. Every so often he turned to the calculating machine. Within an hour he was doing this so often that it clattered and rang like the till in a busy shop. Then it fell silent, and Darvin gazed in gloomy triumph at the notes.

He didn't hear Orro arrive. A short noonday shadow fell across the page, and he looked up.

'I've found your problem,' Darvin said.

'You have?' said Orro. 'Then I forgive the intrusion.'

Darvin jumped up and clapped Orro's shoulder. Orro winced and put a hand to his head.

'Sorry,' said Darvin, pacing across the floor, and turning to pace back. 'It's very simple. You've assumed that the comet is outside the orbit of the Warrior.'

Orro shook his head, then clutched it again. 'I haven't assumed it. It is outside. Not far, but definitely outside.'

'It can't be,' said Darvin. 'That's still too far away from the Sun for a comet to be visible, let alone as bright as it is.'

'Does the anomaly disappear when you recalculate on the other assumption?'

'I haven't got that far,' Darvin admitted.

'I thought not,' said Orro. 'In any case, you needn't bother. That was where I started.' He reached for a shelf above the table, and pulled down another notebook. 'Check that one too if you want. I found the anomaly, and then I realised it couldn't be right, because the comet's path is not perturbed by the gravitation of the Warrior, or of the Queen. My calculations on the assumption that it was much farther out – the ones you've been looking at – are my second attempt. And the anomaly of apparent deceleration is still there. Not only that, but you've just pointed out another one, the comet's visibility and brightness. I tell you, it's enough to drive a physicist to drink.'

Darvin laughed. 'I underestimated you,' he said. 'I thought

you were missing something that would be obvious to an astronomer. You weren't. This is good solid reckoning, Orro.'

'Very well,' said Orro. He looked relieved. He sat on the perch and caught the table edge with his toe-claws and leaned back. 'Let's spit the rind and chew the pith.' He closed his eyes for a moment, with a faint shudder. 'Metaphorically. We have an anomalously bright celestial object, anomalously distant, anomalously decelerating. It is traversing the region of the Queen of Heaven's Daughters, the green stars. What hypothesis springs to mind?'

'None,' said Darvin. 'No celestial object decelerates on its way in towards the Sun.'

'No natural celestial object. Very well then. It must be an unnatural object, or rather, an artificial one.'

Darvin laughed. 'An alien spaceship?'

Orro shrugged. 'Call it that if you must. It may be something not conceived of even in engineering tales.' He pointed over his shoulder at the calculating machine. 'I've sometimes speculated on what could be achieved by such a machine, given a few eights-of-eights of years of progress in the art . . . but leave that aside.'

'Yes, I should think aliens are quite enough to be going on with, leaving aside mechanical thinkers.' Darvin punched his friend's shoulder. 'Come on! This is quite unscientific! It's always better to seek the simpler explanation.'

'You have one?'

'The glimmerings of one,' said Darvin. 'Just as speculative as yours, I admit, but requiring fewer . . . supplementary hypotheses.'

'Give us it then.'

Darvin paced back and forth a few times before replying. In truth he was not as sceptical of aliens as he had sounded. The possibility was an old and respectable one in the astronomy of Seloh and Gevork; even in religion, the green tinge of the

Queen had been associated with life, and the spectroscopy confirmed that. There had even been a delightful legend that the Queen of Heaven's Daughters had been given life by the Queen, and while astronomers discounted that, they allowed that the green tinge of the Daughter stars might indicate the presence of life on any planets around them, while admitting they had no idea how such hypothetical life-bearing planets could filter the light from their suns. There was one outlandish, but established, suggestion that some kind of green plant could grow in space itself, perhaps from the surfaces of comets, but the difficulties of this idea were as obvious as the absence of imaginable alternatives to it.

'Suppose what we have here,' he said, 'is a natural object, but one unknown to astronomy. A new kind of comet. We know that a comet's tail consists of gas glowing in the Sun's rays.'

'Yes,' said Orro.

'Now, the gas is given off as the comet warms up, on approaching the Sun. Now if, if there were a kind of comet or similar body that began to outgas much farther out from the Sun, the flow of gases would – if aligned towards the Sun – slow down the comet and make it brighter than it would otherwise appear.'

Orro closed his eyes and tilted his head back. His lips moved. 'That might just work,' he said at last. 'It would require some damned ticklish and unlikely coincidences: mass, orientation, specific impulse . . . am I right in thinking that cometary outgassings don't normally have any effect on their orbit?'

'You are,' said Darvin. 'This would have to be, as you say, something quite different from outgassings as we understand them. The gases propelled outward by radioactive heating within, perhaps?'

'Radioactivity is a remarkably faint source of power,' said Orro. 'Certainly in any concentrations found in nature, though there have been some experiments and calculations . . . all very speculative stuff, of course.'

Darvin had never heard of work along these lines. 'In Gevork?'

Orro opened his eyes and stared at him; it seemed, through him. 'Speculation.' It wasn't clear to just what Orro applied the epithet. He waved a hand. 'Ignore that. We can only describe what we incontestably have evidence for. So let us describe it.'

'How?'

Orro jumped off the perch, strode forward and clasped Darvin's hand. 'A joint note to the journals? Or failing that, the physics wire? Does not "A Distant, Decelerating Celestial Object: Some Observations", by Darvin and Orro, of Five Ravines, have a certain ring to it?'

'It does,' said Darvin. He returned the handshake. 'If only I didn't suspect that we've both made some ghastly mistake, which some undergraduate will spot straight away, in which case it's a title that'll ring in our ears for the rest of our lives.'

They finished checking the calculations that evening. By midnight they had written the paper. It was brief, detailed, mostly mathematical, and included no speculation whatever about the nature of the decelerating object.

'You know,' Darvin said, glancing it over one last time, 'I can't help thinking this looks a bit trashy and sensational.'

Orro didn't laugh. 'When I close my eyes, I see its title as a screaming headline in large black type.'

'That's fatigue,' said Darvin. He helped himself to some tea. 'But yes, I do worry about the effect on public opinion. In engineering tales, the arrival of aliens is invariably followed by mass panic.'

'That's fanciful,' said Orro. 'It has never been tested.'

'Well, in the nature of things, no,' said Darvin. 'However,

there was one incident back in the Dawn Age, when the first observations of signs of life on the Queen were published. That led to, if I recall my history books, a stock-market bubble, a subsequent collapse, and a brief frenzy of religious persecution.'

'That was the Dawn Age,' said Orro. 'We are now in the Day.'

'So we like to believe. A day in which dirigibles almost too high to see patrol our skies above the Broad Channel. When the Broad Channel itself is patrolled by warships from both shores. A day in which war with Gevork is openly spoken of, and not just in engineering tales.'

'And a day in which many such as you and I co-operate like civilised men.'

'That's true,' said Darvin. 'Perhaps a new kind of comet – even if it was thought to be an alien space ship – would result in wonder rather than fear.'

'How long,' Orro mused, 'before amateurs with telescopes notice it?'

'Several eights of eight-days, even with the best private telescopes, I should imagine.'

'So there is no risk, really, of our discovery's being preempted. We could hold back for a little while . . .'

'I said "private",' said Darvin. 'I'm not willing to see Seloh's Reach being beaten by Gevork on this discovery. Or by any other country.'

'Nor me,' said Orro. He gave Darvin a troubled look. 'Surely you don't think I—'

'Oh, no, not at all,' said Darvin. 'But some of your – their astronomers may already have noticed the anomaly.'

'I doubt it,' said Orro. 'Gevorkian astronomy is focused, you might say, on the stars. Even the planets, leave alone comets, are regarded as almost beneath the notice of serious scientists.'

'The other realms . . .'

'Astrologers!'

'That's the problem,' said Darvin. 'The sky-watchers of the Court of the Southern Rule pay a great deal of attention to comets as portents – their priorities are rather the reverse of your Gevorkians. And their telescopes – say what you like about the beliefs and motives of their builders – are of the highest craft. They were producing detailed sky maps before our Dawn Age – we have one in the university's museum. I should take another look at it, to see if it shows any earlier comets in the Daughters region. It might suggest how the sky-watchers would interpret this one.'

'Well,' said Orro, with a shrug, 'I doubt that we need worry about *their* panicking the populace. Or preceding us into print, for that matter.'

Darvin was not so sure about that. 'Some of their younger sky-watchers are talented and educated men, and they do have their own version of a popular press,' he pointed out. 'They invented it, after all.'

Orro wiped a hand across his tired eyes. 'There's one more thing we can do,' he said. 'That is, to project the path of the . . . object, check it against your latest plates, and work out exactly when it will become visible to amateur astronomers, and indeed to the naked eye.'

'The naked eye!' Darvin had all along assumed that the comet that now bore his name would one day be visible to everyone, but the thought now brought him up short. Since confirming Orro's calculations, he'd begun to think of it almost as a secret.

'Why not?' said Orro. 'A year or so from now, I'd guess. Let's check it.'

'Tomorrow,' said Darvin.

*

In the morning a low fog from the sea overlay Five Ravines. Darvin had to rely more than usual on his proximity sense as he flew to the university. The world was a grey haze interrupted by red flashes. On one sideways turn he noticed how the fog curled away from his wingtip, and reflected on how something like fog – smoke? steam? – might be used in Orro's wind-tube experiments.

But there were to be no such experiments that day. When he'd stepped along the hall, shaking drops of moisture from his fur, Darvin found Orro hanging asleep from the ceiling outside his door. Orro tapped his wing-joint. The other man shuddered, unfolded his wings and blinked up. Inside his wings, he'd been clutching a satchel.

'Have you been here all night?' Darvin asked.

'No,' said Orro. 'Not long. But I needed the sleep.'

He bent upwards, caught the wooden slats of the ceiling with his hands, let go with his feet, and dropped upright and caught the satchel before it reached the ground. Scratching himself, he followed Darvin in to the office. It took them an hour or so to work through Orro's calculations and find where to look for the comet on the more recent plates, those from the past couple of eight-days. Darvin set up the pair of plates, adjusted the blink comparator, and found the comet, brighter than before. Orro noted the degrees of displacement along the vertical and horizontal axes, scribbled in his notebook, and nodded.

'On target,' he said.

They repeated this for nine pairs of plates. The comet's path was exactly as Orro's calculation predicted.

On the tenth pair, there was no jump. Instead, the comet seemed to flash on and off in the same position. On closer examination, Darvin found that it was present on the earlier plate, but not on the later. On the eleventh pair, and all subsequent pairs, it was altogether gone.

FIVE

FAST PROBES

14 364:07:06 08:12

It's strange when something you have been unaware of all your life goes away. Something is missing. It's the minute sideways tug of deceleration, that insensible inclination toward the forward wall that all our lives has troubled our inner ear. You couldn't spot it with a plumb-line and the unaided eye. But now it's gone, and we notice it.

We're in orbit around the Destiny Star. It's hard for me to believe that the journey is over, that we've arrived. It's even harder, I think, for the adults. Four hundred years is a long time to live in one place, even if the place is changing all the time as cities get demolished and landscapes get torn up and thrown into the drive, and new cities and landscapes built, and these in turn . . . So those of us who've known only the final form of the world and who've lived less than a couple of decades in it should be patient with them.

I told myself that earlier this morning as I washed glasses and cleared up bottles. There were snoring bodies all over the place. Some of the younger children had to be cleaned and fed. Aren't adults supposed to be *responsible*? Isn't that the *point*?

I suppose once in four hundred years isn't bad. Or once in fourteen, which is all I can vouch for.

14 364:07:08 22:15

Today the fast probes were launched to the inner system: one each to the ringed gas giant, the waterworld, the asteroid belt, the rocky terrestrial and the mercurial. Funnily enough, it's the one to the gas giant that'll take longest – it's on the far side of the Destiny Star, or the sun as I suppose we should now call it (it doesn't look like one: from out here it's still a star, though the brightest). We won't hear back from it for about ten years. The rest will vary, but they're all in Hohmann transfer orbits (therefore slow) except for the probe to the terrestrial. That one has a fusion drive and a whole atmosphere package. No lander, though there was an argument over that. It's going at a fast clip and should only take half a year (by which time the planet will have moved farther away – right now it's on our side of the sun). Then we'll know what the source of the signals is. If you call them up you can see they're very raw, very messy; they don't look like they've got a lot encoded in them. They don't look like a couple of science packages from a fast interstellar probe reporting back to the Red Sun system.

The latest speculation is that they're *natural*: check out Grey Universal's sim of a pair of permanent electrical storms in stable, long-lasting Coriolis hurricanes.

There's something really strange about that. I can see it in my mind's eye more vividly than in the sim: a whirling tower of cloud, lit up by regular lightning flashes, over the raging oceans of a terrestrial planet. Rain hissing into the white-topped black waves. Around that endless storm (and its counterpart in the other hemisphere) you might catch glimpses of blue sky through gaps in the clouds. And away from it, perhaps, the bald rock of continents, wet or dry, with here and there a yellow splash of lichen or a coppery or green slick of algae, if there's life down there at all.

I wonder what it would be like to walk on that world; to hear through my suit's phones the crackle and roar of the lightning storm; modulated, regular, surging and waning; a sound you could mistake for a signal, and take for a voice.

Genetic machinery was falling out of the sky. It came packaged in tough spheroids a millimetre in diameter, surrounded by aerobraking structures consisting of long wispy cellulose filaments arranged in a radial pattern. The packages landed at random, most of them nowhere near a suitable substrate, or in places where that substrate was already occupied. Horrocks Mathematical thought it a most curious method of distributing genetic machinery. It reminded him of market stochastics, and he speculated that its design had been thus inspired.

As he clambered on all fours across the rubble in the foothills of the now dormant reaction-mass tip by the forward wall Horrocks noticed the source of the genetic packages: plants with green photo-receptors and red insect-attractors. The wind carried the packages away from them in puffy clouds. The plants grew in quite improbable places, in cracks in stones and from crevices between blocks. The dispersal method might not be as wasteful as it looked.

He reached the edge of the tip and hesitated. Ahead of him stretched the monorail line, and beneath its pylons a long, flat strip of grass that merged on both sides with the rolling hills and woods. He had almost had to crawl out of the lift station, and spent hours making his way over the rubble alongside the line. Now he had reached its end, and if he were to go farther he would have to call for transport, or walk.

He was sure he could walk: it was a guaranteed function in his genetic repertoire, though not one he had ever attempted to

access. Like the free fall adaptations of the ground-hogs, it
was included as a back-up. Horrocks didn't know how he'd
acquired his conviction that to walk with his head two metres
above a hard surface in a ten-newton acceleration field was to
risk serious brain damage, but the conviction was there, and
deep. On his hands and feet he made his way on to the grass.
The substrate felt a little spongy and damp. No doubt it served
some hydroponic function, which fortuitously made it fairly
safe to fall on. He walked his hands backward, crooking his
knees, until all his weight was borne on the soles of his feet.
His calf muscles and Achilles tendons stretched as if he were
about to thrust off. In a manner he was. He remained squatting
for a few minutes, turning and rolling his head until he had
the glimmerings of an intuitive fix on the attitude display
and control mechanisms. It was a bit like flying a scooter.

He raised his hands from the ground and stretched out his
arms. Keeping his back rigid and facing directly ahead, he
straightened his knees and slowly stood up. The view was
breathtaking: he could see kilometres farther than he had a
moment earlier. This was easier than he had thought. He
looked down. The grass rushed up to his face, but it was the
palms of his hands that it struck. He rolled, rubbing his wrists.
The pain passed. It was just like misjudging a jump and hitting a wall too hard.

After a few more attempts he managed to stand, then to
walk, and before he quite realised it he was a hundred metres
along the strip and making progress, his head and arms swaying as he moved along. He had just grasped the kinetic
feedback involved when he toppled again. When next he got
up he walked without thinking about it, and this worked.

Every so often a train whizzed past, in one direction or the
other, buffeting him in its slipstream. At one point he noticed
the light darkening. He looked up and saw that a mass of
vapour had obscured the sunline. A minute or two later water

started falling from the sky, in fast fat drops. It was like a shower, except that the water came from only one direction, the vertical, and it was cold. Horrocks tugged the hood out of his collar and over his drenched hair, and turned up his heating. So much for the natural human environment, he thought. The default conditions of a sunliner's final interior surface had been established many millennia ago to emulate those of the Moon's primary, but Horrocks was beginning to harbour a suspicion that some mistake had been made: either the emulation had drifted from the original, or they'd picked the wrong planet to emulate. Surely humanity could not have evolved in such an environment! It was amazing that anyone survived down here without a space suit.

After an hour or so it became evident that he had greatly underestimated the effort required to traverse a given distance by walking. Muscle groups that he seldom used in the axis and in the forward cone ached. Ahead he saw a monorail station. A little elementary trigonometry fixed its distance at about a kilometre. He reached it half an hour later and climbed the steps on hands and feet. When the next sternward train stopped he staggered across the platform, lurched through the door and slumped on to a vacant seat beside a window, facing in the direction of travel. He threw back his hood and shook the water off his hair.

The doors hissed and thudded shut and the train accelerated. Horrocks spent the rest of the trip with his hands clamped to the back of his head, to prevent further injury to his neck. The speed at which the landscape flashed past the windows was another frightening surprise. After his first dozen or so flinches at the rushing approach of some blurred object, a tree or a tower, Horrocks concentrated on the middle distance or the far-off upward curve of the ground. Trees, here growing up rather than out, looked liable at any moment to be borne off on the breeze, like the drifting genetic packages. Habitats and storage units were constructed of heavy, durable substances – stone or wood walls, sheet-diamond windows – in permanent battle with the unpredictable atmospheric conditions and the relentless downward pull of the acceleration field.

He turned away from the window and eyed the other passengers, people for whom such conditions were normal. There were fourteen in the car. Four adult women, three adult men, and the others adolescents or younger children. Two of the women and two of the men gazed into space, their lips moving. The other three adults were sitting around a table, talking and laughing. The adolescents, four of them, were doing the same but louder, and the small children were playing some complicated game that involved running from one end of the carriage to the other. Horrocks was relieved to see that they, at least, wore intelligent clothing that would protect them if they fell. The adolescents were so lightly clad that they evidently counted on luck or reflex. The adults were better covered, but in structured or loose outfits that showed no sign of intelligence or ready adaptability to emergencies, and open at the cuffs or hems at that. All of his fellow-passengers adjusted to changes in the train's motion by subtle muscular reflex, and appeared quite untroubled by its speed.

None of them made to get off the train at Horrocks' destination, Big Foot. He uncurled himself from his seat and walked to the door with as much dignity as he could muster. The platform was empty. He noticed a lift to ground level, but decided to take the stairs, and this time to take them upright. Clutching the handrail and moving hand over hand, step by step, he made his way to the ground. There he sat on one of the lower steps and contemplated his surroundings and his next move. In front of the station stood a couple of self-driving wheeled vehicles with bubble canopies. One of them started up and rolled over to where he sat.

'Do you need a ride?' it asked.

'No thank you.'

The machine backed off.

A path led from the station's paved concourse through a couple of hundred metres of rolling grassland divided by a stream of water and dotted with clumps of trees and shrubs. Beyond that lay the Big Foot estate. Low wood or stone buildings set in gardens with lakes fed by the water stream formed its main living area. Its design drew the eye: curves and lines, light and shade, rough and smooth were integrated as in a complex abstract sculpture. This area was overlooked from a central rise by an imposing three-storey house about fifty metres long, built from wooden planks, with tall and wide windows and a veranda at the front. Somewhere a dog barked. Ponies cropped the park. Strange aromas, not all of them appetising, wafted from the low sheds that housed the food synthesisers. Off to one side lay a long semi-cylindrical segmented hut of glassy black ceramic. That would be the incubator, shielding racks of artificial wombs in a warm reddish dark. To Horrocks' eyes there was something larval about it, almost sinister in its insectile insistence on reproduction. In the cones women carried their own foetuses, but they didn't have the acceleration field and the necessity of rapid increase to contend with.

The estate would have looked even more impressive if its pattern hadn't been repeated, with variations, for kilometres around in all directions. There was something of a relief to the eye in seeing in the far distance, hanging like a pictorial map on the upward curve of the ground, the closer-together and taller buildings of a town. Imagine growing up in a place like this! The first thing you'd want to do, as soon as you could, if not sooner, would be to get out. For the first time Horrocks felt what he'd long understood: the outward urge of the ship generation.

This was what he had come for. Something like this. He

turned away and climbed back up the steps to the platform
and waited for the next forward train.

14 364:09:27 20:38

Sorry about the two-and-a-half month hiatus, everyone. (Note to
self: months, huh? Re primary origin myth question.) I've been too
busy living to biolog. It's all very well for adults, who can stick
their thoughts on a site for anyone to see. Well, not their thoughts
and not anyone, but you know what I mean, and frankly sub-vocal-
isations and saved sights and sounds and smells and such seem
like cheating compared to writing. When all that adult stuff comes
on in my head I'm going to keep on writing. I promise to you, my
faithful reader(s).

So . . . to catch up. I've turned fifteen and I've moved to town.
Only the nearest town to Big Foot, mind you, but it's surprising
how different living among ten thousand is from living with five
hundred. The town is called Far Crossing – another of these pioneer names – and it absolutely rocking fucks, as I heard somebody
say the day I arrived. It's nearly all ship generation, most of them
a bit older than me, not that that's a drawback. And the buildings
and the streets are dense. You can walk a hundred metres and not
see a flower or a blade of grass or another living thing except
people, and that's not a drawback either. You appreciate these
things more when you're not surrounded by them all the time.
When we go out we'll have to get used to that, for a while anyway.
It's like with the shops. When you've had everything you want all
your life you appreciate shops. They're full of things you don't
want but somebody does. Most of them are owned, if that's the
word, by people who've thought of or made something that's
never been made before, and they sell them. Like, you know,
somebody might sell space and time on a training habitat, but it's
strange to see small material objects being sold.

Even stranger to buy them. I now have more bracelets and pendants and hair-slides and clothes and would you believe shoes than I ever imagined I would want, and that's the point I think, I would never have imagined them. I used to get given gifts or take what I fancied from the estate store or make things myself. Even my own business was nothing to do with stuff like this. Atomic's Enterprise (now Magnetic's Magic) used to (still does) trade in phenotypic expression derivatives, which is something so rocking abstract that it bores even me.

But enough about me. You know what's dragged me back to this, it's what everyone else is talking about too. Doesn't matter. Some day we'll look back on this, eventually everybody in our light-cone will know about this and wonder how it felt, so I think it's worth noting our first reactions for posterity and our future selves.

This morning I rolled out of bed and made a coffee to wake up and went down to the cafe along the street to have a proper breakfast. There I met Grant . . .

Let me tell you about Grant. I met him the day I arrived. The thing is, Far Crossing isn't on the monorail. It isn't even on one of the roads. You either arrive by air or on foot, slogging across the estates. Guess which way I arrived?

So there I was, leaning on my rucksack where the road runs out at the edge of town, looking along the streets and up at the towers like, well, like someone who has just walked in from a little estate out In the middle of nowhere. Somebody said hello. He was standing in front of me, a boy about my height and age, with very short black hair and a wispy beard. His eyes were very dark, he had broad shoulders and thick biceps and he was wearing a loose black T-shirt and long shorts and scuffed sandals.

'You've just arrived?' he said.

I looked down at the pack. 'You guessed?'

He stuck out a hand. 'Grant Cornforth Dialectic,' he said. He kind of winced. 'Sorry about the name, but it's mine.'

'Atomic Discourse Gale,' I said, shaking his hand.

He brightened. 'I can see we're going to get on well.'

There's a notion that gets kicked around the cohort that our names have some occult connection with our genotypes, and that names that seem to go together indicate compatibility. It's not one I've ever found plausible, and anyway atomic and dialectic are counterposed. Everyone knows that.

'Maybe,' I said. 'Pleased to meet you. Been here long?'

'Oh yes,' he said. 'Weeks and weeks.'

I stooped to lift the pack.

'Let me take that,' he said.

'There's no need.'

'I need the exercise. Please.'

'All right,' I said. In truth I was glad to be rid of it. I accompanied him into town. Small parks and plazas buzzed with people building ecologies and machines. The buildings were grey and very smooth. They went up and up. Some were angular, others all sweeping curves and elliptical windows and cup-shaped balconies, many of the shapes priapic or vulval or arboreal, a stone dream of the organic.

'Strange smell in the air,' I said.

'Concrete,' he said. He waved a hand at the buildings. 'Structural material.'

'So that's how it's done.'

'Right. I find it interesting because that's what I'm learning: structural engineering. You can use some concrete mixes in vacuum, you know.'

'Water could be a problem.'

'Ice and compression. Proven tech.' He looked at me. 'So, what do you do?'

'I used to speculate in organic futures,' I said. 'When I was younger, I mean,' I added. I knew it sounded tame and obvious, kids' stuff about, well, kids. 'I recently did my micro-gee training and I'm busy trying to plan my future habitat and put together a team. And I write.'

'Biolog?'

'Yes, "Learning the World".'

'I'll check it out,' he said, sounding as if he wouldn't. 'I write too.'

'Not a biolog?' I guessed.

'Just the minimum. If anybody wants to get to know me they can rocking well come and meet me. What I'm really writing is a novel.'

More people say that than say they're biologging. It's a disease.

'What's it about?' I asked. I was looking at shop windows and avoiding collisions. Grant was looking straight ahead and letting other people do the collision avoidance.

'Let's go in here,' he said, stopping and indicating a café. 'It'll take a while to tell you about it.'

I didn't have anything better to do, so I agreed. The place was bright, with yellow tables and blue crockery. It was about half full, with a dozen or so people at various tables. A wall screen at the back was showing airsurfing, or some such sport. The counter was self-service. I got – bought, I should say – a chicken salad and orange juice. Grant shrugged off the pack beside a vacant table and bought a heaped plate of hot processed meats and fried potatoes and a pot of coffee. I could see why he'd jumped at the chance of exercise.

'So tell me about your novel,' I said, when we'd eaten our first few bites.

He leaned forward, gesturing with his fork. I leaned back. He took the hint.

'It's about the previous generation,' he said. 'Our parents' generation.'

'Oh,' I said. 'Old people.'

'That's the beauty of it,' he said. 'Nobody else is interested in it. But there must be stories to tell. Think about it, four hundred years! Cities being built and destroyed! Intrigues, affairs, deals! Secrets! Their past before they took ship!'

'Yes,' I said, 'but who would read it?'

'The *next* generation,' he said. 'The one after us.'

I leaned back again, this time for a different reason.

'That's brilliant,' I said. 'The old people will be, like, legendary, and we'll—'

'We'll just be boring parents. Exactly.'

'So how much have you written?'

'I've done a lot of research,' he said. 'It's not easy. I think, well, to be honest I'd have to have all my faculties before actually, you know, writing about—'

I confess I laughed. He looked taken aback.

'You could write about them from the outside,' I said. 'Don't worry about their inner life, for now.'

He blinked. 'That's a good idea,' he said. 'Thanks.'

But I don't think he has done anything about it. He showed me around the town and helped me to find a place to stay. I met him at a few parties, and sometimes, as now, in the same café.

'Morning,' he said, this morning. He was writing.

I sat down with my pot of coffee and plate of berrybread. Grant absently helped himself to a chunk of the latter and went back to tapping the table. Naked people were doing weird stuff on the screen. I'd finished my first cup before he stopped.

'Working on your novel?' I asked.

'Oh, no.' He waved away the idea. 'I'm writing up a habitat proposal. For IC413.'

'Ambitious,' I said. 'A low-number rock.'

The ship radar has been busy the past few months. Kuiper-belt and asteroid-belt objects are now up in the thousands. Most of the early – thus large and/or near – ones have been tabbed.

'It's more than a rock,' Grant said. 'It's got everything. Metals, volatiles, carbon . . .'

'And nobody's tabbed it?'

He gave me an almost adult look. 'It's not AB, it's IC.'

'All the same . . .'

'It's a waterworld moon, if you can't be bothered to look it up. A very small one.'

'No wonder it's unclaimed.'

'It could become a resort. That's my proposal.'

'A resort? It'll be decades before anyone can afford a resort.'

'Yes,' he said, 'but think about what this could offer them when they do. It's a long-term investment.'

'In what? A place to watch algae patches from orbit?'

'Access to the waterworld,' he said. 'Build a skyhook down. Sailing, swimming . . .'

'*Swimming*? In ten gravities?'

'All right then, surfing. Extreme sports.'

I just snorted. 'Drowning is extreme, yes!'

I was a little disappointed in him. I'd been toying with the idea of asking him on to my team, though I was sure he intended to found his own. I've no intention of going near a gravity well, let alone building a business out of lowering people into one, and the second-deepest in the system at that.

I was telling him all this at perhaps unnecessary length and with uncalled-for vehemence when an unusual irritating chime came from the wall screen. *Forty-Five Free Fall Love Positions*, or whatever the morning programme was, vanished and the World Service Announcement screen came up. Last time I'd seen that, and heard the chime, was when the news about the electromagnetic spectrum sources came through. I felt a pang in my belly.

Seeing the introduction didn't make it go away: all about how the probes en route can send back pictures which – because they're so far apart – can be combined and processed and jiggered with to form an image like what you'd get from an enormous telescope.

'Let go my hand,' Grant said.

'Sorry,' I said. He sucked his knuckles.

Then the first picture came up, of a blue hemisphere whorled with white clouds. We just had time to catch breath when the second came up, and stayed. Strip the cloud layer, enhance, and there it is: a hemisphere almost filled with land.

'Wow,' said Grant. 'A super-continent!'

'Not quite,' I pointed out. 'Look, the top half, you can see it's breaking up.' I counted. 'Six chunks. Island continents.'

'Yes, yes,' Grant said. I could hear he was still sore about his fingers. 'The Southern one on its own is a supercontinent. And the others are so close that a *bird* could fly across the gaps.'

I leaned back, smiling. 'Some day there might be birds. Maybe we should give it to the crows.'

Grant was still staring at the screen. People were shouting and speculating. I was too entranced even to pull out my slate. The brown and green of continents, divided by the narrow blue channels and surrounded by the wide blue sea.

'Green,' Grant said. 'Lots of it. Inland.'

'That's a lot of algae,' I said.

He stared at me. 'You get algae mats on oceans, not on land. We're looking at vegetation. We're looking at *plants*.'

It was then that I saw what I was looking at: a rocky terrestrial with a multicellular biosphere, the first in fourteen thousand years.

'Another Earth,' Grant breathed.

I struggled to place the word, then remembered. It's an archaic name for the Moon's primary.

'Oh,' I said.

Horrocks Mathematical had a gene-complex that processed iron molecules in his head. It lined them up in a delicate tracery that intercepted electromagnetic waves and transmitted electrical currents to his occipital lobes, where they stimulated neurons that formed images in his visual system. The gene-complex was activated at puberty and the resulting structure reached maturity several years afterwards. It was not considered suitable for children and adolescents. It was called television.

He also had natural neural connections formed out of experience, like everyone else. His experiences, also like everyone
else's, were unique. Something in that background of experience – it could have been his studies of biology, his fascination
with terrestrial planets, his skills at habitat construction, his
gambler's eye on the markets, or all of them together or something altogether else – was bugging him. Whenever he looked
at a representation of the signals from the rocky world, he felt
a sensation in his head akin to an itch, or to an incipient
sneeze, or to the feeling that you have forgotten or overlooked
something vital and can't for the life of you imagine what.

SIX

THE QUEEN OF HEAVEN'S DAUGHTERS

The University Museum was a tall cylindrical structure, ringed within by galleries and bristled without by tubes of wood and ceramic that regulated the humidity of its air circulation. Inside, the drip and sigh of this great battery of devices merged to a single vast whisper like a giant librarian's hush. The air was clean and clear, scented of timber and water, and carried the merest whiff of the green algae that flourished under the runoffs of the pipes.

Darvin paced along the Gallery of the Southern Rule, glancing at the treasures of leatherwork and metalwork, of chiselled stone and hammered steel on display. The single great continent south of the equator, on the other side of the Middle Channel's hot, stormy, narrow sea, had laid the basis for an antiquity and continuity of civilisation denied by a more fragmented geography to the reaches and realms of the North. No Long Night – and no Dawn Age, either – had interrupted its protracted and undivided day. Nature itself seemed grander and older there. Gigantic predators, similar to the long-extinct monsters whose log-sized, stone-soaked bones sometimes weathered out of the North's ravines, still haunted its uplands, and preyed on horizon-darkening, earth-shaking herds of likewise gargantuan grazers, likewise long gone elsewhere.

At the cabinets of literature and painting – the distinction was contested, even by experts – Darvin stopped. Parchment scrolls many wingspans long were the main display; every day or two, a museum attendant would wind every scroll forward, to avoid excessive exposure to the daylight. Intricate and colourful, crowded with figurative scenes that sharpened into structures of glyphs before the eye, and with lines of lettering that rioted into characters and animalcules in lush symbolic landscapes even as one tried to descry their rhythm, they glittered with a sensibility at once grave and gay, an outlook solemn and frivolous, a theology horrific and humorous, a philosophy perceptive and pedantic. Darvin hurried past them, seeking another exhibit which he recalled having noticed on his introductory tour.

There it was, a broad, dark backdrop to a tall glass-fronted case of astrolabes and orreries. Of a fine, hard-wearing and unfading opaque black cloth, three wingspans across by three high, it was worked with a multitude of minute separate stitches of coloured wire – silver mostly, some copper, a few gold, and a whole palette of precisely coloured alloys and anodised metals. It could have been a banner, or a wall hanging, or a wrap. It was something altogether different, and more astonishing than even its breathtaking beauty might suggest. It was a map of the night sky, from the northern and the Southern hemispheres both, a seamless rendition of an unseeable scene. Its construction must have taken spans of moons; its preparation, eights of eights of years. From a distance – from the opposite side of the gallery, across the well of the museum tower – it would have looked like a breath of fog, a silver shimmer; in the wrong light, a dull pewter grey.

Darvin peered at the label, a yellowed scrap of curling paper in the corner of the case, the Selohic words lettered in a shaky Gevorkian script, ink faded to brown. The map, looted in some raid on a temple on the northern coast of the Southern Rule back in the Long Night, was as nearly as could be determined one thousand and seven hundred and fifty years old. He nodded to himself and examined the celestial embroidery. The blue-green stars of the Daughters were quite distinct, as were their copper, gold, or silver neighbours. He examined it for any wayward stitch that might represent a comet, and found none. As he assimilated this small disappointment, a quite different anomaly struck him. He knew that patch of sky well by now, and it looked wrong. He took a sheet of paper and a pen from his belt pouch and copied with great care the area of the Daughters, noting the colour of each prominent star. There were only twenty-seven green stars; he knew there were many more.

He gazed at the display for a long time, then folded away the paper, sheathed the pen, and vaulted off the gallery railing. His long swoop across the ground floor and out of the door was accompanied by indignant yells from the attendants, but he didn't care. He flew back to the Department of Astronomy and stalked to his office. His hands were trembling as he riffled through the photographic plates, shaking as he compared one with his sketch. The plate was, of course, black and white, so he had to look the stars up in the ephemeris. He circled them, one by one, on the sheet of thin translucent paper that protected the photograph, and forced himself to count with great care. Of the most visible stars in the Daughters, fifty-eight were classified as green. On his sketch, the other thirty-one were marked as red, or yellow, or white.

He telephoned Orro.

*

'This must have been noticed before,' said the Gevorkian.

'It has,' said Darvin, hunched over an old encyclopedia of astronomy he'd tugged from a high shelf. '"Southern Rule, astronomy of,"' he read out. '"Impressive in the detail of its observations, especially of comets (q.v.) and the sophistication of its instruments (q.v.) but vitiated by its traditional association with astrology (q.v.) and the religious and symbolic basis of its systems of celestial classification, a characteristic instance of which can be seen in the Temple Sky Map (q.v.) with its misleading rendition of the Daughters."'

Darvin flipped over pages, dislodging dust. '"Temple Sky Map: Booty of glorious battle of blah blah . . . astounding workmanship blah blah . . . despite this the colours used for stars in some instances, e.g. the Daughters (q.v.), apparently chosen for aesthetic or symbolic reasons, related to astrology (q.v.) blah blah . . . superstition blah blah . . . sad instance of scholastic dogmatism reminiscent of Seloh's own Long Night blah blah . . . benighted priesthood blah blah . . . nevertheless of great historical interest and remarkable beauty, currently on display in Five Ravines", et cetera.' He looked up. 'Tickets, sweets and souvenirs at the door.'

Orro laughed. 'A "sad instance of scholastic dogmatism" indeed,' he said. 'Even in the Long Night, it was believed that the Queen passes Her green gift to other gods, who become the Daughters.'

'That,' said Darvin, clapping the book shut, 'is precisely why any idea that the stars could change colour in historical time is no longer believed. It's regarded as a quaint superstition.'

'There are variable stars,' said Orro.

'Yes, but they're cyclic. Well understood. Their fires flare and fade periodically.'

'Fires?' Orro looked sceptical, and rather as if he'd caught Darvin out.

'All right,' said Darvin. 'The physics of stars is not well understood.'

'Nor is the physics of radioactivity,' said Orro, with apparent irrelevance. He fixed Darvin in a quizzical gaze for a moment, then sighed. 'Oh well. I suppose we should next investigate some early modern observations – Dawn Age and onward.'

'I've done it,' said Darvin, tapping a finger-claw on a stack of open books on his desk. He stood up. 'Predictably enough, it turns out that some of the Daughters were misidentified as other types of stars, back then. Inadequate telescopes, unskilful observations – you know how it is.'

He dragged one of the books across the desk, pointed at a reproduction of a crude woodcut illustration in which the stars were shown encircled by tiny flames, and marked by tinier letters. The key, written in Orkan but in Selohic script, classified forty-nine of the stars as green, and identified the nine others now included among the Daughters as yellow or red.

Orro laid the tracing of the recent photograph and Darvin's sketch of the ancient map on opposite sides of the book.

'It seems,' he said, 'that we have identified a trend.'

'Is it possible,' Darvin asked, 'that the *modern* classification is wrong?' He laughed. 'I myself have never counted the Daughters. Actually, since I became an astronomer, I've hardly looked at the sky.'

'Let's do that,' said Orro. 'Let's go out on to the high plain and count them for ourselves.'

'The high plain . . .' Darvin said. 'Yes, let us do that tomorrow, and one thing else that we can only do in the day.'

'What's that?'

Darvin grinned. 'You'll see.'

The main cable-car station was quiet the following morning, after the earlier incoming rush of travellers from the plains settlements had subsided. Darvin and Orro, carrying small packs of dried meat and dried fruit and with knives and electric torches clipped to their belts, climbed into a car and sat side by side. A trudge bolted the door and pushed the car around the curve of the terminus loop to face the exit, then tugged a lever to clamp the overhead to the active cable. The car lurched forward into the sunlight outside, rushed up above a steep slope to a stubby pylon at the top, jolted over it then settled into a more gradual ascent to the clifftop pylon that overlooked the town. Darvin poked his head through the open side window and gazed down at the crowded roosts and deep ravines, pondering how different they looked when one was borne aloft from how they looked when flying. The sensation was strange and dreamlike. After a few moments it made him feel queasy. He turned and faced ahead.

The journey to the ochre cliffs of the high plains table-land took about an hour. Halfway up the long catenary that connected the final pylon on the grassland with that of the substation at the top of the cliff, Orro gave a grunt.

'What?' said Darvin.

'I calculate that if the cable were to snap now, we'd have time to take wing before the car hit the ground.'

'Thanks for that,' said Darvin.

The cliff-face loomed, closer and closer. It seemed incredible that they would not crash into it. The car's ascent steepened. Darvin stared fixedly ahead. From this vantage, the ochre sandstone of the cliff was broken and blemished with scrubby bushes and clumps of plants in cracks and shelves, and by great shit-stains of flitter droppings.

Just before the car stopped at the substation Darvin stood up, swaying. 'This is where we get out.'

'Here?'

'Yes.'

The substation was there to provide auxiliary power, but the

cliff was something of a visitor attraction in its own right, so
the cars always stopped there for a few minutes before continuing across the table-land. Darvin and Orro stepped out on the
platform and watched the car's grip glide along a rail and connect to the new loop of the cable. It jolted away, swaying.
There was an open stairway to the ground, for those too laden
or infirm to fly, and a short flight of steps up to a railed view-
ing platform overhanging the clifftop. With wordless assent
the two scientists climbed to it. From there they had a view,
uncluttered by the station or the cables, in all directions: across
the grassland to the glittering sea; along the great sweep of the
cliff; northward, over the high desert table-land, sandy and
barren, breaking in the near distance into wind-sculpted
mesas; and down the eight eights-of-eight drop of the cliff.

'I take it you want to visit the famous caves,' said Orro.

'Correct,' said Darvin.

He hitched his pack of provisions to his belt and clambered
on to the rail. It was too narrow to grasp with his toe- and
heel-claws, but he balanced on it easily, rocking back and forth
on the soles of his feet as he sniffed the wind, scried the shimmer of the heat haze, espied the floating spiral paths of flitters,
and formed somewhere between his brain and his spine a sense
of the shape of the air. He spread his wings, tipped forward,
thrust with his feet, and dived.

The cliff's updraught, on this hot morning, was immense.
He could have hung there like a carrion-eating flitter, almost
without a wingbeat. To fly at this height without the effort of
having climbed to it was exhilarating, with a pleasant sense of
the unearned. The thrum of the airstream on his wings
tempted him to cavort. Instead he tilted and glided downward.
The extra weight he carried sped his descent and he flapped a
vigorous wingbeat or two to adjust. At a couple of eights-of-
eight spans clear of the cliff-face and about an eight-of-eight
down, he banked, beginning to describe a slow spiral. A glance

up showed him Orro following. The physicist waved. Flitters screamed and flocked away. Others, perhaps a different species, fluttered in and out of caves. Darvin scanned the caves. The one he sought was well known and often visited, but quite unmarked, except for the flitter-wire mesh of a gate set a little way back from its entrance, to keep out the wild flying animals.

He spotted it, gestured to Orro, and stooped towards it. He landed with a running thud on the lip of its ledge, and came to a halt up against the mesh. Orro crashed to the same terminus a few seconds later.

'Ha-ha-ha!' he barked. 'That was enjoyable!'

Darvin nodded, panting a little. 'Yes. Well, let our briefly brisker blood-surges power our arms . . .'

The gate was a crude and heavy wooden affair, three heights of a man high; its frame and crossbeams must have been let down from the top on ropes, and likewise with the roll of sturdy-wired fine-holed mesh, much stronger than normal flitter-wire. But rather to Darvin's surprise, the latch was a simple metal hook and loop, and the door swung back on squeaking wooden hinges. The two men stepped through and hauled it back into place behind them, then looked around.

'Stinks in here,' said Orro.

'Dried flitter-shit,' said Darvin. His nose wrinkled. 'Perhaps not *all* dry . . .'

Ignoring what was soft underfoot, he unclipped his electric torch and thumbed the switch. Its heavy *click*, or perhaps the yellow beam, disturbed some things small and dark and swift, that flew chittering further into the cave's depth.

'What do they live on?' Orro wondered aloud, shining his own torch around.

'Dead people,' said Darvin, in a hollow voice. 'Come on.'

A path on the floor of the cave had been worn smooth by the tread of previous visitors. In the electric torchlight, it almost

shone. Darvin and Orro paced along it. The occasional droppings of the small flitters apart, the cave was dry, with nothing
of the dankness and weed that Darvin had half expected, from
some dim association with sea-caves. The air too was fresh;
some of the caves were said to connect to sink-holes well
behind the clifftop, and their occupants – human visitors or
animal tenants – were in danger of being flushed out in the
flash floods of rare rainstorms. The risk seemed small.

'I'm told it's about two eights-of-eights of steps,' said
Darvin.

'When did you start counting?'

'Good point,' said Darvin, and began his mental count at a
double-eight.

But the sight they had come to see was hard to miss. The
cave widened not quite enough for the space to be called a
chamber. High on its walls, and arching over its roof, were
eights-of-eights of coloured drawings. The sketched outlines of
humans were so crude that they could as well have delineated
moths. Animals, prey and grazer, flitter and cursor, were rendered with a colour and tone and line that made one
hallucinate that they breathed. Oddly, they were untouched by
droppings; only a soot-stain here and there sullied them, from
the guttering wooden torches of the first discoverers, scientists – and later, gaping, adventurous travellers – of the Dawn
Age.

It was not the only, or the best, example of the cliff-men's art
in Seloh: new caves were being discovered all the time, right
along the whole edge of the table-land. But it was famous, and
close to wing, and Darvin knew what picture to look for. He
scanned the walls with his beam.

'There!' he said, lighting on a patch about two wingspans up
the wall.

'That pattern of dots?'

'Yes. It's generally supposed to represent the Queen and the

Daughters – they're picked out in a green stain made from, I believe, some kind of copper salt. And of course, being ignorant cliff-men, our clumsy ancestors only bothered to pick out a few.'

He turned to Orro. 'If you wouldn't mind, I'd like to stand on your shoulders for a moment.'

Orro shrugged. 'If you must.'

Darvin backed off, sprang into the air and flapped. He hovered for a few seconds, then lowered his feet on to Orro's shoulders. He resisted the reflex to curl his toes. Keeping his wings outstretched for balance, clutching the heavy torch, he peered at the stone wall. The largest of the green markings was a precise circle about the size of the palm of a hand. He'd consulted the two most reputable books on cave-paintings, and in the brief passages describing this cave the sharp outline was held as evidence that the patch represented the Queen (as well as, less reliably, that the cliff-men had had better eyesight than their modern descendants). Around Her was a seeming random speckle of green dots, each the size of a fingertip. They didn't look like even the more prominent of the Daughters; it was indeed tempting to regard them as a crude indication.

He looked closer yet, leaning forward then almost toppling back, then forward again as he regained his balance. In among the green spots were others, fainter and smaller but definite. Some were made with ochre, some with what he guessed was sulphur, others perhaps with chalk; all of them ground into the sandstone with such force that the markings had left little pits. Red, yellow and white; there was no mistaking the intent.

'Take your time,' said Orro.

Contrite, Darvin hopped off and alighted on the floor. Orro rubbed his shoulders.

'Your turn,' Darvin said. He stepped forward and took a notebook and pencil from his belt pouch and handed them to

Orro. 'Hop up on my shoulders and draw what you see. Make a note of the colour of each spot. I'll shine the torch up for you.'

A minute later Darvin was certain that Orro must be heavier than he himself was. He clenched his jaws and concentrated on keeping the light steady. After another few painful minutes Orro grunted and jumped off. Darvin felt for a moment light enough to fly, and too sore to do so. Orro returned the pad and pencil. Darvin looked at it in the electric light. It was spread across the opening of two pages, a score of annotated circles and dots.

'Neat,' he said. The electric light was fading and yellowing by the minute. 'Let's look at it outside.'

They squatted in the cave-mouth, leaning back on the mesh doorway, facing an abyss of air, a shimmer of grassland, a horizon-line of sea. Darvin felt his every muscle and nerve sing with relief.

'I don't believe the cliff-men lived in caves at all,' he said. 'They're just too horrible.'

'That is a widespread scientific opinion,' said Orro. 'They left their dead in them, or perhaps just their illustrious dead; they may have used them as stores, or as places of worship and meditation; but the popular belief that they inhabited caves is ill-founded.'

'I'm glad to hear it,' said Darvin. He sighed; he was almost reluctant, now, to at last find out whether his own expectation of the caves was ill-founded. 'Well, let's see what we've got.'

He unfolded three pieces of paper: his tracing of the photograph, his sketch of the silk map, and his tracing of the antique woodcut. He spread them on the ground and weighted them with pebbles, then placed the notebook, open at Orro's sketch, beside them. The patterns were not quite identical, and not all the stars shown in one were shown in the others, but as he looked from one drawing to the next, and back, again and again, it was obvious that they were all of the same familiar patch of sky.

The evidence before his eyes was as clear as the jump on a blink comparator: the cliff-men had recorded seven of the stars in the Daughters as green, and the rest as other colours.

'You were right,' he said. 'We have a trend.'

He closed his eyes for a moment, and saw a drifting fleet of dots, as if the images he'd looked at were resonating in his optic nerves, fainter and more persistent than an after-image. He blinked it away and gazed out at the sky.

'In prehistory, the cliff-men saw seven green Daughters. In antiquity, the astrologers of the South saw twenty-seven. In the Dawn Age, mere eights-of-eights of years ago, forty-nine. In the present day, we see fifty-eight with the naked eye, and more with telescopes. And it's not that some are brighter now than they were then — our ancestors saw stars in the same positions, and saw them as red, yellow, or white. These stars have changed from other colours to green, in the lifetime of the human race.'

Orro jumped up and stalked about for a moment, to the very lip of the cave and back.

'Stars evolve,' he said. 'From white to yellow to red, isn't it?'

'I know of that hypothesis,' said Darvin. 'The fire analogy. It's speculative, and going from every other colour to green would knock it right on the head.'

'Not necessarily,' said Orro. 'If the green represents a different evolution: life spreading from star to star.'

'Ah, the comet plants!' said Darvin. 'The vacuum forests!'

Orro shrugged. 'Life is adaptable.' He glared down at Darvin. 'You are testing me with your scepticism. You do not feel it yourself.'

'No,' said Darvin. 'I don't.' He folded the sheets of paper between the pages of the notebook and tucked it away. 'Tell me what you suspect I suspect.'

Orro squatted down again. 'Isn't it obvious? You suspect that the green tinge is caused by life, yes, but by life in some artificial environment.' He outlined a circle with his hands. 'Great globes of glass, perhaps, somehow launched into space, containing complete economies of nature, plants and animals alike, and whatever intelligent inhabitants have built them. That they multiply around a sun, to the extent that eventually they filter all of its light. And that as each sun's environs become crowded, great ships are launched across the voids between the stars, to repeat the process around another sun. Your comet is of course such a ship, decelerating into orbit around the Sun Himself. In years to come, our sky will be crowded with the green globes, and we ourselves may look forward to meeting the mighty builders of worlds, should they deign to notice such as us.'

Darvin looked sidelong at his friend with admiration. 'What a delightful fancy!' he said. 'No, really. And it is a possibility, I concede. But as scientists rather then writers of engineering tales, we should seek explanations in the work of nature rather than the hand of mind whenever possible. I think it's life, certainly, and that it is spreading, but I think it may be an entirely natural process. Because if life − a hardy spore that escaped the atmosphere, perhaps − were to gain a foothold on some rock or comet in space, it could spread. As it did so it would be modified by evolution, and its own actions would modify the paths of the bodies on which it grew. A decelerating comet seems much more plausible if we imagine its outgassing to be controlled − mindlessly it is true − by some life within.'

Orro was shaking his head. 'A journey from star to star would take millions of years. We're seeing stars changing over eights-of-eights.'

'I'm not talking about passive drifting, like spores or downy seeds on the wind. I imagine some much faster propulsion.' He

swept his arms in a circle wider than the one Orro had outlined
a moment earlier. 'A sail of some sort.'

'Propelled by what wind?'

'Light exerts a pressure in vacuum,' said Darvin. 'The Sun
gives forth a fiery stream of other particles.'

'Too weak a one for star-sailing,' Orro said. 'No, Darvin, we
are looking at . . . space ships. And artificial worlds in numbers
that beggar the imagination.'

Darvin felt his knees shake. He did and did not want to
believe it.

Orro took two strips of dried meat from his provisions pack,
passed one to Darvin and started chewing on the other. 'Here
is an idea for further research. We find out the distance of each
of the stars charted in the Daughters region, green or not. We
can see whether the earlier green stars are closer together than
the later ones. From this we can see if a spread from star to star
is actually happening.'

Darvin nodded. 'Obvious,' he said. 'Go on.'

'And we check whether spectrographic analysis exists for
any of these stars. If we were to find that they still show traces
of the spectra from stars with lights of other colours than
green, and they match the ancient records, we'd have made our
case. And then we should find out the composition of the
green light itself.'

'Oh, I know what that is,' said Darvin. 'Its spectra show the
lines of oxygen, carbon, and nitrogen.'

Orro jumped up again. 'But these are the constituents of *life
itself!*'

'Yes,' said Darvin. 'And that's one reason why astronomers
regard life around these stars as possible. That is not the surprise. The surprise, if we are right, is that we have evidence
that it is spreading. Or at least,' he added, struck by an intellectual scruple, 'that it is arising around more and more stars.'

'Why has more not been made of this?' Orro almost

shouted. 'Life around the stars would be the most significant finding of astronomy!'

Darvin thought about it, chewing on the strip. 'Hmm,' he said. 'I suppose because it's all so wretchedly hypothetical, old chap, and so embarrassing to seem to confirm the myths of religion and the . . . sensationalism of the vulgar.'

He smiled at Orro and gestured at him to sit down. 'Let's eat,' he said. 'And then let's take wing, and fly over the high desert, and find some place of comfortable vantage to wait for nightfall and count the Daughters for ourselves.'

It goes all the way down, Darvin thought to himself. Out here in the pitch black of a night before either of the moons had risen, away from lights and smoke, the sky came all the way down to the ground. You could see stars blink into view as they rose above the horizon, and to the west you could watch them disappear beneath it. And in between, in the vault above, the sky was packed with stars. The whole sky shimmered with the massed twinkling in multiple colours. The Shining Path spanned the zenith. The constellations, lost in the crowd, were more difficult to identify than they were at night in Five Ravines.

The Queen dominated the ecliptic, the Warrior a distant second. Between the Shining Path and the ecliptic the Daughters shone green across the eastern sky. He had counted the fifty-eight, and wasn't sure there weren't more. Behind the visible green stars was a greenish haze. In the midst of them, like a ruby among emeralds, glowed the Blood-drop, known to astronomy as Stella Proxima, the Nearest Star.

Orro was staring at it.

'That's where your comet came from,' he said. 'Stella Proxima.'

'If it was a space ship,' said Darvin, 'I suppose it must have done.'

'No!' said Orro. 'There is no supposition about it. Can't you see, man, that's where the trajectory goes back to?'

'I can't see it,' said Darvin. 'I'm no mathematician. But I have no doubt you can show me it, when we get back.' He shivered. 'Speaking of which.'

'The passenger cars aren't running,' said Orro.

'What?' said Darvin, feeling stupid. 'But the overnight mail—'

' Travels in what are known, technically, as *mail cars*,' said Orro. 'So here we stay.'

'We can't!' said Darvin, looking around. He could just about see. He could *hear* things.

'How are you going to get back?' jeered Orro. 'Fly?'

Darvin wrapped his wings around himself. 'What else can we do?'

Orro's eyes showed their whites in the starlit dark. 'You've never spent a night out of cover?'

'No.'

'I have,' said Orro. 'Let me show you.'

He vanished into the dark. A few minutes later – Darvin confirmed the time by the wheeling of the stars, but it seemed longer – he returned with a double armful of brushwood. He stacked some and set fire to it. Rising sparks replaced the stars, and the crackling of twigs muffled the distant scurries.

'We have some food left,' he said. 'And water.'

'Not much water.'

Orro flourished a glass flask. 'Firewater,' he said. 'So called because it keeps us warm.'

Darvin joined him in a huddle over the small fire. Orro began turning a strip of dried meat above the flames. The smell became appetising.

'Where did you learn all this?' Darvin asked.

'Military training.'

'Ah,' said Darvin. He bit off a chunk of the now much more

palatable meat and handed the remainder back. 'This is a delicate question,' he said. 'I hope I don't offend.'

Orro waved the strip, munching. 'Go ahead.'

'I didn't know ironmongers' sons had military training.'

'They don't, generally,' said Orro. He unstoppered the firewater flask, swigged and passed it to Darvin. 'But "scientific civil servant" is a rank of nobility. Hence military training, from the Academy onward.'

The firewater burned in Darvin's mouth and down his throat. 'You're a nobleman?'

'Indeed I am,' said Orro. 'And a not very competent sabreur. I preened myself on being a somewhat more adequate scout.'

Darvin laughed. 'I thought that to be a noble one had to own land.'

'Oh, I do,' said Orro. 'I am entitled to the rent of an acre.'

'How much does that come to?'

'Nothing,' said Orro. 'It's a patch of uninhabited and barren desert.' He laughed. 'Some have become rich from such fiefs. They found rock-oil.'

'So you have a chance.'

Orro shook his head. 'Geologically speaking, and regretfully, no.'

He threw more brush on the fire. The flask passed back and forth. Orro talked about his military training, and about his friend Holder, who had enjoyed it so much that he'd moved from the civil service to the Regnal Air Force. They had remained friends, and it was only Orro's choice of exile that had severed the connection.

'Surely you could write to him,' said Darvin.

'I did,' said Orro. He stared into the fire and spread his hands. 'Some have seen my departure as a betrayal. I don't say he has, but he didn't reply.'

They banked the fire and lay down beside it, wrapped in their wings. At some point in the night, when the moons had risen and crossed the sky and were sinking in the west, Darvin woke to find Orro's wing over him. He wondered what to do, and decided to appreciate the added warmth and go back to sleep. In the morning it seemed like a dream. The two men awoke a wingspan apart, shook the dew off their fur and wings, and flew to the cable station.

'Isn't this impressive!' Orro said.

Darvin gazed at the tangle of wires and torch-bulbs that hung from the ceiling of Orro's laboratory like some demented festive decoration. Now that he noticed, some of the bulbs were decorative, coloured red and green. There were about eight eights of bulbs – no, more, because all of them were paired: one white or red, one green.

'Aha!' he said, as he got the point. 'Now I'm impressed.'

'I thought you would be,' said Orro. 'It took me five days to work out the positions of the stars, and four to wire all this up.' He pulled up a chair. 'Sit here.'

He pulled down blinds at each of the windows, leaving the room as dark as the desert night. He sat down at a bank of switches, and threw one. The bulbs flashed on in a three-dimensional display of stars. Seven were green, a close cluster. Another switch, and twenty more turned green. Then there were forty-nine, and then fifty-eight. In each case the new green stars were farther from the original seven, and themselves adjacent within a ragged arc. Orro repeated the process several times, to display again and again the green spreading like a shockwave. Through it all one small bulb, hanging at the near end of the display in front of Darvin's nose, remained at red.

'The Nearest Star,' said Darvin. He stood up, shifted about, narrowed his eyes until he could see the green bulbs as the Daughters appeared in the night sky.

'Now run it through again,' he said.

The green wave rushed at him. He almost flinched.

'Something is coming,' he breathed. He'd deduced it himself, in the patterns of light and light-years he'd constructed from the ephemeris and the catalogues, but until now he had not quite believed it.

Orro snapped the blinds back up. Light filled the room, leaving the bulbs tawdry.

'How long,' Darvin asked, 'before the Nearest Star turns green? Will we see it, or our descendants?'

'I don't think we can wait that long,' said Orro. He slid some stapled sheets of paper across the table. Darvin spun it around and looked at the title, above his name and Orro's:

A Distant, Decelerating Celestial Object; with Some Observations on the Daughters

'We must publish this,' said Orro. 'Now.'

SEVEN

TELEVISION

14 365:01:13 06:10

Have you seen the pictures have you seen the pictures have you seen the pictures???

14 365:01:13 08:12

Lights on the night side. Nobody expected this. Nobody has any doubt what it means. Not even Grey Universal. Those sims he rattled up in minutes for volcanoes, brush fires, and – wait for it – the phosphorescence of rotting wood are just to show he can. He just likes being contrary, and likes the attention. His Coriolis storm sims had everyone fascinated, for a while, and arguing. But he doesn't believe his latest: I've asked him; he admitted it. He doesn't even buy the other contrary hold-out minority view, that the lights are from some kind of Red Sun robot or download colonies that claim-jumped us. Nobody but nobody would be mad enough to plant colonies on a unique planet, a terrestrial with multicellular life – least of all robots. That's what he told me. He's as excited as everybody else.

Excited is not the word. My hands are shaking as I write this.

There are aliens down there on Destiny II.

I sat and looked at that sentence for ten minutes. I still don't wholly believe it. I still have that particle of doubt. I still feel that I risk being very foolish. Though being as foolish as everybody else is at least not embarrassing. (No, it would be, actually, now that I come to think of it.) All right. If ever I am going to put together a team, and take the lead in setting up a habitat, I'm going to have to build a reputation for being level-headed and thoughtful, as well as of course being the wonderful personality you all know I am.

So I have given this matter some thought already, as soon as we knew about the plants and the biosphere. That was the first hole in the hull, if you'll forgive my crudity. If there really is intelligent life down there it makes things complicated in all sorts of ways, which I'll come to in a minute. But the fundamental shock is finding multicellular life in the first place.

Think about it. Fourteen thousand years – longer, I suppose, because even in prehistory people must have looked at the sky and seen, you know, nothing like the green haze of the Civil Worlds – of expansion into a volume hundreds of light-years across, and we've never found anything more advanced than bacteria or algae or slime moulds or something like lichen. Nothing but rock crust and pond scum.

OK. Now that makes sense, makes sense in a very deep way. It's called the principle of mediocrity. I looked it up. What it means is that multicellular life, leave alone intelligent life, is either very rare, or very nearly ubiquitous. If it were the latter, our whole sky would have been green and the galaxy would have been called the Grassy Path. And because it's not, we know it's almost vanishingly rare. What we have found, all the way out from the Moon, has just confirmed this, over and over and over again. The planets have spoken with one voice, and what they've said thousands of times over is *pond scum pond scum pond scum*. The silence of the sky chimes in with *nobody's home nobody's home nobody's home*. The silence is telling us: there's nobody else out here to talk to.

Now there is, almost certainly. But think about it. Apply the principle that there's nothing special about us. What are the odds against *the only two* intelligent species in the galaxy arising independently within five hundred light-years of each other, and arriving at civilisation (city lights and electromagnetic communications) within less than twenty thousand years of each other? On the scale of the galaxy, we're neighbours. On the scale of evolutionary time, of billions of years, we're in the same generation, the same cohort. More: we share the same birthday, to the hour, to the minute . . .

This is so unlikely that something else, something quite shattering, is more probable: we aren't *the only two*.

It's not just that we're not alone. We, the humans and the aliens, are not alone. *We two* are not alone.

And that means, I'm afraid, that we can't just do the colonisation thing, at least not without thinking about it very carefully. So let's think about it very carefully.

14 365:01:13 13:45

Look, folks, lay off the hate mail, OK? I was just *saying*.

Television, thought Horrocks Mathematical. Like almost everyone else on the ship, he gazed transfixed at the images of the planet's night side, the coastlines and some of the interior spaces of its continents pricked out by light. Unlike anyone else, he jumped to a swift conclusion as to the nature of the enigmatic signals that had been troubling him for months.

Television. That was what it was.

Not the kind of television that gave him pictures in his head, but something quite other and more primitive. But the pictures in his head gave him access to and an interface with the processing power that could reconstruct that suspected source. He plunged into its depths, brushing aside all the confuted hypotheses about codes and encryption, and insisting instead on the command to turn the signal into lines: a few hundred at the most, each at most a few hundred pixels across.

The answer came back in less than a second.

Bat-like beings flew behind his eyes. He closed his eyes, but still they were there, in fuzzy black and white. The flurry settled, dark smudges whirled like snow, and an image stabilised: of one of these beings behind a desk, reading aloud from a sheaf of paper. He heard the voice in his head. Fluctuating from a chirp to a deeper, more measured pitch, it intoned a sequence of phonemes that, even across the gulfs of space and species and speech, sounded like statistics.

It seemed fitting that the first words to be heard might be the names of numbers. That could be a meaty bone for some ravenous heuristic. Horrocks had only a vague idea of what kind of programs would be needed to begin to pick away at interpreting the language, let alone what kind of human skills would be needed. In the population of the ship and in the vaster virtual space of the ship's intelligence repertoire, such programs and skills were certain to be found.

He released the images he'd reconstructed into the ship's nets, with a priority attention override that few people ever cared or dared to use in all their long lifespans. It seemed that he heard a sound like an intense gust, the sound of a million in-drawn breaths, but that might just have been his imagination.

He turned off most of his own input channels and continued

to watch the pictures. After a few minutes the alien laid down the sheaf of paper, said something, and stood up. It came out from behind the desk. For the first time it was visible at full length. With its wings folded it looked like a human being with a furled umbrella tucked under each elbow and angled up behind each shoulder. Its gait was steady, its feet peculiar. Its eyes and ears were prominent, giving it a sharp triangular face. The sole garment it wore was a belt around the hips, laden with scabbards and boxy pouches. Fur, varied in length and shade, covered the rest of its body.

The alien stopped in front of the camera. A hand with three fingers and a thumb loomed, then one of the fingers reached forward and out of shot. The image dwindled to a dot and vanished.

Another image replaced it, not from the alien transmission. Horrocks had never seen Constantine before, but he recognised him.

'I should have you shot,' the Oldest Man said. 'For endangering the ship and everyone on it.'

'How did I do that?' Horrocks asked.

'You sent images from an unknown source to the brains and screens and contacts of everyone on this ship,' said Constantine. 'You released them into the ship's intelligence. Do you have any idea how dangerous that could be?'

'No,' said Horrocks. 'I'm sorry, but I don't. It's obviously a very primitive transmission.'

Constantine passed a hand across his eyes, rubbing his eyebrows with thumb and forefinger.

'That's exactly the problem,' he said.

'I don't understand.'

'No,' said Constantine. 'You don't.' He glared at Horrocks for a few seconds, then smiled. 'Don't do it again.'

*

14 365:01:13 20:19

Well, that's it settled. Aliens.

What a day. There's nothing to say that doesn't sound banal. Is it always like this, on days when the world changes? Did people who wrote, assuming people did write, have this stupid gnawing feeling all the way back to the Moon Caves and before, that your words are inadequate to the events and that anything you say now will shame you in days to come with its inadequacy? What was it like to react to the first starship launch? The first extrasolar colony? The first news of a fast burn?

This changes the world more than any of these. I see from some of the comments I've received that some people don't grasp this at all. They think intelligent aliens are just one more interesting thing out there, like any new biosphere, or a new stellar process, but more exciting and of more immediate import. Quote from D——:

> Isn't this cool? We'll be able to settle the new system with help from an intelligence native to the system. Nobody's ever done that before!

And so on. Lots more like that – check them out.

Look, dear readers: all of that is a possibility. What relations, if any, we establish with the natives of Destiny II is a very serious question and the one that's raging through the air and airwaves as I write. All the boards and committees and juries are in permanent emergency session and everybody has suddenly got an opinion on it and it's driving me crazy.

Because it's not the most important question.

The most important question is this: what does the existence of other intelligent life tell us about the kind of universe we are in?

Yesterday we were in a universe that included us *and lots of cool stuff*: stars, galaxies, plasmas, cometary bodies, planets, and cows and giraffes and AIs and blue-green algae and lichen and micro-organisms.

Today we are in a universe that contains us and lots of cool stuff *and alien space bats*.

That's a different universe.

A universe with a different history, different potentialities, different future from the universe we thought we lived in. We are not living in the universe we thought we lived in yesterday.

We have to start learning the world all over again.

Awlin Halegap entertained in the grand manner. As a speculator, it was expected of him. For the occasion he'd hired a spherical space about a hundred metres in diameter. Horrocks presumed that its shape was why it was called a ballroom. He thrust in, snagged a drink-bulb from a drifting cluster, and floated a few metres away from the entrance, taking stock. The entire inner surface of the sphere was an image of the sky, with the planet Destiny II filling most of one side of it. The planetarium effect was illusory – you looked at the planet's day side, but if you glanced over your shoulder you found that the sun wasn't there or had been edited out – but impressive. Horrocks guessed that it was patched together from the ship's outside view, and the incoming datastream from the fast probe, whose arrival in planetary orbit the occasion celebrated. Almost everyone on the ship would be watching this, with outer or inner eye, but none, Horrocks guessed, would have so spectacular a view.

Hundreds of people floated and drifted in the frosty light. Crows hung, wings steady but for the occasional pinion flick, watched for food scraps and tattled amongst themselves. Hummingbirds, less sentient but more colourful, sipped from the tips of discarded drink-bulbs, and jinked about. Trays of food covered by elastic netting and propelled by tiny electric

fan-jets drifted through the crowd, following simple algo-
rithms of approach and avoidance. Clusters of drink-bulbs
were plucked from and shoved away.

In the two weeks since Horrocks had cracked the television
transmissions he had become famous, and the ship had become
febrile. Its nets buzzed with debate. Factions had formed. In
the crew areas of the forward and rearward cones, fashions:
almost everyone was wearing things like wings, clever pleated
contrivances that fanned out between their arms and their
sides, or simpler rigid structures of cloth or paper. The big free
fall room looked like a butterfly house.

Horrocks scorned the fad. For tonight he wore a rayon
replica of his utility suit, much buckled and multi-pocketed.
He checked out the company as new arrivals drifted or hurtled
past him. On the far side of the room hung a cluster of people
he recognised from personal or fleeting acquaintance or from
their fame: Halegap himself, in earnest conversation with the
Oldest Man; around them some of the science team who had
designed and launched the probes, and one or two from the science jury which had approved it; one delegate from the ship's
Board, looking – even at this distance – a little awkward and
out of place.

Closer to hand, Horrock noticed a group of people he knew
better. He rolled, reached for a passing tray, and let it drag him
to a drinks cluster from which he detached a handful of bulbs
and then sent the rest on their way, and himself in the opposite
direction. A minute later, air resistance brought him to more
or less a halt among the half-dozen people twenty metres away
that he wanted to meet.

'Hi, Horrocks,' said Genome Console, catching his hand.
She wore a filmy pink one-piece, cuffs drawstrung at wrist
and ankle; rings on her toes and her yellow hair in a gold net.
He and she circled each other; he passed her a bulb to coun-
teract his remaining momentum.

'Hello,' said Horrocks. He looked around. The others, like Genome, were all training-habitat builders – colleagues and rivals – except for one man, naked and painted in whorls, with paired jet-packs on a belt. The stranger dipped his head as Genome introduced Horrocks.

'Grey Universal,' he said.

'Ah,' said Horrocks. 'The contrarian.'

'I wouldn't say that,' said the man, and laughed. Horrocks joined in to be polite. Genome let go of Horrocks' hand and caught Grey's, smiling at him in a determined way that Horrocks recognised and was relieved was not directed at him. The Consoles, like the Mathematicals, were an old crew family. Horrocks had played with Genome as a child and felt toward her a vague sense of siblinghood, which he'd sometimes suspected her of not sharing.

'My complaint for the occasion,' Grey Universal went on, 'is that the atmosphere probe whose brave little adventure we're all here to follow is a piece of gross irresponsibility that we'll be lucky to live to regret.'

'Oh, come on,' said Horrocks. 'This has been through a ship-wide discussion, the Board, the science jury and a crew poll. It's settled.'

'Of course,' said Grey. 'I'm still right. What if the bat people spot it?'

'This is a probe three metres long, with a wingspan of two metres, flying ten kilometres up at its lowest point,' Horrocks said. 'A mere dot.'

'But a detectable dot.'

'They don't have radar.'

'They have eyes,' said Grey. 'Very acute eyes, by the looks of them.'

Horrocks shrugged. So far, he'd heard nothing that hadn't been thrashed out already. Some arguments were like that; each side just kept repeating the same points, over and over.

'So they see an . . . unidentified flying object?' he said. 'So what? They may have already seen our retro-flare. The orbiter's thoroughly stealthed, but they may spot it some day. Maybe gradually building up evidence that we're here will be a good thing for them. Better that than us descending one day out of the blue.'

'Assuming we make contact at all,' Genome pointed out.

'All right,' said Horrocks. 'Assume we don't. Assume even that we go away—'

He flinched at the chorus of disapprobation.

'I said, *assume*,' he persisted. 'What then? An astronomical and . . . atmospheric anomaly enters their records. No harm done.'

'Perhaps not,' said Grey Universal. 'We will have changed their history nonetheless. A minute change, you may say. True. But not therefore necessarily insignificant.'

'I've seen your chaos sims,' Horrocks said. 'I'm unconvinced.'

Grey Universal shook his head and squirted wine into his mouth. He savoured it, pursing his lips, and swallowed. 'As a contrarian, I naturally hope you are right.'

The discussion was bypassed a moment later as the cruciform atmosphere probe detached itself from the orbiter and dropped away. A cheer sounded across the room as the view switched to the probe's camera and the planet's atmosphere filled the image in an arc of blue and white. The event shown had happened hours earlier, Horrocks reflected, but still he had the sense that something irrevocable had just taken place.

He had the same uneasy feeling when, a couple of hours later, the probe entered the atmosphere. It went in on the day side, where its friction flare would not be conspicuous, and within minutes it had stabilised in steady, ramjet-powered flight. Around the bulky glass lens of its ground camera the probe had been designed; that, unlike the hardware and software behind it, could not be miniaturised. But it was these that processed and enhanced the images, and that selected – according to the well-established algorithm for interestingness – which to zoom in on, and to show as though from hundreds rather than thousands of metres up.

Over the next hours Horrocks drifted about the room, occasionally joining in one of the formal three-dimensional dance acrobatics that usually ended with all or most participants recoiling off the wall or drifting helplessly and laughing. Every so often a hush would traverse the spherical room at the speed of sound, as the camera viewpoint soared over a mountain range, or panned a herd of gigantic beasts, or zoomed in on a city, or tracked a dirigible, or scanned the horizon-spanning row of volcanic islands in the hemispheric ocean opposite the continents. For much of the time, of course, there was nothing to see but cloud, or the deceptive fractal surface of the sea, or monotonous plains or snowfields.

He was already a little drunk, and more than a little dazed with wonder, when he bumped into the party's host.

'Hello, Awlin,' he said, as they disentangled and re-oriented. 'Congratulations. And thanks for the stock tip.'

Awlin waved a languorous hand, incidentally shaking a ribbed cape of blue silk. 'Not at all.'

They talked business for a while, drinking and observing the scene from the probe, and then the talk turned to gossip: who was in, who was out, who was up, who was down, who was with whom, who was here and who was not.

'It's been a good party,' Awlin said. 'I didn't get everyone I wanted – some of the teams are of course hunched in their cubicles, but that's scientists for you. Still, I've got a lot. From Constantine to the mouthy kid.'

'Who?'

'Atomic Discourse Gale. Something of a rising star among the ship generation. She's been making a name for herself as a writer, with her biolog. In terms of provoking odd-angled thought she is rather snapping at the heels of Grey Universal.'

'Ah, yes,' said Horrocks. 'The mouthy kid.'

She had changed a little in the six months since her micro-gravity training, having become taller and more mature, but she was still the same wiry young woman with a tight mass of curly black hair and a characteristic flatfooter tendency to hunch up as though inclined to curl into a ball. When Horrocks saw her, a few minutes after leaving Awlin to another guest, she was leaning over her knees. Her fingers rippled as she wrote on a virtual keyboard, then flexed as she straightened and stretched and stared at the enclosing screen. She wore shorts and a long-sleeved top, both green. Her keyboard and eyescreen projector stuck out in front of one temple, held in her hair with a fancy jewelled clip.

She saw him and said, 'Hello, Horrocks.'

He smiled at her unsmiling face. 'Atomic, isn't it? Pleased to see you. How are you doing?'

She lifted a drink-bulb almost to her lips and squeezed a few drops, looking at him all the while with suspicion, almost scorn.

'I know you read my biolog,' she said. 'So you know how I'm doing.'

Horrocks spread his hands and affected injured innocence. 'Well, of course, but . . .'

'But you think I'm not telling all about myself?'

'People don't, always.'

'People don't, ever,' she said.

'It was just a friendly query,' said Horrocks. He could feel his face becoming hot. It was infuriating that this girl, six years his junior and still self-conscious about her breasts and hips, could make him feel awkward. 'Anyway . . . I find what you write interesting.'

'That's what people usually say when they disagree with it.'

Horrocks acknowledged the parry. 'All right. All very interesting, but I don't see why you make so much of it.'

'Then you haven't—' she began, then caught herself. 'I haven't made myself clear.' She sawed her fingernails through her hair. 'You remember when the transmissions were detected, you made a joke that they might be from aliens?'

'I did? I must have better foresight than I thought.'

She looked impatient. 'The whole point of your joke was that there are no aliens. It wouldn't have been funny otherwise. Just like if my care-mother had said that something I'd lost in the garden had been taken by the fairies, or the hideaways. If we found fairies in the garden, or hideaways, it would tell us that the world was quite different from what we had imagined. It wouldn't just be a world that had fairies in it, like a different kind of bird or something. It'd be a different kind of world, a world in which fairies could exist.'

'Yes,' said Horrocks. 'So the world is different. So what?'

'So what happens here, around the Destiny Star, won't just decide what happens between the human species and the bat people. I agree, that's quite a responsibility. We're standing in for all humanity here, we're on our own, and we'd better get it right. But the point I'm making is that if one lot of aliens can exist, so close to us in space and time, then almost certainly other aliens do. Lots of them! Some of them may be more advanced than us by the time we reach them, with Civil Worlds of their own. But if they had that already, we'd know it – we'd see their green haze, we'd pick up their transmissions. In the next few thousand years, we may. But in the next few *hundred* years, it'll be planets like this we encounter. Ones on the verge or just over the verge of space flight.'

Horrocks felt puzzled. 'How do you know that?'

Atomic smiled for the first time, exposing a broad row of short white upper teeth. 'I don't,' she said. 'Call it a hunch.'

Horrocks nodded. 'It's more than that,' he said. 'It's what we should plan for. A worst-case scenario. Aliens already exploring what they think of as their system, when we blunder in.' He laughed. 'A good thing for us that the bat people don't even have heavier-than-air flight.'

EIGHT

SECURITY CONCERNS

It was bad flying weather. The morning sea-fog over Five Ravines tasted of smoke, and left black grains on the tips of fur. Frost nipped at feet. Most people walked on clogs which they gripped fore and aft by toe- and heel-claws. Some people walked wrapped in cloaks, like extra wings, made from the skins or woven from the hair of prey. Out in the Broad Channel foghorns sounded, like lonely grazers bellowing.

Darvin strode unshod, wrapped only in his wings and warmed by the memory of the past night with Kwarive. The warmth was emotional; as a matter of regrettable fact, thinking about the night sent blood coursing through his membranes, wasting its heat on the chill air. He didn't mind, but he forced his thoughts to his work. Lecturing and demonstrating to students paid for some of his research. His stipend and the rest of his research expenses, were covered, like those of most scholars, by obscure trickles from Seloh's Bounty. As in most recent years, the Bounty had been pinched at Treasury level by the demands of the armed services, Seloh's Might. Seloh herself – *the* Seloh, twenty-seventh of that name – had made pointed reference in her annual autumnal speech from the Height about the need for stringency in scientific and educational expenditure. Many of Darvin's colleagues had hastened to rephrase their petitions for Bounty in martial terms, with sometimes ludicrous results. Kwarive herself had told him, laughing, of how an entire anatomy course had been justified as research into the effects of lethal or anaesthetic gases. What military applications this could have, gods only knew: the use of gas in warfare was engineering-tales stuff and nonsense, but the air force, Seloh's Flight, had accepted it. Orro's aeronautical experiments had been too hopeless even for such a brazen camouflage, but his mathematical studies, to his surprise, obtained without demur a grant directly from not the Might, but the intelligence agency, Seloh's Sight – alien and suspect though the Gevorkian was. Perhaps, he'd muttered, the Sight wanted to keep an eye on him. He had taken the money and at once used it to pay his debts to certain mechanics and artisans.

Which meant, Darvin guessed, that it had in turn gone straight into putting blood in the mouths of hungry kits. It might as well have come straight from that portion of the Bounty earmarked for relief.

Darvin's own research had found no such excuse, as it had found no planet. His and Orro's paper on the mysterious moving object and on the historical increase in the number of the Daughters had appeared on the physics wire, drawn a wingful of puzzled, point-missing queries, and sunk without trace. It had not been a good summer, nor yet a good autumn, to press the point. The cheap prints buzzed with sensations: a moving star had been glimpsed, not by astronomers; Gevorkian airships had been spotted far inland, not by the Flight; reports of strange slow bolides flew in from here and there; thunderclaps had boomed from clear skies; a ship, its crew all dead of an unknown ghastly malady, had, not according to the navy, foundered on the Channel coast; merchants from Seloh and

Gevork had brawled in some treaty port of the Southern Rule; and a prey calf with two heads had lived an outer-month.

The peril of being associated with such trash had left Orro and Darvin in seething silence.

Meanwhile, Darvin had his own research funding to worry about. He had spent two and a half years already on the blink comparator, and with nothing but the Little Bastards and the mysterious vanishing comet to show for it, he scarcely had grounds for asking his senior to renew the grant, and small motive to. He had toyed with the thought of writing up his meagre results and abandoning the quest to some future junior astronomer with more patience and perhaps better instruments.

Too bedraggled and wearied by his damp walk to fly even the short hop to the Astronomy storey, Darvin plodded up the unfamiliar staircase to the floor, and met at the top Orro. The Gevorkian returned a grim look to Darvin's surprised greeting. Loitering behind Orro were two men, wings poised, arms folded, faces sharp and mouths closed. One of them detached himself from the wall and sauntered to where Orro stood in glum silence. From a pouch on his belt the stranger flashed a small bronze disc with an inset enamel eye. To present even an imitation of that sigil was a slashing offence; Darvin took it as seriously as Orro already had.

'My office?' he said.

The Sight agent nodded. Darvin led the way. As he unlocked the door the keys rattled and jangled. He clenched his fist around them and stalked in. The second agent planted himself in front of the door as soon as it was closed; the first sat on the windowsill. Orro perched on the table, Darvin on his chair. An awkward party they made, distributed thus about the cluttered room.

'Well, officers, how can we help you?' asked Darvin.

The one on the windowsill gave his cheekbone a meditative rub with his wing-wrist.

'For you to say, I should think,' he said.

'I don't understand.'

The Sight man looked around the room. 'Did they pay you much?'

Darvin misunderstood. 'I have my stipend, various Bounty grants, some teaching fees—'

'Not what I meant.'

The one at the door made a lurch. The other warned him back with a frown.

'Your friend here, now,' he went on, 'he's a Gevorkian. All quite understandable. But you, that's the puzzle. Hasn't Seloh given you enough? Hence the question.'

Darvin understood at last. 'I haven't the faintest idea what you're talking about,' he said.

Another lurch from the door, another frown from the window. The fog swirled outside.

Orro clapped a hand to the top of his head. His ears went back. 'Oh!' he said. 'I remember now.'

He extended a leg to the floor, stood on it, swung the other from the table, and paced behind the blink comparator, as though its brassy bulk could afford him some protection. He looked from one agent to the other, his glance pausing only for a remorseful fraction of a second on Darvin.

'I wrote to my friend Holder, in the Regnal Air Force, about our . . . ah . . . results,' he said.

'Which results?' asked Darvin.

Orro waved upward. 'The comet and the green stars.'

'That's all?'

'That's all. He replied, and I discussed it further. Nothing else.'

Darvin let out a sigh of relief. He had been afraid Orro had noised abroad something about his aeronautics – which, futile though it was, might have made some unsleeping Eye prick up his ears.

'There you are, gentlemen,' he said. 'No defence significance. A scientific enigma, that's all, related to a former colleague across the water. My friend here hasn't abused his position in the least.'

'What's of defence significance,' said the Eye at the window, 'and what's an abuse of position, is not for you to judge. Nor me, come to that.' He combed an eyebrow tuft with a claw. 'But you did sign the university charter, did you not?'

'Of course,' said Darvin.

'Correct me if I'm wrong, but that does include a clause or two about having due regard for the interests of the Reach?'

Darvin tried to remember a page or eight of small-print boilerplate. 'If you say so.'

'I do say so, and rightly,' said the agent. He made a sad sucking noise through his teeth. 'And, in my layman's opinion, some unknown object hurtling out of the outer darkness straight towards us might just possibly be of some moment to the weal of the Reach.'

Darvin felt like laughing with relief. 'In that case, I've done my duty,' he said, 'and so has Orro. We've published a full account of it.'

'That,' said the Eye, 'is your problem.' He drummed his heel-claws on the wall, then slid down to stand again on the floor. 'Published. You've no idea the trouble you've given us. If you're feeling a bit put out that it didn't get much of a response, don't blame your colleagues. Except, maybe, for a certain lack of fortitude about having their arms twisted.'

'The Sight did *that*?' said Darvin, outraged. 'Suppressed discussion?'

'That and more,' said the agent. 'That and more.' He shook his head and sighed. 'It's a cold morning,' he said. 'Brew us some tea, would you?'

Startled by the shift in tone, Darvin complied. As he wiped stains out of old mugs with a rag dirtier than the crockery, he tried to calm his thoughts. He was certain that nothing either he or Orro had done could count as a crime before any just tribunal, but the Sight was not reputed to be just. Nor, on the other wing, was it considered arbitrary. It did not persecute. It seldom pried. He suspected, therefore, that he and Orro were being given a shaking to see what fell out from under their wings. Or – aha, that was it – to soften them up for a softer approach.

The suspicion was soon confirmed. The agent at the door sat down on the table, the other returned to the window, and both sipped the tea with evident relaxation. The one who had spoken before spoke again.

'All right, gentlemen,' he said. 'You seem to have got yourselves into some trouble. Quite innocently, I reckon, from what you've said. You don't act like guilty men. But that's just my opinion, and I don't know if it'll be shared by the higher-ups, if you see what I mean. So let's see if I can help you to help yourselves, so to speak, and maybe matters will go no further.'

Orro flashed Darvin a warning look; Darvin nodded, unsure of what he was being warned.

'Good,' said the Eye, taking the nod as his. He laid down his mug on the windowsill and fingered a sheaf of fine, crackling papers from the largest of his belt pouches. Darvin and Orro peered over the first sheet as he spread it on the table. The other agent stared over their bowed heads, out of the window.

The paper was squared, with two numbered axes, and marked with minute, also numbered crosses in ink. The crosses had been joined with a pencilled shallow curve.

'What do you make of that?' said the Eye.

'It's an arc of an ellipse,' said Orro.

The Eye looked at him. 'That, I could have told you,' he said. 'A little more detail, if you please.'

Darvin looked closer and recognised what he saw. The axes were the familiar celestial ones, and the numbers on the crosses were dates and times that registered a series of observations – a series that reached to the day before yesterday, and began half an eight of outer-months ago in early summer, around about the time when the comet had disappeared.

'Hey!' he said, straightening up so fast that the crown of his head almost collided with the Eye's chin. He rushed to his desk and scrabbled through the papers there, and brought out an off-print of his and Orro's article. Flicking through the pages, he found the diagram he sought, and laid it beside the new picture. The dates overlapped, the numbers matched, and the lines—

Orro needed no more than a glance to see what Darvin had seen.

'Deceleration,' he said, 'followed by a free elliptical orbit – deceleration *to* orbit! Orbital' – he sought a word – '*insertion*.'

Darvin's hands shook. He reached for the paper to see what lay underneath. The Eye grabbed his wrist.

'Later, maybe,' he said. They all leaned back and looked at each other.

'So you recognise our intruder.'

'In principle,' said Orro. He reached for his tea and slurped. 'You've shown us a plot of a path it could have taken. But it continues after it vanished from sight. How could the subsequent points be observations?'

'Never you mind,' said the Eye. 'For now, let me assure you that they are. Or so I've been told, by people who don't mess me about.'

The hitherto silent agent stifled a laugh.

'Not,' the Eye went on, 'that many do.' He waved aside the sudden return to menace. 'Anyhow. These very folks have also told me, most definite like, that this thing here is no natural object. No way, no how, no matter which way you turn it – and they have, gentlemen, they have.'

'This is wonderful,' said Orro.

'You could say that,' said the Eye. 'What the Sight says, and the Might says, and the Flight says, and for all I know to the contrary, what her soaring majesty herself says, is that this thing is of — now how did you put it? — defence significance.'

'Of more than that, surely,' said Darvin, appalled at this blinkered view. 'It's of world importance. It's the most significant and exciting event in our history!'

The Eye gave him a look.

'Examined it, have you?' he said. 'Communed with it, perhaps? Confident, are you, that it means us no harm? Thought not.'

He leaned over the table again. 'Next picture.'

The grey-and-black sheet he spread out might have been a photograph of a series of small photographs, arranged in three rows of six; Darvin had not seen its like, and was unsure how it had been done. The pictures showed a pointed cylindrical object with two rectangular attachments midway along it. A white line of smoke or steam began a little behind the blunt end. In the first pictures the object was foreshortened, then in the second row it appeared in full view, and in the final row it was foreshortened from the back, eventually dwindling to a dot. The trail was in all the photographs. The series gave the irresistible impression of something like a flechette hurtling past. Darvin imagined how they would look run as a series of kinematographic frames, and realised that that was what they were.

Orro looked so expressionless that Darvin suspected he recognised what he saw; but the Eye's quizzical gaze was on Darvin, as though suspecting that *he* knew what it was.

Darvin shook his head. 'I'm baffled,' he said. 'What is this?'

The Eye turned a glare on Orro. 'I'll tell you one thing it isn't,' he said. 'It's not one of your precious *self-propelled flechettes*.'

The Gevorkian started. 'I know nothing of such.'

'As well you shouldn't.' He twisted a smile at Orro, and jabbed a finger at the paper. 'You know what altitude this was flying at? Five by eight by eight by eight wingspans.'

It was a figure you thought of as a distance, not a height.

'Travelling about that distance in about eight-and-two seconds,' the Eye went on. 'Faster than a speeding cross-bolt, you might say. Its length is reckoned to be about a wingspan and a half.'

'How were photographs of something so small taken at such a distance?' Darvin asked.

'None of your business.'

As soon as he said it Darvin formed a guess: a camera attached to a telescope, and tracking very fast – a new gunsight, no doubt. As secret on the Selohic side as the self-propelled flechettes – whatever they might be – were supposed to be on the Gevorkian. It saddened him that military technology was so much more advanced than he'd ever imagined.

'All right,' he said. 'So . . . what is it?'

The Eye looked impatient. 'We're asking you.'

'You really don't know?' Orro sounded disbelieving.

The Eye clasped his hands on the top of his head, in a gesture of frustration or surrender.

'No,' he said. 'We wrapping well don't know, and that's no ploy.'

It occurred to Darvin that the man, and whoever had sent him and his silent comrade, was afraid.

'I know what it is,' said Orro. 'It's a self-propelled aerial vehicle. A heavier-than-air flying machine, but one that flies without flapping.'

'We should have you in the service,' the Eye said.

The sarcasm was wasted on Orro.

'It must work on the same principle as the self-propelled flechette,' he said.

'And what might that be?' asked the Eye.

'It is not for me to say,' Orro said. 'You no doubt know, in any case, but—' He passed his hand across his lips. Then scientific excitement seemed to overcome patriotic scruple. He snatched the paper and held it up to the light from the window, his head swaying as he scanned it, narrow-eyed, back and forth. 'I think I see it.'

'See what?' asked Darvin.

'It's undergoing a sort of . . . power-assisted gliding.'

'Artificial thermals?'

Orro shook his head. 'Of course not.' He laughed harshly. 'Not a bad idea in itself, in terms of military applications. Burning towns provide thermals enough . . . but no, this is quite different. This line coming out of the back appears to be a jet of steam. Now, a jet of steam, under sufficient pressure, could propel the object forward – action and reaction, see?'

'Yes,' said Darvin, 'I quite see that, but—'

'And what,' interrupted the Eye, 'would be the heat source for this flying tea-kettle?'

'I don't know,' said Orro. 'Something beyond our present comprehension. It doesn't matter. It could as well be . . . the mode of propulsion of the . . . ah . . . self-propelled flechette, but that has . . . um . . . certain practical limitations, which, um . . . forget about that for the moment. The point is that one can separate the two functions of a wing – lift, and power.'

'That's a difficult idea to wrap one's mind around,' said Darvin.

'There's a certain truth in the old saw,' said Orro, 'that if the gods had meant us to build flying machines, they wouldn't have given us wings.'

Darvin recalled flying in the wind tunnel, flapping hard into the blast of air from the cannibalised airship propeller. This conversation gave him the same strange, frustrating feeling of flying on the spot.

'You mean that chiroptery has all been a mistake?'

'Not entirely,' said Orro. 'Now let us think. If this *jet* propulsion is impracticable for us, we need to devise, as well as the static wing, some other form of, of . . .'

'Propeller?' said the Eye.

Orro and Darvin rounded on him and shouted as one. 'That's it!'

The Eye backed away, taking all of the pieces of paper with him. His companion bristled and backed in the opposite direction, to the doorway.

'All right,' said the Eye. He picked up his cup again, sniffed at it, and put it down. 'I'm sure you've both just made some remarkable leap of logic. Very gratifying, but not my immediate concern. Nor, right at this moment, should it be yours.'

'What do you mean?' Darvin tried to keep his excitement from leaking aggression into his voice. He wanted nothing more than to rush out of this room to Orro's laboratory.

'I mean, gentlemen, that you're still in trouble. Not the trouble you thought you were, though that's still hanging over you, so to speak. You've seen things, and had ideas, that we don't want spread around.'

'I understand,' said Orro. 'You have my word that none of this shall go to Gevork.'

The Eye shook his head. 'Not good enough, I'm afraid. Which is sad. If I'd been sent to expel you as *persona non grata*, I'd have gladly taken your parole and not so much as bothered to escort you to the quay. But we're in stormier skies here.' He sighed. 'Stormier skies. This is where your troubles begin.'

Keeping his gaze on them, he stepped forward to the table and took from yet another pouch: a small folding knife, a thin iron rod with a curled end and a wooden handle, a box of matches, a dip pen, a candle stub, a stick of sealing-wax, and two sheets of paper. He flicked the knife open and flourished it in their faces. The blade looked very sharp. Darvin wondered what he was about to do with it. He thought of Orro's military training. Behind him, he heard the solid click of a hand-held crossbow being cocked.

The Eye pushed a paper towards each of them.

'Read, sign and thumbprint in blood, and seal,' he said. 'Or die here.'

Five minutes later Darvin and Orro were sworn to Seloh's Sight.

'This is outrageous,' said Darvin. 'You've betrayed your country.'

They perched together at the top of the faculty's tower, out of sight and earshot of anyone within view. Orro's calm gaze didn't deviate from the fog.

'I have not,' he said. 'What would Gevork give, to have a Gevorkian within the Sight?'

'I'm sure they have agents in place already.'

'No doubt. So you see, I have nothing to worry about.'

'Seems to me you have everything to worry about.'

'It does get complicated,' said Orro. 'There are mathematical functions for such matters.' He shrugged, and steepled his wings. 'I can keep track.'

Darvin thought of spies spying on spies. It made him dizzy. Perhaps it was his duty to report on Orro. Perhaps this was a test, to see whether he did report on Orro. Perhaps Orro had all along been suborned to the Sight. Or, maybe, everything was as it seemed. That was something he could never again take for granted. He decided he would.

'All right,' he said. 'You keep track. What worries me is what we're both betraying.'

'And that is?'

'Science.'

Now Orro did turn to him, eyes bright. 'Oh no,' he said.

'Not at all. Isn't this the most marvellous opportunity we could ever have been given, to discover new knowledge?'

'There can be no secret science,' said Darvin. It was one of the platitudes of the Dawn Age.

'Whoever tracked the comet,' said Orro, 'and whoever designed the camera that took those pictures, worked in secret.'

'Well *obviously* military research—'

'Why is that an exception?'

'It's engineering, not science.'

'Battle is the forge of tools,' said Orro. He said it like a Gevorkian proverb.

'Peace and not war is the father of all,' Darvin shot back. Another platitude.

They both laughed.

'But we've seen the pictures,' said Orro.

'Yes,' said Darvin. 'We've seen the pictures.'

He had a lust to see more pictures. According to the Eye, the project promised more. More secrets, more hidden knowledge, the most knowledge and the deepest secret there had ever been.

'And we know how to build a heavier-than-air craft,' added Orro.

'In secret.'

'Yes.' A note of regret sounded in Orro's voice. 'But you know,' he went on, 'Gevorkian though I am, noble though I am, when I think of the Regnal Air Force officers who laughed in my face, I can't help gloating over the shock they'll some day get.'

That worried Darvin, but he said nothing. The two of them were not, of course, agents of the Sight, not Eyes; their recruitment to it was a formality, whose only differences from say, activating Darvin's membership of the Reserve were that the Gevorkian too could be validly recruited, and that the penalties for betrayal or desertion were far more severe. What they had been recruited to was a project to investigate all aspects of the alien arrival. None of it would, they were assured, be compartmentalised: the whole point was to integrate all the diverse sources of information and insight. It was to be called Project Signal, which Darvin thought something of a giveaway, but one that had a certain ring to it.

There was a camp in the high desert. It consisted of four identical barrack roosts, a central lecture ring, a shooting range, a prey paddock, and a huddle of ruins used for close-quarter combat training. Except for a few guards, the troops had been moved out. By the first night there Darvin had a fair idea of where it was, just from looking at the stars and applying rudimentary navigation. This made the way he had arrived – in a windowless cabin of an airship – a quite futile exercise in security, but he knew better than to say so. The senior military and security officers of Seloh's Reach were more flexible in their outlook than those of, by all accounts, Gevork, but they had as little sense of humour. To his relief the inaugural Project Signal meeting was organised not like a military briefing but an academic conference. About eight-by-eight scientists and engineers were present. On the first evening, everybody talked about anything but what they were here for.

The following morning, Darvin and Orro hung side by side on the lecture ring with the others and fixed their attention on the man standing in the middle.

'Good morning, colleagues,' he said. 'My name is Markhan. I am a research scientist with the Flight. My field is one of which few of you will have heard, because its very existence is secret. I refer to telekinematography, the transmission of moving images by ether-waves. It potential use in military communications is self-evident; so much so that our own developments are closely paralleled in Gevork.'

Even Orro could not forbear to laugh.

'However,' Markhan went on, 'we are, I venture to believe, a little ahead of our friends across the water in the matter of building sensitive receiving equipment. A few outer-months ago, during a routine test of this apparatus, one of our technicians – young Nollam over there – noted a strong source of etheric interference from a point in the sky. Now, it should be noted that celestial sources of etheric waves are not rare, and include the Sun Himself. To the best of our knowledge all of these sources are natural. What Nollam spotted was that this source was strong, had a distinct pattern, and moved from night to night. The pattern was a regular pulse, with a period of precisely two point seven beats. It was moving in the plane of the ecliptic, and was thus, almost certainly, an astronomical object.'

Nollam had taken the data to Markhan, who had then made discreet enquiries and hasty searches through the stack of prints from the physics wire – which had turned up Darvin and Orro's paper. More recently, extraordinarily faint echoes of the secret Selohic experimental transmissions had been detected from the sky – as if Ground had acquired a third moon, as Markhan put it – shortly followed by the detection of the high-altitude aerial vehicle.

'Does anyone dispute,' Markhan asked, 'that all of this, taken together, is evidence that we are being visited and observed by travellers from another world?'

No one did. Darvin guessed that any who might have done so had been excluded – or had excluded themselves – from the project.

'Very well, ' said Markhan. 'The question that now arises is: what are we to do about it?'

On this, opinion was divided. Only one voice, that of a

stubborn old biologist, was raised in favour of opening the whole matter to the public and to the world. Markhan pointed out that Seloh already stood to gain some military advantage from the existing observations – he didn't specify how, but Orro nudged Darvin at this point – and there was no telling what might be gained in the future. For the rest, the suggestions ranged from attempting communication with the aliens to building some unspecified gigantic weapon to shoot them out of the sky. The great majority, however, put forward practical suggestions for continuing to observe the craft – Orro, to Darvin's surprise, urged an attempt to detect it visually, now that its location was continually betrayed by its emissions – and to build more sensitive etheric apparatus; to investigate further and if possible to emulate the powers of flight displayed by the aerial vehicle; and to establish a network to centralise reports of any other unknown aerial or celestial phenomena.

Markhan summed up the emergent near-consensus; the combat military and security officers present endorsed it; the token high political figure from Seloh's Height made an inspiring speech; and the great project began.

NINE

RED SUN CIRCLE

14 365:05:12 11:17

It is now a year since I started this biolog. Happy birthday to
'Learning the World'! Last night I stayed up all night reading it.
Well, skimming it, to be honest. So much in it is self-absorbed and
self-indulgent. Sometimes I gave you all too much information.
Any fully adult reader must have found it painfully limited. I can
see that now.

But, you know, it's surprising. Seeing is seeing; reading is reading; and being able to see through everything and read anything is
still seeing and reading. You can have the illusion that you're thinking faster, but it's not you who carries out the calculation, or the
search, or the transformation — it's the system doing it for you. So,
now that I have more of my adult faculties, I will not be patronising
towards those who have not. Which isn't to say that I don't appreciate the added richness, the texture, the depth that the virtuality
genes (and, I suppose, in due course television and all the rest)
give to the world. (Or do they? Is knowing (that you can know all
that is known about) what you are looking at, is the labelling and
tagging and indexing an *impoverishment* of experience? Does it

carry the risk that we miss what might be new and unknown and fresh, even about familiar things? Whenever I test that seductive thought by turning off the virtual overlay, I seldom experience any enrichment: the world just loses a dimension, and looks flat.)

But I've told you all that already, in now embarrassing breathy excitement when the genes at last kicked in a couple of months ago. Enough.

To serious business. Life has become strange. It is not how I had expected it to be. I and everybody I know is working on their plans and proposals and trying to pull together a team or find one they'd like to join, just as we always expected to be doing. But overlaying all this – kind of like the virtual overlay, now that I come to think of it – is our preoccupation with Destiny II. In one sense it's the most exciting thing that could have happened. In another it's a big distraction from what we all thought was all we wanted in life.

The first probe images were distracting and fascinating enough. Since the probe returned to the orbiter with its atmosphere samples (high partial pressure of oxygen, which supposedly explains how the bat people fly and the megafauna are so, well, mega), and the analysers got busy sequencing the aerial bacteria (they have (yawn) a unique genetic code) and the orbiter started spraying out glass-beaded atmosphere-entry assembler packages to build microprobes with compatible chemistries and the little bugs started reporting back . . . well! You know what it's like. You can get lost in exploring Destiny II.

I hesitate to say this, but the bat people are *horrible*. The filthy roosts they live in are bad enough. What really disgusts me is that they keep *slaves*. It's a word I'd only encountered before in the context of ants. I have since found out that originally this usage was a metaphor, and the term 'slave' applied in the first instance to human beings – the prehistoric races used to do it to people. And the bat people do it to these poor mutilated drudges. But still, I suppose we should not be too sweeping in our condemnation: human beings used to keep human slaves almost up until the time of the Moon Caves. So our ancestors were just as disgusting when they only lived on the surface of the primary. It may become important to bear this in mind.

This morning at breakfast in the café with Grant and as usual talking about the big argument – is there really anything more to say? If so, I'll find it – when I wondered what the Contract has to say about resolving disputes that divide the whole ship. (Notice how we all now think of it as the ship? And not the world?) So I looked it up. Part of my mind, I guess, must have been on the subject of contact, because I must have subvocalised the word, and that was what came up:

> *11378(b): Alien contact shall be treated as an emergency. 'Alien contact' means the acquisition of information in any form direct or indirect which indicates or suggests the presence in any region within operational or communications range of the ship of any form of intelligence not of human or post-human origin. 'Emergency' means a situation as defined in Clause 59 paragraph (f) above; wherein it is declared, that the duly constituted Council at the time of the declaration or discovery of emergency may take any action internal or external which it deems fit with a view to resolving the emergency; such action to be answerable to the entire Complement and to the Civil Worlds in due course. In a situation of urgency (q.v.) within a state of emergency executive action may be taken by appropriate members of the Crew. Such urgent action shall be referred at once to the Council. A state of emergency may not be maintained for more than one calendar year as heretofore defined unless renewed by express permission of a poll of the entire Complement, normal canvassing procedures being available on a regular and non-emergency basis for*

the duration of the pre-poll discussion, which shall
not be less than seven calendar days.

'Look at this!'

Grant was in a trance of his own, doubtless refining the design of his waterworld scheme (it now has a name, The Last Resort) or (hah!) his novel, but I overrode it with a zap. He came out blinking and shaking his head as if he'd really been swimming in his ludicrous ten-gravity water.

'What?'

'Look at this.' I patched him the link.

Breath indrawn through teeth. Trouble is, he was chewing at the time. (Yes, Grant, this is to embarrass you.)

He swallowed and came back into focus.

'Does this mean what I think it means?' I asked.

'If what you're thinking is: "Has the ship been in a state of undeclared emergency for the past four months?" and if "shall" and "or discovery of emergency" mean what they normally mean, yes,' he said.

'Oh good,' I said. 'So the Council is a lawless dictatorship with only eight months to go before it has to put all its actions up for scrutiny.'

'I don't see what's good about that,' said Grant.

'The "only eight months to go" part.'

'Do you think the Council is aware of this?'

'Of course it is,' I said. 'It has to be. What amazes me is that the Contract has a clause about alien contact at all.'

'It has clauses for all sorts of unlikely events,' said Grant. 'Fast burns inside or out, capture of ship, memetic plague, meteor strikes, you name it. Even war.'

I had to look the word up, but the internal dictionary is so fast it just looks like a blink, not a trance.

'You mean, something other than clade conflict with fast-burn spin-offs?'

'Yes,' said Grant. 'Organised hostilities between relatively stable societal entities.'

'But there hasn't been one of these for thousands of years!'

'Not in the Civil Worlds, sure. But some societies may have fallen out of them. Fast-burn survivors and so forth. And some ships go bad, we know that. So yeah, mad as it seems, the Contract has the appropriate provisions.' Grant grinned. 'War is a state of emergency.'

I can't really imagine war. I can imagine having to fight some swarm of zombie machines or snarling horde of posthuman fast-burn wreckage or whatever, but not two or more actual human societies actually fighting each other. I'm aware that people did that, before history, before the Moon, but it seems irrational. One side would have to believe they had something to gain from destroying or damaging the other, which just doesn't make sense: it runs up against the law of association. And more to the point, each individual on any side would have to believe that they bene-fited from participating even if they died, which doesn't make sense either. I suppose kin selection could make genes prevalent that made people vulnerable to that kind of illusion, but that only makes sense with animals that don't have foresight. Even crows aren't that stupid, at least not the ones that can talk. You have to get down to ants and such like before you see that kind of genetic mechanical mindlessness.

But this is a digression. I wrenched the conversation back on topic.

'All right, ' I said. 'And alien contact is, too.'

'The Council hasn't behaved like we're in a state of emergency,' Grant said. He waved a hand at the wall screens. 'Everybody's still arguing, there have been no decrees or anything.'

'That is not the point,' I said. 'Everybody should know what the real situation is.'

Grant shrugged. 'If you say so. The emergency looks more vir-tual than real at the moment.'

'To be honest, I'm not sure why this bugs me so much,' I said.

But it did. So I sent my message – you may have seen it – to every newsline I could reach: *Are We in an Undeclared State of Emergency?*

And I await an answer.

It was a place of blue tiled domes and white stone walls; of arches and arbours, orchards and courtyards, of narrow alleys and broad avenues and wide stairways, of aqueducts and fountains; of limes and oranges, figs and pomegranates. The fruit was eaten by birds and monkeys or rotted where it fell. (It had something to do with recycling.) White City was a haunt of the older generation. That made it a more happening place than the child-rearing suburbs or the teen-cohort towns. In that respect it reminded Horrocks of the free fall cones. Some of the house prices that appeared in discreet virtual tags here and there showed higher numbers than any of his deals. He walked its streets with caution, taking care not to collide with even virtual presences. He took care, too, to keep his balance. Since his first adventure in walking he had become competent and confident, though here in White City the smoothness of the paving was as reassuring as the hardness of its stone was troubling.

The founder generation, the First Hundred Thousand as they sometimes styled themselves, dominated the streets and plazas. Salons discoursed in shaded sidewalk cafés, as much meaning carried in virtuality-freighted glances as was conveyed in speech. In other cafés business was done, under an aspect of leisure. Lovers strolled arm in arm, or entwined each other in nooks. Musicians of heartbreaking talent performed in small green patches of park. Sculpture and murals were displayed, or were being created in processes that struck Horrocks as contrived in their difficulty. In the cones the subtle arts of the matter-composer were carried on with refinement and panache – what went on down here, he thought with some disdain as his sandals crunched marble chippings, was *cutting-edge* stuff.

When they weren't exerting themselves in primitive art and architecture or disporting themselves in courtly assignations or vexing their brains with hyper-intelligent hyper-chat the founders indulged in likewise artificial risk-taking. Hanggliders and microlights soared above the town. Bicyclists and roller-skaters whizzed along the otherwise pedestrian streets. There was even a combat sport, a form of wrestling whose bouts consisted of long minutes of watchful poise followed by a move almost too swift to see, which in playback unpacked into a flurry of lethal-looking blows, grips and throws, and ended always with one or both participants stretchered off.

The other thing the founders did was conspire in cliques. It had long been established in the Civil Worlds that public business was to be transparent, and personal matters opaque; but it was as well recognised that the two would always have a turbulent interface, and that the clique, the caucus and the conspiracy were as ineradicable features of civility as the Council or the committee. The confabulation of elders to which Horrocks had been invited was known, where it was known at all, as the Red Sun Circle. He had been given to understand that the invitation was a privilege, but he was not much impressed. The politicking of the founders was not their only proclivity that struck him as adolescent. Only his respect for Awlin Halegap, who'd delivered the invitation, and an itch of curiosity, had brought him here.

Here, where the guidance ware in his head had led his feet. He stood in front of a plain green double door in a white wall. The paint and the whitewash had bubbled and flaked. The nailheads and fittings were of pitted black iron, as was a knob at waist level. Horrocks placed his palm against it and wrapped his fingers around it. Nothing happened. He thumped the door with the heel of his fist, in the time-honoured manner of dealing with a recalcitrant mechanism. A sliding noise and a click came from the door, and it swung open to reveal a woman holding something behind the door's edge.

'Come in,' she said. 'You're expected.'

'Thank you,' said Horrocks. He stepped past her into a courtyard and watched as she pushed the door shut and turned another knob, this one on the inside. Again the sliding noise and the click. The woman looked somehow familiar, though Horrocks was sure he had never seen her. Small and sturdy, she had a mass of black curly hair, some of it caught by a clasp and piled on top of her head. Her shiny green shift was simple, as were her sandals, which showed underneath the hem. She pivoted and held out a hand.

'Synchronic Narrative Storm,' she said. Her grip was firm, her eyes amused.

'Horrocks Mathematical.' He hoped he didn't look as embarrassed as he felt. No wonder he had almost recognised her. Atomic Discourse's care-mother had sent him a very sharp note when the girl had been training in his habitat, and something of her appearance and demeanour had accompanied it like a synaesthesic scent.

'Ah, sorry about—'

She released his hand and waved in front of his face. 'Forget it,' she said. 'I was just being overprotective. Care-mothers do, you know. Come on in and meet the gang.'

She led him past a long stone-walled pool in which fat, lazy mullets swam in salt water, to an area behind it at which a dozen or so people had gathered in the shade of orange trees. Some perched on the pool's wall, others stood or sat around a few round white-painted wrought-iron tables. In a corner chicken flesh sizzled on a barbecue. Horrocks recognised only Awlin Halegap, who sprang up to welcome him and introduce the rest. They were all founder generation, their skins deeply tanned, their teeth bright, their dress casual. Six men and seven women. Horrocks shook hands, filed names, tabbed faces, accepted a tall glass of clinking ice and flavoured dilute alcohol, and tuned his perceptions to the conversation.

As he'd expected, he couldn't follow the buzz. It was not a question only of his elders' higher bandwidth. Even in normal speech they carried more information than he could process. These people had known each other for centuries. Allusions zipped past his head like deflected meteors. He found himself missing jests, or laughing loud and alone. He began to wonder why he was there. It was only after the last gnawed chicken femur had been thrown on the coals and the last finger licked that Synchronic turned to him with an explanation.

'You've gambled in terrestrials,' she said. 'So have we. Of course none of us expected such an interesting terrestrial, any more than you did. But unlike you, perhaps, we've leveraged some of our stakes into long futures – decades, even centuries in some cases.'

Horrocks nodded. 'Wouldn't be much use to me,' he said. 'I expect to be out of here well before then.'

In ten or so years of normal development, the sunline's power supply would be switched over from the engine to a purpose-built power plant drawing on the Destiny Star system's indigenous resources, most likely some combination of solar and fusion power. The cones would disengage from the great spinning cylinder, which would become an autonomous habitat and, in all probability, the hub of the system's culture and commerce. The crew would construct a new cylinder, almost fill it with the right mix of asteroid rubble, metals and organics, populate it with whoever wanted to be part of the next founder generation, fire up the engine to generate a new sunline and away they would go, to repeat the whole process another few centuries hence.

'You don't intend to stay?'

'No,' said Horrocks. 'I'm crew, and that's all there is to it.'

Synchronic gave him a teasing look. 'You're sure of that? Some of the crew always elect to stay.'

'And some of the founders always choose to go.'

She smiled at his riposte. 'True enough. And it's always a surprise, even for them, or so I'm told. But for now, you're certain you don't want to stick around here?'

'Yes.'

'Good,' she said, with a hint of regret. 'That puts you in a good position to be objective. You see, our interests are potentially in conflict with those of the ship generation.'

Horrocks was shocked. The harmony of interests between the crew, the founder generation and the ship generation was almost an axiom. He put down his empty glass and, without thinking, refilled it.

'I don't understand,' he said. He looked around at the ancient faces and found no clue in them.

'You know the ship generation,' Synchronic said.

'Not as well, surely, as you,' he said.

She smiled, with a trace of impatience. 'You've seen a lot more of them since they grew up than I have. You've trained scores of them.'

Horrocks nodded. 'Hundreds. I've been favourably impressed. They're enthusiastic, eager to learn, quick to pick up.'

'I should hope so,' said Synchronic. She glanced around the others. Something flashed between them, too fast for Horrocks to decode. 'They were raised for this adventure; they were, in a sense, bred for it. That's our problem.'

'I still don't see the problem.'

Chandrasekhar Limit Lamont, a habitat design entrepreneur in a blue skirt and a buzz-cut, leaned forward, elbows on knees, spreading greasy fingers.

'They're eager to start colonising,' he said. 'The ship is like a seed-pod about to burst.'

Horrocks nodded. 'Of course,' he said. He wondered if the man knew of his wonderment at the plant genetic machinery dispersal system. Unlikely – the image would be familiar to the flatfooter. 'If I'd grown up in one of the small settlements, getting out would be the foremost thing on my mind. Apart from sex, I suppose.'

Synchronic laughed. 'It's the same thing.'

'Still,' said Horrocks. 'The problem with that?'

'Is that we may have to delay colonisation,' said Chandrasekhar.

Horrocks had heard the option being bandied about, on the margins of the raging debates about whether or not to contact the aliens. Hearing it put forward as a serious possibility startled him.

'If you want to know how the ship generation will react to *that*,' he said, 'you don't need me to tell you. You already know the answer. They'll not stand for it. They'll be furious.'

Chandrasekhar nodded. 'That's what we expect, yes. We were curious as to whether you would confirm it. Nevertheless, it's a step we may be forced to, in the . . . awkward circumstance.'

'Why?' Horrocks asked. 'Everyone's tooled up for the usual sky-down approach. We don't have to go near the terrestrial for centuries. Or any of the planets, come to that. Apart from scooping helium 3 from the gas giant. The aliens don't even have to notice us.'

'Oh, they'll notice us,' said Armstrong Phillipic Natura, an artist. She regarded him over the rim of her glass. 'Unless we stealth all our comms, which is impracticable. And as soon as we start doing things, they'll see the industry.'

'What if they do?' Horrocks asked. 'It still doesn't *affect* them. Not until they get space travel, anyway. And when they come out, we'll have plenty to offer them, and no doubt they us.'

'It'll affect them long before they get space travel,' said Chandrasekhar Limit.

'We know this?' Horrocks asked.

The three who had just spoken to him exchanged looks.

'How much,' asked Synchronic, 'do you know about what people did before they lived in caves?'

The shade had covered the sunline. A few lights had come on in the courtyard. Small insects had become bothersome. Horrocks stood staring into the pool. Mullets nibbled at what he had spewed in it. The sight failed to disgust him. He felt cold. He did not look again at the pictures that Armstrong Phillipic had conjured in his head, but their images remained in his memory. It wasn't that they were news to him. He'd known, in the abstract, that terrible things had happened in the deep past. Everybody did. It was part of education. But – wisely, he now thought – the teachers and care-parents and even the history texts had never brought it home to him; never rubbed his nose in it; never given him the full picture.

The pictures were bad enough, but it was the mentality that had produced the reality they depicted that had shocked him. His prehistoric ancestors seemed more alien than anything down on Destiny II. No, that wasn't it: they were precisely as alien, and the aliens as prehistoric.

The clique had long dispersed, but for Synchronic. He heard her light footsteps, felt her arm across his back and her hand on his shoulder, her head against his upper arm. He took a deep breath. Her scent was motherly, with a faint erotic tang.

'Feeling better?' she asked.

'Not really,' he said.

'I can tell by your tone that you are,' she said.

He shrugged away from her and paced around the pool, all the way around and back. She had sat down on the wall. He sat beside her.

'I am better.'

'And you know what we would like you to do?'

He could see her register her mistake as soon as the words were out of her mouth. His flare of anger subsided. Anxiety had driven over her tact.

'No,' he said. 'I don't. And even if I did, I'm not sure I'd agree to do it.'

'That's fair,' she said.

'It's knowing that their just knowing that we're here will drive them to – all that.' He clenched his fists. 'It makes me want to go down there and tell them to stop – *make* them stop – teach them the law of association – *make* them see it—'

Synchronic laughed. 'That's one option, yes. Only the most dangerous one. The reaction we most want to avoid.'

'"We"?'

'The Red Sun Circle. And others of our generation, of course. But the first priority is to have a moratorium on colonisation. At least in the inner system. We might get away with starting in the cometary cloud. They might not be so worried about us there, even if they detect us, which they will.'

Horrock snorted. 'Ask people to wait fifty years while we trundle back out there? No way. And the crew wouldn't be too happy either, I can tell you that.'

The cometary cloud was usually the last of a system's resources to be exploited. Though vast, it was far too thin a gruel to satisfy a ship generation keyed up for asteroids and moons and planets. Horrocks doubted even that it would be practicable to colonise it, without the power and resources of an inner system at one's back.

'All right,' said Synchronic. 'Scratch that. So – shall I tell you what we want you to do?'

Horrocks felt a momentary combination of dismay, at what he might be enjoined to do, and self-importance, that these ancient and powerful people should need his help. It faded as he reflected that he was, in all likelihood, far from the only one of his generation who would be thus approached.

'Please do,' he said.

'As a microgravity trainer,' Synchronic said, 'you have some influence and respect among the ship generation. You have credibility. Especially because your speculation on terrestrials was so profitable to you. It gives you some glamour.'

'That was Awlin's doing.'

'Nevertheless, it exists. Call it a halo effect. We would be very grateful if you would use what influence you have to ask the ship generation to be patient, to forego colonisation for as long as it takes for us to work out some solution. Bear in mind, we expect some good informed and considered advice to come from the Red Sun system in less than eight years.'

'And how long would it take to implement this expected advice?'

'We don't know.'

'It could be decades,' said Horrocks. 'Frankly, even asking them to wait eight years would be like – well, as your friend said, like telling a seed-pod not to pop.'

'It has to be done.'

Living half a millennium, Horrocks thought, could put a lot of steel in a voice.

'All right,' he said, 'but even if I did try to do that, I have no way of using my influence. Except talking to people I know. I'm no public writer or speaker.'

'You can start by talking to someone who is,' said Synchronic. 'Atomic Discourse Gale.'

He stared at her, feeling he was either being teased, or had been caught in a wile. 'She detests me!'

Synchronic's gaze was unfathomable. 'I know. It's only to be expected . . . at her age.'

Now what did she mean by that? He chose not to enquire.

'She's very likely to argue against anything I say, take the opposite position just because it's me who's—'

'Yes, yes,' said Synchronic. 'Let us worry about that. You do your bit, make your case, and let the law of unintended consequences take care of the rest.'

'All right,' said Horrocks. He rose to his feet. Synchronic remained seated.

'Don't go yet,' she said. She smiled, looked down, and looked up. 'All this talk about seeds popping.'

14 365:05:14 20:10

'Your thinking is metaphysical.'

Thus Grant, this morning. I stared at him. That's the first thing he's said that I couldn't understand. We had met, as usual, by the newsline hotspot on the corner of Fourth and Curved, and were walking, as usual, to the Yellow Wall Café, reading our grabs as we went. I blinked away columns.

'What?'

'Abstract, not rooted in experience.'

'Oh, you mean about the contact clause?'

I'd concede that: my query, though published in several significant outlets, hadn't drawn so much as a comment.

'No,' he said. He shoved his hands in his shorts pockets and walked on along Fourth. 'In "Learning the World".'

'You've read it?' I said, with what I hoped was the right mix of appreciation and sarcasm.

'All of it,' he said. 'Last night.'

'Oh,' I said. 'Well, thank you. So what's metaphysical about it?'

'Your arguments about what the existence of aliens tells us about the universe. You start with the principle of mediocrity – that we are in no unusual situation, not privileged observers – and conclude from that that if there are aliens with an origin and level of development so close to ours, the galaxy is about to light up with alien transmitters.'

'Nothing metaphysical about that. Two close together is unlikely unless there are lots all over the place.'

I held the café door open for him.

'Oh, but it is,' he said, breezing through and barging for the counter. 'Metaphysical.'

'I still don't understand what you mean by that.'

'You start from some point of logic and try to deduce something about the nature of the world.'

'As in, one plus one makes two?' I put the corresponding pieces of berrybread on my plate, one by one, under his nose.

'One and a half, now,' he said, chomping.

We got our coffees and sat down.

'Let me give you an example I trawled up,' he said, half a cup and several rounds of argument later. '"From the principle of plenitude, we conclude that God would have created aliens. From the Fermi Paradox, we conclude that if there are aliens, they would be here. But there are no aliens. Therefore God does not exist. Discuss."'

I nearly choked on a mouthful. 'That isn't a metaphysical argument! It isn't any kind of argument! It's a rocking string of non sequiturs!'

'So it is,' he said. 'And so's yours.'

'Where did you drag that up from anyway?'

'Prehistory,' he said. 'Early decades AG, anyway. And it was, I suspect, a parody of arguments even older than that. Or perhaps contemporary. Consider this one. If humanity is to fill the galaxy, the human population at that time in the future will be many orders of magnitude greater than the present human population. Agreed?'

'OK.'

'Therefore the probability of being alive in a future galactic human community is billions or trillions to one greater than being born now, when humanity only fills a tiny fraction of the galaxy. But we are alive now, which is very unlikely unless there is no vastly greater future human population. Therefore humanity will soon become extinct.'

I pounced on a too obvious flaw. 'It might just stop expanding.'

Grant shook his head. 'You still get far more future humans than present humans, even if we stay with the same population for say the ten million years it would take to fill the galaxy. And thus, the same desperate improbability of our existence among the first, unless we're also among the last.' He looked around, shoulders hunched. 'Doom lurks unseen.'

'That's even more stupid than the last one!' I said. '*Somebody* has to be among the first. It's just a brute fact.'

Grant leaned back, patted his belly, and smiled. 'Exactly.'

If he'd made a point I didn't see it.

'I mean, somebody could have made that argument when they were in the caves.'

'It was made before the caves, actually,' said Grant. 'But don't you see? Your argument is of the same type.'

'No it is not,' I said. 'That argument starts with a completely arbitrary notion, the "probability of being born", which is probably meaningless in the first place, and tries to deduce *without any additional facts . . .*'

At that point I ran out of road. I could see where I was going.

'All right,' I said, with ill grace. 'Point taken. So how do you explain it?'

A serving machine beeped. Grant took the coffee pot from its top and refilled our cups. He fingertipped the machine and it wheeled on.

'Maybe it doesn't have an explanation,' he said. 'It doesn't have to. We can in principle explain how life arose and developed and so on on both planets of origin. What else do we need to do? Do we need a separate explanation of why it arose on two so close together? Why? It's just a brute fact. It happened. Things do. Events.'

'It's still a big coincidence.'

'Yes,' he said. He gazed at me with a serious expression, unlike his habitual flippancy. 'It's *a big coincidence*. It's *something we can't explain*. But as far as we know that's all it is. And if it isn't, we'll only find out by discovering more facts, not speculating, no matter how logical that speculation might seem. The way to learn the world is to *look at the world*.'

I could hear some criticism there, some tone of disappointment and reproof. And (sorry, Grant, if you're reading this) I did not take it well, and I had no intention of letting him take it further.

So I resorted to saying: 'You're a bit intense this morning, Grant Cornforth.'

'Yes,' he said. He sipped his coffee. 'Sorry.'

I took this undeserved apology with a gracious wave of the hand.

'That's all right. Well, I have work to get on with. Same time tomorrow?'

'Of course,' he said. As I stood up he added: 'Nice dress, by the way.'

I looked down at the rippling emerald satin shift. 'Thank you,' I said, stepping away.

'Good choice,' he called after me.

'Yes, but the choice wasn't mine,' honesty made me admit, over my shoulder. 'My care-mother sent it to me.'

TEN

ABOVE TOP SECRET

Kwarive on the telephone: 'There's something you might like
to see.'

'I'll be over,' said Darvin, and put the receiver down. He
knew from her tone that nothing more effusive was expected,
and that something important was up. They had agreed on how
to convey such matters. Getting clearance to tell Kwarive a fraction of the truth had required a fight with the Sight of which he
could tell her nothing. His security handler had been rather too
enamoured of his own clever idea for a cover story, which was
that Darvin should tell Kwarive that he and Orro had male-
bonded. Darvin had sometimes speculated that Orro was a
male-bonding male – in parts of the Gevorkian armed and civil
services and nobility it was almost a requirement – but he had
no wish whatsoever to violate his friend's privacy and reticence.
He had made this point with such vehemence that the handler
had asked him, not in jest, if the suggested cover story was in
fact true. Darvin assured him it was not. The tale was in fact
tempting – it would have reassured Kwarive that Darvin and
Orro were not using their frequent mysterious absences for any

dangerous or unsavoury purpose – but it would have been, Darvin knew, intolerable to Orro. So, with great reluctance and much scratching of floors and stamping of papers, the handler had agreed that Kwarive, as Darvin's girlfriend and prospective roost-partner, could not be kept out of the circle. He was still enjoined to tell her nothing of the aeronautics, telecommunications and other projects that the discovery of the alien visitation had stimulated; and he had sworn to that effect.

The Life Sciences Building smelt of flitter and skitter droppings, of preserving fluids and warm hay. Skulls and skins decorated its corridor walls, as in the roost of a plains hunter. Kwarive, as a student, didn't have an office, but she had a regular place of work, the laboratory annexe of the department's museum. Her part-time job there gave her valuable training in practical skills as well as a small wage.

Darvin hurried past the dusty glass cases and stoppered glass jars and into the room at the far end. Shelves lined its walls, laden with preserved animal parts, bones, chunks of mineral, and stacks of paper. Its door faced the window, and between door and window lay a long table that, except for the electrical lamps and dissection microscope, looked a lot like a prey-merchant's counter. Bloodstains, gashes, sharp tools, animal parts. Kwarive looked up from the far end. She gestured to a shelf near the door.

'Pick up the telephone receiver,' she said. 'Hold it to your ear.'

Puzzled, Darvin complied. He heard nothing but the expected whining whir. Kwarive, holding a closed basket, paced down the room towards him. As she approached the telephone's note changed, overlaid by a faint buzz that rose in volume with every step she took. When she held the basket beside the receiver the buzz dominated the sound of the empty line. Kwarive smiled at him and retraced her steps. The buzz diminished.

Darvin returned the receiver to its cradle.

'What have you got in there?' he asked.

'Guess,' said Kwarive.

'Some electrical device?'

'Come and have a look.'

His hand on the basket lid, he hesitated.

'No trick?' he asked.

Kwarive looked indignant. 'Nothing's going to jump out at you.'

On the floor of the basket was a shittle. A common grazer-dung-eating insect about the length of a thumb, it was in no way different from any other shittle Darvin had ever seen: stubby feelers, sturdy nippers, two camera eyes, four legs on the thorax, four on the metathorax, shiny blue wing-cases along the abdomen.

Darvin closed the lid and raised his brows. 'Yes?'

'You asked me to tell you about anything unusual,' Kwarive said.

'Well, it's certainly an interesting discovery,' Darvin said. 'I bet nobody knew shittles have an electrical field. Maybe they use it to find their way around in the shit, like electric fish do in murky water, or perhaps it's a defence—'

'Shittles don't have an electrical field,' said Kwarive.

'How do you know?'

Kwarive jumped on to the perch at the end of the table and huffed. When her wings had settled she pointed to another identical basket on a shelf.

'There's a whole basket of them there,' she said. 'See for yourself.'

Darvin checked that the basket indeed contained a crawling mass of the ugly brutes, and carried it to the telephone. He picked up the receiver and heard only the whir. He returned and put the basket back.

'Maybe it's a different species.'

Kwarive chittered her teeth at him. 'I'm the biologist here.'

'All right,' said Darvin, abashed. 'Sorry. So tell me how you found this one.'

'The delivery trudge came in with the full basket – it's a consignment for an insect physiology practical – just as I was on the telephone to the administration office. That's how I heard the buzz. Now, I immediately jumped to the same conclusion that you did – that I'd accidentally discovered a new fact about shittles. However, being a good scientist, I decided to check it by putting half the shittles in an empty basket. One buzzed, the other didn't. So I kept splitting them between various empty containers' – she gestured at a collection of jars, boxes and dissection pans among the clutter – 'and narrowed it down to this one specimen.'

Darvin found a stool and sat on it and looked up at Kwarive on her perch.

'And you think an electric shittle is relevant to the, ah, big picture?'

He had a vague worry that he had let slip some information about the telecommunications aspect, to which – Kwarive might have thought – an electric-field-producing insect might be of interest. A dim notion floated past him of somehow training the little beasts to act as signalling devices for sabreurs in flight. A sort of portable wireless . . . yes indeed, the Flight might be interested in that . . .

'I think it came from up there,' Kwarive said. She rolled her eyes upward, as – with a different significance – did Darvin a moment later.

'Perhaps the visitors are very small,' he said.

She hopped off the perch and shook him by the shoulders. 'Stop making fun of this!' she said. 'It's like you're making fun of *me*!'

Darvin put his wings around her and nuzzled the top of her head.

'I'm sorry,' he said. 'But it's all so—'

She stepped out of his enfolding. 'I know,' she said. 'I find it hard to believe what you tell me, even though you've shown me some of the evidence. You know, there are times when I wonder whether your big secret story isn't a cover for something even stranger.'

'I wouldn't do that to you,' said Darvin.

'I know, I know. Anyway. Sometimes I swear it seems easier to believe that you're a spy for Gevork or . . . or something, than that what you tell is true. Even though I do trust you.'

'You know I have not told you everything,' said Darvin.

'Oh, I know that. I'm sure the military are flapping their wings all over this.'

Darvin nodded. 'It's their job,' he said. 'Their duty.'

'And it's yours not to tell me about it. Now let's dissect this bug.'

She could change course like a flitter, Darvin thought, but he was glad of it.

She tipped the shittle on to a bloodied square of board and flipped it on its back. Its legs waved. Kwarive reached for a long pin.

'Stop!' said Darvin.

'What?'

'It might give you an electrical shock.'

'That little thing?'

'There might be some kind of capacitor inside it.'

Kwarive looked dubious, but held the pin in a pair of wooden tongs when she skewered the shittle, and rummaged up a ceramic probe and knife. Then she took the board to the binocular dissection microscope and switched on the light. She slit the underside of the animal lengthwise, through the hard thoraxes and the soft, segmented abdomen, and eased the sides of the cut apart. The legs stopped twitching.

The tips of the probe and the blade stirred almost

imperceptibly in the innards. Darvin recognised a tiny gut being lifted to one side. The probe's tip snagged. Kwarive grunted and her hands made more minute, steady movements.

'Will you look at this,' she said, her voice calm. She stepped back from the instrument.

Darvin adjusted the eyepieces and the focus. The shittle in the magnified field filled his sight. Beside the teased-apart digestive and circulatory systems, amid the gunk and bits that biologists called connective tissue because they didn't know what it did, lay a peculiar complex of red and green glassy-looking crystals and a thin copper-coloured strand, about the thickness of a fine hair. Darvin held out a hand and Kwarive placed the probe in it. He tapped the crystals. They were hard. He poked at the coppery strand. It was too strong for gentle pressure on the probe to break. He slid the tip towards the head end. The strand went all the way to the top of the thorax.

He relinquished the microscope to Kwarive. She placed the edge of the knife between the nippers and brought it down, cleaving the head.

'The strand bifurcates,' she said. 'It goes to each of the eyes.'

Darvin looked and confirmed this.

'Can you lift the whole thing out?' he asked.

She could. She took a water bottle with a tube through the stopper and washed the thing a drop at a time. It lay gleaming on the slab beside its now headless and eviscerated host.

They stood together and looked at it for a while.

'What sense do you make of it?' asked Darvin.

'Well,' said Kwarive, 'it's plainly artificial. That coppery strand is *copper wire*.'

'Are you sure?'

'Sure as I can be without a materials lab.'

'Easy enough to check,' said Darvin. 'But what could the rest of it be?'

'I have no idea,' said Kwarive. 'No, I do have an idea, and

I've had it ever since I noticed the electrical effect. But it's too far-fetched.'

Darvin glanced again at the glittering mechanism.

'Nothing could be too far-fetched to explain this.'

'Very well,' said Kwarive. 'I think it's a transmitter, of wireless telephonic or telekinematographic etheric waves. It is using the insect's eyes as cameras.'

'That's certainly far-fetched,' said Darvin. 'No wireless telephone, let alone telekinematographic apparatus, could possibly be this small.'

'How do you know that? You might as well say that your object in space could not possibly be so large.'

'I suppose, if we are dealing with a technology so much more advanced . . .' A thought struck him. 'But even so, the signal produced must have been very weak. How could it reach – so far away?'

'I wouldn't know,' said Kwarive. 'I know nothing about telekinematography.'

'Come to think of it,' said Darvin, 'how do you know about it at all?'

'Orro told me,' she said. 'He says it's being developed by the military . . . in Gevork.'

'Hmm,' said Darvin. 'That's all right, I suppose. Please don't talk about it loosely. Anyway . . . from the little I know, it involves rather heftier equipment than this.'

'I wonder if it's still active,' Kwarive said.

They repeated the telephone experiment. The electrical interference was gone.

'It may have drawn its energy from the shittle's body,' said Kwarive.

'Or we broke it,' said Darvin.

'That would be a shame. It would be irreplaceable. No, wait, it wouldn't. We can find more, and I know just how to do it.'

'How?'

Kwarive smiled and shoved the empty basket to him. 'Fill it up,' she said. 'I'll call Orro.'

Not being a biologist, Darvin didn't have Kwarive's confidence in statistics, and after an hour scooping shittles from the dung in the gutters of the wintry streets he didn't like it either. He washed his hands and feet in the chill canal before returning with his reeking burden. By this time Orro had joined Kwarive and was hunched over a handful of scrawled paper. The telephone receiver had been dismantled. Parts of it lay beside the dissected shittle and its alien innards. Neither of them looked likely to be put back together any time soon.

'What are you doing?' Darvin asked.

Orro looked up. 'Trying to work out wavelengths from the circuitry of the receiver.'

'Laudable but premature,' said Darvin, putting down the basket. 'We need a working receiver right now.'

Orro fussed for a moment.

'Oh, good lady above,' said Kwarive. She snatched up a screwdriver and had every component in place and the receiver back on its flex within minutes.

'Now then,' she said, holding it up, 'the basket, if you please.'

Darvin hefted the basket and walked towards her. Kwarive smiled.

'The buzz is back!' she said.

This time the tedious sorting procedure sifted out two of the electric shittles (as they'd started calling them). The three scientists peered down at the two unprepossessing insects. The two insects – Darvin couldn't but fancy – looked back.

'Hello,' he said. 'Greetings from Ground.'

Orro grabbed his shoulder so hard that it hurt.

'We could do that!' he said.

'Do what?'

'Use the electric shittles to communicate with the visitors.'

Darvin burst out laughing.

'What's so funny?' demanded Kwarive.

'Oh, nothing,' Darvin said. 'It's just that I had a sudden vision of a conclave of scientists and security men jabbering and capering in front of a glass case floored with shit and crawling with shittles.'

'Well, why not?' asked Orro.

Darvin sat down on a stool and looked from Orro to Kwarive and back. He scratched the fur on the back of his calf.

'No reason why not,' he said. 'It's just that I sometimes find it hard to believe. You both evidently don't.'

He stood up and paced around, scouting for tea.

'For one thing,' he said, 'the signal these little – and I stress little – blighters put out couldn't possibly reach . . . its supposed recipients.'

'You're doing it again,' said Kwarive. 'Saying what they can and can't do without evidence. We've just seen evidence that they can do things we can't. The pot and the brazier are behind that stuff on the ledge, by the way.'

'Oh, thanks.'

'No, he's right,' said Orro. 'It's a question of output power. There are theoretical limits to how much electrical power can be extracted from chemical processes.'

'And you know these limits, I suppose?' asked Kwarive.

'I do, as a matter of fact,' said Orro. He brushed at his eyes as if weary. 'I wrote the paper on it. Nevertheless, there is a way in which such weak signals could reach our, ah, supernumerary moon, if not farther.'

Darvin fiddled with gas taps and water taps. 'And what's that?'

'Amplification,' Orro said.

'You astonish me,' said Darvin, sparking up the flame under
the brazier. 'The question we're all agog to hear the answer to
is what such an amplifier might be.' He waved a hand at the
window, at the view of buildings and trees. 'Given that we
don't see telekinematographic transmission towers mysteri-
ously springing up all over the place.'

'Oh!' said Kwarive. She hopped on a perch and spread her
wings. 'We do!'

Darvin, unable to wait for the tea, pushed some leaf under
his tongue and grunted a query.

'Trees,' said Kwarive. 'Look at the shape: the tall central
spire and the upward-curving floret of branches. Does that
not remind you of something, Orro?'

'I concede the resemblance,' said Orro. 'Doubtless it inspired
the design of the transmission and reception antennae.'

'You never told me this,' said Darvin.

'No, I never did,' said Orro. 'I was, ah, discussing Gevorkian
science with Kwarive one day and it slipped out. I have since
then guarded my tongue more carefully. However, this is not
the point. The point is that I don't see how trees could be so
used. Wood is not, after all, renowned for its electrical con-
ductivity.'

Kwarive hunched like a hunter watching prey from a
branch. She scratched behind her ear. Darvin, knowing the
signs, said nothing more until the pot had boiled and he had
served the tea in three containers that (Kwarive assured him)
were only used for that purpose, and not to hold any of the
unsavoury liquids and pulps that the room's other identical
beakers contained.

'So, Kwarive. You were saying.'

'I think I have it now,' she said. She blew and sipped. 'If
copper wire can be formed inside a shittle, why can't it — or
some other metal — be formed inside the branches and spire of
a tree? Along the capillaries, perhaps?'

'Why do you say it was formed?' asked Darvin. 'I had imagined it was somehow implanted.'

'If it was implanted,' said Kwarive, 'our visitors are a great deal closer than we think.' She laughed. 'They fly among us.'

'That's a possibility,' said Orro. 'I can imagine, say, a mechanical flitter. Like one of my chiropter models, only successful. With tiny manipulative hands, like a real flitter.'

'Oh yes,' said Darvin. 'I can see it now, preying on the shittles among a flock of real flitters, and stashing some away to vivisect in its nest!'

'Why not?' said Orro. 'We are agreed that calculating machines may make great progress in ages to come.'

Kwarive extended and quivered her wings, almost spilling the tea.

'And does it mine the copper and whatever substance the coloured crystals are made from? Or does it perhaps steal them from shops?'

Orro was immune to her sarcasm. 'Some species of flitters are notorious for stealing odds and ends of material for their nests.'

'Oh, for the Queen's sake, gentlemen,' said Kwarive, 'will you stop this idle speculation and listen to my – to my—'

'*Your* idle speculation?' said Darvin.

Kwarive laughed. 'Indeed. But listen. How I had imagined it was something quite different. Fix your attention on a congenial subject for a moment. Sex. The male, as you may know, produces a sticky fluid with which he impregnates the female.'

Darvin gaped at Orro. 'So *that*'s what happens!'

'Shut up,' said Kwarive. 'As you also know, the life-bearing seed is a microscopic animalcule. And yet somehow, from this tiny invisible seed comes, in due course, a litter of kits.'

'The seed has to combine with the female egg,' said Darvin, entering into the spirit of conveying no news.

'Which is larger but still microscopic,' said Kwarive. 'And

somehow, from one or both of these come a clutch of living things, each large enough to hold in your hand. Which, as they grow up, display characteristics similar to those of their parents.'

'Fascinating,' said Darvin. 'The mystery of life. The miracle of reproduction. I don't know why I didn't learn all this in school.'

'I did not,' said Orro. 'I read it in an imaginative but broadly accurate illustrated treatise inscribed, if memory serves, on the wall of a municipal pissery.'

'Each to his own,' said Kwarive. 'My point, if I can momentarily distract you, is that reproduction is *not* a miracle. The life principle in the germ-plasm somehow organises and controls a mass of matter that but yesterday was the mother's food, and transforms it into another living organism. Forces that we do not understand shape every organ and limb, and in a manner which is inherited from the parents. The vehicles of that inheritance are without doubt the tiny egg and the still smaller seed.'

'I see,' said Orro. 'You are suggesting that the seeds or eggs of the shittles have somehow been influenced to produce small electrical devices, as if they were bodily organs. And that a similar influence may be exerted on the growing-power of certain trees, albeit ones already mature, perhaps due to the greater plasticity of the botanical cell-plasm.'

'Yes!' said Kwarive, sounding surprised and relieved. 'That's exactly it.'

'But – *copper wires?*' said Darvin.

'That's the easiest part of it,' said Kwarive. 'There are copper salts everywhere. Other mineral salts form naturally on dung. We all have a tincture of iron in our blood.'

Darvin drained his dubious cup. 'That,' he said, 'is the wildest speculation I have heard today. It makes Orro's intelligent mechanical flitters seem like a sound and sober possibility. That's why I think you're right, Kwarive.'

'You do?'

'Well, it's that or something wilder. We must take this to the project.'

A few days later an airship of Seloh's Flight flew slowly over Five Ravines. Adults spared it a glance, and gained from that glance a touch of reassurance. Gangs of kits tried and failed to reach its altitude. After criss-crossing the town a few times it flew away to the north. The following day, here and there about town, men with the municipal crest on the buckles of their crossed straps were observed, or rather, not noticed, flying into certain trees, sawing off the branches they perched on, and flying away. That evening, a telegraph machine rattled in Darvin's office, and spat forth a message that, when decoded, read: FRUIT ON SCHED PREP DESP URGENT.

The device was like an enormous flechette or flighted cross-bolt, several wingspans long. With its backswept wings – or stabilisers, as the techs insisted on calling them – it resembled a crude copy of the alien flying machine in the photograph. Pointed at one end, open at the other; rivets making small elliptical shadows on its burnished steel plates. It lay atop a trolley on a railed wooden ramp with an upward slope. Heavy electrical cables trailed from the ramp. Somebody counted backwards. At zero flames sputtered from the open end, then roared forth like an opened furnace door. The device rushed forward and hurtled into a shallow ascent of several eight-eights of wingspans on the horizontal and about two eights on the vertical, then tilted downward, hit the desert, performed a couple of spectacular cartwheels and exploded with a deafening bang.

Ears still ringing, Darvin heard a cheer from the small crowd of project members who, with him, watched at a supposedly safe distance.

'Impressive, isn't it?' said Nollam, the young telekinematography technician.

'You could say that,' said Darvin. 'Also expensive, futile and dangerous.'

'All of these,' said Nollam. He rubbed his hands and shook out his wings. 'This is our top-secret self-propelled giant flechette project. Officially called Project Cross-bolt. And us lowly types have been officially told to unofficially call it Project Piss-crystal.'

'Saltpetre?'

'Yes,' said Nollam.

'Why?'

'In case any news of it leaks out.'

'I should have thought,' said Darvin, strolling back to the huts of the project's desert camp, 'that naming it after the device's shape and after a component of bomb-powder rather gave the show away.' He stopped. 'Oh,' he said. 'I see.'

'You do,' said Nollam. 'Gives great cover. The Gevorkians must know we're up to something up here, and that's just the sort of rind to throw to them. Besides,' he added, 'it might just work.'

Orro, who had watched the display from the air, swooped to land beside them.

'Wonderful!' he said. 'I must tell you, this is substantially better than what I know of such work in Gevork.'

'That's a relief,' said Nollam.

'Of course my knowledge is years out of date,' said Orro, sounding worried. He brightened, and clutched the technician's arm.

'Has anyone thought of launching the device straight upward?'

'Firing it at the sky?' said Nollam. 'Whatever for?'

'It could be a method of reaching extreme altitudes.'

'I'll pass it on,' said Nollam. He didn't sound as if he meant it.

'Seriously,' said Orro. 'It's important.'

'All right, man, all right.'

The ground was hard. Their breath puffed in front of them. The tips of Darvin's ears, toes and fingers ached. He still preferred the pale clear blue of the desert winter mid-morning sky to the dripping clouds and fogs of the warmer and moister coast.

Kwarive, now seconded to the project since her biological discovery, had chosen to watch from the still safer distance of the camp. She met them at the gate.

'It's a good start,' she said. 'But I don't see it ever reaching the sky.'

'It doesn't have to,' said Nollam. 'It just has to reach a Gevorkian gas-bag.'

Kwarive, Darvin gathered, was not to be told of the misdirection.

'How horrible!' she said. 'I'm glad my — our part of the project isn't so destructive.'

Her, or their, part of the project now dominated the barracks square, though to a casual observer, the transplanted tree by the lecture ring might merely have been there to provide a pleasant sight of home. The blimp, moored eight-eights wingspans above it and trailing cables, might have been a lookout over the flat dry plain. The grazer dung from the prey paddock heaped around the tree's foot might have been to fertilise the barren soil in which this coastal tree improbably grew. A hardy evergreen, its lean spire and parabolic array of branches and leaves seemed almost to yearn for the sun. Instead, as Nollam's telekinematographic reception apparatus cabled to a big wire frame in the tethered blimp monitored, the tree — or rather, the fine network of unknown alloy that permeated it from the roots up – was sending a continuous stream of incomprehensible etheric information skyward. None of Nollam's equipment could make more of it than a flickering screen of snow.

Eights upon eights of electric shittles burrowed in the dung, and now and then poked their unblinking eyes out upon the world. No attempt to attract their attention – whether with bright-lit pictures, earnest discourses, or people jumping up and down – had elicited the slightest response. Kwarive had observed and recorded the insects' reactions over two days and nights, and the best statistical methods she could apply showed that their gazes, as much as the radio waves which they continued to pulse forth, were random. They bore no relation to the putative objects of interest presented to them. At any given time there would be a few shittles peering outward, but that was what shittles did.

What the scientists working on the other aspects of the project made of all this bizzare activity Darvin, Orro and Kwarive occasionally speculated on, but took care not to ask. Knowledge within the project was as compartmentalised as an insect's body.

'I'm going to try something new today,' Kwarive said, stopping beside the wheeled screens that surrounded the base of the tree.

'What is it this time?' Nollam asked. 'Obscene photographs? Religious texts? A careful heaping of stones in eights, to show them how we count?'

'No,' said Kwarive, in a tone that suggested she might have considered these. 'Maps.'

'Isn't that a security risk?' asked Darvin.

'Oh yes,' said Kwarive. 'I've cleared it with Markhan.'

Orro and Darvin looked at each other and shook their heads. Neither of them had so much as spoken to the chief scientist since the project began.

'We'll leave you to it,' said Darvin. 'Good luck.'

'Bring me some tea,' said Kwarive, spreading a large sheet of paper on the frosty ground and kneeling beside it with ink-bottle and brush. 'Hot and soon.'

The three men made their way to one of the barrack roosts. Its sleeping-racks empty by day, its interior space had been turned into a long laboratory. Cluttered tables filled the aisle. Between them snaked dangerous trailing cables that originated in the blimp and ended around the back of the cable-festooned mass of the telekinematographic receiver. This device was a wooden cabinet the size of a meat-cupboard with a glass screen like a window, a couple of handspans wide, in the front near the top. The glass looked thick and somewhat convex, with rounded corners. At the moment it displayed a random flicker of spots and lines that hurt the eye if you watched too long. Nollam joined the technicians trying to make sense of the tree's data stream, Orro studied the results of the latest aeronautical experiments – the real ones, being carried out far away at a place unknown – and Darvin headed down an aisle to the tea urn. He took tea out to Kwarive, who had already completed an impressive sketch-map of the Selohic coast. Just as he arrived she added, in the empty middle of the map, a stylised, chevron-winged flechette.

'Now that looks like a security risk,' said Darvin.

Kwarive shook her head. 'It was Markhan who suggested it.'

Darvin shrugged and gave her the steaming cup. She nuzzled his hand and he returned to sift through the day's reports from the physics wire. It was the second time this outer-month that he and his friends had travelled to the camp. The university authorities had been told, by much higher authorities, that the two scientists' and the student's services were required for military training and preparation, and that no demurral would be brooked. In that outer-month the project, with a soldierly dispatch that impressed and baffled Darvin, had set up the experiment with the transplanted tree. What he was doing now, though, could just as well have been done at Five Ravines, and – with no results from the experiment – Darvin chafed to get back. Under cover of his continuing planet search, he had accumulated a stock of paired plates that showed the Object. Now that its position was known, it was indeed, as Orro had guessed, detectable as a distant companion of the Camp-Followers, the asteroids, but one somewhat beyond the orbit of the Warrior. Ground's much closer visitor, the third moon, though betrayed by its etheric echo, remained invisible.

An hour or two had passed when Kwarive laid a cold hand on his shoulder, making him jump.

'Come outside,' she said. 'There's something you might like to see.'

Darvin followed her out as she marched back to the foot of the tree. Her completed map hung from one of the wheeled screens. Eight eights of shittles faced the map.

'Watch,' said Kwarive.

She wheeled the screen a little way around the tree. As she did so other shittles emerged and faced it. She wheeled it around and around, until the base of the tree was surrounded by a phalanx of outward-facing insect eyes.

Darvin stared at them, and then at Kwarive. She was shaking.

'I think—' she began.

Through the open door of the barracks roost and across the square they heard Nollam's yell.

ELEVEN

ALIEN SPACE BATS

14 365:05:22 22:15

I don't know about you, but I've been neglecting my habitat planning and proposals lately. Yes, that was a joke. I can see from a
glance at the markets that everyone's doing it. Well, maybe not
everyone, but a majority of the founders and a significant minority
of the ship generation. Planet-watching eats your time and drains
your sleep. I see the bat people in my dreams.

What follows is not a dream. It's based on some notes I took
last time I entered a virtuality of Destiny II.

It feels like real time. It isn't, of course; what I'm seeing and hearing happened hours ago, the information from countless bugs in
numerous disguises uplinked to the satellite and beamed thence
to the ship, where it's been processed and reconstructed and the
gaps filled in by guesswork and best fit until it's a seamless seeming, ready to be studied by science teams and traipsed through by
the rest of us.

I'm in a coastal industrial town. The air is hazy with carbon particles. In the distance, at the edge of town, smoke drifts in thick

streams from tall chimneys. My POV is at its default height off the ground, that of my own eyes, but I expect I'm going to vary that if I'm to see things from – literally – their point of view. I begin, though, at ground level. It's an eerie feeling, as if moving among them unseen.

That in itself isn't half as weird as standing on a surface that looks flat and is actually convex. It curves away down to a horizon, as I can see whenever I glimpse the sea between the buildings, instead of curving away up. And above that horizon is nothing but empty (well, cloudy and hazy) sky, instead of the other side of the world. About sixty degrees up in that sky I can see the Destiny Star, like a sunline rolled up into a ball.

(And this in turn, incidentally, isn't half as unsettling as standing in a virtuality taken at night. Of course such virtualities are even more artificial and reconstructed than this one – our little bugs are for the most part not nocturnal, nor do their eyes focus to infinity – but I'm assured what we see is what we would see in that very position at that time of night. Now, in a sense it's only what you see when you link to the ship's outside view to look out through the ship, in the right direction, give or take a few AU difference in POV. But when you use your imagination and really think of your-self standing there, on the outside surface of a planet, with nothing but a thin skin of atmosphere between you and the raw vacuum . . . the Civil Worlds glowing green, the Red Sun in their midst burning red, and the rest of the stars in all their naked native glory winking at you . . . it shakes you to your CNS, that's all I can say. So just try it, OK?)

But back to today.

I'm on what might be called a street. The road is metalled, the sidewalk elevated, and vehicles move on the one and pedestrians on the other. It's filthy. Looking down I see the droppings of the big beasts that haul carts, and the different ordure of the slaves who carry loads and run errands and haul cabs. Add rotting rinds, bones, and scraps of paper – all of which receive close and competitive attention from a variety of insectoids and different species of flying rat – and it makes me very glad I'm not really setting foot here. All this garbage may serve to manure the peculiar paraboloid trees, which sprout everywhere. An open-topped car rushes towards me through the ruck and press of carts. I see its radiator grille like bared teeth, and the flat glass plate of the windscreen. I hear the roar of its internal combustion petroleum engine, interpersed with the braying blare of its warning instrument. As it passes through my POV I glimpse the faces of its driver and two passengers, and the vehicle's interior. The seating is two wooden bars. The driver operates controls with hands and feet. I turn to watch it. From behind, the occupants have a look of cowled people with high-set, pointed ears. The warning instrument sounds again, and one of the bat people leaps into the air in front of the car, takes wing and lets it pass beneath him or her, and settles again on the road. Then it hurries to the sidewalk.

I drift the POV to above the sidewalk and bob along at the local walking pace. I'm two or three heads taller than most of the bat people. Seen close-up, their faces are like a somewhat flattened face of a fox. They have more in the way of jaw and snout than most humans, balanced by much larger eyes. The fine fur on their faces is patterned with stripes and spots, and their fur colours vary – grey, white, black, brown, reddish and so on. Some of these colours and patterns may be from artificial dyes. Their eye colour, oddly to our eyes, varies little. It's a clear yellow, one of their many features – like walking along eating chunks of raw meat, or scratching each other's fur, or chittering their teeth – that strikes us as animal-like. Their speech comes across as a continuous trill of chirps and squeals, with some low growling notes.

The slaves, trudging along with their burdens and their slashed, atrophied wings, look even less human. Their eyes are duller, and they say little. Their jaws are heavier and more prominent, as are their sagittal crests. Their limb muscles are bulkier. But these differences, which may not even be genetic, are quite hard to spot.

You have to watch a lot of bat people before you can tell instantly which is slave and which free – ignoring the mutilations, of course.

Slaves apart, many of the pedestrians are pregnant or nursing females. The former waddle with ponderous dignity and a certain ferocity of countenance. Everybody steps out of their way, even – especially – the slaves. The nursing mothers stride along more briskly, each with three or four tiny infants clinging to her chest fur and usually plugged in to her nipples. Three rows of paired nipples, litters of offspring, pregnancy itself – again, it all reminds us of beasts, and we have to watch out for any subconscious prejudices in this regard.

On the other hand . . . they're disturbingly not alien. They don't breathe methane or have twenty legs. They're mammals like us. Clearly there's been a lot of parallel – or is it convergent? I can never remember – evolution. They're made by DNA coding for proteins, albeit by different pathways. Their amino acids even have the same handedness as ours. We could – viruses and bacteria aside – eat the same food. (After cooking it, something they don't do much of, though they dry and salt meat and sometimes heat it up to eat.) Is this a coincidence, or is it evidence of some deeper connection? After my talking-to from Grant the other day, I'm not sure whether to speculate. No, I positively don't want to speculate. I want to observe and record.

OK. Street level is not where the action is. The buildings are tall and narrow. They go up to ten or more storeys and look rickety. Most of them are built of wood and are as if on stilts. The ground floor is usually open on all sides and, here at any rate, is used as a tip or as a shop or as a stable, heaped with the fodder for the huge beasts – they look more like hypertrophic rabbits than anything we might recognise as cattle – that the bat people eat. The real building begins at the next floor. Most floors are linked by ladders or stairs, but they usually have narrow landing-ledges where the bat people alight, to go in and out by the openings in the sides. These openings are fitted with awnings and screens of woven straw and basketwork, or of some kind of translucent parchment. Some of these screens are decorated with pictures of flowers and foliage. This decoration seems distinct from the big pictures that many of the buildings have on their frontage or sides, usually of bat people eating or drinking, or of devices and vehicles. They also bear symbols that are reckoned to be the aliens' script, in very large font. They're kind of like tags, but actual rather than virtual.

I levitate the POV and drift it into one of those first floors. The reception is patchier here – fewer vermin for our bugs to parasitise – all I can really make out is a row of bat people perched on a low bar and hunched over a long table, on which they are inscribing stuff in a paper book. In the corner there's a big clunky machine that takes oblong cards in and spills a long roll of paper out. It could be a mechanical computer, or it could be a machine for printing wallpaper. I drift out the other side, over another and similar street, and look up. The streets are criss-crossed with cables, some of them electrical or telephonic (that's power and coms) but most of them carrying little wood-frame cable-car contraptions that sometimes contain loads and sometimes have bat people sitting on, perching on, or clinging to them. I think most of the people on these are infirm in some way. Their bodies deteriorate with age. Their skin hangs loose, and they get diseases from bacteria and viruses. It's amazing how deftly the flying bat people avoid the aerial obstructions, and each other in flight. Many fly much higher than the buildings, of course, and can ignore the traffic patterns below. Higher than them, very occasionally, I see dirigibles, but no other aircraft.

In among all the low flyers are the flying rats and flying insectoids. There are no birds in this sky, no birdsong in the air. Only the squeaks of the flying rats. The rats come in several sizes and one colour, a dirty dun. To my eyes and ears it's a strangely impoverished sky. And in among the flying rats, dodging them and catching them and sometimes *eating* them, are the bat people's young. They seem to start flying when they've grown to about a quarter the height of an adult – knee-high to a bat – and they roam the air in flocks, line the ledges of buildings, chitter and scream. We only know they're the young and not some bigger species of flying rat from close observation, and seeing them fly back to their parental roosts in the evenings. (Where, it has to be said, the parents treat them with what looks like affection, enfolding them in their own big wings, stroking and grooming them and feeding them titbits.) They have no adult supervision whatsoever, at least until they reach about half adult size, when you can see them lined up, upside down, on the rafters of some low buildings which are evidently a sort of primitive school.

I see one of these down the road, and in sudden curiosity I zip towards it. Inside it's quite bright and the floor is covered with straw and droppings. The view is quite clear. The young bat people hang from beams overhead, bright eyes swivelling as they follow the actions of an adult who struts and frets beneath them, indicating diagrams on the floor – scratched in the dust, often, with the foot-claw or some tool clutched in the foot – shouting and pointing. Sometimes the adult flies up and attacks some hapless youngster, beating fists against its huddled wings. I turn away and zip out, feeling nauseous, and blink out of the session. This sight has upset me. It makes me want to teach *them* a lesson.

A temptation we must learn to resist.

'Thanks,' said Horrocks, swinging off the rear saddle of the two-seater.

'Any time,' said the pilot, whose name Horrocks had failed to catch. The pilot glanced back and gunned forward, and the microlight bumped across the grass and rose into the sky.

Horrocks waved, turned away, and looked across a couple of hundred metres of parkland to the edge of Far Crossing. Complex voluted towers, tall trees, radial streets whose roadways ran out in a dribble of macadam on the grass as though their builders had lost heart. Atomic Discourse had called it a town, but she had been mistaken. It was a concentrated, condensed city. It had all the exciting parts of a city: the shops and studios and theatres and cafés, the lofts and cellars, the laboratories and nanofactories, and none of the dull bits: the dormitory suburbs, the marshalling yards, the car ports, the residential streets, the industrial parks. What White City and its like were for the older generation, Far Crossing and its like were for the young.

Horrocks followed floating virtual tags to the loft where Atomic worked. It was in a building near the centre, above a row of shops. Up two flights of stairs, which he negotiated with a firm grip on the handrail. The loft was about thirty metres long, with high sloped windows at either end. In this dim space a score of people worked on design units. Those old enough for their virtuality genes to have kicked in could have done it all in their heads, but all of them used screens or holograms: display, advertising, was part of the process. One or two showed modules or specialised areas – recycling plant, gardens – or mining schematics tagged to particular claims. Others had conjured up more ambitious schemes, for orbital habitats or surface projects for one or other of the system's moons, or gas-mining processes for the ringed gas giant, or power stations for the mercurial. One even had a wild scheme for lifting water from the waterworld. For most of those here, as for most of the ship generation, such schemes and dreams would never be realised. They would be tested to destruction in the ship's memory, stocked as it was with millennia's worth of contingency and circumstance. Most of the minority that survived however many iterations of what it took to weed out the unfeasible wouldn't attract enough interest or venture capital to make them viable. In developing them, however, their young creators would learn their own interests and abilities, their strong and weak points, perhaps to change or improve them, or to bring them to whatever project they eventually joined.

It was heartbreaking to watch.

Atomic, not to his surprise, sat beneath a vivid display of an entire habitat. Though built around a typical carbonaceous chondrite, it was unusual in having a transparent exterior and an outward orientation of the living-space. Bright and beautiful, but too open and vulnerable.

The girl sat staring into the spaces behind her eyes, shaping and tweaking her design with her hands and mind. She wore, Horrocks noticed as he padded up behind her, a green dress that looked identical to the one Synchronic had worn the night she'd seduced him. Stepping closer, he fancied he caught a faint whiff of Synchronic's unmistakable and unforgettable scent. He wondered if it was the same garment. The ancient and cunning care-mother was, he reckoned, quite capable of such a gesture, or a manipulation; capable, even, of weaving her characteristic pheromones into the fibres for time-release. But on the other hand, if that was the case the card had been palmed with a flourish so blatant it was difficult to credit her with it, or to imagine her imagining its not being noticed. Unless . . .

He stopped, smiled to himself, and shook his head. Trying to outflank the twisted ploys of one of the First Hundred Thousand was as pointless as it would be unprofitable. Let the law of unintended consequences take its course – that was what she'd said, before she had, with doubtless intended consequences, taken care of him.

Some involuntary movement of his – a shift of stance, a sigh, a grunt – must have alerted Atomic to his presence. She snapped out of her dwam and spun her seat around, looking startled, then recovered almost at once to a polite incuriosity, a mask of cool.

'You can walk!' she said. The way she said it, she regretted she didn't have a wider audience.

'It's taken me a lot of hard work,' said Horrocks. 'And a few falls.'

'So what, besides your legs, brings you here?'

'I wanted to talk to you.'

'That's sweet. What about?'

Horrocks temporised. 'Rather a lot, actually. Perhaps over lunch?'

'Be my guest.'

He wasn't familiar with the phrase, but it sounded like agreement. He gazed above her head. 'That's a beautiful habitat—'

'I hear a "but" coming.'

'It's too exposed.'

She enhanced an array of sensors, a battery of lasers and a cluster of missiles. 'Meteor defence, see?'

Horrocks shook his head. 'Beside the point,' he said. 'People straight out of a ship need the sense of substrate – a good few metres of regolith at least – between themselves and the hard stuff.'

'Ah, but do they?' Atomic jumped to her feet. 'That's what I think might be changing, with so many of us jaunting in virtualities where we walk under sky.'

The thought made Horrocks uneasy. Despite his interest in the planet, he'd shirked the terrestrial virtualities.

'I've only just got used to walking on ground,' he said, 'and I'm not so sure.'

'I'll tell you all about it,' said Atomic. 'Walk with me.'

'Do you realise,' she said, looking up from the foot of the stairs as he made his way down, 'that for thousands of years people have been living in caves?'

Horrocks didn't answer until they were out on the street. He handwaved upward.

'This doesn't feel like a cave. It doesn't feel enclosed.'

'That's just because you're used to living in the cone. It feels open but it's like you said, it's the reassurance of regolith. Compared with this, standing on a planetary surface is, like, totally exposed.'

'And living in a habitat with a glass roof isn't?'

She laughed. 'It isn't glass, it's diamond. And it's less exposed than a surface. Especially one like Destiny II, which doesn't even have asteroid defence. Yet that's what lots of us are subconsciously getting used to.'

'I don't think so,' said Horrocks. 'At a deeper level we know it's virtual.'

'Imagination can overcome that,' said Atomic.

They walked on down Fourth. The street was quiet. Music throbbed from nodes in the air. It made Horrocks yearn for wide spaces and pioneer toil. Music could do that.

'Do you imagine the bat people feel exposed?' he asked.

'I suppose they do,' Atomic said. 'Those of them who understand what the sky is, at least. I guess some of them still think the sky is a roof.'

'They don't seem that primitive.'

'Some of them are, in the back country.'

'All right,' said Horrocks. 'What worries me is the more advanced ones. How do you think they would feel, under that open sky, if they saw us colonising? Changing their asteroid belt, the moons of their waterworld and gas giant? Some of the solar power collectors would look like new planets even to the naked eye. To say nothing of fusion reactors.'

'New stars!' Atomic laughed.

'Yes indeed,' said Horrocks. 'And your diamond habitat would shine like—'

Like your eyes, he almost said.

'Like an asteroid with a high albedo,' said Atomic.

'Yes.'

She walked so fast that the green shift didn't ripple, like it had on her care-mother: it shook. Horrocks thought he could see every bone and curve of her small energetic body inside it if he looked long enough. He almost tripped.

'Sorry,' he said. 'Could you slow down a bit?'

She slackened her pace.

'I've been thinking about that too,' she said. 'But perhaps the idea of other intelligent life isn't as strange to them as it is to us. Not as alien, you might say. After all, they'll have seen the Civil Worlds for millennia. They'll have seen the green scum on the waterworld. They might even think we come from there. Oh! And I almost forgot – they have television, so they may have detected our deep-space radar. Anything interesting shown up on their transmissions?'

'Not really,' said Horrocks. 'Some grainy shots of scenery, sometimes with bat people flitting across it, then back to someone talking to camera. The heuristics think he's talking numbers, and they've got some consistent results, but the rest of what's said is as obscure as ever. The other source, funnily enough, looks very similar – scenery, talking head – but sounds somewhat different. Two languages, almost certainly.'

'Here we are,' said Atomic, stopping outside a café with a big front window and yellow interior walls. She lifted her hem to go up the step and Horrocks opened the door for her, almost falling through it in the process. The café was about half full of ship-generation kids, talking loud. Horrocks blinked to a particular perceptual mode and saw the air was as filled with data-interchange streams as it was with food smells. The data streams were almost all between hand-held or head-worn machines rather than heads. He closed his eyes and opened them, back to normal sight. Atomic turned at once to the table by the window, where a young ship-generation man sat drinking coffee. He stood up and smiled at Atomic, stuck out a hand to Horrocks.

'Grant Cornforth Dialectic.' Chunky muscles, firm grip, a wavy straggle of beard, wary eyes.

'Horrocks Mathematical.'

'The microgee trainer?'

'The same.' Horrocks turned to Atomic. 'What'll you have?'

'My treat,' she said.

'Thanks. Black coffee and whatever you recommend.'

She went to the counter and Horrocks sat down.

'So,' said Grant, 'what brings you among us flatfooters?'

'Getting flat feet,' said Horrocks. He rubbed his calf muscles.

Grant laughed. 'But really.'

'Delivering a personal message to Atomic,' he said.

Grant glanced down at his cup. 'Do you want me to leave?'

'No, no, not at all!' said Horrocks. 'Please.' He waved a hand at the rest of the clientele. 'I'd have everyone around the table if I could.'

'But you can't?' said Grant.

Horrocks tightened his lips for a moment and nodded. 'Call it semi-private. You're her friend, you're definitely welcome.'

'I see.' Grant didn't sound happy.

Atomic returned with two mugs and two plates with meat pasties. Horrocks tasted.

'Very good,' he said. He'd forgotten how hungry he was. Grant leaned over and took a chunk of Atomic's pasty.

'Horrocks says he's here to deliver a message to you.'

'I'm not surprised,' said Atomic. 'I bet it's from my rocking care-mother, yes?'

Horrocks put down his mug so that it didn't splash.

'Yes,' he said. 'In a manner of speaking. She convinced me of something, and asked me to convince you of it.'

'Well, what is it? That you and I are destined to be soul-mates?'

'What?'

'Oh, I know her,' said Atomic. 'She's an incorrigible genetic speculator. When she sent me her used dress, I knew a boy couldn't be far behind.'

Horrocks didn't know where to look. He thought her very forward. It must be the city life. Only a few months ago she'd thought him uncouth for mentioning her genetic parentage, and now she talked like this! At least she hadn't said 'a used boy'. He ate another bite or two with a dry mouth, sipped coffee.

'It's nothing like that!' he said. 'Well, I can't be sure of her intentions, but—'

'She sent you on some quite different pretext? That's her way.' She stretched across the table to brush a crumb from Grant's lip.

'No,' said Horrocks. 'This isn't a pretext. This is really important.'

'So spit it out.'

'All right,' he said. 'The aliens, the bat people, are at a stage of development very similar to that of our ancestors in the age of world wars. Internal combustion engines, radio, the beginnings of television, airships, steamships, mass urbanisation. In at least one city, the probe has detected traces of crude attempts to concentrate radioactive isotopes.'

'Yes, and?'

'Some of the founder generation think the aliens too may be on the brink of an era of war.'

Atomic stared at him. Grant rapped a finger hard on the table.

'Speculation,' he said. 'And wooden-headed technological determinist speculation at that. We know nothing of the aliens' social relationships, apart from the apparent slavery –

which incidentally is far more widespread than at the same stage in human development, which rather undercuts your suggestion. They could be a single world empire, or a federation of anarchies, or a happy global co-operative commonwealth for that matter. We just don't know.'

'What about the slaves?' asked Atomic. 'Don't they count?'

'We don't even know they are slaves,' said Grant. 'They could be beasts – very similar animals to the dominant species but without speech or self-awareness.'

'Hah!' said Atomic.

'Excuse me,' said Horrocks. 'That's beside the point.'

'And the point is?' said Grant.

'The point is, if these bat folk are going into their own Twentieth Century, their whatever-it-was century BG, then we can expect trouble down there. And out here.'

'Oh, come on,' said Atomic. 'You don't seriously expect them to come swarming up on – what? rockets? – brandishing nuclear explosives? Or building particle-beam projectors in their deserts?'

'Yes,' said Horrocks. 'That's exactly what we – what I do expect, in a few decades, if they don't blast each other back to barbarism first!'

'Oh, right,' said Atomic. 'In a few decades, huh? By that time we could be trading partners. It's not like we don't have plenty to offer them.'

'I'm afraid that's still missing the point,' said Horrocks. 'For people in that stage, control is everything. Each power centre would use whatever they gained from trading with us to get one up on rival powers, and at the same time they'd see our colonisation as an invasion of their space.'

'How can they believe that the planets of this system are theirs? They haven't even landed probes on them!'

'Look at it this way,' said Horrocks. 'If an immensely more powerful species or clade or whatever set up shop in some unclaimed part of the system, wouldn't we feel a little uneasy?'

'It happens in the Civil Worlds,' said Atomic.

'Yes, but this is not among the Civil Worlds. This is what comes *before* the Civil Worlds. This is life on the primary. War, conquest, grabbing territory because if you don't somebody else will—'

'They're flyers,' said Atomic. 'Maybe they don't have the same territoriality as we do.'

'Birds are territorial,' said Grant.

Atomic glared at him for moment. 'Point,' she conceded.

'Besides,' Horrocks went on, 'the whole issue of controlling airspace, and by extension outer space, might be stronger with them, it'd be just about instinctual . . .'

'You're forgetting something,' said Atomic. 'Law of association. Extended markets. Division of labour. Mutual benefit.'

'You're the one who thinks they have slaves,' said Horrocks. 'But whether they have or not, I very much doubt that the bat people have learned the law of association.'

'Why not?' asked Grant. 'Apart from the airships and steam engines, that is. Like I said, that kind of technological determinism doesn't convince me.'

Horrocks looked from one to the other, nonplussed. 'All right,' he said. 'Let's put it a different way. We need to be sure they do understand all that before we do anything that might set them at each other's throats if they don't. In our own interests, we need to be sure they are not going to come out and attack us in a few decades. I know we could improvise some kind of weapons against them – something like meteor defences, I guess – but we haven't fought a war for thousands of years, and if I'm right and you're wrong, they're about to become *really good* at it. Just like our ancestors were before they went to the Moon.'

Atomic drained her cup. 'Putting it that way, maybe you're right. So what do you propose that we do about it?'

This was the crux. Horrocks nerved himself.

'Something you once suggested yourself. Hold back on colonisation until we're sure the aliens can handle it.'

Atomic looked regretful, and Grant thoughtful.

'I did hint at that myself once,' Atomic said. 'Read my hate mail sometime.'

'Have a good look at what intra-species war was like – sometime.'

'I don't need to or want to. I already have the general idea, thank you.'

Horrocks closed his eyes for a moment. 'Perhaps you need more than the general idea,' he said. 'I know I did. But even based on the general idea, as you say, do you really think the annoyance and frustration of our ship generation weighs much in the balance?'

'It's not so much that,' said Atomic. 'It's that the annoyance and frustration, as you put it, might be quite enough to produce a war all by itself. A war amongst ourselves.'

Horrocks was startled at how shocked he felt. He wanted to tell her to wash out her mouth. Not, on reflection, the most tactful thing to say.

'That may be putting it a little too strongly,' he said at last.

'Is it?' said Atomic. 'The founder generation, yes, they're our gene-parents and care-parents and we love them and they love us. But we know very well what they bred us and raised us for. To go out, to conquer the system, while they carry on their doubtless fascinating little intrigues and affairs and deals in this lovely habitat that feels to us like a hot room with too many people in it. We need vacuum on the other side of our faceplates to feel we're breathing *fresh air*. And the thing is, that's exactly what we were bred and raised to feel! If the founders try to stop us, they're asking for trouble.'

'I *know* that!' cried Horrocks. People turned and stared. He lowered his voice. 'The founders know that too. What we're –

what I'm asking you is whether you can see a way around that, some way to maybe channel all that energy and urge to explore into something other than . . .'

His voice trailed off in the face of their set, sceptical smiles.

'I can tell you this,' said Atomic. 'And you can tell my care-mother and her clique and anybody else you care to: if we don't get out, our energy and urges are going to be channelled into something *they won't like.*'

Grant nodded. 'You said it, Atomic.'

Atomic stood up. 'I think we're finished here.'

Horrocks watched them leave.

The Engineer's Dream was known as a deep hang, a disreputable venue near the axis of the forward cone, popular with habitat trainers, microlight pilots, maintenance co-ordinators and other low-responsibility crew-members. Horrocks drifted through the hatch into its hazy air and narrow-spectrum artificial light and toed off for the drinks wall, where he broke off a bulb, crooked his elbow through a loop and turned to survey the scene. Time of day wasn't an issue here, the entire circadian rhythm being based on on-shift or off-shift, but the place was in one of its phases where only a score or so of people were in. Good: he wanted that sense of drinking at the wrong hour.

He exchanged nods with a few people hanging in the central mesh, none of whom he fancied talking to, and then noticed Genome Console at the far end on her own. Focused on an inhaler, she didn't see him so he pinged her. She turned, saw him, waved and rolled to place her feet on the wall. One swift thrust brought her over. A neat somersault docked her in the same loop as himself. She wore something like an opaque black sphere with holes for wrists, ankles and neck, but a sphere that had crinkled and shrunk inward to cling here and there, mostly there. Her fair hair floated wild.

'Well, hello,' she said. 'Where have you been? The gang all thought you'd gone flatfoot.'

'It was just for a few days,' said Horrocks.

'A few days at a time,' she said. 'You've been going down there for weeks.'

'Doing business with passengers.'

'I don't believe that for a minute. Fancy a sniff?' She waved her inhaler. Horrocks checked the cartridge: red clouds and a lightning flash, an obscure brand-name.

'No thanks.' Horrocks swigged a squirt. 'But you're right. I got caught up in something.'

'Ah!' said Genome, her eyes bright from her sniff. 'You and that flatfoot girl.' She tilted her head back, sighting him along her nose. 'She's trouble.'

'She is that,' Horrocks said. 'How do you know about her, anyway?'

'She's biologged your little contretemps already.'

It had been hours. 'You follow it?'

'I track the feeds. Bad habit I picked up from Grey.'

'Oh,' said Horrocks. For some reason it was a name he didn't welcome hearing. 'How is he, by the way?'

'Perverse,' said Genome. 'Like all that Red Sun crowd.'

'Red Sun crowd?' Horrocks had an alarmed moment when he thought she alluded to his dealings with the Red Sun Circle.

'You know, all the people from back there.' She waved over her shoulder. 'The old crew-hands are as bad as passengers sometimes.'

'Oh, right. They've been so long in the ship it's like—'

'They have to make life more complicated than it needs to be,' she said.

'You're right there,' said Horrocks, with more force than he'd meant.

'Ah!' said Genome again. 'Her care-mother got under your

skin, did she?' She grinned at his open mouth. 'Atomic biologged that, too.'

Horrocks had to laugh. 'What do you think of the substance of it?'

'The argument? Huh.' She took a long sniff and stared into the distance. 'I sure don't want these little flatfoot breeders on the ship for much longer. Or their parents, come to that.'

'Just go ahead as planned?'

'Yup.'

'What about the aliens?'

'Rock the aliens,' said Genome. 'Look, in fifty years they'll have data colonies and science robots and all that Civil Worlds shower crawling all over them. They might as well get used to us in the meantime. Let it sink in that they're not – *ta-da!* – alone in the universe, and they'll soon sort out their little squabbles.'

'Suppose they have a little squabble with us?'

'So what?' Genome said. 'What are they going to send up against us? Kites?'

'I'm sure you've heard what I've said on that score,' said Horrocks. 'I'm more concerned about what fighting them would do to us.'

Genome shrugged. 'We'd have plenty of time to prepare. Discuss. Sort out the morality of the thing. It's not something you can do anything about now.'

Horrocks broke off another drink. 'I suppose not,' he said. 'I have a nasty feeling I've been inveigled into one of these founder intrigues that has nothing whatever to do with the ostensible bone of contention.'

'Yeah,' said Genome. 'Probably some speculative ramp at the back of it.' She sighed. 'Grey was always doing things like that. Watched the terrestrials market like a crow eyeing a caterpillar, every time he fired off one of his daft rants.'

'Past tense now, is he?'

She shifted in the loop. 'As far as I'm concerned, yes.'

Horrocks guessed he mirrored her embarrassment. They gazed at each other for a minute. Having known Genome since childhood no longer struck Horrocks as a difficulty. In a sense he had not known her at all. Her directness was refreshing, her sharing of his age and background attractive. He told her so.

She waved her inhaler under his nose. 'It's a strong anti-inhibitor,' she said. 'And you've been sidestreaming it for half an hour.'

'You have me at an advantage,' he said.

'So I have,' she said, and took it.

TWELVE

VIEW FROM A HEIGHT

'Tapes!' Nollam shouted. 'Tapes!'

As Darvin and Kwarive rushed in to join the growing huddle around the telekinematographic receiver, two of Nollam's fellow technicians scrambled and fumbled to load and thread what looked like two kinematograph reels, one full and one empty, with no projector between them.

Darvin peered over Orro's shoulder, conscious of Kwarive's chin and hand-claws digging into his.

'We should have had them ready to roll,' he heard Orro grumble. He paid no attention. The screen demanded it all. The press was still growing. Behind and around him people were clambering up racks and leaning forward.

The moving picture was a grainier black and white than a kinematographic film, yet less jerky, more fluid and realistic. It showed the map Kwarive had drawn, and peering over it their own staring faces from a minute earlier, then them turning and running out of view. An uneasy laugh went up.

The image changed again, to a figure like a human being without wings, and with small eyes, ears, and nose. The face appeared hairless, with a tuft on the crown of the head. Its mouth was moving, it seemed in synchrony with the sound that boomed from the loudspeakers of the apparatus: *EEE UUUUMMMM IIIIHHH EEESSS EEEEE* . . . it went on like that, a sound like surf in a cave. It was hard to hear, for a moment, as everybody in the room gasped or cried out, Kwarive loudest of all. Darvin shook with astonishment. Thus far he had not so much as imagined the aliens, and the vague swirl of images in his head that he'd associated with them had been of things far more alien than this.

The alien turned and pointed. What had seemed baggy, wrinkled skin on his arms and chest slipped and moved, revealing itself to be a body covering, like a cloak but fitted and shaped. The picture became for a moment incomprehensible, a patchwork of varied shapes interspersed with bright surfaces and overlaid with fuzzy white blobs. It rotated about a vivid white line drawn from the top of the screen to near the middle, and gave way to much a darker area dotted with clumps of bright spots. This was repeated several times, alternating light and dark.

'It's the inside of a cylinder,' said Kwarive.

The view snapped into perspective. A cylinder: of course.

Orro jumped. 'It's the inside of the ship!'

'That's ridiculous!' said one scientist. 'Where are the occupants? Where is the machinery?'

'Too small to see!' shouted Orro above the hubbub. 'The white puffs are *clouds*. The bright patches are lakes. We're looking at a landscape rolled like a map.'

At that point everyone fell silent. The similarity of the scene to a view, from a greater height than any of them had flown, of an entire country curving upward and wrapped around overhead was irresistible.

'The thing is vast,' breathed Markhan, pushing forward from the back of the crowd.

'We knew that already,' said Darvin. 'For it to be visible by telescope at its distance.'

The alien voice continued. The viewpoint zoomed downward. As it sank they all saw what seemed to be a gliding man, which as it passed closer turned out to be a small flying-machine with a propeller at the front. Orro turned and grinned into Darvin's face. The viewpoint reached ground level and settled on an open space, beyond which lay low buildings. A few of the aliens walked in and out of view, their legs long, their gait limber. They showed no awareness of the viewpoint, which Darvin presumed to be a camera.

The voice stopped and the picture changed again, to a scrolling display of line diagrams and row upon row of symbols. After some minutes of this the crowd began to relax and break up. Some who had rushed in drifted away, or hastened to their neglected duties. Some of the scientists went into immediate huddled conferences. Others remained transfixed by the incomprehensible sigils on the screen. The telekinematograph technicians paid more attention to the apparatus than to the display.

Markhan called one of them over. 'More tapes!'

'Sorry, chief, we only have a couple more reels, and they're right here.'

'How long does a tape last?'

'About half an hour.'

'Put out a call for more. Airship them in. Meanwhile, scrounge around for any used tapes. I don't care what's on them. Have them ready to tape over.'

The technician left, muttering under his breath.

'Might be a waste of time,' said Nollam. 'Begging your pardon, chief, but even if we could read that, which we can't, it's flying up the screen too fast.'

'Couldn't we run the tapes slowly?' asked Kwarive. A couple

of the technicians laughed. Nollam gave them a sharp look and nodded to Kwarive.

'We couldn't do it now,' he said, 'but maybe with a bit of tinkering . . . I'll think about it.'

'If necessary,' said Orro, 'we could film the screen and then analyse the film frame by frame.'

'Not much use if we can't read the script,' said Darvin.

'Forget the script,' said Markhan. 'These diagrams we glimpse here and there might tell us much.'

Kwarive scratched Darvin's back and moved away from behind him. She walked over and stood beside the receiver.

'What,' she asked Nollam, 'was the first clear picture that came up?'

'Ah!' he said. 'That map thing you drew.'

Kwarive smacked one hand on to the other. 'As I thought,' she said. 'What we're seeing here is a reply. Somebody recognised the map as a communication, and sent it back as an acknowledgement, then responded with its own message: first the wingless alien, then a view of the interior of the ship, then all this data.'

'But that map wasn't your first stab at communicating,' said Markhan.

'No,' said Kwarive, 'but it was the first one they recognised. They recognised the map because it corresponded to something they'd already seen – the coastline of Seloh's Reach, from space.'

'You're right,' said Orro. He stalked forward and joined her. 'And I'll tell you something else: this is not a communication *with us*.'

'I don't follow,' said Markhan.

'If it were,' said Orro, 'I should expect, perhaps, some simple pictograms. A series of numbers, like that idea we had about stacks of stones. A diagram of the solar system, a drawing of the ship, a sketch of the aliens' anatomy. Instead, we get what may be a greeting in the aliens' own language, followed by screeds of text, also in their own language. It's as if it's addressed to somebody on Ground, all right, but somebody who understands.'

'Maybe it's meant for the electric shittles,' said Darvin, in a tone lighter than he felt.

Orro shook his head. 'No. If it were, it would be on the same etheric wavelength as the previous transmissions. This is on the same wavelength as our own telekinematography, and is evidently intended—'

'No,' said Nollam. 'Same wavelength and frequency. Started coming through clear, that's all.'

'That's makes my point just as strongly. It's not directed at the shittles. It's directed at us, or rather, at someone or something else for which they mistake us.'

Darvin felt the fur on his back prickle. 'You're saying that someone or something else is among us?'

'No,' said Orro. 'Merely that the aliens think there is.'

'Perhaps,' said Kwarive, 'they think others of their species, but not of their . . . expedition are here?'

Orro laughed. 'They may have rival powers, like us! It's as if a ship from Seloh saw a signal from a beach in the wilder parts of the Southern Rule, and thought it came from a Gevorkian landing-party, whereas in fact it was from the natives.'

'Very neat,' said Markhan. 'And entirely speculative. Please watch the screen, record with as few interruptions as possible, while I confer. Let me know at once of any developments.'

He hurried out. The remaining two-eights or so of people in the room stood or perched around the receiver.

'Well,' said Kwarive, after another glance at the enigmatic screen, 'at least we know what they look like.'

'Or what they want us to think they look like,' said a familiar voice.

Darvin turned to see the Sight agent who'd recruited him.

Bahron, he called himself. He hung around the camp and gave vague explanations about site security. Everybody knew who he was and what he did, but kept the pretence that they didn't. Darvin hadn't noticed him in the room earlier, and guessed he'd just arrived, or that his penchant for the shadows had kept him unseen.

'Why do you see deception everywhere?' said Orro.

'It's my trade,' said Bahron.

'In this case, you're letting it get in the way of . . . seeing,' said Kwarive. The tiny barb drew smiles from the scientists and techs, and a flicker of irritation from Bahron. 'Why should the aliens wish to deceive us?'

'If they're big ugly monsters, or little ones for that matter, they might want us to think they looked more like ourselves.'

'Then why wingless?'

Bahron shrugged. 'For the very reason you raise the question. If they looked too much like us, we'd be suspicious.'

Kwarive folded her arms and steepled her wings. 'Fine,' she said. 'It's your job, as you say, to look for lies. It's ours to look for truth, and until we have more to go on, we'll go by what we've got.' She looked around. 'Did anyone spot how many fingers the alien had?'

'Five digits on each hand,' said Orro. 'One of them opposable.'

'You're sure?' asked Kwarive.

'Positive.'

'Good,' said Kwarive.

'We can check later,' Nollam called out. 'Soon as we can play back the first tape.'

'All right. So we can guess that their number system has an eight-and-two base.'

'Awkward for arithmetic,' Orro chuckled. 'For the base to divide into odd numbers.'

Kwarive laughed. 'See how much we're learning? We know

they're wingless quadrimanal bipeds, that their speech comes from their breath like ours, that they have binocular vision, poor eyesight and hearing, and that they make a sorry fist of arithmetic!'

'But possibly more dextrous than us,' someone said. 'With the extra fingers.'

'Good point,' said Kwarive. 'Any more ideas?'

Others began throwing in their own shaky deductions: that the deep voice showed a more resonant, and thus larger, chest cavity; that the aliens saw in the same wavelengths as humans; that from a biomechanical analysis of their gait it might be possible to work out their mass; that the same could be cross-checked against their flying machines; that they had slower reflexes than humans . . .

'Seeing we're playing this game,' said Bahron, 'I can tell you they're warm-blooded, too.'

'I'd assumed they were,' said Kwarive, 'but why do you say that?'

'No fur,' said Bahron. 'Except on top of the head. But they wrap themselves in some kind of insulating material.'

Kwarive looked at him with a little more respect. 'I hadn't thought of that.'

'Tell you something else,' said Bahron. He climbed up on a rack, spread his wings, and hopped off to alight on the floor again. 'They can't do this. They can't fly, except in machines, right? So they must be afraid of falling, and ground must matter a lot to them. I mean, you could keep them out of any patch of ground with just a fence or a wall, like grazers and trudges.' He gave an evil smile. 'Or in. So what I figure from that, see, is they're likely to be very interested in our world: in . . . Ground.' Another nasty grin. 'See, this is my job after all.'

'Wait a moment,' said Darvin, alarmed at the drift of Bahron's deductions. 'They have an enormous vessel in which they've lived in space for a long time.'

'Yes,' said Bahron. 'A long time. And in all that time, they've been spinning their vessel, to give them ground to walk on and weight to carry. Now, Orro, how long do you reckon they've been in space, if they did come from another star?'

'Oh, many eights of eights of years, at the very least.'

'Generations, then?'

'They might have very long life-spans,' said Orro.

Bahron turned to Kwarive. 'You reckon that's possible?'

She shrugged. 'I wouldn't rule it out, but it seems fanciful.'

'Words out of my mouth, lady. In any case, they've had plenty of time to adapt to living in space, weightless you might say, and what do they do? They live as much like on the ground as possible. They give themselves artificial weight. Now, what reason could they have for doing that, if they don't intend to walk again on a world?'

'There could be all kinds of reasons,' said Kwarive. 'Perhaps all animals need gravity for some reason we don't know.'

'Ah! Some reason we don't know? You said we should stick to what we know. Now, I'm no medical man, nor no scientist either, but it seems to me that floating about weightless – and not even having wings to fly with – would cripple you from walking again. Muscles waste away when people have to be laid out, when they're too sick even to hang. If you never need to walk, no problem. Float free as a fish or a flitter. But if you do mean to walk again, like I said, you have to keep in shape. These wingless wonders mean one day to walk on the ground, and I do mean Ground.'

There was a brief interruption while Nollam and his assistants changed the recording-tape. Everyone stared at the screen, as though to memorise whatever was missed.

'So what,' Darvin asked, 'does it matter that they wish to come here?'

Bahron hunched, fingers curled. 'When a shipload of adven-

turers from here or Gevork turns up on the coast of some wild
area of the Southern Rule, they don't usually have the well-
being of the locals at the front of their minds. I don't see why
the wingless should be any different.'

'Oh, I object!' cried Orro. 'That is speculative and unjust!
Any race capable of the great achievement of crossing the space
between the stars must surely be too advanced to merely wish
to extend a reach! How could so great a project be compassed
without a vast enterprise of co-operation? What mere material
end could make so long a voyage profitable?'

'In any case,' added another scientist, one of the etheric spe-
cialists, 'if they did invade us, or wish us ill, what could we do
to stop them?'

'Fair questions, gentlemen,' said Bahron. 'And I'll allow,
they perplex me. What *need* brought the wingless here, and if
Darvin and Orro are right has brought them from star to star
already? Curiosity or some such I could understand, but why
so vast a ship, big enough to hold a great many of them?' He
hesitated, then continued as if determined to have his say.
'What first comes to my mind – a mind that's paid and
pledged to be speculative and unjust, I admit – is that it might
be what's brought people to every land of Ground: population
pressure. Now *there* would be a reason for wanting a fine world
like ours, a habitable world. As to what we could do to stop
them – it's true, as long as they are in the sky and we are here,
there's nothing. But if they're here and we're here, it's a different story, is it not?'

'It is not,' said Orro. 'We know the power of their engines,
the scale of their work, the subtlety of their etheric communications, and the ingenuity of their contrivances. Their flying
machines alone – the one we saw inside the ship, to say nothing of the one that was photographed high in the sky – could
wreak havoc on us. Put aside all thought of fighting them. Our
only chance is to communicate with them, to come to an

accommodation, and to hope that their greater power is a sign of greater wisdom.'

'Fine sentiments,' said Bahron. 'So, no doubt, thought the ancestors of the back-country folk when the sails of the first Seloh's fleet speckled the Broad Channel.'

'You sully the glorious future by equating it with a savage past!'

'Do I?' said Bahron. 'So much the worse for the glorious future. My duties are to the present. If you will excuse me, gentlemen, ladies.'

After he'd left, the conversation continued, but it had lost its sparkle. Everybody knew that Bahron's concerns would be mooted at a level far above their influence. Some might have shared his concerns. Darvin knew that the other scientists, most of them aligned with various military institutions, took a darker view of the alien arrival than he and Orro did. At the same time he found himself wrestling with a prejudice. It was difficult, having seen the aliens as wingless, to see them as a superior race. The flightlessness that they shared with the despised trudges – about whose fate and use, dumb beasts though they were, he'd never been comfortable – reduced the aliens' imputed stature and status. He wondered whether this would induce a dangerous contempt, or a more dangerous fear. The notion of an intelligent and articulate trudge – a *rebellious* trudge – was a staple of moralistic satire and engineering tale alike. Such tales betrayed, he thought, an unease that had haunted the conscience of his race since that terrible and glorious moment in the dawn of time when mankind had first battened upon the physical strength and mental weakness of his closest animal relative to make of that brother a beast of burden.

What, he wondered with a chill prickle of fur, would the aliens make of *that* relationship?

Another half-hour of tape rolled by. Nollam was just changing the reels when Markhan returned, agitated.

'We've sent calls,' he said, 'to other locations where telekine-matography is being developed. They've tuned to the same etheric frequency and wavelength, and they're receiving the same message.'

'What I'd expect, chief,' said Nollam, straightening. 'This stuff must be beaming down from the third moon. Gives it quite a spread, I should imagine.'

'Indeed,' said Markhan. 'Which means it's also beaming down upon Gevork.'

Darvin noticed how all eyes turned to Orro, and didn't like it.

'What reason,' Darvin asked, 'do we have to think that the receivers of Gevork are also tuned – so to speak – to this message?'

'Why, none at all,' said Markhan. 'Except the well-known scientific prowess of Gevork.'

'They're a bit hidebound,' said Orro, sounding defensive. 'That's why I'm in Seloh's Reach, after all.' His folded wings quivered. 'Unless you refer to the fact that this very installation is, ah, in some respects arranged around the presumption that the eyes of the Realm are upon it?'

A silence – embarrassed in most cases, puzzled in others – fell on the gathering. The rocket scientists had no more of a clue than Kwarive did that their work was diversionary.

'No, no!' cried Markhan. 'That's a misunderstanding, Orro, for which I ask your pardon. The layers of subterfuge employed by the Sight and the Might are, I fear, far too subtle for mere scientists like us.' He flapped a wing. 'Please don't trouble yourself with them. All work here is secret, and truly so. No, I only speculate that Gevork might have learned of the visitation independently.'

'It's certainly possible,' said Orro. 'I don't—'

'Look!' shouted Nollam.

The image on the screen was no longer of scrolling lines of

symbols, but a jerky pattern of squares and rectangles. After a moment, it was replaced by a flicker of black and white, the random spume of etheric surf.

'Has the third moon gone below the horizon?' asked Markhan.

Nollam shook his head. 'It'll be up for hours.'

The hiss from the loudspeaker was drowned out by a loud fizzing and crackling from outside. Kwarive ran to the door. Darvin followed.

The communications tree smouldered. Smoke rose around its foot.

'Stay back!' Darvin shouted. Kwarive ignored the warning. She stooped over the small dungheap, and turned with something held between the claws of her thumb and forefinger. As he came up to her she held it out and dropped it on the palm of his hand.

Still almost too hot to hold, the dead shittle's carapace was split and carbonised. The curious device inside it had melted to slag.

'They're all like that,' Kwarive said.

Behind her the tree caught fire.

They sat, that evening, around another fire and waited for the return airship to Five Ravines. Darvin, Orro and Kwarive talked in low voices. After a while Nollam joined them. Behind them the camp went about its routine. The project would continue. News or rumours of the aborted contact had spread to everyone, and a late-afternoon emergency conference had thrashed out its implications to no one's satisfaction. Bulletins on the Might's wireless network had told of unexplained fires breaking out all over the country, and abroad. In the coastal cities, the seasonal rain and damp had ensured damage was slight. Elsewhere, brush and forest fires burned out of control. No explanation had been given, but no doubt some would be found. Darvin placed a mental bet on a coincidence of lightning strikes and hunters careless with fires.

'You know,' said Orro, turning a joint of dried meat on the embers with a stick, 'we now have no evidence of what happened. It could all have been a dream.'

'We have the tapes,' said Kwarive.

'The Might has the tapes,' said Orro. 'I am certain we shall never see them again.'

'Too right,' said Nollam. 'Markhan's stashed them in a safe in his office.'

'There's still the Object,' said Darvin. 'And the third moon. Speaking of which.' He turned to Nollam. 'Something you and Markhan said, about the third moon having to be in the sky?'

'We did, did we?'

Darvin ignored the ploy. 'Which means that the ether waves used in telekinematography are line-of-sight only.'

'I couldn't say,' said Nollam. 'Here, Orro, pass me that meat. The smell's making me dribble.'

He bit off a chunk of the fragrant meat and passed the hunk to Kwarive. It made its way around the circle, becoming gnawed to the bone. Darvin laid the bone at the edge of the fire, alert for the sound of a crack that would let whoever snatched first get at the marrow.

'I wonder,' he said, staring up at the rising sparks, 'what practical *use* a line-of-sight communication system could have. One even more unwieldly than wireless telephony, and without its range and versatility. Pictures, yes – but if it's only line-of-sight, what's wrong with a telescope?'

'Forward artillery spotting,' said Orro. 'Among others. Or so it is said in Gevork.'

'Let your fancies run free,' said Nollam. 'I'm not telling you a thing. Mind you, they do have some sharp thinkers over there in the Realm. So it's said.'

Darvin saw out of the corner of his eye a red glint in the sky and thought it was the landing-light of the airship they awaited, but as he looked up he saw it was only the gleam of the fire reflecting off the tethered blimp. It reminded him of the etheric reflection off the third moon. That passing thought stirred the same obscure excitement in his mind that he'd felt the day he'd invented the wind tunnel, and failed to invent the aeroplane.

He rocked forward on his haunches. Orro's hand darted for the bone, then returned disappointed. Darvin twitched his lips at his friend and stood up and walked slowly away into the dark. This time, he was determined not to let whatever insight he'd glimpsed flash away like a fish. Once outside the firelight he could see the stars, and the underside of the blimp. He sprang into the air and flapped upward, and turned. He soared above the fire – his friends looked up and called out – then began circling it, climbing in the warm thermal updraught until he was almost at the height of the blimp. He flew back and forth above the quiet, busy camp. Flying helped him to think, and there was objectivity in that view from a height.

Height! That was it! Height and sight!

He dropped.

He landed beside the fire in a whoosh of wings and a flurry of smoke and ash.

'Hey!' complained Kwarive, fanning the air in front of her eyes.

'Sorry.' Darvin settled beside her, put a wing around her and spread the other wing and both hands before the fire to feel the warmth.

'What was that all about?' asked Nollam, who had mean-time won the bone.

'Just a thought,' said Darvin. 'One that might occur to a

bright young tech like yourself. An idea that could get a man noticed.'

Nollam sucked a greasy finger and regarded him. 'I'd be interested.'

'Oh, I don't know,' said Darvin. 'Maybe I'll keep it to myself. Guard it, you might say, like some tasty morsel.'

Nollam tossed him the charred femur. 'There's some left.'

With a show of gallantry Darvin handed it to Kwarive.

'All right,' he said. 'Far be it from me to pick your brains for military secrets. But the marrow of the thing, one might say, is point-to-point, line-of-sight communication. Hilltop to hilltop, like beacon fires. Now, I don't ask you to say that's what it is. All I'm saying is, if that's all the Might is using it for they're missing a trick.'

'Go on,' said Nollam, ears pricking.

'Today the message from the sky was received over a wide area, or so Markhan gave us to suppose. By receivers that were nowhere near within sight of each other.'

'They were all within sight of the third moon,' said Nollam. His ear twitched and his brows rose. 'Aha! I see what you're getting at, but we can't put transmitters or transmission aerials in the sky.'

Darvin looked upward, slowly enough to let Nollam track his gaze. The blimp glowed red above them.

'Can we not?' he said.

THIRTEEN

CONTACT CLAUSE

The summons had a priority override that lasered it through layer after layer of firewall: from the No-Trace on the recipient's location, through the Do Not Disturb aura around his room and several subtler obstacles in his head, to finally penetrate the last barrier, sleep. Horrocks woke with heart pounding and eyes staring. In the dark a ghastly hallucination of the Oldest Man blazed in front of him, demanded his presence, and vanished.

The jolt of his awakening had disturbed Genome. She rolled, mumbling. Horrocks caressed her shoulders.

'It's all right,' he said. 'Conference call.'

'Talk quiet,' she said.

Her fingertips trailed across his back and thigh as he pushed away. He split the side of the permeable cocoon they'd shared and drifted across the still-dark room to the utility wall. The cocoon sealed itself again behind him. He docked with his clothes while sucking a hot-enough coffee. Its dim infra-red lit his way to the hatch. The corridor's daylight strip struck him like a rush, its wavelengths rebooting wakefulness faster than the black drug. He finger-thrust the wall and launched himself along; grabbed a handhold outside the first unoccupied nook, fifty metres along; swung in, braced himself against its curving walls like a child between the trunk and branch of a tree, and closed his eyes.

The summons' track-back pulsed in front of him like a migraine. He tagged it and was yanked into a hasty telepresence. Constantine glowered from its the far pole. Eleven other people were already there, of whom Horrocks recognised two by sight: Awlin Halegap the speculator, and Amend Locke, the science-team boss for the Destiny II probe. A quick scan of their tags identified the others as team members or brokers in terrestrials. All science and finance, then; and all crew. All except himself were old hands.

'Jury is quorate,' said Constantine. 'We thank the youngest member for his prompt arrival, all things considered.' The spark of humour faded as fast as Horrocks' surge of alarm flared. A jury! And not one chosen by lot! Whatever this was, it was serious.

'We must proceed with all dispatch,' Constantine continued. 'Not fifteen minutes ago I learned, to my great displeasure and dismay, that the Destiny II probe has made contact with the inhabitants. More precisely, the inhabitants have made contact with it, and it has responded.'

Shouts rose all round; if it had been a real space, they would have echoed. Constantine ignored them and flashed a file into common view. The clamour died in a moment of silent study. The first picture was a white rectangle unequally divided by a jagged, curving black line with an isolated arrow-like shape well above it, somewhere about the middle. On to the rectangle, a second or two later, a coloured picture was overlaid: a planetary survey photograph. Blue sea, green coast, brown desert. The jagged line fitted the coast, the arrow marked a spot in the desert. The image zoomed to the spot. Under maximum resolution it picked out a dusty polygon of low structures, which on enhancement resolved to buildings and ramps.

'The sketch-map was the signal, and the spot you're looking at was the source,' said Constantine. The view pulled back from the first picture to include it, as a piece of white card or paper, in a raw bug's-eye view of two of the bat people staring straight into camera. 'The natives are using our own surveillance devices to communicate with us. The response from the orbiter was this . . .'

Horrocks almost laughed to see a pre-recorded image of the Oldest Man himself in his best silk formals, announcing that the expedition came in peace and showing off a view of the interior of the sunliner, followed by a brief download of the ship's specs and the latest news from the Red Sun system. That last was still running when Constantine flicked the view off.

'Who is responsible for this?' Constantine demanded.

'I am,' said Amend Locke. 'You recorded the introduction for me about three hundred years ago. It's the standard courtesy call to a claim-jumper or a data colony.'

'Yes, yes,' said Constantine. 'I remember that. What I don't remember is authorising its use here and now.'

'It's a default,' said Amend Locke. 'As soon as the probe detects a clear attempt to hail it, however obscure, it fires off the standard message.'

A flicker of corroborating data interchange accompanied the dialogue. Horrocks didn't bother to do more than glance at it, but filed it for later.

'If there was a wall here,' said Constantine, 'I swear I should now be banging my head against it. We knew by the time the probe went into orbit that we weren't dealing with a claim-jump or a data colony. Why wasn't that default . . . amended, Locke?'

'It was overlooked,' she said. 'The responsibility is mine. The default is buried deep in the probe's software and, well, with all the new information coming in we—'

'All right,' said Constantine, with a wave of the hand. 'Next question. From a swift study of these latest pictures I see that the bugs are borne by some kind of beetle, big enough and common enough for the inhabitants to notice. How did that happen? And why didn't *we* notice?'

'That's straightforward,' said Hardcastle Wood, the biologist. 'The bugs are adaptive and opportunistic. In all hitherto existing situations they've never had anything bigger to work with than single-celled organisms or slime moulds, and natural prominences – rocks, essentially – for their amplifiers. When the assemblers encountered a fast-breeding and ubiquitous insectoid they seized upon it. Likewise with trees. As for why we didn't notice . . . the virtuality software is seamless independently of the quality of the incoming data, and, ah, the lay viewers just referred casually to "bugs", and we ourselves—'

'Defaults, defaults, everyone's got defaults,' chanted Constantine. 'Tell me about it. Don't tell me about it. I know what fifteen thousand years of confirmed conjecture can do to harden paths and bury assumptions. And speaking of assumptions – I take it there is a size limit on these bugs? We are not talking about bat people, or even the little bat beasts, fluttering around with wires in their optics?'

'No,' said Wood. 'Although if they were left long enough to mutate . . .' He looked thoughtful. 'No, I don't think so.'

'Good,' said Constantine. 'Glad you've got that well in hand. Now: action?'

'We could cobble together a more comprehensible and apt message,' said Amend. 'After all, now that we know they've detected us, we might as well talk back to them. There's a standard CETI package somewhere deep in the vaults.'

'Riddled with defaults and assumptions, I'll warrant,' said Constantine. 'No thank you. Let me remind you that the ship's complement has yet to decide what we're to do here. The matter is moot. I move that we terminate the message at once, and the surveillance.'

'The surveillance?' Hardcastle Wood asked, outraged.

'Yes. Burn out the bugs.' Constantine paused, frowning. 'They do have a self-destruct mechanism?'

'Oh yes,' said Amend Locke. 'It's a default.'

Constantine glared at her, but Horrocks could see in the interchange that Constantine had accepted the dig as payback for his earlier pun on her name.

'But why should we do it?' protested Wood. 'Terminate the message, yes, but the surveillance?'

Emphatic nods all round, except from Horrocks and Constantine.

To Horrocks' surprise, a prompt from Constantine flashed in front of his eyes: *you tell them*.

'Two reasons,' Horrocks said, before he'd thought of one. He paused and raised a finger to stall while he gathered his wits. 'Ah, first, there's no telling what the aliens will learn from studying the bugs, now that they've figured out what they are. They've grasped electronics but haven't yet achieved miniaturised circuits, let alone nanotechnology. The bugs could inspire them to these and more, at an earlier and even less stable stage of development than our ancestors did. Second . . . this has more to do with us, but I think immersion in the Destiny II virtualities is becoming bad for morale.'

Constantine's private ping flashed: *Yes!!!*

Which was more than Horrocks felt. He had made his second point without thinking, and without having thought of it before. But, now that he'd said it, it made sense of a lot of what he'd taken from his encounter with the Red Sun Circle, and with Atomic and Grant. It even made sense, at some still obscure level, of why he'd spent the night with Genome.

'Why do you say that?' asked Claudin Empirio, one of the scientists.

Over to you, Horrocks flashed to Constantine. He could see himself getting used to this mode of surreptitious, footnoted conversation.

'What our young colleague is driving at,' said Constantine, 'is that immersion in the doubtless fascinating details of the lives of the bat people is undermining our objectivity. We are becoming fractious, my friends. We have decisions to make about what we do in this system. We already know all we need to know to make them. We already have far more data than we could process in a decade. Further immersion in Destiny II can serve only to raise the emotional temperature. Once more, I move to terminate the message and the surveillance.'

'May we take that in two parts?' asked Hardcastle Wood.

'No,' said Constantine. 'If we don't end the surveillance, it *becomes* the message – and one over which we have no control. Both parts stand or fall together.'

'Further point of order,' said Amend Locke. 'If we burn out the bugs, other stuff is certain to burn. Damage to life and property is inevitable.'

'We must all accept full responsibility,' said Constantine. 'Before the bat people themselves, if it should come to that. My whole case is that the consequences of leaving them in place could be incalculable and severe.'

This seemed to satisfy everyone, though Horrocks suspected it was because harm to the bat people did not feel real, and facing their justice – if they had such a thing, which they probably did – seemed a remote prospect indeed.

A minute or so of discussion ensued, all electronic and too fast for Horrocks to follow. It reminded him of the final moments of the wrestling bouts he'd seen in White City. The result was as swift, and as final. The vote went nine to four in favour, with Wood, Empirio, Locke and Halegap against.

Constantine's finger stabbed at a virtual key somewhere the second the vote was taken.

'Done,' he said. He smiled around at everyone. 'Jury dissolved. Now it is we who are on trial. Goodbye and good luck.'

The virtuality broke up. Horrocks blinked out of it and gazed for a while past his knees at the wall of the nook. Then he elbowed out of it and into the now-busy corridor and joined the traffic flow in the direction back to his room. He wanted one last untrammelled fuck before he became notorious.

14 365:05:25 10:20

It's like being jolted awake from a dream.

And then to be shown a glimpse of another dream, and to have that dashed too. The Yellow Wall is full of angry voices and quiet weeping. Not from me.

Of course I'm furious about them crashing the virtualities. I'm even more upset about them breaking off the contact. The bat people *contacted us*! Surely that counts for something about their maturity? Their desire to learn from us? That map with the arrow in the middle – what else could it have been but an *invitation*? This is where we are; please drop in! I'm shaking with rage at the jury, especially Horrocks Mathematical. I'd have expected better of him.

But I must stay calm, and so must you. A lot of you are outraged about the decision, and so am I, but we should base our arguments on facts. And one thing that is not a fact is what many of you believe: that the decision was illegal.

It wasn't.

So to calm ourselves down, let's think about the ship's constitution. I started reading up about the Contract after coming across the contact clause. (Still no response on that, by the way. Don't any of you *care*?) You'll notice I said reading *about*. Reading the Contract itself would take years. In fact, only software *can* read it all and understand it, and that software is itself very old and much modified. (You see where this is going? But that's a problem for future generations – who will of course be ever so much smarter than us. We hope.) The Contract is vast, and it's vast for a reason, as I've found. I found it by starting with kids' stuff that I learned back on the estate, and refreshing my knowledge of that and working my way up.

Forming a ship's complement partakes both of launching a company and founding a new world. Over fourteen millennia it's been done many, many times, and we're all descended from people on ships whose Contract worked; or, if it went wrong, could be changed to make it work. Successful changes became incorporated in other ships' Contracts, and so it went on. Social evolution!

That's why the Contract is full of patches and makeshifts and amendments and exceptions, like very old software or the DNA in a natural genome, and far too long to read. But the basics are simple, robust, time-tested and hard-wired. You start with one or two or three hundred thousand people who (hope they) are willing to spend about four centuries in each other's company, completely isolated (apart from comms) from everyone else in the universe. They're willing to spend that time turning a gigantic reaction-mass tank into a comfortable habitat, by means of turning it again and again into properties that inevitably end up as reaction mass. Along the way, some might do very well, and others – by bad luck or incompetence – might lose out. Which is, as you know, all well and good and the natural order of things, but for some reason people are a little unwilling to sign up for it (and when they do, in desperate situations, the ships go bad. We know that now).

Hence the Contract. What it boils down to is that nobody can end up owning nothing, nobody (no individual, no group, and no everybody) can end up owning everything, and every adult gets a say in decisions. Not all decisions (which would get you back to everybody owning everything) and not even all big decisions, but all decisions 'within everyone's competence and wherein everyone has standing' (it says here).

Such decisions, it turns out, are few. (Compared to all decisions taken, that is. The ship's Council is not short of work.)

Others are up to individuals and smaller groups, and one type of group is the jury.

And yes, I'm afraid it is within the competence of a jury of scientists and financiers and rocking Horrocks Mathematical to decide to trash our virtualities from Destiny II.

Which doesn't mean we have to agree with it, or let it stand, and I for one don't mean to do one or the other. Neither should you. Not because it's illegal, but because it's insincere. The reasons given in the public record aren't those for which the decision was taken. Nor do the spoken deliberations have anything to do with the real arguments that prevailed. These, of course, remain in people's heads, where not even a Council subpoena can get at them. We're all watching the Council debates at the moment, but I can't help thinking they're debating without all the relevant information.

Look at the transcript! Do they really expect us to believe that the probe team *didn't know* about the pre-recorded message? That they *didn't know* the bugs would parasitise large organisms and that the aliens would find the bugs? Or, for that matter, that they decided so casually to start *fires* on Destiny II?

What really went on at that jury was *not* what we've been told.

Horrocks Mathematical's head rang with incoming messages. Filtering them made it ache. A scanty sampling had determined him to ignore most of them. He now knew what

Atomic had meant by 'hate mail'. The strange thing was that here, in the Engineer's Dream where he'd taken refuge, he was the toast of the company.

'This'll get the little breeders back to work,' someone had said. The sentiment was general. Microgee trainers had seen a significant slackening of business as the alien virtualities had gripped the ship generation. Constructors' orders for seeding vessels had dried to a far lower level than even the preliminary trickle that would be expected at this stage of the process.

Horrocks closed his eyes and shook his head. He suspected he had drunk too much. When he opened his eyes he found Genome looking at him with curiosity and concern.

'You can turn it off, you know,' she said.

'What?'

'Your headphone. The messages will just re-route to your externals.'

'Oh, right. Of course.'

He'd never had so much incoming to handle; the bombardment itself had prevented him from recalling how to cope with it. He closed his eyes again, focused his mind, searched his options, found the choice and made it. For some reason the cut-out presented itself to his natural sensorium as an aural hallucination of a distinct *clunk*. The silence was joyous, the relief ecstatic.

'It's like when you're a little kid,' said Genome, 'and you bang your head on the wall just for the feeling you get when you stop.'

'You did that?' said Horrocks, baffled.

'When I was very small,' said Genome. She looked like she wanted to change the subject. 'Speaking of kids, your favourite flatfoot has been bad-mouthing you again.'

Horrocks swigged. 'I'm not surprised. Nor interested.'

'Take a look anyway,' said Genome. She sent him a ping and outlined with her forefingers a rectangle in the air; the ping carried the data, the gesture evoked the page for him. As he scanned the text a cross-reference niggled at his mind, too persistent to brush away. There was some real urgency there, of the kind that most people would blush to attach to a mere angry note.

'She sent me a call, too,' said Horrocks. He grinned at Genome. 'Mind if I share it? I might need some moral support.'

She squeezed his shoulder. 'Go ahead.'

Horrocks sent a tightly specified query into his log of stored calls. It returned as text. Atomic had wasted no bandwidth on voice, let alone video. That was what he thought first, then he noticed the heavy cladding of encryption around the message: she'd had no bandwidth *to* waste.

Hello, Horrocks, she'd written. *If I know you, what went on in that jury went right over your head, just as it would have gone over mine. The difference is that you have it* in *your head. I urge you to take some time to take a look at it. When you've done that, I'm sure you'll know what to do, and I wouldn't dream of trying to influence you. But do please take a look. Regards, Atomic Discourse Gale.*

'At least she's polite,' said Genome.

'There is that,' said Horrocks. 'I expected my ears to burn.'

'Are you going to do what she asked?'

'Yes,' said Horrocks, dreading the prospect of wading through screen upon screen of elliptical, high-density discourse. 'When I'm sober.'

Genome ran a hand along her bandolier of inhalers and extracted a slim green cylinder.

'Snort this,' she said, holding it up in a billow of blue sleeve. It smelt like pine.

Horrocks felt as if he'd wakened from a deep, refreshing sleep eager to tackle an absorbing job of work. The room became sharp and clear, a tawdry hang of red-tinged light and lolling bodies and loud, empty talk.

'Don't look at me like that,' said Genome.

'Sorry,' said Horrocks. 'It isn't you, it's—'

'I know,' said Genome. She gave him a conniving smile and a hard shove. 'Go away and read your transcripts before it wears off.'

Her push sent him to the exit. He caught the jamb on the way through, swung around and thrust off, looking for somewhere quiet. The corridor was wide, elliptical in section, and heavy with colour-coded utility piping and small bulk-transport conveyor belts. A practice-habitat component a couple of metres across moved past him, its glum owner straphanging behind. It was heading away from the locks that led to the main cylinder. Horrocks drifted, kicked, drifted again. He noticed an unobtrusive tag marking an access tube that went off to one side in an inward direction. It was labelled as leading to the engine vault.

The engine vault was a place for quiet contemplation and discreet assignation, a place where people tended to go when they were very young or very old. Like the rare transparent panels in the outside of the cone where one could look at the stars as directly as it was possible to do through metre upon metre of flawless sheet diamond, and experience – or at any rate appreciate – the very photons from the stars themselves impact upon one's own retinae, the engine vault was a site of natural wonder, and one whose awe few presumed to blunt with undue familiarity.

He jack-knifed into the tube and pushed along it. After twenty metres he reached the open far end. He jammed his hands against the sides and moved forward so that his head projected out into the vault. He found himself somewhere near the middle of the wall of the vast space, a couple of hundred metres above the floor and as much below the ceiling. Other such pinprick holes were visible here and there on the inward-curving sweep of the wall below as black dots. A few tens of metres from his face, the engine loomed like a cliff, stretching off into a blue-hazed distance half a kilometre on either side. In its complexity too it looked like a cliff-face, but Horrocks knew that every curve, every hollow, every flange and protrusion, every minute pit in it was not the random result of weathering but features whose function he could not guess, but might some day centuries hence aspire to learn.

Sublime as the sight was, it took a knowledge of what it did to take the full measure of its magnificence. Like its polar counterpart in the rearward cone, the titanic engine was a cosmogonic machine. At its core was a process that – second by second when it powered the ship's flight, hour by hour when, as now, it powered only the sunline – compacted the equivalent of a multi-megaton nuclear explosion into a space the size of a hydrogen atom. Its primary effect was to accelerate the reaction mass to relativistic velocities. As a side-effect, invisible but inevitable, it generated universes. From each compacted explosion, like a stray spark from a hammer, a new singularity exploded out of space-time and inflated in an instant to give birth to a new cosmos. Some inconceivably minute fraction of the energy of that inflation could be tapped to make the engine self-sustaining. Invented in the Moon Caves, the cosmogonic engine had given man the stars. At one level efficient beyond cavil, on another it was the most profligate of man's devices: it blew multiple universes like bubbles, for the mere sake of moving mass, and at an average speed of 0.01 c at that.

Horrocks gave these considerations a moment of due respect, wedged himself comfortably in the hole, accessed the transcript files in his mind and settled down to read. It didn't take him long to discover that the only thing he could reliably make sense of were the names. The actual dialogue was so elaborate, so allusive, so technical and at the same time so playful that it would have taken him years to parse it, decades to uncover evidence of a conspiracy or a hidden agenda. For all he could tell, this entire arcane undertow to the exoteric proceedings of the jury might have served only to reinforce and document what had been spoken in the open. After struggling with it for a while he pasted the entire transcript to a call and sent it to Atomic.

'Do what you want with this,' he said.

14 365:05:25 18:15

I'm in a dilemma. A fix. A trap. A cleft stick.

I have what may be incontrovertible evidence that the jury was a sham and that some elements in the crew have been less than candid with the rest of us.

I have every reason to think that I was meant to get and release this information, and that doing so will only advance the next item on someone's agenda.

But if I don't, then I'll be party to something else. Some other twist. No matter which way I turn, I'm advancing someone else's purposes, wittingly or not.

I'll have to think about this and get back to you.

14 365:05:25 19:20

All right. Here it is. I'm releasing this to all channels and all newslines and to the Council's live feedback. Read this if you can make sense of it.

[Link to attached documentation.]

Here's my educated guess.

As I've told you before, and as you can easily see from the public record, most of the founder generation – which means, let's be clear, most of the voting-age population, what the Contract calls the

Complement – are interested in a moratorium on colonisation. Most of the ship generation, to put it mildly, aren't. What we hadn't factored in was that the crew are on our side in this – they tend to steer clear of public debates, so it wasn't as obvious as it should have been.

Obviously, these are crude generalisations, but the breakdown of consensus is along the following divisions:

The founders are going to be in this system a long time. They have a lot of speculative and venture capital riding on our projects, but for the long term stability is their watchword. They want – need – to be absolutely sure things are not going to blow up with the locals before we venture forth. They also have, it's fair to say, a genuine humanitarian – if that's the word – concern about the locals. They don't want some ghastly global conflict on their consciences, and nor should they, and nor do I.

We, dear readers, have a rather different calculus of concern. We want to get out there, and we're confident we can handle the consequences. I mean, come *on*! In a decade or two we'll have settled a good tenth of the asteroids, industrialised most of the moons and have advanced projects under way around the gas giant and the waterworld. We'll have a power station on the mercurial that'll outshine the bat people's global energy output every *second*. We'll have started building a long tube. And with all that we can't even *intimidate* them into behaving decently – to each other, and to us? Let alone what our power and example of peaceful co-operation and progress could do to show them the way.

The crew have their own interest and their own code. They want us out there, because they need us to harvest the resources and breed the replacement population for the next journey. They have no long-term investments outside the ship. They don't plan to stick around for long, and to them – marvellous as the discovery of aliens is – our dealings with each other and with the bat people are just one more instance of the sort of intra-system bickering they've made it their life's business and the habit of centuries to walk away from. (If you already feel that way yourself, consider joining the crew. A minority of every ship generation does, just as a minority of crew become system-settlers.)

So, on this issue, the crew are on the same side as the ship generation.

The Destiny II virtualities became an arena of that conflict of interest. Remember I warned that we would get very frustrated without something to channel our energies and urge to explore? The virtualities were on the way to becoming just that: we were all slacking off on our projects and exploring Destiny II. It's not just that the founders want us immersed in virtualities until the bat people are set on some kind of stable path. It's not just cynical. By understanding the bat people and the planet in more depth, we'd be better prepared to contact them, communicate with them and if necessary intervene when the time came to do so. Who knows how long that would be – years? decades? But until then, the founders want to avoid contact, and any too obvious activity in the system, at almost any cost.

Some well-placed people in the crew, I suspect, have done their best to rock this.

What I can't understand is why they summoned Horrocks to the jury, unless they knew he'd leak the proceedings – the real ones – and wanted him to do so. They must want the founders and the Council to know. Why?

Send me your ideas.

14 365:05:26 00:00

To the reader: This message was not posted by the author of this biolog. It is being posted to all channels of live communication simultaneously. This biolog and all other private one-to-many channels are temporarily suspended with immediate effect. Private (one-to-one) communications are not affected or monitored. For the next twelve hours, only emergency calls are being routed. A state of emergency exists. The contact clause has been invoked. For documentation and Contract verification, query ship memory on relevant phrases. For further information, please locate and use regular public news channels. Expect service interruptions.

FOURTEEN

THE EXTRAORDINARY AND REMARKABLE SHIP

In the third outer-month after the turning of the year, in the early spring, a ship flying the golden lizard pennant of the Southern Rule sailed up the Broad Channel from the west. It made port first at Low Lassir, the great harbour of Gevork, linked by river to its inland capital; then after three days of lading and unlading tacked across the Channel and – somewhat to the surprise of informed observers – made for the jetty at the mouth of Long Finger River at Five Ravines.

Among the low barges, grubby coalers, and gay sailboats that shared that backwater, the ship stood out like a lordly roost above stables. Its steam engine gave off little smoke, and its propulsion churned the sea at greater depth than any known propeller. Its sails rose bright and white in odd-angled but harmonious shapes, like pieces of a geometric puzzle. Though its hull and superstructure were wooden, and its paint gaudy, its lines displayed something of the elegance of a leaping fish and the camber of a well-poised wing. As soon as its topmast rose above the horizon it attracted attention; by the time its hull was in full view it was an indispensable sight for anyone with the least pretension to being abreast of events; and when it sailed into the harbour it had almost as many adult sightseers circling its masts at a respectful and admiring distance as it had screaming kits chasing the sea-flitters that followed in its wake.

Before it had hove to, an eager crowd lined the jetty. Every merchant of drugs and spices in town had sent at least a boy with a list and a line of scrip; ladies and gentlemen of fashion hastened to the quay in hope of fine ribbons, bright buckles, keen blades and grotesque belts; reporters from the local press came in search of distant news and outlandish opinion; draughtsmen from the cheaper journals did not scruple to snatch the sheets of newsprint in which the wares were wrapped, and steal from their coloured woodcuts inspiration; students and scholars sought exotica and erotica. Few in that crowd were disappointed, and fewer still noticed a member of the ship's company balance on the rail, peer this way and that, check a bearing with tilted eye and levelled compass and an investigative sniff at the air, then take deliberate wing to the university quarter.

Darvin watched the students who had attended his lecture swirl skyward, shuffled his notes together, and sighed. Most of the students might have understood his presentation of the method of estimating stellar distances by parallax, but he was certain that some would not. A few essays would come his way explaining that it was done by looking at stars through binoculars and closing one eye at a time. He switched off the projector, stuffed his notes in his belt pouch, and began clambering up the expanding concentric rings of the lecture tower. He didn't have the energy to take a running jump into the air.

The winter months had been trying. Since the collapse of the contact he had not been called upon to do anything for

Project Signal. Debarred from publicising his only significant discovery, the Object, Darvin had lost enthusiasm for his search for the hypothetical outer planet. That research project falling fallow, he'd turned more of his time over to teaching. It was a measure of his avoidance of contention that he conducted, not advanced seminars with his peers who might have shown interest in his own work, but lectures to novice students. Their reminders of himself a few years earlier irritated and depressed him.

Orro, on the other wing, had spent half his time away on aeronautical research, at some distant strip in the desert. On his returns to the university he'd been too preoccupied with catching up with his teaching — about which he was conscientious — to say much, even of the little the project's secrecy permitted. Once, after a second or third stumblefruit, he had confessed to feeling burdened by the deaths of two test pilots in flying machines of his design. He understood perfectly the moral logic of his innocence: he had given the designs his best, the pilots were enthusiastic volunteers who knew the risks, and they were all working at the limits of the known; but he could not shake off the sense of culpability. The lucid imperatives of civil and indeed military ethics warred in his conscience with the gallant, foolish ethos of the sabreur.

Halfway up the slope of circular rails Darvin clutched with his feet, leaned forward and launched off. He swooped, then climbed, and flitted out between the lip of the pit and its canopy. As soon as he was out of the tower's shadowy interior, with the sun on his face and the fresh wind rushing through his fur, he felt better. As he banked towards the Faculty of Impractical Sciences he spotted a new and tall ship down at the quay. He guessed from its lines that it was a Southern Rule ship, and then noted with satisfaction the long triangle of the banner that confirmed his guess: green, with a gold wavy line that he couldn't make out in detail at this distance, but knew to represent a stylised lizard, symbolic of the Southern Rule's vaunted antiquity. He made a mental note to visit it later, and dived to the department's ledge.

Outside his office door a stranger waited. The man wore bright beads on the bristles of his ears and a belt made from the linked scales of some gigantic grazer around his hips. Within the belt was stuffed a curved scabbard, from which projected a chased handle. Around his neck hung a broad leather satchel, its lower corners secured by coloured tapes to the belt. Spider-silk ribbons were knotted below his knees. Silver sheathed his toe-claws. As Darvin approached he raised his arms and erected his wings in an excess of welcome.

'Do I have the honour,' he asked in flawless but accented Selohic, 'of the presence of the renowned astronomer Darvin of Five Ravines?'

Darvin stopped before the stranger and spread his own hands. 'You flatter my fame beyond all reason, sir, but I am Darvin.'

The stranger pressed his palm against Darvin's. 'My name is Lenoen, sky-watcher to the super-lunary survey of the court of Narr, a province of the land you call the Southern Rule and we' — at this point he smiled — 'call the Roost of Man.'

'Your presence honours me,' said Darvin. 'My disorderly office, I fear, is unprepared for such a guest, but if you would deign to enter, the freedom of it is yours.'

Another glint in Lenoen's eye assured Darvin that he had caught the right note, and that the formality of self-deprecation amused the stranger as much as himself. He pushed the door open and ushered Lenoen within.

'Take a perch,' he said. 'Or a seat.'

Lenoen chose a seat by the table, and watched in silence as Darvin prepared tea. It was only after his first sip — at which he failed to quite suppress a wince — that he spoke again.

'You feigned surprise at your renown,' he said, 'but I can

affirm that you need do so no more. Your name is between the teeth of every sky-watcher in the South who is more than a scryer of portents.'

'You astonish me,' said Darvin. He dreaded what was to come next. 'My sole contribution to the science is the discovery of a handful of the Camp-Followers. Are they, perhaps, of some astrological significance unknown to me?'

Lenoen's beaded bristles rattled. 'To fence well takes a balanced sword,' he said.

Darvin set down his cup. 'You catch me off guard,' he said.

Lenoen nodded. He opened his satchel and withdrew a sheaf of papers, from which he selected a stiff, glossy sheet and placed it on the table. Darvin stepped over and looked at it. White spots speckled the shiny black background. In the centre, small but distinct, lay an irregular blob, whitish with dark spots. It was the clearest and largest picture of an asteroid that Darvin had ever seen. For a moment he hoped against hope that this impressive achievement was all that his visitor had come to show.

'That is a photograph of one of what you call the Camp-Followers,' said Lenoen. He laid on top of it a similar sheet. 'Here we see another.'

In the centre of this one was a long rectangle with a triangular point at each end. Though fuzzy – it was at the limits of magnification – the object tantalised with a hint of internal structure, of lines and panels.

'More of the same.'

One after another, Lenoen slapped down eight-and-four more sheets. They showed the object – the Object, Darvin knew with cold certainty – from a variety of angles that made it obvious that it was a cylinder with two conical ends.

'This,' said Lenoen, 'is the distant decelerating celestial object of which you spoke in the now justly famous paper by you and your esteemed colleague Orro.'

'I'm astounded,' said Darvin. 'Our best telescopes can resolve it to no more than a dot.'

Lenoen leaned back and looked Darvin in the eye. 'You are surprised at the resolution, but not at the shape revealed?'

Darvin knew he had blundered. 'Hints of structure have been inferred,' he said. 'From, ah, changes in its albedo and . . . and so forth.'

'And so forth,' said the Southerner. 'I do not doubt it.' He tweaked the elaborate bow at his knee. 'May I ask what the astronomers of this great Reach of mighty Seloh think it is?'

'I don't know,' said Darvin. 'There has been little discussion of it. None, if I am honest.'

Lenoen raised his brows.

'I speak the truth,' said Darvin. He waved a hand at teetering stacks of offprints. 'See for yourself – take the papers, I'll be glad to have them off my hands.' A thought occurred to him. 'How did you come across ours? Do you receive the physics wire?'

'Not directly,' said Lenoen. 'Until telegraph wires are strung across the equatorial ocean, we must perforce rely on copies of the prints. Which make their way to us, by one or other route.' He slapped his knee, setting the fixed ribbon ornament aflutter. 'But enough. What is your own opinion?'

'I suppose,' said Darvin, 'that some gigantic crystal, formed in the far reaches of the system by processes beyond our ken, could perhaps account—'

Lenoen guffawed. 'I beg your pardon,' he said, 'but I remind you of the proverb of the sword. You slash, you flail, you are in danger of spinning out of the sky.'

'Sir,' said Darvin, 'it is I who should ask pardon of you. Despite appearances, I do not trifle with you. Let me say only that an obligation heavier than that to science overshadows me.'

'I quite understand,' said Lenoen. 'I too am loyal to my lord.

Hailed be the name of Narr! Very well. Let me tell you what the sky-watchers of the Southern Rule make of it, if I may.'

'Please do,' said Darvin.

'It's a ship from another star,' said Lenoen. 'Probably the one you call Stella Proxima.'

Darvin said nothing. His mouth was too dry for speech anyway.

'Its arrival in our system,' Lenoen went on, 'is probably connected with a number of anomalous incidents of the last year or so — odd aerial phenomena, strange portents, the recent outbreaks of fire, malformed beasts, the birth of a trudge kit with the power of human speech, the—'

'A trudge kit with – *what*?' asked Darvin.

'Speech,' said Lenoen. He waved a hand. 'A rustic rumour, I must admit, recounted in one of our sensational prints. Still, I am struck once more with what it takes to surprise you.'

Darvin spread his hands. 'In our fencing you leave me, I fear, a broken heap on the ground. But I am sworn to silence on such matters as you mention.'

'Yes indeed,' said Lenoen. He stood up and began to pace around. 'Let us talk about that silence of yours. I expected it. I encountered this week a similar silence on the other side of the Channel.'

'You've just been to Gevork?'

'Yes. In the port of Low Lassir, and upriver to High Lassir, where I spoke both with Gevorkian astronomers and with the embassy of the Roost of Man. It is of the latter I would speak, for a moment.' He sighed and sat down again, his silvered claws tapping the floor in a manner that betrayed some unease. 'You are aware, I take it, of the state of affairs between the Reach, the Realm, and the Rule?'

Darvin shook his head. 'I take small interest in politics,' he said. 'The subject repels me.'

'The ways of the starry heavens are indeed more uplifting,'

said the Southerner. 'However, as a court sky-watcher, it unfor-
tunately behooves me to keep one eye on affairs here below.
The merchants and adventurers of both your great reaches of
the Sundered Continent knock upon the doors of our trade
with ever greater importunity and, if I may say so, impertin-
ence. And in those narrow doorways, and indeed in other
entrances less regular, they jostle each other and trample the
unwary. Their rivalry alarms the wise among us. Our emissaries and . . . travellers . . . to northern shores have noted
indications that the alien presence has become an object and
occasion for a rivalry as intense as it is covert. On this, the wise
among us are on the verge of beating their heads with clenched
claws!'

He raised a hand and rose again to his feet, then stooped
over the table on which the astronomical photographs were
spread, as if to spare Darvin the shame of avoiding his eyes.
'You need not comment. I come here only to pay my respects,
and as a token of it to give you these photographs of your
wonderful and never-to-be-forgotten discovery of the extraor-
dinary and remarkable ship.'

'Thank you,' said Darvin. 'Your kindness overwhelms me.'

The Southerner placed some more paper on the table.

'I have also,' said Lenoen, turning around and straightening,
'left you a humble attempt at an interpretation of the object. A
woodcut diagram, with captions, and a page or two of expli-
cation. Perhaps fanciful, but a preliminary effort, for your
justly critical but I hope indulgent perusal.'

'Once again, you are too kind.'

'Not at all,' said Lenoen. He edged past the table. 'On the
contrary, I am clinging by a single claw to the limits of the
courtesy due one scientist to another, let alone to my sense of
honour and self-respect.' He pushed open the window and put
a foot on the frame. 'I tremble to tell you that even as we
speak, copies of these photographs, and of our interpretation of

them, are being distributed by our merchant seamen to the
representatives of your local press at the quay, and at this same
moment by our emissaries in Lassir to the popular press, such
as it is, of Gevork.' He stood on the ledge, speaking over his
shoulder. 'I ask your pardon for the presumption, your understanding for its necessity, and offer my thanks for your time
and your tea, and bid you, without further ado, farewell.'

He dived off.

Darvin stood for a few minutes studying the photographs
and comparing them with the diagram on the front page of the
document. When the telephone rang he ignored it. When a
knock came to the door he rolled up the document, stuck it in
his belt and left the room by Lenoen's route.

The previous spring Kwarive's sister had had five kits, of
whom only two had died in their first year. When Darvin
couldn't find Kwarive around the university, it was a fair bet
that she was at her sister's roost. So it proved that afternoon.
Darvin pushed aside the safety mesh and ducked under the
awning of the side entrance to find Kwarive on her back on the
slatted floor, batting up with her hands as the three yearlings
flew around the room, yelling and bumping into the walls
and each other. He sometimes suspected her of becoming
broody, but she had always insisted on completing her studies
before she'd consider taking a roost.

'What's the matter?' she asked, looking up at him.

He told her. ('L'noen!' squeaked the kits. 'Lassir! Emissary!'
They grabbed new words like bright toys.)

She sat up. 'This is serious,' she said.

'You've said it.' He laughed. 'Now we'll find out if the engineering tales got it right about mass panic.'

'Oh, not that,' said Kwarive. 'That's all piffle anyway. No, I
meant that story about a talking trudge kit.'

Darvin clasped his hands across his head. 'I don't take *that* seriously! It's all of a piece with portents and dead men's ships and two-headed prey-calves. It's the loss of secrecy that concerns me more. The whole project—'

'Project! Project!' shrieked a kit whizzing past his ear.

'Let's take this somewhere else,' Darvin said.

'Good idea.' Kwarive walked over to a barred cupboard, hauled out a struggling flitter, snapped one of its wings and tossed the hapless creature in the air. The kits brought it down and bit and clawed into it. Its screeches stopped in a second, the immediate feeding-frenzy a few seconds later. The kits raised their heads.

'Good Kwarive! Good Kwarive!' they called with bloody jaws.

'I'm too good to them,' Kwarive grumbled on the way out. 'My sister would have a fit. Breaking its wing like that.'

'She objects to the cruelty?' Darvin asked.

'No,' said Kwarive. 'The loss of the chase. They need the exercise.'

Darvin and Kwarive perched on the rail of the roost's balcony.

'You were saying?' said Kwarive.

'The project won't be secret any more. That's got to be a good thing.'

'Wishful thinking,' said Kwarive. 'The *occasion* for the project is no longer secret. The actual content of it is. Do you think Orro's aeronautics will suddenly become open to public discussion? Nollam's etherics? And whatever else is going on that even we don't know about?'

'I don't know.' He pulled Lenoen's document from his belt. 'Have a look at this.'

The document consisted of three sheets of paper, held together by a cunning cut and fold in the top left-hand corner. They peered at the top page. It was headed: 'A Grave and

Truthful Discourse Upon Some Recent Unusual Events'. Beneath that was a fine woodcut of side, front and three-quarter views of the Object. The labelling gave the scale, and interpreted the front and rear cones as engines, and the central cylinder as spinning to provide an effect of weight. A brief note below recounted the discovery and location of the object, referring to Darvin and Orro's paper and also to some reports in the various tongues of the Southern Rule. The vocabulary of the note, and the size of the print, gave every indication of being aimed at the simplest of readers.

The second page listed a series of anomalous events, in the same straightforward style, as if taken from naive eye-witness accounts.

The third page stated:

From reliable reports of travellers and friends, the Wise of the Southern Rule believe that the esteemed over-watchers of the northern realms have been breathed upon by a great wind of invention and skilful work from their knowledge of these events. In the Reach of Seloh, honour to her name, those of craft and knowledge have set about the following mighty works: building flying machines of fixed wings; sending moving pictures through the ether; searching the sky for etheric messages from other worlds; new methods of reckoning the descrying of portents from numbers. In the Realm of Gevork, praise be to its ancient fame, the following: building large rockets of metal; sending moving pictures through the ether; obtaining heat and light from certain rare and poisonous minerals; building etheric machines for reckoning and comparing, and for the construction of subtle secret codes.

It is the heavy dread of the Wise of the Southern Rule that these wonderful works, and more we wot not of, may be intended to improve the arts of war. It is our humble and fervent hope, upon which our holy men daily and nightly beseech the blessing of the Most High and the beloved gods below and above the moons, that our dread shall prove unfounded and that the realms remain at peace.

The lower half of that page consisted of two woodcuts. One showed a fixed-wing flying machine with a propeller at its nose, the other a rocket of metal – someone had taken pains to show the plates and rivets – with flames shooting out of the back. They appeared to be on a collision course.

Darvin's hands shook as he turned the papers back to the front page and stared at the drawing of the ship from another star.

'How did they find this out?' he said.

'The Southern Rule,' said Kwarive, 'must surely have something like the Sight.'

'If I were in the Sight,' said Darvin, 'I'd be searching now for Southern spies inside the Sight itself.'

'You *are* in the Sight,' Kwarive pointed out.

'So I am,' said Darvin, 'to my rue, and perhaps my ruin.'

'What do you mean?' cried Kwarive.

'I'll be under suspicion. So will you. So will we all.' He was thinking of Orro.

'Perhaps we should disappear. Your relatives in the back country—'

'No!' said Darvin. 'That's just about the worst thing we could do. If the Sight seeks us, it'll find us – depend on it. The best we can do is act as if we're innocent – which we are.'

From the balcony they could see the Southern ship. Kwarive gazed at it.

'Why did they have to do this?' she asked. 'What did they hope to accomplish?'

'Exactly what they said – peace.'

She gaped at him. 'That's so naive!'

'Is it? "Naive" is not a word I associate with the Southern

Rule. Superstitious, perhaps, traditional, yes, maddeningly set in their ways, certainly – but not naive.'

'I meant you are naive. They must have a hidden motive.'

'This is why I have no politics,' said Darvin. 'I can't think in those terms.'

'Then maybe it's time you learned to, and fast!'

Her anger sounded sodden with distress. Darvin wrapped a wing around her.

'Tell me why you were concerned about the tale of the talking trudge,' he said.

'It reminded me of the electric shittles,' she said.

'How?' He didn't see it at all.

'If the wingless ones can influence the life-force of a shittle, to make it grow an electrical device, why couldn't they influence the life-force of a trudge, to make it grow whatever part of the brain is needed for the power of speech?'

'No reason why they couldn't, I suppose, but why should they?'

'The shittles have failed them,' she said. 'We detected them, and we started sending messages back. That's why they were destroyed – because the observation had become contaminated by our awareness of it. So now they're trying again. What better way to watch us than through the eyes of trudges?'

Darvin shuddered. 'That thought gives me the creeps,' he said. 'However, it doesn't explain why they should want a trudge to speak, assuming it really happened and wasn't some drunk farmer's bad dream.'

'Well, going along with that . . . I must admit it doesn't fit.' She laughed. 'So like a good scientist, I have another hypothesis: the aliens are sentimental like you, and think of the trudges as a sort of strong and very stupid people, and not as beasts.'

'Ah!' said Darvin. 'In that case, why should they *give* them speech? If they know that have no speech, they know they are beasts, so giving them speech wouldn't be seen as helping people. It would be seen as turning beasts into people.'

'They may not see speech as the issue. Perhaps it's a side-effect of raising the intelligence of the trudges.'

'And why should they want to do that? Queen of Heaven! If trudges became intelligent, or if a coming generation of trudges were born intelligent, they would – they would—'

'Slaughter us,' said Kwarive. 'Without hesitation, without mercy, without scruple. And then, when they had wiped us from the face of the Ground, they would welcome – for a time, at any rate – their benefactors from above. And if they didn't, they would have even less chance than we would of resisting the invasion.'

Darvin felt almost as shocked that Kwarive could imagine such a thing as he was by the sanguinary vision itself. The malevolence or incompetence it ascribed to the aliens also disturbed him, in part because it rang true with his own earlier dark suspicions. If the wingless aliens looked like trudges to human eyes, was it not possible that the aliens might themselves feel akin to the flightless trudges?

'This is a morbid fancy,' he said. 'I will hear no more of it.'

'Not very scientific of you,' she chided. She clutched his shoulders and looked him in the eye. 'Oh, Darvin, I've been thinking about what Bahron the Eye said, about how the aliens want our world. He may be right, you know. All life is a struggle for existence. Why should it cease to be a struggle if it spreads among the stars?'

FIFTEEN

HOLLOW SPACES OF THE FORWARD CONE

LEARNING THE WORLD in exile # 100

14 365:11:02 10:43

Issue 100! That's not a number I ever expected to reach when I switched to mailing. Nor did I then hope to have *more* readers than I ever did when anybody could access it. So thanks to all who've subscribed, and to all who've spread the word. I still miss the biologs, though. The newslines do their job but it's all professionals and much less exciting than the buzz. So I appreciate all the mails that come to *me*, and the mailing lists, and so on. And I know it's not just me – I know there are hundreds if not thousands out there writing and speaking and performing against the emergency and the embargo, people whom I've never heard of and who've never heard of me. (How do I know? From the number I do hear about, and how I hear about them – by chance, by word of mouth, and by the people I meet when I go to other towns or who come to Far Crossing, and I find whole communities of people in the same fight. And from the songs.) It's not the same, but it gives us heart, it keeps up our spirits, and helps us realise that this dark time will soon be over.

Nearly six months of State of Emergency; just over six months to go. Soon? It seems a long time, I know, but remember that in that time even more of us will have turned sixteen, as I did a couple of months ago, and we'll not just be able to vote in the referendum on the emergency but petition a recall and throw out the entire Council. *Throw out the Council!* I want to write that in virtual letters across the sunline. It's going to happen. It's unfair – most of the people on the Council are good people. (I'll get hammered for saying that, I know, but it's true, so don't bother.) But it's the price you pay. If you keep your ship generation cooped up in the ship, your ship generation grows up like grass under your feet and a huge cohort of it comes of age and *votes you out*.

What have we accomplished in the past six months? There are those who'll say, nothing much. We're still stuck here, the embargo's still in place, the emergency's still in place. To those – I'm thinking of S—— and H—— here, and you know who you are – who think like that, just think back to how it was that midnight when the contact clause was invoked and the boom came down. Or think about the morning after it. It was worse than when we lost the virtualities. It was as if the sunline had gone out and then the lights had gone out. We were stumbling around in the dark. Suddenly everyone was all alone. We couldn't see in an instant what others all over the world thought. All we had was the people around us and the talking heads on the newslines.

I remember that morning. I never wrote about it at the time because it was too depressing. But look back at it now, compare it with this morning, and it's downright encouraging. Here is how it was.

Something woke me before the sunline came out, about six in the morning or so. I really needed a bite and a brew, so I climbed into some clothes and pulled on a pair of springy shoes and spiralled down the stairs and jogged off down Windy and on to Dark (is how it felt at the time) and didn't even pause to pick up the day's newslines at the hotspot. In the half-light of the farside I noticed people standing in small groups on the street, talking. I didn't know, maybe I'd missed a big all-night party or something. There was an odd sense of quiet, and I couldn't quite understand why. I could hear voices, the sounds of early risers rising and early birds reaffirming their property rights, the hum of an engine and the hiss of tyres in the next street.

And then I noticed. The quiet was in my head. Most times of course you don't listen to the buzz. You don't read the chat. But you know it's there in the background, like distant surf, like far-off lights. I stopped for a moment, my heart thumping much harder than the running justified, and closed my eyes and interrogated my inner ear. Nothing. No sound, no lights, nothing in my head but me. I could taste myself like the roof of my mouth.

Maybe I hadn't quite woken up. I didn't think anything was seriously wrong. A vague, half-formed thought floated through my fuzzy mind that the comms might be down due to the previous day's bonfire of the virtualities. An even vaguer thought drifted by that it served them right; 'them' being, of course, the jury who'd pulled the plug and the Council that had endorsed their decision. It may have been the first time I ever thought of the founders, the older generation, as 'them' with quite that emphasis.

As I jogged along a curious thing happened, which had nothing to do with anything that happened later, and nothing obvious to do with anything that had happened immediately before. Looking back, I can see that it may have had something to do with that alone-in-my-head feeling. What happened was this. I became very much aware of being me, and it felt strange. It was as if a wider, cooler mind had found itself in my head, and was surprised to be there behind my eyes. And yet that larger mind was mine. Very odd. It passed in a few moments, leaving me a little shaken, curious, and quite unable to recapture it. I have never found a name for this experience, and though I've had it several times since I can neither induce it at will nor prevent its recurrence. When I tell people about it they either look blank or say: 'Oh! You mean you have that too?' But it isn't a bond between us, not a secret, just a peculiarity, an anomaly, perhaps as random a feature of our minds as the ability to roll one's tongue is of our bodies. It solves no problem, conveys no insight, and yet leaves me with an impression of significance. It has an aftertaste, but no taste. That impression, that aftertaste, may be its empty secret: it may be a tiny glitch in the process by which our brains find meaning in sense.

But I digress.

I pushed into the Yellow Wall and found the place crowded. Knowing how gradually it fills up even from about seven or so, this was a surprise. It was full of people who looked like they'd been up all night, and not at a party. Nobody talked much. The place reeked of coffee and inhaler fumes and sweat. The loudest noise came from the wheezing labour of the air-conditioner. It was the most squalid atmosphere I'd breathed since my microgravity train-ing. Most people looked down at visible or invisible comms or watched the video wall. The scene came from outside the Council Hall. As I made for the percolator I twitched my ears to pick up the audio. You know what I heard. The cup I dropped was empty. Its crash made everybody jump.

Faces turned toward me.

'You didn't know?' asked Far Sun Park. One of the New Lamarck kids. I was with her at our last big shock, when we first received news of the transmissions. (Why all those flashbacks to training?) She cried then, and she looked like she'd been crying now, for all that she'd matured in the meantime.

I shook my head. 'Has it passed?'

'Ninety-eight to thirty-five,' she said. 'No abstentions.'

I summoned a brave face. 'Thirty-five? That's more than we could have hoped.'

Some people looked at me as if I was talking nonsense, but most looked like they wanted to hear what I had to say.

'The emergency can only last a year,' I said. 'We can design and train like we expect to go out tomorrow, and by the time it's up, we'll be more ready to go out than we've ever been.'

'They won't let us go out,' said Far.

'Who's they?' I said. 'A year from now, most of us will have the vote.'

'By that time, they'll have convinced most of us that the moratorium is a good idea.'

'They're not the only ones who can do convincing.'

At that point everybody just laughed. I turned away and gathered the shards of the broken cup. Then I got myself the coffee and snack I'd come for. I sat down with it and wrote my first 'exile' post and sent it to everyone who'd ever contacted me. I had plenty of time to do it, because nobody wanted to talk to me.

Compare that to how it is now. This morning I rolled out of bed, leaving Grant to sleep, and grabbed my breakfast here. I went to the workshop and did a couple of hours on the habitat virtual tests. I wasn't the first person in, and the loft filled up fast. When I looked around the real and virtual spaces were more crowded than the desks, with projects big and wild. Grant's waterworld resort no longer looks outrageous – there's a scheme for farming the algae that has so far survived three feasibility studies; an even wilder project for exporting water by whipping waterspouts to escape velocity (don't ask); some very neat work with using gas giant slingshot effects to get a head start on the long tube; all of which are attracting some founder capital – which of course does its bit to undermine the pro-embargo coalition, by vesting interests in colonisation and getting out. On the cultural side there's a small school of artists over in the corner data-mining Red Sun transmissions – four years behind, obviously, and four hundred years of cultural drift off, but that's what makes what they make of it interesting, even beautiful.

I'll tell you a secret: we've gained by losing the virtualities. Without that distraction we're more focused on our work and on our plans. Some of us. The truth is, the workshop is crowded not because too many people are working on projects, but because not enough are to justify opening another one.

And therein lies a problem, one I was reminded of it as I walked to the café just now for my morning break. The streets and parks were busy. What worries me is what they were busy with. Fun, games, music, talk talk talk. Half a dozen kids loafing, passing an inhaler around, giggling. Nothing wrong with that at a party, but this was ten in the morning! Saw one guy cross-legged on a bench, whittling a bit of bent branch into a vague semblance of an animal. Doubtless he thinks it's art and that he's accomplishing something. Not everyone is into starting projects. Some always take more initiative than others. That isn't the problem. The problem is that too many people who should be initiating projects aren't, and too many people who should be checking out which project they want to join aren't bothering. They don't have plans and they don't bother even to study. They're out there playing under the sunline.

Who can blame them? Well, we can, and we do. We busy folk call them slackers and birthrighters, because they're living on their birthrights and not earning or learning. But they didn't just happen to be born with idle bones. They're idle because they don't believe they'll ever get out, at least not for decades. So should we blame the founders, and all those who voted for the embargo?

No! We should blame ourselves! We're not doing enough to convince them that the embargo won't last more than another six months. All we have to do is vote. The voting-age cohort of the ship generation is enough to tip the balance.

I've just had an awful thought. If we don't shift that crowd of slackers, they might vote to *keep* the embargo.

Think about that. Actually, when I think about that, I get such a terrible sense of suffocation that I gasp. And I think about killing.

I really feel as if I could go out and choke slackers with my bare hands.

I'm as shocked as you are.

Synchronic Narrative Storm was showing a group of five-year-olds the big machine that turned bales of mown grass into milkshakes and meat patties when a shadow darkened the sunlight from the doorway. She turned and saw Constantine.

'You grace us with your real presence,' she said, in an electric message with a sharp edge. He smiled and stepped out of sight. Synchronic passed the five-year-olds to the charge of two ten-year-olds, who took over the demonstration so quickly that Synchronic could smell the sizzle before she was out of the door. She found Constantine leaning on the side of the barn, in a pose that needed only a chewed straw between his teeth to complete.

'You have some nerve coming here,' she said.

'Yes, my lady,' he said. He straightened away from the wooden wall and gestured to the pathways. 'Care for a stroll?'

'If you must.'

'Thank you.'

They walked between gnarled trees. Mowing machines like large trilobites with baskets on their backs trimmed the verges.

'Feed for the nanotech cow,' remarked Constantine. 'A cumbrous process. In the cones we grow food straight from the gunk.'

'You didn't come here to pass the time of day.'

'No, my lady, I did not.'

'I still haven't forgiven you, and I'm not going to, so don't ask.'

The subterfuge of the surveillance still rankled; its exposure, at least, still embarrassed him. She could see his blush in the infra-red.

'I didn't come to ask forgiveness,' he said. 'Nor to offer mine.'

'You think I need any?'

'Not particularly.' He looked sidelong at her. 'Business is business. Can we put all that aside for the moment? Accepting it as unfinished business?'

She shrugged. 'If you insist. So what did you come for?'

'We're in danger of losing the ship generation.'

'I'm aware of the problems,' she said. '"You can't tell the boys from the girls, they have no respect for their elders, their user interfaces are garish and unwieldy, everybody is writing a book, and their music is just noise." Found scratched on a potsherd in Sumer.'

'All true as it ever was,' he said, 'but it's more than that. They were ripe to go out, and now they're overripe, to the point of becoming somewhat rotten. A significant number are demoralised. Another and better fraction are becoming angry and organised against the founders.'

'And whose fault is that? They were conveniently distracted and constructively occupied with the virtualities until you crashed them.'

He raised a hand in front of him, palm facing her. 'I know, I know,' he said. 'Let's not recriminate. As we agreed, yes?'

'Yes.'

'So the question is what's to be done about it. I think we have to give them hope, and we have to give them constructive work. Real work and real hope.'

'Planning and designing is real work.'

'Yes, and it's killing their spirits. The better they are the more they yearn to put their plans into practice.'

She stopped dead on the path. Constantine took a couple of oblivious steps forward, then noticed and turned around. She glared him in the face.

'Don't open again the question of colonisation. We're not

doing it until at least we get advice from the Red Sun system.'

Constantine spread his hands. 'You know you haven't won the young people over to that. When the emergency goes to referendum they can vote it out, and vote your people off the Council, and colonise anyway.'

'They can vote all they like,' she said. 'They can't force us to invest.'

She thought she detected a flicker of amusement at this, but no note of it reached his voice. 'Don't put them to that test,' he said.

'So do you have anything to propose?' she asked. 'Some real work that isn't virtual?'

'Yes,' he said. 'I propose that we let them get to work on real asteroids, but not out in the system.'

'Oh?' she said. 'And where would we find these real asteroids? In the slag mountains?'

'No,' said Constantine. 'In the hollow spaces of the cones.'

She knew about these asteroids, of course. It was because she had classified them in the wrong mental category that she hadn't thought of them.

'That sounds very tempting,' she said. 'I think we could sell that to the Council. On one condition.'

'Yes?'

'That it counts as colonisation, with the settlers emigrating as if they were going into free space. They are, after all, leaving the habitat.'

Constantine smiled. 'And therefore can't vote? Yes, I had thought that aspect would appeal to you.'

'I can see how we benefit,' said Synchronic. 'What's in it for the crew?'

'Same as for the kids,' said Constantine. 'Work. Something useful to be getting on with. Trade. Resource extraction.'

'You know,' said Synchronic, 'it might be best if the

suggestion were to come from the ship generation themselves, and then be acceded to by the Council. So that it seemed less like a palliative offered by us, and more like a concession won by them.'

'I'll take steps,' said Constantine.

The town, or miniature city, of Far Crossing had changed since Horrocks had last visited it. This time he arrived in his own hired microlight. He dragged it across the field and parked it at the edge of town, then walked in along the same street he'd walked six months before. Sternward Avenue, that was it. Its familiarity underlined how much about it had changed. It was more crowded and less busy than he remembered. The paintings and writings on the walls were no longer harmonious and decorative. Angry slogans flared in jagged letters. *Rock the founders. Rock the aliens. Room to live. Space for us.* Elaborate illuminations of names and obscure words. Obsessive, detailed pictures of habitats, fantastically encrusted with weapons; of the aliens, with speech bubbles enclosing improbable dialogue. *Trompe l'oeil* murals of climbing plants. The loss of much of the usual electronic buzz and background chatter had shifted illustration and emphasis and communication out to the actual.

Music thudded or moaned from every shopfront and open window, or so it seemed. The air floated pheromones of frustration and molecules of narcotics, stimulants and hallucinogens. The people in the street affected in their attire a studied casualness – space-rigger fatigues, mesh and nanofibre – or the louche, bedraggled formality of ill-matched, half-fastened outfits like those of people returning drunk from a party. Some of them, Horrocks realised with disdain, *were* returning drunk from parties. It was the middle of the afternoon.

He felt pinched and short of the ready. The stuff in the shops was out of his reach. Six months of seeing terrestrials stock tank and not much in the way of training fees had left him not poor, but cost-conscious in a way he hadn't been before. The thought of Constantine's scheme put a bounce in his step.

The Yellow Wall held a surprise. It had changed in a different direction. Most of the tables were occupied by two or three people, but it was as quiet as a library. A lot of reading and writing was going on. Some heads were even bent over physical books: pages printed out and bound in codices. Horrocks had come across this before, as a work-around for certain access restrictions. He couldn't see it as anything but bad for the eyesight.

Atomic sat alone near the window. She stared in front of her, fingers tapping, a neglected coffee cooling. Her hair was tied up by a complex braid of threads, her make-up colours clashed, and she wore a thin vest and long shorts. A bulky crew-surplus jacket hung on the seat back.

Her eyes blinked and refocused as he sat down. He had two fresh coffees; he pushed one across the table.

'It's good to see you again,' he said before she could say anything, and before he had thought of what to say. Her smile surprised him, but it conveyed detached amusement more than welcome.

'I knew you'd be back,' she said. 'What brings you here this time? Another message from Synchronic?'

'No, no, nothing to do with her. And no message. Just an idea.'

Eyes narrow, seen through a wisp of steam. 'What kind of idea?'

'One that's been kicked about in the crew quarters for a while,' he said. 'You know I got a lot of stick for supporting the embargo, though what I did on the jury kind of offsets that.'

Atomic snorted. 'Not as far as I'm concerned!'

'I know,' he said. 'Anyway, we're all hurting from the

embargo. I am, for sure. By this stage we should be raking in asteroid organics, and construction consultancies and training fees. Some of us were grumbling about all this when somebody pointed out that we can get hold of massive chunks of asteroids and chondrites and cometary dirty ice and so forth, in vacuum and free fall, without going outside the ship.'

'Where?'

'In the reaction-mass tanks in the cones. They're not exactly a reserve, but they're a bit extra over and above what was in the cylinder. They were full at the start, and now they're much depleted, but there's a good bit of rock and ice still in there.'

She gave him a sceptical smile. 'Oh, come on, what does that add up to – a few boulders?'

He pulled over the cold cup, dipped his finger in and drew a triangle on the table, about ten centimetres to a side, and dropped a perpendicular from the apex.

'That has the proportions about right,' he said. 'The sides represent the space that's used around the surface and rear of the cone, for living space and machinery and so on. The perpendicular contains the engine, and more living quarters and amenities. The empty spaces stand for the tank. So we're looking at a conical volume sixty-odd kilometres across the base, less the spaces I mentioned.' He looked up. 'You do the math.' He noticed her gaze go blank. 'I didn't mean literally.'

'How much rock is in there?'

He shrugged. 'Millions of tons. The tanks aren't full up. Maybe a tenth of the volume is solid, the rest vacuum – well, very thin gases. The rocks are kind of piled up against the surfaces the deceleration pressed them against – the top of the forward cone at the front, the base at the rear.'

'You're thinking of us working on them?'

'Yes,' he said. 'Colonise them, if you like. Stake claims. You could build whole habitats, mines, fabrication units, fusion plants. . .'

She breathed in sharply. 'Wow – I can see that, but I can't imagine working or settling on rocks all bumping about—'

'They wouldn't be,' he assured her. 'The first job would be to stabilise them. Move them out a little – you'd get that as a by-product of working them, or we could fire off a tiny acceleration burn on the drive, move the ship in relation to them – then tether them in place with massive buckyropes.' He shrugged. 'Or use attitude jets. It's an engineering detail.'

'But what would be the point? I mean, OK, we could mine them, but what's the point of settling them? Inside the ship? It would be just playing at colonisation.'

'Even if it was it would be good practice,' Horrocks said, 'but they needn't be inside the ship for ever. The cone surface is segmented. Whole sections of it can swing open. That's how the rocks get loaded in the first place.'

'So we could settle and some day . . . move out?'

'You got it.'

She leaned back, gazing above his head. 'That sounds wonderful,' she said. 'So what do we have to do to get this going?'

'Well,' he said, 'like I was saying, it's just an idea that a few of the crew have come up with. I'd want to see it discussed a bit more widely, among the old hands especially. Thrash out the feasibility. And I suppose you'd have to get the Council's blessing, though technically I'm not quite sure if it has standing in regard to the rocks. Raise funding from founder capital, maybe by swapping for other stakes that are . . . at a discount right now. Oh, and I guess you'd have to see if any of the ship generation were interested.'

'You must be joking! They'd jump at it!'

'I've seen a few today who wouldn't.'

She waved an airy hand. 'The slackers? They'll join in too, you'll see, but who cares if they don't? You'll get enough of us going for it, that's for sure.'

'Great!' he said. 'Ah . . .'

'What?'

'There is one drawback. The legal situation.'

'How's that?'

'When we first came up with the idea we checked the Contract.'

'You're telling me it has no provision?'

'Oh, it has a provision all right. Not for this situation, exactly, but it's very specific about who can vote and who can't. About who is in the Complement. Crew, of course. Founders and ship generation over sixteen, as long as they live in the habitat. The habitat, not the ship. It definitely has provision for people moving to nearby celestial bodies in the same orbit. Which applies to the rocks in the tanks.'

'You're saying we'd lose our *votes*?'

'Possibly. Very likely.'

He expected her to baulk or bridle at this, but she just stared off into space for a moment.

'Hmm,' she said at last. 'How many of us could move out in six months?'

'Oh, a few thousand, I should imagine.'

'Ah!' Her face cleared. 'That's all right. There'll still be plenty behind who can vote.'

'You know how they'll vote?'

'Once this gets going – oh yes.'

'Well, I'm sure you know how to spread the word.'

Her face fell a little. 'Yeah. It's just a lot more difficult these days.'

'There's a rumour going around,' he said, 'that the Council is thinking of lifting the comms restrictions.'

'I haven't heard it.'

'It's bandied in the cones.' He drained his cup and rose to leave.

'Do you have to go?'

'Yes,' he said. 'To be honest, this isn't the only place I want to visit. Spread the word in person.'

Her nod was firm, her look a little disappointed. 'Good idea. Come back sometime, OK?'

'Sure.'

When he looked back from the doorway she was already writing.

14 366:02:12 00:17

Haven't written much recently. Nor received many comments. Is anybody still reading this? Is anybody else still *biologging*?

Oh yes. I see you are. Those of you who haven't come out here yet, and are still just talking and planning, planning, planning.

Well, this is for you. I haven't written much because I've been *doing things*. And because it's exhausting out here. It's exhausting but it's fun. It's pioneering. It's what we were born for.

Out here . . . Let me just pause for a moment and clarify a point of terminology. Words are important. I see from a quick search through the biologs that most of you refer to us in the cones as 'in there'. We're not 'in there'. You are: you're in there in the habitat. We're *out here*.

It's not outer space. But it's hard vacuum (well, hard-ish), it's free fall (well, microgravity), and it's black all around. An aperture on the sunline burns in the sky like a nearby sun. The rocks we're working on are hundreds of metres across. Most of them are less than a kilometre apart from each other, so it all looks like a child's cartoon illustration of an asteroid belt rather than the real thing, with millions of klicks between one and the other. It's a bit like being in a Ring, but without the collisions and the ablation and the micrometeorites going like sandblasters and the dying full of holes in a cloud of blood and stuff.

But it's still the real thing. If you want the full illusion of being outside, you can tune your eyes to the external view and see the stars – and those of the planets that are visible at the moment – just as they would be if they were outside your faceplate. That's cool, but admittedly you can do that anywhere in the ship. And somehow, we don't feel the need to. Being in this enormous space is enough.

Because we really are pioneering. These rocks have never even been prospected! If they'd ever had to be processed, they'd have been refined and sifted for useful minerals and organics before the slag was thrown in the drive. But I'm sure a lot would have been missed. Apart from anything else, we're doing real science. These rocks are after all from the Red Sun system, and some of them date back to its formation, and we're actually finding out stuff that I'll bet their own scientists back there haven't got round to yet. Well, maybe not, but it's new to us, and it's fun finding out secrets four billion years old. Delicate crystal formations; complex organic molecules; microscopic bubbles trapped in the rock or ice, of gases with curious isotope ratios; shock patterns that indicate or suggest that at least one rock out here was chipped off a larger body, which some have identified from the records as likely to be Red Sun VII 14.

All right, that's exciting to me, but maybe not to you, and anyway we're not out here to do science. Science is a sideshow. The main event – events, rather – is mining and extracting, synthesising and building. We're building habitats! Real habitats we're actually living in, and that one day – soon, I hope – may orbit freely around the Destiny Star on their own.

Nobody's got the habitat of their dreams. (Mine needs a *much* bigger asteroid.) Everybody has had to divvy up or share. For this rock we're on it's a team: me, Grant, a few people from Far Crossing, and the New Lamarck crowd. Of course there are more machines than people, which makes it feel more crowded but also makes things happen fast. We've already got a beautiful cluster of diamond bubbles that look green from outside with all the plants within.

Nobody's doing the exact project they'd planned. Again, most of these are tagged to specific features or moons or rocks, so they're not relevant at the moment. That doesn't matter. There's a whole lot of projects we're working on with the crew, both because it's valuable experience and because it's trade for the expertise and resources we get from them. (Any accountancy software experts still hesitating? There's work for you out here.)

Oh, and speaking of work, anybody with power-engineering ambitions should just drop everything and emigrate here, because you'll never get a better chance to hone your skills and serve a sound apprenticeship with old crew hands. Fusion power plants aren't strictly necessary here, but they'll be useful in the future. Same goes for missile and laser batteries. We're building plenty of them, there's a whole industry going on (amazing the explosives and fuels you can cook out of gunk from carbonaceous chondrites, and the reaction and refinery paths are way complex and cool). They'll be sold around when we move out. Likewise the power plants. Like I said, the opportunities in that line are amazing.

We are building a *lot* of fusion power plants.

It had been a long three months for the Red Sun Circle and its associates. For a time the entire scheme had hung in the balance, with the more energetic elements of the younger generation divided between those who most wanted to get on with constructive work, and those whose top priority was ending the emergency and voting out the Council. Synchronic wasn't sure how much effect her care-daughter's passionate appeals for the former option had had, but she couldn't discount them.

Now, the stream of young settlers to the hollow spaces of both cones was steady; the lifting of comms restrictions had allowed first an outpouring of discontent and then its gradual fading; and among the majority of the voting-age cohort who remained behind, a growing minority had begun to voice a grudging recognition of the wisdom of the founders in vetoing colonisation until future relations with the aliens could be sorted out.

Her one disappointment was that almost all the ship generation had lost all interest in the Destiny II virtualities now that they no longer had a live feed. The archives of the virtualities were vast, and in large part unexplored. An immense amount of information of undeniable future use lay untapped. She'd expected that this hoard of insight into the very first alien civilisation – and indeed multicellular biosphere – to come within the ken of humanity would lure many bright young minds. But few indeed still entered it. It was as though it was old news, and that only the constant unfolding of the planet's present moment could seize attention.

She'd have been tempted to write this off as the superficiality of the youth of today, but her own contemporaries in the founder generation were almost as remiss. They too were entranced by incoming live data, in their case from other planetary probes and system surveys. Speculation on resources remained brisk, though with long futures. There was even a market in shorter futures, betting on the possibility that the embargo would be reversed; Council discouragement and disapproval of this dubious activity had merely and predictably given rise to secondary and tertiary markets in moral hazard.

So she herself had taken to doing what she'd once hoped the ship generation would become absorbed in doing. In hours of relaxation and recreation she roamed the vault of uplinked and recorded and synthesised impressions, trying to make sense of the bat people's world.

Today she haunted the simulacrum of an upland settlement, somewhere in the typical altiplano of the continental hinterlands. Scrub and brush on the hills, a richer and greener vegetation in the hollows that might have been the local analogue of grass, grazed by the big four-footed beasts. A narrow, rickety tower on a hilltop, surrounded by fenced and hedged orchards and a scatter of low sheds. You couldn't call the place a farm: the bat people didn't practise agriculture. They tended tiny plots of herbs and berries; they built fences and walls that kept the grazers out of patches of ground, wherein fruit trees sprang up, with parabolic inverted-umbrella layers of branches turned to the sky like some ancient SETI radio-telescope array; they herded and hunted, chivvied and chased the grazers, swooping and hallooing around them, driving them with slashing clawed kicks and occasional bites that looked like a vampiric refreshment. When a beast was selected for slaughter, and driven close to the settlement and set upon with tooth and claw and blade, the crowd of wings and the frenzy was such that it seemed a surprise how much meat remained to be cut up and carried off, to be hung and salted and smoked and sent on its way to the cities on the occasional passing cart hauled by machine or slave traction.

She rotated the POV and drifted it towards the shed that she guessed was the slave pen. As the door came closer – it was wooden, the lower half of solid planking, the top barred – the POV fell through a sudden and disconcerting rift.

Her viewpoint was now behind the bars, looking out. The time of day, perhaps the day itself or even the season had changed. The shadows looked shorter, the hillside scrub thicker than they had a moment ago. The quality of the image had sharpened, had become more detailed, dense with verity. It was as if she looked directly upon a real scene, rather than a seamless but speculative construction stitched together from numerous flaky, tiny inputs. The sound quality had improved too: she heard a sound like breathing, louder and closer than the grassy arboral hiss of the upland wind that carried the lowing of far-off alien kine.

And, as if from around a corner, voices.

High-pitched and fast but with almost recognisable syllables, quite other than the bat people's chirruping patter.

As she strained to hear, the view before her tipped forward and filled with a crossbar and a pair of four-digited hands. The hands, encumbered about the wrists with a sort of ragged fleshy sleeve, squeezed between the bars and twisted around with a disregard to their own damage that made her flinch. Blood slicked the boards. There was a grunt, and then a rattle and squeal of metal, and a hard rap.

The hands were wrenched back through the slats. For a second or so her gaze fixed upon raised wrists, scratched and scored, spiked with splinters, bleeding back to the elbow. Then the wrists reversed and the hands slammed forward, thrusting the door open with a thud. The POV rushed straight ahead, jolting as if from a camera on the forehead or shoulder of someone running. Trampled mud, grass, a ring of cyan fungi, a fence looming, a leap and a frantic scrabble—

A shout from behind.

'Hey – the trudge is out!'

'After him!'

Before Synchronic could assimilate her shock at understanding the words, her vision became a confused, blurred rolling as the viewpoint topped the fence and fell down the other side, then more running.

Then wings, a glint of teeth, a clawed foot jammed straight into the viewpoint. A flurry and a welter. Sky and a sunlight flash on a downward-stabbing blade. A long, deep, full-throated scream that ended on a rising, resonant pitch, as if a soul had streaked upward to the bright, blank blue that was the last image to fill its sight.

Darkness and silence.

SIXTEEN

THE ANOMALIES ROOM

Kraighor, the capital of Seloh's Reach, lay a long way around the coast from Five Ravines. Darvin had been there once, when he'd been a little kit, and his memories of it were an unstable mix of the vivid and the vague. Loud streets, sharp tastes, a smell of burning coal, a high and roost-encrusted hill, trees with dark and twisted leaves. He and his parents had arrived by cable-car from inland, and it was his memories of the station that he felt were reliable: if it hadn't changed much he could still find his way around it. The city itself was a blur.

This time he travelled there alone, and by the coastal packet steamer. It made the trip every three days; the voyage took from the early morning of one day to noon of the next, with three or four stops at small ports along the way. Such halts gave the passengers – about an eight-of-eights – a welcome opportunity to stretch their wings; flying off the side of the boat was discouraged, because of the danger of falling behind. Tedium, motion sickness, yelling kits, sleeping-racks in which everyone swayed and bumped into each other like ill-matched pendulums, salted meat and bruised fruit, travelling salesmen who liked to talk . . . Darvin took with him plenty of reading matter.

The physics wire offprints were there to salve his conscience. The bulk of the papers he stacked on the slopped table of the steamer's saloon came from an eight-days' worth of the press of the town and the Reach. The local sheet, *The Eye on Five*, had been first with the story of the Southerners' communiqué, which had been picked up a day later by the weighty Kraighor *Voice* and its popular counterpart, *The Day*. As he traced the story through the pages, Darvin found none of the reactions he'd have predicted, in part – he had to admit to himself – on the basis of his adolescent reading of engineering tales.

Scepticism hadn't so much as twitched an eyebrow. All of the papers reported the Southerners' story as serious and probably true. The Height had made no public comment as yet, but Darvin suspected that an official word had come down. Panic and hysteria had remained in their roosts, with barely a flutter. The news of the alien presence in the system was treated as Ground-shaking and portentous, but as an occasion for sober vigilance rather than alarm. Priests of the cults – who, to Darvin's exasperation, were quoted as often as scientists – had hailed it as confirmation of the ancient dogmas of life's plurality and the Queen's fecundity. He himself was quoted too; having been referenced in the Southerners' brochure, he could hardly avoid it; he had suffered several interviews, in which he'd presented the facts about his discovery, and no opinions. The government's secrecy and continued silence on the subject was ascribed to caution and wisdom rather than any sinister purpose. Where worry was expressed, it was about not the aliens but Gevork. No persecution of Southerners had broken out, nor any suspicion fallen on the luckless trudges; at least, none that the press saw fit to report. This was consistent with his own experience, if not with his initial fears: Darvin had heard nothing from Orro, and his handler for the Sight had said nothing untoward at his most recent contact.

The engineering tales were false. That hadn't stopped the most popular pulp in Five Ravines, *Other Worlds*, from rushing a special edition into print so fast that the ink still smelled sweet and fresh on the page, like honey-gum. The cover pirated the pictures on the Southern pamphlet and headlined a story whose title, 'Invasion from Infinity!', bore witness to a brash disdain of doing right as much as a blithe contempt for having being proved wrong. Darvin noted the depiction of the invaders as giant wingless humanoids. He felt an irritated temptation to draw the Sight's attention to it as evidence of a security lapse, more for the discomfiture this would inflict on the reckless editor than because it mattered. But he put away the unworthy impulse before he slept.

The ship rounded the eastern headland of Kraighor Bay under a high sun. Airships speckled the sky. His keen first glimpse of the city disappointed Darvin. Between the harbour and the foot of the central Mount most of it lay under a yellowish haze from which only the upper storeys of the taller buildings stood out. The Mount itself rose clear above it, crusted with the Height. The lower levels of that tall, spreading, ramshackle edifice were of stone, the upper and more recent of wood, almost as raw as scaffolding, a structure always growing and never finished, stone replacing wood from below as in a tree that calcified as it grew. The analogy of form and function had been a gift to satirists and a cliché of cartoonists.

As the ship drew closer the smell of waste fumes from the rock-oil distillate that fuelled the numerous motor-vehicles became so pervasive that the keenest nose lost all sensitivity to it, and only the throat felt it, like grit. Darvin was so eager to get off the ship that he abandoned his papers and took wing a minute's flight from the shore. He alighted coughing on the quay, pushed his way through waiting passengers – the ship would continue down the coast, to return the following morning – dodged the importunities of cab-drivers and trudge-handlers, and stalked into the city. He made his way to his destination by several stops of a cable-trolley, a flight across a park, and a short walk, following a route he cribbed from a map he'd been told to burn. Where the Sight's headquarters were he did not know, but he knew that the office to which he'd been directed was not it.

As he walked down a back street towards that address it occurred to him, not for the first time, that he might be heading into trouble: a debriefing with prejudice, as the Sight cant went. But short of turning back, there was nothing to be done. The entrance he sought was above a row of victuallers' shops, not of the best quality. Flies buzzed in air haunted by the smells of meat that had hung too long, of fruit that was past ripe, and of dried herbs gone damp. Shopkeepers eyed Darvin through drifts of laughterburn, bored. He sprinted his last few steps, rose a few wingbeats, turned and swooped to the door. It opened, as instructed, without a knock.

Inside, he found a broad corridor of fresh-painted wood, whose far end opened on a balcony above a courtyard. He could see daylight and a tree. Along the corridor suspended electric globes every few spans cast a clear cold light. On each side of the corridor were four doors, marked with the names of obscure commercial properties: import-export agencies, brokerages and the like. He knocked on the third left. It opened a little and an elderly woman peered around it.

'Come in,' she said. She had red fur and a dappled chest. 'You must be the famous Darvin.'

He nodded. 'And you?'

'Arrell,' she said, after a moment's pause.

The room was long and wide, windowless and brightly

lit. Shelves lined its walls. Racks interrupted the aisles between tables, over which the bright lights hung. Eight and two people worked there, most turning great stacks of newspapers and journals into scissored heaps of waste paper and small neat files of clippings. Others processed letters and notes from (Darvin guessed) informants. Four of the people were middle-aged or older, the rest young. A teleprinter machine clattered in a far corner. Here and there, telephones flashed rather than rang, and were answered at once. Tea braziers smouldered and pots bubbled. It was a place where much leaf was chewed.

'Welcome to the Anomalies Room,' said Arrell. 'Tea?'

'Thank you,' said Darvin. He looked around, marvelling. 'Has the Sight always done this?'

'You should know better than to ask,' said Arrell, threading her way between tables. 'But since you do,' she added over her shoulder, 'yes. But not on this scale. This is our new office — with, as you see, some new staff.'

As he followed her Darvin glanced at the words lettered on the open boxes into which the researchers placed their clippings or reports; these he glimpsed: *Sky. Water. Weather. Lights. Signs. Ground. Imponderables. Wonders. Powers. Dust. Falls. Foreigners. Monsters. Unusual Acts. Mental.*

The system of classification eluded him.

'I regret,' Arrell said, over tea, 'that you couldn't tell us your area of interest.'

'It was something I didn't want to mention on the phone.'

Arrell laughed. 'Who but the Sight would be listening?'

'Good question.'

She looked back at him with a minute increment of respect. 'True,' she said. 'So, what is it?'

'Trudges,' said Darvin. 'Unusual behaviour of.'

'See under "Monsters",' said Arrell.

She led him to a small table to one side and left, to return with a deep cardboard box, so heavy that he sprang to help her. The thump of box on table made people look up and frown.

'The file has grown,' she said. She reached up and pulled a cord to switch on the table's overhead light. 'Let me know if you need anything.'

The question of the trudges had preyed on Darvin's mind ever since Lenoen had raised it. He had no one to talk with about it except Kwarive. He didn't *want* to talk with anyone else about it. If anything could create the kind of mass panic that the news of aliens hadn't, it had to be this. He himself had begun to give every trudge he passed a wary glance, and now and again had seen, or imagined he'd seen, a spark of thought or anger in their eyes. One day he looked back at such a trudge, to find that the trudge had turned its head to look back at him. That moment he had decided on the course that had brought him here.

The box was divided by loose cardboard partitions. Almost half had one for each outer-month, with the cuttings stacked vertically between them. There were already eight and one of them, taking the record back to the previous year. The other section was of everything from before that year, and thin stuff it was, though it went back many years and made up most of the bulk. Why the Sight had kept track of curious events for all that time Darvin didn't know, but he could guess. It had nothing to do with a scrying of portents; it was that the circulation of strange tales and rumours gave clues to the popular mood: ripples of anxiety or hysteria, cold, deep currents of belief and doubt.

In that early archival section he found a handful of trudge oddities: instances of albinism, of wingless freaks (there had been some speculation that the acquired characteristic was becoming inherited; Kwarive would have smiled); of travelling

performers who showed off trudges capable of counting or
other unusual feats; of nests and entire colonies of feral flying
trudges that had reverted to their ancestral physique and mode
of life. None mentioned the use of speech, though some
claimed understanding. Most of the reports were of sports
thrown up by other breeds of domestic beast – he lost count of
two-headed calves – and of sightings in the wild: sea snakes,
lake lizards, mysterious man-like beings of the mountains or
deserts, great winged things in the sky. That there were
unknown species in the world Darvin didn't doubt, and
Kwarive had told him of a growing interest among biologists
in mutants, which some thought had a bearing on questions of
evolution; but most of this was most likely clutter: misper-
ception and misreporting, rumours hardened to fact and
become precedent and template for others, and downright
hoaxes and lies.

He sighed, wiped dust and ink from his fingers, and pro-
ceeded to the more recent files. The parade of monsters was
now longer and weirder, capering across his inner vision and
gibbering. He dismissed all but the odd trudges, who were
present in the parade in force.

A veterinary surgeon had lost an eye when a trudge kit had
lashed out with its foot when its turn came to be spayed.
Another kit had screamed 'No!' when its wings were slashed,
had gone into a decline and died. An old woman who lived
alone had been found strangled by powerful hands; suspicion
had fallen on her (now missing) trudge. A trudge in an upland
farm had unlocked its stable door, and had had to be stabbed
by the farmer and his boy as it fled across the meadows. A
second-generation (it was thought) feral trudge, wings
unslashed, had haunted the skies above a back-country village
for many a night, evading nets and dodging cross-bolts.
Mutilated carcasses of cattle had littered the vicinity.

That was in the first outer-month. Albeit that the reports

came from all over Seloh and Gevork, and one (the strangling, recounted by a returned sailor) from the Southern Rule, it was a troubling tally. Over the next eight outer-months it increased, not month by month, but overall.

He leaned back and stared up at the ceiling mats, where tiny skitters ran upside down with sticky toes, catching mat-bugs in long looped tongues. The real world was wonder enough, and seemed light-years distant from the crazy tales he'd read.

The woman Arrell's face loomed above him. He rocked forward.

'Finished?' she asked.

'For now,' said Darvin. 'May we talk?' He tipped his head back a little.

She nodded. 'Outside.'

She led him down the corridor to another door, which opened to a small office. Flat panels of float-bark covered the walls. The room had more light fixtures than seemed necessary. Arrell switched on two of them, perched at the back of a desk, and motioned Darvin to a seat.

'We call this the interview room,' she said, with a slight smile.

'For debriefings with prejudice?'

'Yes. It's not as sinister as you may have heard. Be that as it may, you're assured of privacy.'

'All right,' said Darvin. 'What I must ask you first is: how much analysis do you make of all these reports? How does the Sight handle them?'

'In ancient times,' said Arrell, 'Anomalies was a department of divination. Today it remains a small but significant element of statecraft . . . I'm sure you understand why.'

'To gauge the susceptibility of the populace to rumours and alarms?'

'Not at all!' said Arrell, sounding surprised at the suggestion. 'Because the Sight needs to know about all unusual and untoward events. We sift the dross for nuggets. To take some banal examples: a mysterious flying light could be a Gevorkian airship; a strange man of the mountains an infiltrator or a rebel; a sea-snake the wake of an unseen ship.'

'But – two-headed monsters!'

She shrugged. 'A new disease? A false rumour? It doesn't matter. The Sight wants to know of it.'

'What do you make of this year's increase in unusual events involving trudges, then?'

'I don't try to interpret,' she said. 'My job – our job, rather – is to summarise, tabulate, and report.'

'So this matter has been reported?'

'Among others. Monster tales are many this year.'

'Why?'

'Why? Well. In my experience, any one strange event results in many spurious reports. One Gevorkian airship over the coast, whose presence we can confirm independently, gives rise to a double-eight of sightings from leagues around, from places that could not have seen it, and could not have heard of it at the time. Rumour flies faster than sound, as the saying goes.'

'Or is backdated in recollection?'

'That too.' The creases around her eyes quirked. 'What is your theory about the trudges, by the way?'

He didn't know how much she knew about the project. Possibly she had never heard of the ether-wave emissions from insects and trees. It was not his place to tell her.

'I think,' he said, 'that something connected to the event has begun to increase the intelligence of some of them.'

She didn't quite conceal her surprise.

'How could that happen?'

'I don't know,' he said. 'But I would very much appreciate it if you were to bring all such reports to the specific attention of the higher ranks.'

'Of course,' she said. 'Anything else, before you go?'

'I understand,' he said, 'that the Sight, at times, finds it necessary for the security and stability of the Reach to . . . discourage public discussion of certain matters. I submit that this trudge business may be one of them.'

'I'll pass your suggestion upward,' she said. 'Will that be all?'

It was the second hint. He saw himself out.

Late-afternoon sunlight slanted through the heights and roosts. The first stirrings of the evening breeze off the Mount and the range behind Kraighor had begun to shift the day's haze offshore. More people eddied among the shops and stalls, and the street didn't smell so stale. As Darvin walked among them he felt his sense of himself shift, like the flip of a blink comparator, from lowly agent of the Sight to visitor to the capital, a free man with time on his hands. The city had a great and fine university. Its department of astronomy was a place he had long intended to see. His reputation now preceded him. He could be sure of a welcome, even at this hour, and a convivial evening. The dining-hall would be ample, the alcohol-laden fruit abundant, the laughterburn mellow, the talk stimulating. It was all there, a few stops away on the North-East Cable.

He considered it, and reckoned it would be an opportunity missed. He could meet scholars and students any day of the eight. The city's temples, the complex, piled-up stone roost of the Height, the maze of back streets – these he had to see. He turned away from the thoroughfare and headed back along the side street, deeper into the city.

Clinging with both feet to a rattling cable-bar that squealed for lack of oil, Darvin turned his head from the swaying bodies

likewise suspended in front of him on this cheapest of trans-
ports and peered down at the market beneath his nose. A few
stalls of cheap domestic stuff: mats, burners, brushes. Not
worth a look, and in any case packing up. It was the end of the
day's third quarter, the hour halfway between noon and midnight, the time when people headed home. There was a
peculiar division in the transport. Tired workers from the
shops and factories clogged the cable-bars and trolleys; civil
servants from the Height darkened the sky, welcoming the
chance to stretch their wings after a hard day behind the desk.
Darvin had in just the past hour roamed the perimeter of the
edifice, which he'd reached by cable-car. He'd watched the
regular wheelings of the sabreurs of Seloh's Guard, and the
comings and goings of airships at the skeletal copse of mooring-masts on the slope below. The Height was a busy place,
but how much of its activity represented something real, and
how much really symbolic, was another matter.

The cable-bar swung over a square puddled with yellow
lights around trees, tables and stalls. Smells of tea and stumblefruit wafted up. A few workers in the line ahead of him,
who had dozed, feet reflex-locked to the bars, jolted awake and
let go, gliding down. Darvin followed. The momentum of the
cable's rush carried him forward as his back flexed upward and
his wings braced. Down he spiralled. Tiny green spear-points
of new growth bristled the dusty trees. He alighted on cobbles
and strolled to a tea-bar. There was room for his feet at the
perch and for his elbows at the counter. The serving-girl was
bright and brisk. A trudge squatted just beyond the end of the
counter, leashed to the leg of the stall and gnawing on a bone
while its master drank with friends at an adjacent table. Some
people at the counter talked and laughed; others, solitary like
Darvin, sipped in silence.

From a nearby temple the sound of many voices singing
echoed: there was a trick they had, of concentrating the sound

by focusing the crowded singers' wings. Darvin listened to the hymn with a mixture of enjoyment of its beauty and disdain of its content. He was no scoffer: at the sight of the galaxy, Deity seemed the most evident and insistent of deductions. Like most astronomers, he was devout. Like almost all, he had no truck with the cults. It was not only that they still held a grudge against astronomy, the science that had stolen heaven from their very hands, though the more enlightened were ever eager to honey-gum the antique myths in symbolism. For the priests, one god was never enough, nor a good life a sufficient offering. For them there had to be sacrifices, conducted with sickles and herbs at the new moons and knives and calves at the new year; and songs at evening and morning.

Varlun, a noted philosopher of the Dawn Age, who had lived three eights-of-eights of years ago in Gevork, had written of the passages from day to night, and night to day. At night, he wrote in his essay, 'What is Dawn?', the starry skies above told you all you needed to know about the might and mind of Deity. By day, the Sun's kindly warmth told you all you needed to know of its creator's goodness. And in the evening hours and in the dawn the promptings, indeed at times the pains, of conscience told you all you needed to know of right and wrong. For this the priests had had him locked up for seven years.

Darvin examined his conscience for stirrings and found nothing that pricked. His unease about the trudges had ceased to be a moral pang and become a practical concern. How different, he wondered, would life be if there had been no trudges? No tractable, versatile beast to do the heavy and dirty work? Some engineering tales had speculated on that. Sometimes they averred that the art of invention would have developed faster, culminating in a society little different from that of today, but with two-legged, two-armed machines in the place of trudges; for some tales of the future such machines had become a part of the furniture. Others, darker and more daring, had made the blunt point that if there had been no trudges to bear the load, some men would have been forced to bear it, slashed and lashed, leashed and chained, some gelded and spayed. And as that came to revolt the conscience, or became too clumsy a method to work in manufacture, why then they would have been turned loose, and hunger having taken the place of all other inducement, they would have done the same work for pay. The usual refinement of such tales was in finding ingenious ways to exclude the freed human trudges from nature's bounty of fruit and prey. The crudest involved enormous fences and aerial barriers; the subtlest, debt.

None had given thought to what a future without trudges would be like; a future that did not begin with a convenient mechanical analogue to take the trudges' place.

Darvin stayed at that counter for three-quarters of an hour, drinking two glasses of tea, his ear cocked to conversations. He heard not a word about trudges or aliens, Gevorkians or Southerners. Gossip and shop talk, and the party politics of the Reach. He moved on when he became convinced that the trudge tethered to the stall was listening too.

'Bahron! Arrell!'

Bahron sprang towards him and clapped him on the shoulder.

'In the name of the Sun and the Queen,' the Eye hissed in his ear, 'shut the fuck up. We aren't called that around here.'

'Oh. Sorry.' Darvin heard his apology coming out slurred. He'd had one too many stumblefruits.

'What'll you have?' asked Bahron, louder.

'A sharp fruit, thanks.'

'Coming down,' said Bahron. He shoved Darvin towards a table. 'Talk to the lady.'

Darvin sat down so hard it hurt his buttocks. 'Hello.'

'A whiff, I think,' said Arrell.

She waved under his nose a smoking bowl of laughterburn. Darvin inhaled. On the instant the world became lucid and wondrous. Stars flickered in the gaps between tree branches. Rings of poisonous-looking fungi probed up from ground littered with leaves and rinds. He was in a stumblefruit orchard in the university area, to which his ramble had, quite without conscious intent, taken him.

'So much for avoiding scholars and students,' he said.

She didn't get it, but Bahron, returning with three small ripe fruits, did.

'Hah!' he said, sitting down. 'Been trying to pick up clues to the popular mood, have we?'

'Yes.'

'Not your job,' Bahron said. 'But I don't doubt you've done it well. Let's see now . . .' He bit into the fruit and let the juice dribble into his upturned mouth. 'Ah, that's better. You heard very little about the subjects on your mind, but what you did hear told you that people are pretty sceptical about this so-called alien craft, think the claim about it is some kind of manoeuvre by our friends in the South, and if they're worried about anything beyond their own troubles, it's Gevork. Trudges? Far from becoming smarter, all you've heard is the odd grumble about how some trudge or other is acting even more stupid and recalcitrant than usual.'

Darvin almost choked on his own first sip of the bitter juice.

'Exactly!' he spluttered. 'How did you know?'

He had the sudden, embarrassing suspicion that the Sight had been tracking him ever since he'd left its secret offices.

'From the letters column of *The Day*,' said Bahron. He waved his hand over the smouldering bowl, inhaled, and regarded Darvin with narrowed eyes through the smoke he breathed out. 'A lesson, eh, astronomer?'

Darvin laughed. 'Lesson learned,' he said.

'Cab-drivers are another useful source,' said Arrell.

'I don't suppose,' Darvin said, 'you have any idea when we are going to get, you know, some definite view from the Height?'

Bahron ran a finger-claw up and down the side of his nose. 'Watch the skies, astronomer,' he said. 'Watch the skies.'

Later that evening Darvin noticed a public telephone near the orchard's exit. When she was on her own Kwarive had the habit of working late in the museum annexe. Sometimes she even slept there. It seemed like a good idea to call her. Darvin fumbled for coins and fed them in, connected to the operator and told him the number of the room. After much clicking and clunking the call went through.

'Hello?' Kwarive's voice sounded sleepy.

'Hello, it's me.'

'You woke me up. Is everything all right?'

'Yes, everything's fine. I just wanted to hear your voice.'

'You're juiced, Darvin.'

'Well, yes, but—'

At that point the line went noisy with a buzz that became louder. Darvin held the earpiece away and looked at it. The connections seemed secure. He could still hear the noise. He recalled how the electric shittles had been detected, and glanced around, half expecting to see one nearby. A trudge walked past, wheeling a barrow of stumblefruit gourds. The buzz peaked and faded.

Shocked back to sobriety, Darvin returned the receiver to his ear.

'What was that?' Kwarive asked.

'Nothing, darling,' Darvin said. 'Just some interference. Look, my coins are running out. Good night. I'll see you the day after tomorrow.'

'You mean tomorrow,' said Kwarive. 'It's after midnight. Good night. Sleep well.'

'You too.'

He hung up the receiver and walked back to the table. Bahron and Arrell were licking the stickiness off their hands and clearly getting ready to leave.

'Everything all right at home?' Bahron asked.

'Yes,' said Darvin. 'Everything's fine.'

Darvin spent the night in a cheap lodging – little more than a bowl to wash in and a rack to hang from – and at dawn, wakened by a pre-arranged and persistent telephone, waited at the quay for the return packet. The sky was red and the air was cold. Trudges lugged packages and bales to the quayside. None of the trudges showed a glint of intelligence, but, Darvin reflected, nor did many of the humans there. He doubted that he did so himself.

The steamer rounded the western headland. As he gazed at it, Darvin's attention was caught by a golden gleam high in the sky, far out above the Broad Channel. It came from the low sun reflected off an airship, a big one, moving fast in the morning wind off the sea. After a few minutes, and long before the steamer had crossed half the bay, the dirigible was in plain sight, sinking towards Kraighor. On its underside at the front was a greenish dot, which Darvin knew to be the blue and green roundel of Gevork. The steady note of the airship's engines sounded from the sky.

A louder, harsher throb came from the air in the shoreward direction. Darvin heard shouts. He turned and looked up, and shouted too.

Four flying machines with double wings passed overhead. They looked like the aeroplanes he had imagined, and the experimental airframes Orro had described. Painted on their red wings was the black claw of the Reach. A thrill shook Darvin from head to foot. Nobody here, he was sure, was as amazed as he.

The four craft buzzed seaward and climbed with a rising snarl to meet the descending Gevorkian. They passed it and turned around, sunlight flashing off their tilting wings. Their engine note changed, like that of a motor-car throttling back. Two above, two below, they took position on either side of the airship and escorted it down. They looked like flitters beside a grazer, but that was a matter of mere size: the relatively tiny machines gave an impression of concentrated power that the vast wallowing gasbag couldn't begin to match. Even their engines were louder.

The aircraft passed overhead again, the four aeroplanes pacing the dirigible as it dived towards the mooring-masts high on the Mount. A cheer rose from the quay, and from the esplanade, and from the houses round about. The steamer left a half-hour late that day.

SEVENTEEN

FIRE IN THE SKY

'You did *what?*'

Not in five hundred years had Synchronic felt such fury. Her hands shook and the world darkened in her sight. Constantine looked back at her with a calm she was certain he would not have dared to affect if his presence before her had been physical.

'Reverse-engineered from the language module,' he repeated.

Synchronic's hands mimed strangling him. Shocked, she calmed herself with several deep breaths and a moment of flash meditation. This could be dealt with. This disaster was not irrecoverable. This was not beyond her power. She could get on top of this. They all could.

Futile rage gave way to urgent enquiry.

'How?' she asked. 'How is that *possible?*' The anger again. Another moment of the hard-learned mental discipline. Calm.

'Quantum-level effects,' he said. He shrugged, waggling his spread hands, palms down. 'Crew scientists, you know what they're like. I don't claim to understand it. I'm told it's a refinement of brain interface techniques. If that helps.'

"'If – that – helps!'"

Brain interface techniques indeed! I'll give you brain interface, you arrogant fool! Her brain interface was right now transmitting all she saw and heard to her fellow members of the Circle, and thereby to the Council, on which two of its members sat. Anger flared and calm restored. She returned a serene gaze to the spectre in the sunny garden. She had to keep it this way. They were sharing information. They were solving a problem together. Constantine was not on trial. *Not yet.*

She reviewed what he had told her, replaying the words and sentences her anger had whited out and shouted down the first time.

The problem, the intellectual problem, was this. No Rosetta Stone existed for the bat people's language. No amount of observation, no iteration of linguistic heuristics, could decode an unknown language from recordings alone. For mutual understanding, there had to be mutual interaction. One had to know directly what one side of the conversation was trying to say, and that meant one side of it had to be you. Faced with this impasse, the crew's scientists had, in all too characteristic a fashion, worked around it. Their solution had all the grubby fingerprints of a brute-force kludge.

The neural structure of the human brain's language-processing module, named in deep antiquity Chomsky's Conceit, had been known since the Caves. The genetic code of the Destiny II biosphere was known from aerial micro-organisms returned to the stealth orbiter. The amount of information and genetic instruction that could be packed in a nano-assembler was vaster by far than even the vast amount stored in natural genomes and machinery, cluttered as they were with redundancy and junk. The information processing hardware capacity of the ship was beyond all human conception, and the amount of information its science software could extract from the slenderest and most fragile of evidence was limited only by the ingenuity of the human enquiry that initiated it.

So . . . they'd had the means to install Chomsky's Conceit on any big enough brain down below. They'd had the means to generate radio transmitters within host bodies, as they'd done with the dung beetles. And faced with the crash-and-burn and banning of that project, they'd skipped blithely ahead to a bolder one. They couldn't install Chomsky's Conceit on the brains of bat people – the aliens' brains already had a language module of their own. That would have given rise to wetware conflicts and deep grammar errors, and anyway, ethically, that would never have done. Oh no. That would have been wrong. That would have *interfered*. What they had done, bless their reckless little souls, was to set up the machinery to install the module on the brains of the *slaves*, who had (they'd figured) no language module (and who were, therefore, not slaves but beasts). And once they'd received and filtered and processed and quantum-handwaved the information coming back from brains *learning* the bat people's languages, the translation protocols had been –

Reverse-engineered from the language module!

Holy rocking shit.

It was turning into a big day for flash meditation. Much more of this and she might attain flash enlightenment.

'You realise what you've done?' she demanded. 'Do you have the faintest conception of the harm this will cause?'

Constantine nodded. 'The disruption will be immense. It'll destroy the entire slave economy.'

'But they're *not* slaves!' Synchronic said. 'If they had been, I could see why we might want to interfere. But you've taken what are by your own admission mute brutes, and given them language. Deep grammar. Self-awareness. Human consciousness. You've *made* them slaves.'

'Yes,' said the Oldest Man. 'Slaves that will try to free themselves.'

Synchronic had already shown him the breakout she had witnessed. She flashed him a pointer to the file.

'Like *that?*' she said. 'When these poor creatures become aware of what they are and what has been done to them, they will suffer terribly. They will flee, they will fight – kill their owners . . .'

Constantine agreed again. 'That may all happen,' he said. 'The owners have it coming.'

Synchronic just stared at him. 'How can you say that? How can you be so destructive?'

'We didn't do this to be destructive,' said Constantine. 'We did it to reduce suffering, and to increase intelligence.'

'The suffering of brutes? When did that become urgent?'

'The last time I visited you,' said Constantine, 'you were showing the kids the meat and milk machine. Why don't we just raise and slaughter cattle?'

'Hah!' said Synchronic. 'Convenience.'

'No moral reason? Perhaps a mere shudder of distaste, a fastidiousness we can afford. Very well. I can still tell you that these brutes suffer, whether they're conscious of it or not. They are treated with cruelty and disdain. Their situation is much worse than that of the grazing animals the bat people prey on. These are predators and prey after all, it's a natural relationship and the beasts have natural lives. The relationship between the bat people and their related species is nothing like that. It's artificial, it's unnatural, it's wicked and it's got to stop.'

'As no doubt it will,' said Synchronic, 'in a few decades when we've made contact. By then, they might have invented robots for themselves. They're an inventive lot.'

'Indeed they are,' said Constantine. 'Well, we are not willing to wait a few decades. We're here now, we have the means to stop the suffering, and therefore the duty to act.'

'For all you know, the bat people might be able to *keep* them in slavery. I'm sure they'll come up with all kinds of rationalisations, if the human precedent is anything to go by.'

'Then they're no worse off, and they have the benefit of intelligence and language to help them escape or resist.'

'That poor thing I heard called a trudge didn't exactly *benefit*, from what I saw and you saw.'

'Oh no?' said Constantine. 'It lived five minutes as a free man. That's five minutes more than it would ever have had without us.'

Synchronic was astonished at the ruthlessness of that argument. It was so outrageous and unexpected that she couldn't begin to answer it. She concentrated instead on the appalled promptings now pouring in from her allies.

'Even if we grant everything you say,' she said, 'why did you and the scientists not take this to the Council?'

'It would never have passed. You would never have permitted it. So we did it without asking your permission.'

'That's outright rebellion!'

'Is it? There's been no ruling on it. It isn't a contact. It's surveillance, but a different project from the one that I had stopped.'

'It's more than a contact. It's an intervention!'

'An intervention, without contact, doesn't break the letter of the law.'

'We'll see about that!'

Constantine shrugged. 'It's a fait accompli. You would do better to consider ways to limit the damage.'

'We most certainly will,' said Synchronic. 'Just as you did with the beetles.'

The ambiguity of the remark seemed to escape him.

'You can abort the transmitters, yes,' said Constantine. 'You can't burn out the new neural structures. And you can't stop the nano-infection spreading. We made sure of that.'

'How?'

'The assemblers don't have self-destruct mechanisms. So the only way you can limit the damage is to intervene before the whole situation gets out of hand – a servile insurrection, a massacre of the slaves, or more likely, both.'

'I know what this is about!' Synchronic said. 'It has nothing to do with concern for the brutes! It's all about the interests of the crew. You want to bounce us into making contact, because then you can go ahead with your projects.'

'Believe that if you like, my lady,' said Constantine. He grinned. 'Look on the bright side. When you make contact, you'll at least be able to talk to them.'

Synchronic said nothing. She was scanning the Contract in ship memory for an arcane legal term that had just become relevant. Ah, there it was.

The word was *arrest*.

The all-hands call brayed through Horrocks' brain and woke him with a jolt that set him bouncing off the elastic mesh of the free fall hammock. Genome woke in the same way, with the same result. She grabbed him on their second collision.

'What's happening?'

'I don't know.' The conditioned reflexes of emergency training overrode everything. 'Suit up! Suit up!'

He thumbnailed the hammock open and they both dived to the opposite corners where their spacesuits were stashed. Into the loose garment feet-first, close it, hood over head and faceplate sealed. It took five seconds and felt like longer. They had both been drilled in this since childhood; for their final crew qualification, in explosive decompression and the dark. But as the suit hardened around him, going from the look of loose cloth to the feel of metal and glass, Horrocks could see nothing wrong. The room and the lights were normal, no alarm sounded, and the suit monitors were nominal.

In the corner of his eye the crew circuit light flashed. He chinned the pick-up.

'All available crew to the reserve tanks! If you think you're not available, check the following list of exemptions . . .'

He didn't need to look at the list scrolling down the corner of his eye to know he wasn't on it.

'. . . Everybody else – to the tanks!'

Virtual tags guided them as they kicked, drifted, strap-hanged and just plain got carried along to the nearest mass airlock. The lock could cycle a hundred through at a time. They had to wait three cycles, and still the press behind them piled up. Still nobody knew what was going on. Wild theories flashed around: a collision, a viral outbreak, an accident. All that was known for certain, because queries were flying back and forth the length of the ship, was that a similar scramble was going on in the rearward cone.

Horrocks and Genome stayed together in the crush inside the airlock, and together in the surge out. For three months they had lived and worked together; the training-habitat business had boomed as more and more of the ship generation had chosen the confined but real opportunity the cones afforded. The fees earned had more than made up for the collapse of Horrocks' small fortune in terrestrials shares.

Now, for the first time, Horrocks saw the cone's interior hollow space with his own eyes. Its vast volume overwhelmed any sense of confinement. Above the swarming thousands of crew members emerging from the access locks scores of rocks hundreds of metres across hung in what he could only see, looking up, as the sky. Bubble shack habitats beaded most of them. Structures and construction equipment bristled from every side: booms, manipulator rigs, mineheads, power plants, greenhouses. In the spaces between the rocks the habitats' builders, the ship kids, on scooters or rocket packs or lines or tumbling free, milled about like gnats. Threaded through it all were numerous long and thick cables in a complex three-dimensional mesh like the web of some gigantic drunken spider, strung from wall and brace.

The impression of chaos didn't last more than the first few seconds. The crew circuit lit up with a message of a kind that Horrocks had only seen in drills and sims: an Order of the Day. The top-level objective cleared up any confusion about what was going on, and left Horrocks for a moment slack-jawed: separation of the cones from the habitat in the shortest time consistent with component integrity. Target completion time: ten hours.

Successive levels of the Order spelled out what that meant. The top priority was to shift fusion plants to the axis. The next was to have these on line and standing by to replace the drive in powering the sunline after separation. Third was to have the cones' auxiliary and attitude jets fuelled and ready to fire. The fourth was to have the cones' anti-meteor defences on full alert. Fifth and finally, the habitats and other constructions in the tanks were to be evacuated. On completion of the tasks, or on command at any time, everyone was to return to the normal living and working quarters of the crew.

Beneath these general levels and breaking down the tasks into a rational division of labour, an organisation chart proliferated like an inverted tree. Each person had a job to do, highlighted in the version of the chart that reached them. For Horrocks and Genome it was scooter and tug work, ferrying people and equipment.

As soon as he tabbed his acceptance, a message flared across Horrocks's faceplate:

Your performance of this task and others in fulfilment of the above Order of the Day is covered by the below-cited emergency clauses in the Contract covering a breakdown in relations between Crew and other sections of the Complement. If you do not wish to take part for any reason you are required to stand down at once. No sanctions will apply and arrangements for evacuation or resettlement will be made on request and implemented as soon as possible.

A scrolling screen of legal boilerplate followed. Horrocks didn't even skim it. What mattered was the digital signature at the foot, authenticating the entire Order and signing off on it: Constantine the Oldest Man.

Horrocks looked across at Genome and chinned their private band. 'You in?'

'I'm in if you are.'

'If Constantine asks it, that's good enough for me,' said Horrocks.

'OK,' said Genome. 'Let's do it for the Man.'

Synchronic expected trouble as soon as the call to arrest Constantine went out. She expected grumbling from the crew, protests from citizens, and angry exchanges in the Council, already in an uproar over what Constantine's brazen admission had revealed. She was right. Lost in the virtual spaces in which she followed these developments, she didn't hear the distant thunder until a small girl ran in from the garden and shook her shoulder.

'Mummy mummy there's a fire in the sky!'

Synchronic scooped the breathless, anxious child up in her arms and rushed outside. Looking up, all was normal: the sun-line shone, white clouds drifted, the far side of the habitat lay in a dim shade pricked by faint clusters of light like a washed-out image of a night sky.

The infant squirmed around and pointed towards the central

ring of the forward end of the cylinder. Synchronic almost dropped her.

Around the rim of the spinning axial plate, kilometres wide, that joined the cylinder to the cone, lightning flared and flickered. Thunder rolled down like the sound of a waterfall. In the electric inconstant light from far above the remaining shards of the slag-heap, all the way around the bottom of the cylinder's endplate, flashed black and white like broken glass. On the more distant rearward plate a similar ring of fire encircled the far end of the sunline.

Apocalyptic and unexpected as the sight was, Synchronic recognised it. She would have seen such a spectacle at some point in the next few years. The gigantic electromagnetic baffles of the frictionless flange between the axial plate and the rest of the endplate within which it spun were being readied to lock down and friction-weld into place, sealing the ship and turning off the field at the moment when the cones disengaged.

Synchronic made a supreme effort to retain her composure in front of the fast-growing crowd of her younger care-children. Knowing that most of her older care-children were now on the other side of that fiery barrier did nothing to help.

She put the little girl down on the ground and stroked her head and smiled around.

'Isn't it exciting!' she said. 'What an amazing sight! And listen to that thunder!'

'What is it, Synch?' somebody shouted. The cry was taken up.

Synchronic waved her arms. 'It's all right,' she said. 'It's just some engineering work. The crew have to do it every so often. You're all too young to have seen it before. Say, why don't you all fetch your cameras and make some pictures of it?'

All but the smallest children, and one or two of the older, were satisfied with that. She told Magnetic Resonance and the other older ones a less than complete truth about what was going on, and set them to work distracting their younger care-sibs. Then she went inside and sat down and tried to take stock before returning the insistent calls of her friends and allies.

This was mutiny, total and irrevocable. Worse, in a way, than the secret scheme of Constantine and his cabal of crew scientists. That at most had seemed – only hours earlier, in her furious confrontation with Constantine – a probably illegal and certainly unethical and underhand circumvention of the established, albeit contested, will of the ship's community. This was the literal break-up of the community itself.

The personal betrayal left her with a dark sense of abandonment. Constantine had not been her lover in a long, long time; but in their centuries of friendship she had felt she had come to know him to the bone. Cities had risen and fallen around them, fashions and philosophies had come and gone, fortunes had been made and lost, styles of art and customs of courtship and subtle techniques of intrigue had been refined and trashed like the buildings in which they'd flourished and faded. At the end of the great enclosed adventure of the two-generation generation ship that had turned the emptying of the tank into the founding of a world, she stood here on what they'd made of the last dregs of the regolith and the mulch and realised she didn't know him at all.

Above and beyond that, less personal but more disquieting and disorienting, was what the mutiny told her about people in general. Separating the cones could not be done without a sustained co-operative effort of the crew, and no doubt of the ship generation on the same side. In all her long life politicking had been polite: the fights fierce, the stakes small. You went along with decisions you'd been defeated on and expected others to go along with those you'd won, because there would always be another round of the game, another roll of the dice.

Was this all an illusion? Did it all come down to personal influence in the end? If so many people were eager to troop along when a coal-black alpha, a respected senior, the Oldest Man, kicked over the table and walked away – then it seemed so.

If that much of her experience had fallen, far more still stood. She began taking and making calls. The Red Sun Circle and its allies would give Constantine the fight of his life.

Awlin Halegap had been surprised to find himself directed to his normal work-space by the Order of the Day. He'd always considered his work as vital as anyone's, but he'd never have expected 'speculator' to be a reserved occupation in an all-hands call. He regretted missing the fun: a day spent shoving and stopping large and dangerous masses sounded like sport.

He slid into his cubby-hole, invoked java on his hot drinks feed, and with a flexure of hands and fingers conjured the markets to the real screens around his head and to the virtual screens within.

'A choppy day,' he said.

The great ship's exchanges already looked segmented. With most crew and all the settlers in the cones mobilised to what amounted to manual labour, their trading had been left in the hands of agents, demons, and bots. It lacked panache. In these early minutes no one could be sure how the day would end, how much would be honoured and how much written off.

In the habitat cylinder, by contrast, immense disturbances stirred in the depths, visible on early trades like the upward bulge of a stretch of ocean that foretold a tsunami on a distant shore. Sharp fluctuations in raw materials prices agitated the surface. Established disreputable futures markets in bets on an early end to the colonisation embargo supplied the windblown froth.

Moments ahead of most of his fellow-traders, Awlin saw the arbitrage potential of the flatter markets of the cones. Even discounting for uncertainty, it was a sure thing that the gross misallocations imposed by the mobilisation would open up gaps that it would be profitable to correct when the dust had settled. He spent a happy hour chasing them, and then was almost caught short by a wave of selling. Wrenching his perspective, he traced that wave to a sharp activity spike in the habitat, to whose markets the selling wave rebounded in seconds. The three parts of the ship were connected again, and not in a good way. The wealthiest cartels of the founder generation were driving down cone futures, leaving only the most risk-prone speculators to shark up the slack. Within minutes they too began to buckle.

In the screen segment devoted to physical activity in the cone reserve tanks, snarl-ups and stoppages reddened the nodes of the decision tree.

'They're cutting the kids off without a penny,' Awlin muttered. At the sight of their economic futures subliming like carbon dioxide ice before their eyes, some of the settlers were getting cold feet and shaky hands. He didn't blame them. Having your head ring with frantic calls from your finance bots while you scrambled to shift fusion plants and salvage machinery from the possibly doomed habitats – Awlin was sure the settlers had no illusions as to the likely fate of the contents of the reserve tanks, once separation was accomplished – couldn't be anything but crushing. Although the settlers were on the crew circuit and working off the same chart, they didn't have the crew ethos and morale. But without their continuing involvement the whole thing would bottleneck.

Awlin flashed a comment around the traders' loop: 'This is downright economic warfare.'

Enough agreement came back for him to float a company and co-ordinate a counterattack. The markets rallied, but not enough. Awlin contemplated an array of downward slopes and a continued flare of red lights on the project board and decided matters were out of his hands. He liquidated the company and kicked the problem up to a finance jury.

The deliberations didn't take long, and the response crackled with an impatience he suspected was Constantine's: *What are you waiting for? This is separation! So separate already!*

Awlin sucked in a deep breath. This was the nuclear option. He hesitated for a moment, then sent out the proposal that would sever financial ties between the cylinder and the cones: currency reform.

The forward cone went through three distinct commodity bases for an autonomous currency in as many seconds, and settled on a basket of carbon, nickel-iron and helium-3. At once all values of goods and services in the cone were reckoned on the assumption of access to the system's resources and independence from – and the irrelevance of – habitat capital. The stimulus was in part illusory; it was almost certainly inflationary; but Awlin and his collaborators had bet that it would be enough to carry along the human and virtual agents. He waited for the markets to turn.

They did. The habitat economy went into a sharp downturn while that of the cones shot upward, at least as far as expectation were concerned. For the moment rich and hopeful again, the ship kids began to make good. The red, blocked nodes on the physical chart flipped to green. The cone was as yet a long way from separation, but already its markets had rocketed away from the ship.

Synchronic watched the cones' break to financial autarky with her knuckles pressed to her mouth. She and the Red Sun cartels had tried to steal the ship generation away from Constantine. Now the crew cartels had stolen them back. She wasn't worried

about the integrity of the habitat. The crew's work to ensure it
was obvious. It was its future as a trading and cultural centre for
the new system that had just taken a severe blow. Relations
with the settlers, and with whatever market was eventually
established with the aliens, could be chaotic for years – perhaps
decades. By the time the data colonies and fast probes arrived the
habitat could have lost all the advantages of its prime location
and become a backwater, vulnerable to hostile bids and outright attack. She was not complacent about the aliens' prospects.
They seemed a fierce, fast-learning species, and the knowledge
that space travel and molecular technologies were possible might
have them swarming out of their gravity well long before the ill-
equipped, ill-prepared colonisation that the crew evidently
contemplated was complete. The premature separation had left
whole cohorts of the ship generation stranded in the habitat, and
having seen how badly their elder brothers and sisters had
behaved in a less fraught situation, Synchronic didn't look forward to their likely reaction.

She summed up her proposal for the Circle:

*Capitulate and negotiate. Offer reforged links, limited colonisation,
and accelerated contact.*

Her voice was one of many from various cartels that called
for a similar policy. The Council, still shaken by the news of
the crews' clandestine intervention and further rocked by the
impending separation, considered it seriously. The main alter-
native proposal shocked her:

*To allow crew mutiny and unauthorised colonisation a free run sets
a very bad precedent. Cripple and recapture.*

Synchronic's outraged demand of *How?* was met with a likewise laconic retort: *EMP*.

Electromagnetic pulse.

Nukes. It would work, she was assured. It wouldn't even
harm anyone, if they got the distance right, and the meteor-
defence system was good at that.

The proposal passed. Synchronic was having none of it. She zapped through a warning to the cones seconds before communications were cut off.

Hours later, she stood in the garden with the children and waited. The circles of lightning flared and died. A sound too loud and brief to be called a scream split the air. For a moment a red ring glowed in the endplate as the friction welding seized. A vast shudder passed from the ground to the top of every head. In the same second the sunline died, giving a moment of total blackness longer than a blink. The sunline flickered like an old fluorescent tube, steadied, and shone on as if nothing had happened.

Synchronic spoke vague comforting words to the children. She switched her vision to the forward outside view, which was filled with the slowly shrinking circle of the base of the separated cone, and waited for the flash.

14 366:02:23 22:00

These are moments I will always remember in the present tense.

We have the fusion plants in place and on line. All the equipment that can be saved from the interior settlements is piled on the forward side of the rocks. We head for the huge exit airlocks as fast as we can, clinging to scooters and rocket packs and gas-bottle rafts in a great and now empty-seeming darkness. Our little round window on the sunline, our false star, has gone out. Hope your virtual and infra-red vision is in synch. The airlocks loom. Brake if we can, jump if we must.

We tumble in heaps of hundreds into the locks. The cycle doesn't bother to conserve air.

Into the corridors and rooms. Lights again. Find a corner, a cable, a cubby-hole, a creeper, anything. Cling and brace.

There's a moment like when we entered this sun's orbit, a

moment when something that has always been there goes away. The engine that has powered the sunline all our lives goes off. There's nothing, not a flicker of the lights, not a vibration of the bulkheads, not a sensible clue. But we all feel that eerie absence. I have the passing fancy that the shutting down of a machine that makes universes should feel like this: like the sudden silence of a god.

The mystical moment passes in a blare: *All hands! Stand by for separation!*

There's a shriek and a vibration that set your teeth on edge and rattle them at the same time. Then a faint backward pressure, a small sense of weight, increasing. We're on our way now, running on auxiliary and attitude jets. With the cosmogonic drive's jet no longer channelled to the sunline, we can't use it until it's pointing away from the habitat, which it could cut like a laser.

All hands! Brace for manoeuvres!

The floor lurches, the vertical tilts. Unsecured objects and people skid sideways. The whole cone is tipping over. I'm busy imagining this until I realise I can watch it if I want. I patch in the feed from the cameras on the base of the cone. The habitat cylinder is shockingly close, spinning lickety-split. I can just see along one side. Ruby lights flicker. We're taking raking laser fire! It can't hurt us, I think, it can't burn through metres of plate and regolith. Then as the view degrades I realise: they're burning out lenses, blinding our defences. Farther back, more lights and another kind of movement.

My surge of angry adrenaline comes at a lucky moment—

All hands! Stand by for acceleration!

The god's presence comes back, and with it weight, weight like a sack of soil on your chest, weight like people piling on to you. I'm looking ahead, eyes closed, seeing in the direction that is now *down*. I see the white rapier of the jet stab to infinity. Far away, another jet crosses it, as if in parry. The habitat dwindles beneath our backs. I see the cylinder entire now, rolling on its axis like an abandoned fuel tank. There are other lights, red and white, but they're hard to tell apart from the bright dots in front of my eyes. Except they're moving faster.

The habitat shrinks to a white streak like a star on a long-exposure plate.

The weight becomes so much that I feel my ribs are about to break. I think I'm blacking out.

My sight fills with soundless vast spherical explosions of white light far below.

Something, somewhere, fizzes and cracks.

Then there's a sense of absence and blessed relief as the weight goes away. The call still rings through my head:

All hands! Stand by! Free falling!

And the lights below us fade.

EIGHTEEN

SABREUR

The legend went that the Queen of Heaven had given Her children the green gift, the gift of life; but that it was the Sun Himself who had given the red gift, of fire and intellect. Darvin and Kwarive now sought hidden sparks of that gift in the streets and markets, with a radio receiver. The apparatus was one Orro had cobbled together during the great shittle hunt. It was less bulky than the ones most people had in their houses. It had earpieces instead of a loudspeaker. None of this made it inconspicuous, and as he lugged it around Darvin found himself pestered by kits and glowered at by stall-keepers.

'What is their problem?' he muttered as a piece of rotten rind skittered past his foot.

Kwarive fiddled with the loop antenna. 'They think it's some new kind of health inspection.'

'Well, that makes sense.' Darvin aimed a half-hearted kick at his other tormentors. 'Flap off, you little imps!'

'Great,' said Kwarive. 'Now they'll go screeching to their mothers.'

'Yes, it's their mothers I'd like to speak to. These kits should be in school and not skulking around the – wait a minute.' Something had buzzed in his ears. 'Back a step. Hold it there. Rotate.'

The buzz came back. One side of the antenna faced a blank wall, the other an alleyway.

'Down there.'

The buzz grew stronger as they hastened down the alley. Around the corner of the far end stood a small cart, laden with bricks. The trudge who stood between its handles looked at them with a brighter gaze than most of his kind. When his master returned from a nearby refreshment stall the trudge bent his back to haul without demur. As the cart moved off Kwarive turned the antenna. The trudge was the source all right.

'Follow it?' Kwarive asked.

'Not this one,' said Darvin.

'Why not?'

Darvin wasn't sure why not. 'Too risky. We're not trying to intervene. Not until we know more.'

Kwarive shrugged. 'You're the one carrying the wireless.'

They walked on down the street. Lined on one side with stalls, it was a narrow shelf along the bank of a rivulet at the bottom of the Second Ravine. Lichens and fungal growths splashed garish scarlet and cyan circles on the cliffs and the wet ground. The stream, normally sluggish, was spring-spate swollen, sediment-brown, lapping the banks. As they followed it upstream the goods became ever shoddier: trappings in cracked leather, malformed pots with glazes in colours Darvin didn't have names for, electrical implements with rusty components and dusty handles, cages of listless flitters. At least here the wireless apparatus drew no attention. It looked like something they might have come here to sell.

The earphones buzzed, but faintly. Darvin glanced at

Kwarive and raised a finger. They stood facing the torrent for a moment, mud under their heels, vile suds hissing and popping around their toe-claws. Kwarive pointed a diagonal finger across her midriff.

'That way.'

They turned and walked a few eights of paces on, looking at every stall and trestle, until they came upon a table stacked with barred boxes. At first glance it looked like another stall of flitters, live prey for small children. Then Darvin noticed their thick fur, sturdy limbs and odd, baby-like faces.

'Trudge kits,' breathed Kwarive.

The old woman behind the stall rattled her bony wings. 'That they are,' she said. 'Healthy and uncut. Train them from small, it's always the best. Nice young couple like you, any of these'll be well tamed by the time your own kits come along, just don't feed it live meat, that's what I always say, you hear some terrible stories sometimes, that Queen forbid may happen to you, but don't you worry, it won't, because . . .'

Kwarive let her prattle on while moving the antenna about in front of the wooden cages. Darvin waited until he was sure from which the buzz originated, then nodded.

Kwarive pointed. 'I'll have that one, please.'

As the old woman shifted boxes she noticed the looped wire and the radio.

'What's that you've got there, dears?'

'The very latest thing,' said Kwarive. 'An etheric dowsing-box. To pick up good-luck vibrations.'

'Don't hold with that there etheric dowsing, dear, that's Southern superstition, that is. But if it works for you, who am I to say, young people these days . . .'

As she spoke the woman deftly knotted a string handle around the box.

'Fifty selors,' she said.

Darvin fumbled out the money.

'Thanks,' said the vendor, counting the scrip and tucking it in her belt. 'Well, best of luck with that one. I've found him a bit of a handful myself.'

They walked back down the path, each with their own load.

'*Etheric dowsing?*' Darvin asked, as soon as they were out of earshot.

'It was something I made up,' said Kwarive.

'It'll be all the rage,' said Darvin.

The box stood on a shelf in Kwarive's museum annexe room. Among all the bones and stones, skins and pickled scraps it didn't look out of place. The small black animal inside it clutched the bars with tiny fingers and peered out with big eyes. It stank somewhat. It didn't scratch itself much, and it licked its fur a lot. This seemed reassuring about its health. Every so often Darvin waved the aerial in front of it, while holding one earpiece to his ear. It always buzzed. He still found it hard to believe. This belonged with the weird tales in the Anomalies Room.

'So what are you going to do?' asked Kwarive. 'Dissect out the transmitter?'

'Gods above!' said Darvin. 'Don't *say* things like that. Not where it can hear them, anyway.' He leaned towards the cage and crooned: 'Don't you listen to the naughty lady, she won't hurt you, I won't hurt you, will I? No, no, no – ow!'

He rubbed his nose where a tiny claw had scratched it.

'Oh, you nasty little beast!'

'Iodine,' said Kwarive. 'Now.'

She unstoppered a bottle and dabbed Darvin's nose with a rag. 'There.'

'Thanks,' he said.

'Well, what *are* your plans for this bit of a handful?'

Darvin eyed the cage. 'Treat it with kindness,' he said. 'Talk to it. See if it talks back.'

Kwarive snorted. 'Men!'

'You have better ideas?'

Kwarive passed him a pair of thick leather gloves. 'You wash him in the sink,' she said. 'Use the rock-oil tar soap. I'll clean out the cage.'

A few minutes later she added, without having to look around: 'With *warm* water.'

Sitting wrapped and restrained in a hand towel, its ear fur still bedraggled, the trudge kit looked almost cute. Darvin considered the appearance deceptive. Kwarive pointed proudly at the box, now scrubbed down inside and lined with fresh straw. The whole room reeked of disinfectant soap.

'Well, Handful, what are we to do with you now?' said Darvin. 'Oh, I know. Back in the cage with you.'

He stroked the top of its head with a gloved finger. To his surprise the kit rubbed back, rolling its head so that the stiff fingertip seam scratched behind its ear.

'Mmmm . . .' it said in a small throaty voice.

'I suppose that's a response,' said Kwarive. She picked up the still-wrapped animal. 'It's disturbing how much he looks like a human kit.'

'How old is it anyway?' asked Darvin.

'About a year, I'd guess. About the age human kits start talking.'

'I remember,' said Darvin.

Kwarive sat the kit down on the straw in the box and tugged to remove the towel. The kit mewled and clung hard to the rough cloth.

'Oh, all right,' said Kwarive. 'Hang on to it if you want.'

She closed and locked the cage door.

'Maybe it's cold,' said Darvin.

'Or maybe he just wants to feel held,' said Kwarive.

'You think it misses its mother?'

'Maybe.'

'Just don't ask me to cuddle him.'

'He must be lonely.'

'Hungry, too,' said Darvin.

'Well, don't stand there,' said Kwarive.

When he came back with a scrap of raw meat and a small slice of fruit the infant trudge had fallen asleep. Darvin slid the food through the bars. The trudge's nose twitched but it didn't waken.

'Let him rest,' said Kwarive.

They went out. As they walked through the museum Kwarive laughed.

'What?'

'We're padding about like a couple with a new-born litter.'

'Don't even think about it,' said Darvin. 'One handful's enough.'

'What's the point of all this, anyway?'

'We have to prove it,' said Darvin. 'Strange tales are one thing. Right in front of your eyes is something else. We have to show a talking trudge kit to the Project high-ups.'

'You know what they'll say?' said Kwarive.

'Yes,' said Darvin. 'They'll say: "What an ugly child!"'

'This is hopeless,' said Kwarive, the third morning after they'd bought the trudge. 'He's just not talking.'

Handful sat on now grubbier straw, grooming his wings. He'd taken to rattling the cage door whenever Darvin or Kwarive entered the room, but other than that treated them with wary disdain. Every so often he would clutch the towel and chew the corner of it.

'Three days isn't long,' said Darvin. 'In astronomy.'

'I think we should let him out,' said Kwarive. She closed the slatted screen over the window space and moved to open the cage door.

'Hang on,' said Darvin. 'He'll crash into things and crap all over the place.'

'You know what?' said Kwarive. 'I don't care.'

'On your head be it.'

Kwarive opened the barred door of the box. Handful watched, still sitting. He crawled forward and looked out over the edge of the shelf. His head recoiled. Then he stood upright, spread arms and wings, and leaned into the drop, eyes closed. He tipped forward and fluttered to the floor, where he sat down with a bump and peered around.

'Ow,' he said.

He stood up, rubbed his skinny buttocks and opened his wings again and flapped hard. After getting nowhere for a bit he walked over to Kwarive and stretched his arms upward.

'Up,' he said. 'Up.'

'Did you hear that?'

'Yes, I did,' said Kwarive. 'No need to yell.'

She stooped and held out her fists, thumbs extended. The trudge kit grabbed on and she swung him up above her head. Handful made a harsh cackling noise and let go. Suddenly he was flying. Around the room once, not hitting anything, and back to the box.

The telephone rang. Darvin picked it up.

'Museum annexe,' he said.

'Hah!' said Bahron's voice, 'They said I'd find you there. I told you to watch the skies, astronomer.'

'What's happened?'

'Come to your office and I'll tell you.'

'No,' said Darvin. 'You come down here. Kwarive and I have something to show you.'

'Heh!' snorted Bahron. 'All right.'

Bahron arrived a few minutes later. He had company: Orro and a stranger.

'Orro!' Darvin said. 'How good to see you again.'

'Likewise,' said Orro. He looked more than pleased. He looked like a different man. 'Darvin, Kwarive – allow me to introduce my good friend Holder, from the Regnal Air Force of Gevork.'

The stranger, tall with uniform brown fur over which he wore a complex leather harness with a long sabre at each hip, spread his wings and hands.

'Delighted to meet you,' he said. 'I've heard much of you both.' His diction was clear, his accent stronger than Orro's.

'I've heard much of you,' said Darvin. He looked around. 'Please, everyone, take, uh, a perch or whatever . . .'

Bahron, as was his wont, made for the windowsill. As he rattled open the slatted shutter Kwarive latched the cage. Darvin saw Bahron take notice, and glance from the cage to the wireless receiver on the table, and the hint of a self-satisfied smile. The Eye missed nothing, and knew it.

'Consider the sabreur one of us,' said Bahron.

'I . . . see,' said Darvin, hating the awkwardness in his voice.

Bahron laughed. 'Nothing like you think. Signal is a joint project now – between Seloh, Gevork, and the Southern Rule.'

'I'm not going to fall for that,' said Darvin. He looked sidelong at Kwarive. 'This is a test, yes?'

'Stop acting the amateur,' said Bahron. 'The Sight does not indulge in petty intrigues, or set little traps. The word from the Height will come down later today. The situation is far too serious for flapping about. Tell them, Holder.'

The Gevorkian frowned into the distance, as if inspecting a complex display flight.

'As Bahron mentioned,' he said, 'we shall hear officially later today. I arrived in Kraighor five days ago by airship as a guard

on a diplomatic mission. The instructions of our plenipoten-
tiary were not divulged, but I was given to understand that the
moment was fraught. Suspicion had been evinced that Seloh's
Reach had entered into direct relations with the aliens. I admit
that some wild talk was indulged regarding our military
advantage in the field of rocketry. The impression among the
Air Force personnel was that we were in a position to negotiate from strength, as the phrase goes. When our mission was
met and escorted down by four flying machines, such talk was
heard no more. Within a day of landing at the Height, I was
summoned to the embassy to be told that I had been assigned
the post of scientific-military liaison to your Project Signal, on
behalf of our own Project Portent, of whose existence I had
been unaware until that moment. I can only speculate that I
was chosen on the basis of my position of, ah, personal trust
with Orro.' He smiled. 'Be that as it may, my instructions are
simply to share all that we have learned. Portent and Signal are
to be merged without delay or reservation. A treaty of mutual
assistance between the three great powers has been signed and
will be proclaimed. We face a situation where our previous differences are of no account.'

'I couldn't agree more,' said Darvin.

'Oh, you could,' said Bahron. 'You'll agree a lot more when
you see this.'

The paper was of poor quality, the picture poorer. It was all
dots. Narrowing his eyes, Darvin could just about make out a
rectangle and two triangles.

'It's the Object!' said Kwarive, over his shoulder. 'And it's
broken up!'

'Well done,' said Bahron. 'The two conical bits are moving
very fast. Not our way, thank the gods. To the little rubbish
planets – the Camp-Followers.'

Darvin held up the sheet of paper. 'Where did this come
from?'

'It's a wireless photograph from our embassy in the Southern Rule. The Gevorkians also have a copy. The original was handed in by one of the court astrologers. I understand it's a lot more detailed. Like I said, you should have watched the skies.'

'Indeed I should,' said Darvin. 'When did this break-up happen?'

'Four days ago, I gather.'

'Then there may be photographs from the observatory in my office—'

'Yes,' said Bahron. 'I was kind of hoping there would. What *have* you been doing lately, if I may ask?'

Darvin gestured at Kwarive. 'We've been investigating the trudges.'

'Brilliant,' said Bahron. 'And what have you found?'

Kwarive held up an earpiece in one hand and the loop antenna in the other. 'Listen,' she said.

Bahron came over and put his ear to the buzz.

'Is this some kind of trick?' asked Bahron.

'Trick,' said Handful. 'Trudge trick. Bad trudge!'

In the moments that followed, the trudge kit heard some new words which Darvin rather hoped it wouldn't learn.

They walked between the towers to the Faculty of Impractical Sciences. They walked as a courtesy to Kwarive, for whom Handful was now an armful. When they'd made to leave the annexe the little beast had set up such a pathetic wail that nobody could bear to leave him behind. Kwarive walked beside Bahron, in earnest conversation. Behind them Darvin walked with Orro and Holder. Darvin observed on the faces of people walking the other way a predictable shift of expression. As they approached, their faces tended to bestow the standard vague indulgent smile of noticing a young woman and a small kit. As they came closer and passed, the faces of those who noticed what Handful was froze, intrigued or shocked or outright disgusted. Darvin maintained a strut and glare that defied remark. It seemed to work, though he allowed on reflection that Holder's swords and Orro's martial bearing helped.

'Make yourselves at home,' he said when they crowded into his office, and left them to sort themselves out while he made tea. The stacks of unopened envelopes of celestial exposures, still sent every eight-days from the observatory, nagged at his conscience. He'd kept the order up for the sake of some future student who wanted to take up the search for the outer planet, and had never bothered to examine them himself. A packet had been in his basket as they came in. He thumb-clawed it open as the pot heated up. There was no room to spread them out. He flicked through them pair by pair. Orro's arm reached over his shoulder.

'That one,' he said.

'How do you know?'

Orro gave him a puzzled look. 'We solved the equations last year.'

'So we did, Orro, so we did,' he sighed. 'Could you take care of the tea, old chap, and I'll fire up the blink comparator.'

He positioned the plates and adjusted the focus and started scanning, faster and with less care than usual. By luck or intuition, he found the three adjacent moving dots within a minute. He spent longer staring at them.

He wondered how much difference there was between his mind and Orro's. Where did any normal person stand in relation to someone who could visualise orbits from equations and recognise small patches of sky from memory and place the orbiting body in the right patch after half a year? Orro wasn't doing mathematics quickly; he found calculation as laborious as the next fellow; but once he'd done it, he *saw*. Was the working of Orro's mind as different from Darvin's as his was from that of a trudge? It wasn't a superiority in reasoning. It was like having another faculty, as alien to the normal human as language to the brute.

He looked up. 'It's confirmed,' he said. 'I'll have the photographs sent daily, so we can track what's going on.'

'That would be good,' said Bahron, from the windowsill. 'Going to the Observatory would be better.'

Orro handed Darvin the tea.

'Thanks. What next?'

Bahron jerked his head at Holder. 'Ask the sabreur.'

Holder, standing by the door holding a mug as if not quite sure whether to drink from it or piss in it, glanced around all the expectant faces.

'As a Gevorkian, I feel somewhat awkward giving directions to—'

'Don't,' said Orro.

'Thank you,' said Holder. 'Forgive me. This is all very new. Once the treaty is proclaimed, the whole security aspect changes. The new project will be public. Much more work will be done openly. Our etheric calculators and systems of rocket guidance may prove invaluable, when combined with Seloh's advances in aviation and etheric telekinematography. The secret sites will still be used, but it will be possible to ship in far more personnel and equipment now that there is nothing to hide—'

'Excuse me,' said Kwarive. She looked up from giving drops of tea on her fingertip to Handful.

'Yes?' Holder didn't sound like a man used to being interrupted.

'You say there's nothing to hide. That's true – between us humans. We have nothing to hide from each other. What about hiding from the aliens?' She stroked Handful's back. 'This little creature, for example, is transmitting etheric waves as we speak. I don't know if it's getting back to the third moon, but it could be. Other trudges are doing the same, on a scale we don't yet know. It's going to be bad enough dealing with intelligent trudges, without worrying about trudge . . . intelligence, if you see what I mean! If we're going to keep what we're doing secret from the aliens, we have to do it out of the sight and hearing of trudges.'

'What do you mean, hearing?' asked Holder.

Darvin recalled Lenoen the Southerner's comment about what it took to surprise him.

'Well,' said Kwarive, 'if this little one is learning our language, and transmitting to the aliens, who's to say the aliens aren't learning it too?'

'That is a good point,' said Holder. 'I have seen etheric calculators, and I am not inclined to set limits to what a more advanced science may do. However, it changes little, because we have no intention of concealing our activities from the aliens.'

'What?' cried Darvin.

Holder made a helpless gesture. 'Bahron? You can explain it better.'

'Don't know about that,' said Bahron. 'But I'll try. See, I and the science boss, Markhan, and smarter folks than me, like Arrell, we've talked a lot about this. Especially after the shittle affair. Other parts of the project have looked long and hard at what that germ-plasm fiddling tells us about what our friends up there can do. We never forget that they're up there, looking down, seeing us as sharp as a hunter fixing on a skitter. We never forget that their eyes are down here – maybe in the trudges, maybe shittles again, maybe things we can't see at all. When I was a little kit, and even a big kit, we knew there was ether, right, it's self-evident, but we had no idea there was such a thing as etherics. Invisible waves passing right through us and all that. We know the aliens use etherics, but don't know what else they may use. In other invisible realms, so to speak. So we could be hiding away in caves and under roofs and screening for all the things we know about, and the wingless could be just watching us and smiling behind their big hands.'

He slid off the windowsill and laughed. 'You ever get that creepy feeling of being watched from above? Like, when you were little? Kwarive tells me it's nature's way of overprotecting us, if I understand her right. You're safer to be wrong that way lots of times than wrong the other way once. Well. There's no point trying to hide from the aliens. We're not going to try. We're going to do everything right out in the open. It's our only chance.'

'For what?' asked Kwarive. 'Scaring them off?'

'In a word,' said Bahron, 'yes.'

Darvin and Kwarive laughed. None of the others did.

'It's not as mad as it sounds,' said Bahron. 'The wingless may be driven by population pressure, like anyone else, but there's no reason to think Orro was wrong about their being peaceful – at least in their past experience. That big world-ship of theirs doesn't look like it was expecting trouble. Markhan and Nollam have had a chance to go through the pictures and do some calculations, and it looks like a big tin drum full of their women and children. It's not the sort of thing you'd send first into an unknown system if you had any idea there might be somebody shooting back. So regardless of what their capabilities are, they might not have much stomach for a fight. If they see us tooling up, building rockets and aeroplanes and such, they might just back off.'

Kwarive laughed again. 'That's quite a supposition!'

'Like I said,' Bahron replied, 'it's our only chance. And anyway, what have we got to lose?'

'Lose!' echoed Handful. 'Lose!'

Bahron fixed a glare on the kit. 'There is that, of course. I don't see how turning trudges into men is anything but hostile. But now we know what's going on, we can deal with it.'

'How?' Kwarive asked. She held the kit closer as she spoke, wrapping a wing around it, Darvin noticed.

'The Sight is on the case,' Bahron said. 'What the Height intends to do has to be kept secret from the public until the last minute. That's all I can say for now. I would advise you all very strongly to say nothing on the subject.'

With that ominous admonition he left.

Darvin had last spent time at the Observatory when he was a student. The popular image of the astronomer as nightly star-gazer had never had much truth in it, and in modern times it had even less. Observation was still the basis, but the long-exposure camera had become a much more fruitful source of observation than the telescope alone. Much observation could be done by poring over photographs and spectroscope readings, and besides, it was in the application of mathematics to the results that such progress as occurred was being made. The science was in one of its difficult periods, when new observations didn't so much solve problems as raise them. What fuelled the stars? Why did they show such a regular sequence of colours? What was the nature of the nebulae? What subtle property of the ether made the light of distant stars and nebulae shift toward the red end of the spectrum? Compared with such questions as these, Darvin's search for the outermost planet had been trivial: a postgraduate project carried too far into the early part of his professional career, more out of a certain stubbornness – and the lure of knowing that, if he did find the planet, it would forever be associated with his name – than any true scientific urgency.

Now he had his fame, for what that was worth.

In the Observatory, what it was worth was that he had had complete control over the telescope for four outer-months. All other work had been set aside for the Project's priorities. Night after night Darvin and his colleagues scanned the skies and took photographs. Day after day they inspected the plates in a blink comparator. The diminished Object – the cylinder, according to the Southern data – remained close to the orbit of the Warrior. Of the two cones that had broken away, no trace could be found. None of Orro's calculations – and there had been many – had successfully predicted their new location. There had been moments of excitement, whenever a new body was found among the Camp-Followers. But when its location was sent by radio to the Southern Rule, to be viewed through the superior telescopes of the antipodean astrologers, it was always resolved as yet another natural asteroid.

While Darvin cursed his luck, every other aspect of the Project raced ahead. The treaty proclamation had been greeted more with relief about the prospect of a lasting peace with Gevork than with anxiety about the aliens. People still, Darvin suspected, didn't quite believe in the aliens. Not even the publication of pictures from the aliens' indecipherable message had shaken the popular complacency. The existence of aliens had for so long been the subject of a lax assent – or article of faith, for cults and pulps alike – that its confirmation unsettled no prejudice and provoked no panic. It was quite possible that what people thought they saw in their everyday lives was progress stimulated, perhaps inspired by the aliens, rather than the massive co-ordinated military mobilisation that it was. Taxes had gone up, prices risen, but the great manufactories and their penumbra of backstreet workshops had full order-books. The sight of an aeroplane over a town no longer brought all activity to a halt. The most visible sign of great change was the sight of the tethered balloons that had sprung up on every horizon as TK relay stations. All the larger towns now had at least one huge public screen, upon which every night telekinematographic pictures were projected. They showed the work at the desert camps and proving grounds: the rockets rising and crashing, the vast arrays of etheric aerials, the test flights of experimental airframes; they gave nightly glimpses of the day's debates in Seloh's Roost; they had begun to carry lighter, more trivial news items and even theatrical performances later in the evening.

Whatever was going on among the trudges had stirred no unrest. The question was never raised in the Roost, nor discussed in the papers. The Sight was no doubt kept busy. What it was busy doing, Darvin did not want to think about. He felt himself a coward for that. In the cluster of buildings around the Observatory, there seemed no grounds for worry. Handful had become something of a mascot. Kwarive's instructions for her part of the Project had simply been to go on studying the infant trudge's language acquisition, and she had moved to the same accommodation block as Darvin in order to study it discreetly. Handful flew around freely indoors and out, picked up new words and formed short sentences, and thrived. The only danger he faced, and that was slight, was of being attacked by one the long-winged, long-necked flitters – carrion-eaters and opportunistic predators – that circled the thermals of the high desert.

It was a hot evening, after a hotter day, near the turning of the outer-month. The sun had set, and the pylons of the cable-car system clicked and rang as their metal cooled. Nocturnal animals stirred and chittered in the scrub and sand. Soon the sky would be dark, the air chill. Darvin looked forward to it as he prepared the night's observations. His eyelids were gritty with lack of sleep, his fur damp with sweat. The technician working beside him was equally exhausted.

Handful flew in through the open window and perched on the telescope's circular railing.

'Darvin! Darvin!'

'Hello, Handful.'

'New moon! New moon!'

Darvin smiled, the technician laughed. 'That's a smart trudge all right.'

'Clever Handful,' said Darvin. He reached over and scratched the trudge's ear. 'Clever boy, Handful.'

'No,' said Handful, grabbing the hair on Darvin's wrist and tugging. 'New moon. See new moon.'

'I've seen them lots of times, Handful. Please go away. Be a good boy.'

'New moon!' The tugging became painful.

'Give me a minute,' said Darvin to the technician. 'I'll just take the little pest back to his — back to Kwarive.'

He scooped the trudge into the crook of his elbow and stalked out. Handful pointed to the blue-black sky, in which the first stars pricked into visibility and, just above the last glow of sunset, the Fiery Jester burned bright. Darvin's exasperated glance followed the pointing finger to the south. The inner and outer moons hung like sections of white rind. Close to them and a little above, a tiny but distinct triangle glinted like a faceted gem brighter than the Queen.

'New moon,' said Handful.

NINETEEN

A FULL AND FRANK
EXCHANGE OF VIEWS

14 366:02:25 11:37

Even after two days—

There are several lines of thought and conversation that could begin with these words.

So let me start with the easy one.

Even after two days, crew quarters are a strange environment. It's unlike the habitat or the settlements. The habitat is a ground environment, a pseudogravity environment, an imitation – strange as it may seem – of a planet's surface. Yes, the ground curves up and over your head, which I know from the virtualities would seem as strange to anyone from a real planet as a real planet with sky overhead would to us. But that difference is less than it might seem – all on the surface, you might say. Think of the things they have in common: lakes, vertical buildings, plains, forests and parks, tame and wild animals roaming about, trees growing upward, rain falling downward, sun(line)-light from above. The eye and the inner ear tell you the same thing, most of the time.

The microgravity homesteads were different again. The living-spaces are small. They feel like site huts, not yet like homes. Everything was a bit raw, even though we were beginning to grow plants. Everywhere smelled of rock dust, except where it stank of leakage from organic cycles. And no, living in space suits or smart-fabric clothes all the time is not a solution.

The crew quarters of the cone are quite unlike either. This is a mature free fall environment. It's like a rainforest canopy. And it's old. The habitat's present landscape has only existed for a few decades. The settlements, only a few months. This place is thousands of years old, almost as old as the ship, and behind it stretches another ten thousand or so years of precedent and practice. Millennia of trial and error, of artificial and natural selection, of genetic and mechanical engineering, until the long backward view fades out in the haze of legend: of Skylab and Mir, of the space stations and the Moon Caves. You see trees that buckle steel plate. You see ecosystems that have grown up around a water leak or a warm spot. You see sculptures whose details have eroded in the flow of air from a ventilator. You meet people who have lived thousands of years and never been outside not just the ship, but this cone. You encounter activities that are either immensely slow, subtle tasks or symptoms of wetware crashes. You see women with foetuses growing inside them. You hear children talking and not sounding like children, nor acting like them, but working together with adults. There are no child-raising estates here, no teen cities, no full-time care-parents. Small children zoom around in a chaotic, tumbling, noisy and unsupervised way that reminds me of the bat people's young. Of course there are not many children, but they make their presence felt out of all proportion.

That sounds a little cantankerous. The fact is, I like it here. Even after two days—

That phrase again. OK, now for the hard part:

Even after two days, I can't understand or forgive the Council. I can hardly believe it.

They tried to nuke us!

It may have been 'only' an EMP hit, but the effects of that could still have killed people. Suppose some critical systems had gone down? Suppose the nuke had gone off a fraction of a second too soon or too late? I can't believe that the founders would risk killing people just to get their way. This will not be forgotten or forgiven.

I'm almost as shocked, in a way, with what Constantine and his scientist clique have done. They used us (obviously – lots of fusion plants, huh). They went behind the backs of the Council. They've left us no choice but to make some kind of intervention. I can see why the Council members were furious. But how anyone on the Council could have thought that the crew would allow Constantine to be detained I don't know. Maybe what I now see of the crew, and the crew quarters, helps to explain it. The founders just didn't understand how different and strange the crew are. Only people as clannish and devious as the crew could have come up with the scheme to enlighten the slaves and translate the languages. Giving them speech and then reverse-engineering from the language module! I ask you. Not to mention using as amplifiers, of all things, the underground bodies of fungi and lichens: fairy rings.

But, you know, kudos for the panache.

Horrocks Mathematical's viewpoint hung in space, looking down at ruins. Even though he was safe inside crew quarters, guiding a tiny telemetry probe, it helped to think of himself as looking down, and not as looking straight ahead – or worse, up – at a vast unstable cliff. Most of the rock at the base of the reserve tank had remained trapped by the web of buckyrope cables. The mesh had been devised to hold the asteroid and cometary chunks in place under normal acceleration and manoeuvres. Under the five or six gravities of the cone's headlong flight from the nukes, the entire content of the tank had slammed against the base, the impact cushioned somewhat by the gigantic elastic cables. As soon as the drive had been turned off the cables had recoiled. Most of the larger rocks had remained trapped, but broken-off masses of rock had been catapulted against the sides of the tank. The fragile material from carbonaceous chondrites and cometary ice had been smashed and partly melted. Smaller fragments had ricocheted around, their gradual ablation under repeated collisions pitting the interior walls and filling the space with drifting dust and granules.

As for the habitats and machinery, everything that had not been salvaged to crew quarters had been flung about or crushed. Dust-covered diamond bubbles bulged from the wreckage, but anything inside might as well be written off. The original plan had been for the separation to be prepared in clandestinity and to be sprung as a surprise. A gentle acceleration would have left the habitats and fabrication units intact, for later release into the asteroid belt or among the gas-giant moons. Now colonisation would have to proceed from scratch. At least the ship kids now had some real experience under their belts, but their disappointment would be deep, and their financial losses severe.

'Compensation claims,' Awlin Halegap said when Horrocks backed out of the view and gave him his assessment of the disaster. 'No problem.'

'What?' said Horrocks. 'It could be years before we get compensation out of the founders.'

'Assuming the legal software even agrees,' added Genome. 'The issue of who broke the Contract, or if anyone did, is so complex . . .'

Halegap looked at both of them and shook his head. 'You're so naive,' he said. 'We start a *market* in compensation claims. The ship kids can sell their claims for ready cash. They'll lose out on the discount, but they'll still raise enough capital for start-ups.'

'Oh yes?' said Genome. 'And who will they sell their claims to?'

'Me, for a start,' said Halegap. 'I hope nobody has thought of it already. Excuse me . . .'

His virtual presence vanished with a sound-effect of rubbing hands. Over the next seconds Horrocks watched with his inner eye and virtual vision an entire financial sector flare out of nowhere like a nuclear explosion in the void. He grinned at Genome and turned to the crowd of ship kids behind him. The telemetry room was an irregular shape and strung with lianas. Water bubbled through transparent piping. A score or so of former settlers hung in the organic mesh at all angles. Others were no doubt watching from elsewhere, or following other probes.

'What was all that about?' asked a young fellow with a cockatoo crest of blue plumes. They had seen the devastation on their own interfaces, but most of them hadn't been able to follow the swift spectral byplay with Halegap.

'Speculation,' said Horrocks. 'The guy's a friend, and I'm no adviser, but . . . I'd advise you to keep your options open if somebody offers to buy your compensation claims any time in the next, oh, week or so. By then you might get a good price for them.'

'I don't want compensation!' somebody else shouted. 'I want my habitat back!'

Rattlings of lianas, drummings on the bulkhead, shouts.

'Yeah, everything's ruined!'

'We should go back and kick out the Council!'

'Rip some stuff off the old ship!'

'What about the crew? It's all their fault in the first place!'

Horrocks blinked and shrank back from the hubbub. Genome pushed forward.

'Shut up!' she yelled above the din. Her pitch and volume made Horrocks flinch. A startled silence fell. 'That's better,' she went on. 'I know you're upset. I'm upset. Horrocks is upset. We helped build these habitats. We don't like seeing them wrecked any more than you do. It's terrible. But the fact is that they are badly damaged and there's no easy way to get them back. We can salvage some of what's down there, but it's going to be hard, heart-breaking work. And we're millions of kilometres away from the old ship. We're not going anywhere near it until we've struck enough deals to make ourselves safe. One of these deals will be compensation, OK? There are people willing to give you money now, or next week as Horrocks says, just on the off-chance that we'll make these deals – who knows when! That's your good fortune. We're heading for the asteroid belt and when we get there you can get busy on some real settlement, right out in free space. That's what you all want, right? And until then, *don't* let me hear *anyone* talking about "the crew" as if the crew are some *other* group of people. When you agreed to carry out the Order of the Day, you joined the crew. You're all crew now, as long as you're in this ship. And for the moment, this cone is the ship. We're all in it together – literally. So rocking well grow up, OK?'

Her gaze swept the room like a spotlight, stopping here and there.

'Everybody happy?' she asked.

Silence.

'Anybody *not* happy?'

More silence.

'Good,' said Genome. 'See you around, crewmates.'

She arrowed to the exit hatch. Horrocks followed, looking straight ahead. Outside in the corridor and out of earshot he caught her ankle and pulled up to face her.

'Where did you learn to do that?' he asked.

'I guess I've had younger trainees than you in the past,' she said.

'That yell—'

'Yes,' she said. 'It's the training-habitat voice.'

'How do you know we're going to the asteroid belt?'

'Aren't we?'

14 366:02:28 17:20

One advantage of being detached from the ship is that we can skip around the system like a flea on a griddle. Right now we're headed for the asteroid belt at such a clip I doubt we show up as even a streak on long-exposure photographs. Even so, we won't be there for weeks. In the meantime . . .

I think the crew are at a bit of a loss as to what to do with us. They must have expected the settlements to survive the separation, with any repair work to be quite enough to keep us occupied until the rocks could be decanted into independent orbit. Right now we're poor, idle and fending off investors offering rock-bottom (hah!) prices for our compensation claims. Exploring crew quarters is fun but after a while that's bound to pall. Salvage . . . I don't have the heart for it, though Grant does. He enjoys the challenge.

But there's one thing we can do that is more than just killing time. We can go into the new virtualities, the ones uploading data from the slaves – the trudges, as I gather we're now supposed to call them.

I'm surprised the crew haven't suggested it. Maybe they think it's too reminiscent of how the founders tried to keep us occupied. Maybe they want to make any decisions about intervention without any pressure or clamour from us. I take their point. But we are, after all, the ones who are going to have to live with the consequences, long after the crew have gone. So I think we should at least know on what basis the decisions are made.

Another thought: I miss those of us who were left behind. I miss, in particular, my three-quarter-sister Magnetic. We used to talk and write to each other a lot. It's not something I ever mentioned here. It was private. But I miss her, and I'm saying so now because it's about time someone did. There's been a lot of tough talk about how the kids who didn't make it to the cone settlements are ones who were slackers or birthrighters anyway. This is nonsense. Most of them were just too young, or had you forgotten that? And cut out the talk about how we don't need them anyway. There are enough of us here to make viable settlements, for sure. But we need the rest of the ship generation to fulfil our plans and hopes – and theirs. There are tens of thousands of our younger brothers and sisters stranded back there in the habitat. We are not going to abandon them.

So don't give up. Don't turn into a new kind of slacker. Get stuck into those virtualities, try to observe what is going on down there, and keep up the pressure on the crew to come up with an explanation of how we are going to get the rest of our generation back.

'It's time to re-open contact,' Synchronic had said, two days ago at a meeting of the Red Sun Circle at the villa in White City. The others around the pool had, to all appearances, engaged in glum counsel with the mullets, or divination with the wrack. Then one by one they had looked up and nodded. The Council had, after a likewise unfathomable deliberation, come around to the same decision.

But as she sat in the estate garden, real thumb poised over a virtual switch, Synchronic found herself hesitating. When you'd lived long enough, she'd sometimes reflected, when certain habits had become ingrained no matter what refreshment of the neural pathways the immortality genes could bestow, ethics and etiquette became ever less distinct. Hitherto the involuntary equation had read one way, in disproportionate pangs of conscience over a small breach of manners. Now the terms had been inverted, and she felt over the Council majority's horrible, criminal, potentially murderous mistake the sort of acute embarrassment that might have been appropriate for some ghastly faux pas. *Dreadfully* sorry, I'm *such* a ditz about these nuclear attack protocols . . .

Oh well. A week had passed since the separation, a day since the decision. She had deliberately not followed the exchanges between crew and Council. She presumed any initial awkwardness had been got over, and negotiations opened. The full brunt would have passed. Constantine, at least, would have calmed down.

She sighed and opened the channel. There was a moment of light-speed lag.

'You've got a rocking nerve,' said Constantine. 'Showing up here.'

He lounged in some real-world environment beside a centrifugal wheel of water. In the background she could see people swimming, up and over, around and around. The Man was naked. Discarded drink-bulbs drifted around him. It had been a long while since she'd seen him like that.

'Excuse me?' she said. 'I sent you the warning.'

'Well, whoop-de-do,' said Constantine. 'That was good, but it's not good enough. It was you who tried to have me arrested. It was you and your clique who set out to ruin our finances. That you drew back from the brink is very much to your credit, Synch, but it was a brink you'd brought us to.'

There was this to be said for comms delay: it gave you cover for speechlessness.

'I could recriminate too,' she said at last. 'But I won't.'

'Glad to hear it,' said Constantine. He took a squirt of his drink. 'Do you have anything constructive to say?'

'We can discuss a timetable for contact and colonisation, to minimise—'

Constantine had had his hand up, she reckoned, by the time she had said 'discuss'.

'Not up for discussion. What I and the crew are waiting to hear about is the steps you've taken to have the Council deposed, arrested and slung in the brig.'

She blinked up a couple of words in her dictionary.

'Out of the question,' she said.

Constantine reached forward to cut the connection.

'Wait!' she said.

'Go ahead.'

'We can't possibly unseat the Council. My position was in a minority.'

'So? Last I heard, the Council had a couple of hundred members. You have tens of thousands of ship-generation kids. No contest.'

His words conjured up an absurd image of a crowd surrounding the Council building, marching in and carrying off its members. At that point her imagination failed, and she knew she had him on the run.

'That's absurd,' she said. 'The Council has nothing with which to enforce its will but its moral authority and the agreement of the Complement. If that goes, on what does whatever replaces the Council rely? Armed force?'

'I'm not asking you to use armed force, or unarmed either. Heaven forfend that civilised people like us should resort to violence. That could escalate all the way up to nuclear. No, you can do it constitutionally. Raise a petition to have them impeached. Trigger a recall referendum. Whatever. It's all in the Contract. I don't care if you succeed or not, as it happens. In a few years the ship generation will all be old enough to vote. But what I want to see now, and I think I speak for most of us, is some evidence of good faith on the part of the Council minority. Some real protest at what happened. Not some apology and let's put it all behind us and move on. Until we see that we'll continue to put you behind us and move on.' He chuckled. 'At some considerable velocity.'

'We could demand the same of you, about the intervention.'

'You could, but it would be a waste of breath. The situations aren't symmetrical. We are in the right, your majority is in the wrong even if we made a mistake, which I don't think we did. So we're going to sort out the consequences of what we've done, with or without the rest of you.'

Synchronic sat silent for a moment. This was a private channel. She didn't need or want the advice of the Circle. The situation looked like an impasse. Neither side could physically damage the other, even if – unthinkably – they'd wanted to. Their anti-meteor defences were more than adequate to handle the other side's turning their own missiles and lasers to offensive use. That had been for millennia part of the minimum spec, in the light of the possibility of ships going bad. It had only been the close proximity of the escaping cones that had made the intended EMP hit even a possibility.

The cylindrical habitat was self-sufficient. Not indefinitely – it would need system resources in at most ten years – but it could hold out for the time that mattered. It had the finance, the resources and the experience to make colonisation a fast and smooth process. The trouble was, the cones had all the most enterprising and energetic colonists. Without economic links to the future settlements and industries, the habitat was doomed to be a backwater. And a backwater occupied not just by frustrated founders, but by an ever-growing crowd of frustrated would-be colonists.

Physically it was secure. Socially, it was a sealed vessel with pressure building up. Enough pressure to—

Enough pressure to blow the place apart.

She smiled.

'I think we'll do the same,' she said. 'Keep in touch.'

She cut the link before Constantine could do more than open his mouth.

14 366:04:10 12:32

Six weeks since separation. Grant's been working in salvage a lot. We have a place in one of these complicated arboreal arrangements. Even the water supply oozes rather than flows. Capillary effects, right? Grant says it's like working in a cave and coming home to a tree. He seems to enjoy it.

I've been doing what I can with our diminished funds, scouring the exchanges every day, and talking to as many people as I can reach back in the ship – it's good to make contact again, but with the comms lag old friends seem oddly distant. Well, not just the comms lag. We may be growing apart as fast as we're moving apart. They feel, for now at any rate, that they're in it together with the founders, but more than that (and I can tell there are tensions with the founders already) they feel that we have somehow abandoned them and let them down. We feel we're in it together with the crew. The main reason I keep in touch is to reduce that feeling of abandonment, but it's a struggle.

Which leaves the virtualities. These are not as entertaining a diversion, or as useful an occupation, as I'd expected. This is not because they aren't vivid. They are.

There are two problems with them. The first, and the most annoying, is that the thrill of hearing translated words soon wears off when you find out how few words are translated. The trudges are learning language, but mainly language spoken to them. So you see a bat person and hear him or her shouting:

'Pick that up and put it over there!'

And you see hands picking up some heavy object, a juddering walk, and hear a crash.

Then you hear a number of other words, including: 'brute', 'stupid', 'fuck', and 'off'.

The other problem is that although you see streets and fields and so on, most of the time you're seeing the inside of some dark, dull and dingy place: a cellar, a barn, a factory, a back room. The work done by the trudges is brutal, physical, and repetitive. Even watching it is tedious and exhausting. The only bit that's interesting, in a way, is seeing the viewpoint of a trudge pulling a passenger cart. And that's just too distressing to watch, because all the time you hear the crack and see the lashing tip of a whip.

14 366:04:13 22:47

I wish I could delete that. But in a way it's good that I posted it, because I got a flood of (well, seven) messages telling me I'd been looking in the wrong place, and pointing me to the newslines. Everything is so different here you don't imagine newslines. You think, this is crew quarters, everything runs on hint and rumour and scuttlebutt and that's why I'm out of the loop, and you never think, there are people here who make news their work. But I digress.

Something strange, fascinating, and disturbing is going on.

But before I get on to that – well, you know what I'm going to get on to. Everybody's talking about it. Alien television.

Did they learn it from us? Did they somehow pick up from our download the idea that there's more to be done with television than use it for two-way, point-to-point communication? That you can *broadcast*?

Because that's definitely what they're doing now. We know that because some of the trudges from whose bodies we get transmissions see the big public screens, though they can't be said to watch them, exactly. Those that do watch tend to get cuffed about the face and yelled at. So it's something glimpsed sidelong. But we can see them, direct, from the aliens' television broadcasts.

And what broadcasts! I think the long boring bits are the most significant. They tell us what *they* find important. A slow sweep of a camera around a vast conical chamber ringed with concentric stepped circular bars gappily lined with bat people hanging upside down and now and again making a lot of noise and flapping – it has to be a Council, a parliament. I know Grey Universal says it's a lecture theatre, but that's just him. What his interpretation has going for it, I admit, is all the other stuff: the quaint rockets that go fast and explode; the peculiar multi-winged box-kite aircraft not much bigger than our microlights and obviously, painfully heavier; the strange balloons and dirigibles.

It could be, I suppose, some enormous system of public lectures on aviation and rocketry.

Except that you see the same sort of thing in two different languages, from the two separate parts of the divided continent. (Nothing from the big continent in the other hemisphere.)

And what you see, through the trudges' eyes, in and above the cities: the bomb-catapults and giant crossbows wheeled through the streets on carriages drawn by straining teams of trudges, or huge coughing steam-engines; the new flying machines very occasionally, the dirigibles floating overhead much more often than they did on our first surveillance, and the co-ordinated flights of great masses of bat people, swooping and wheeling in unison.

I know I've sometimes been controversial, but never for the sake of it. I'm no contrarian. What I see there is what most people see there; what I see in front of my eyes.

What I see is two powers preparing for war.

But that isn't the worst. The worst, the most sinister development, is what's happening to the trudges.

Reports from all over, of course – check the newslines – but here are two from me.

First one: I was in one of those dull virtualities I complained about the other night. The trudge was working at the back of a shop where they sell fresh meat. A huge carcass of one of the grazing animals had been tipped from some kind of truck into a stone-flagged yard, where two of the bat people cut it up with knives that look too small for the job. Their skill was impressive – they slide the blades into the joints and slice through the ligaments, and suddenly a whole limb falls off; or they slit the belly and all the guts spill out – but, as you will by now appreciate, it was a bit disgusting to watch. Anyway, the trudge whose POV I was getting and another were lugging the chunks to the front of the shop, where they threw them down on a big marble-slab counter. Back and forth, back and forth. And 'my' trudge leans over to the other and says: 'Get knife.'

The other trudge looks back and grunts. My trudge looks away and goes on with the work. But every so often, the POV focuses on the two bat people's bloody blades. I'm just beginning to wonder whether I'm about to see something exciting when two more bat people drop out of the sky. They land in the yard. Both are wearing smart belts. One of them has a chest harness on which is mounted a box. Cables go from the box to his ears. He tweaks some kind of knob on it and looks straight at me – as I can't help feeling – and walks straight up to one of the aliens working on the carcass.

I hear something like this: 'You [*chirp growl*] boss?'

'[*Twitter*] to you?'

Then a lot of stuff that doesn't translate.

The new arrival hands the blade guy a bundle of pieces of paper. I recognise it as the stuff they use as money.

They walk over to 'my' trudge and point to the front of the shop. 'Out.'

So the trudge shuffles out, past the counter, past a small queue of bat people, out into the street and into the back of a motor-vehicle. Then the virtuality crashes. No input.

I replayed it, taking more care to look, freezing images now and then, and I noticed something interesting about the interior of the van. It contained a big box of metallic-looking mesh, with a door that stood open as the trudge was hustled in.

It might just be a coincidence, but that box would work as a Faraday cage. It would block all radio transmissions.

Shaken, I did some prowling around, and found a scene where I'm looking out of a wooden barred box. There are other trudges in the box. They look strange and out of proportion, and I realise all of a sudden that they're juveniles.

A hand reaches in, there's a second or two of going head over heels, and then an open metal cage and then nothing.

Check the newslines. It's happening all over the place. Check the virtualities. They're dropping like a stone in a gravity well.

Our inputs are being cut off one by one. The trudges infected by our nanotech are being rounded up. Beings to whom we have given language and self-awareness.

We can't let this happen.

14 366:04:14 06:08

We're going in!

This is the first time in my life that I have felt proud that Constantine is my half-father.

Grant is not so pleased. He's just gone off to work in the tank, after having been told – along with everybody else – that salvage work is over for the duration. Instead, every available hand has been mobilised to co-ordinate a fleet of those big spidery crab-like machines in tearing up the carbonaceous chondrites and working the buckyfibre spinarets to make twenty thousand kilometres of rope. Not to mention breaking stuff up for reaction mass.

14 366:04:14 07.10

Damn. Just checked my incoming. I'm on the reserve-tank work roster too. Well, at least they didn't send one of those all-hands calls to my head. Fourteen-hour days for the next week. And in one gravity at that, as we boost across the system on main drive. No news as to the intervention plans as yet, but I think it's a safe guess we're going into geosynchronous orbit.

Talk to you after the war, I guess.

TWENTY

SECOND CONTACT

The camp had changed. New launch-ramps had been built, a long balloon-cable ascended from the middle of the square, new sheds and barracks had been thrown up. Fresh craters and wreckage littered the test-ranges. Flattened and tarred strips of what looked like roadway had the tiny crosses of airframes clustered at their near ends. An enormous parabolic structure of wood and wire mounted on an arrangement of iron-wheeled carriages on a circular rail turned hither and yon, like a hand-cupped ear to heaven. The greatest difference, Darvin reflected, was that he was looking down at all this from the cabin of the descending airship. The location was no longer a secret.

Along with the secrecy had gone the complacency. Not much room for that with an extra moon in the sky. Darvin glanced upward and sideways at the thought of it. He could-n't see it in the bright daylight sky, but he knew it was there. Unlike the natural moons, and for that matter the invisible third, artificial moon, this new satellite did not rise or set. Its orbital period was one day, to the minute. Through even a good amateur telescope its conical structure was unmistakable. Darvin wondered where the other cone from the gigantic world-ship had gone. The obvious presumption was that it was being held in reserve. Bahron, when he'd telephoned to summon Darvin to the camp, had made the point that if the aliens were holding back half their forces, this meant they thought there was a chance they might lose the other half. Darvin didn't find this notion convincing, but he hoped Bahron was spreading it around. It might help morale.

The airship drifted, nudged by its rotors, to the perimeter mooring-mast. The engines feathered down. The door slid open. Eight-and-four passengers – the rest had all been close-mouthed scientists, leafing through pages of small-print formulae – made their way to the exit and dived out.

As he glided groundward Darvin spotted Nollam walking across the central square. He banked, flapped, sideslipped and alighted beside Nollam in a puff of dust.

'Show-off,' said Nollam.

'Watch your lip, techie.'

'Less of that,' said Nollam, straightening so much he almost leaned back. 'I've been awarded a degree, I have. Master Scholar.'

'You?' said Darvin. 'Well, allow me to congratulate you. I'm a mere Scholar Ordinary. Have you been studying in your spare time?'

Nollam gave him a look. 'I got it for my work.' He waved a hand, indicating the giant parabolic aerial in the middle distance.

'Ah, for the design—'

'No,' said Nollam. 'For founding a new discipline. Etheric astronomy.'

'First I've heard of it, but again, congratulations.'

'Oh, you won't have heard of it,' said Nollam. 'It's all under wraps. Morale reasons. But they gave me the degree to keep me happy and quiet, knowing I was recognised and would be

remembered even if the whole field stays a secret until after
I'm dead.'

Darvin wasn't sure if the young technician – correction,
Master – wasn't tugging his wing.

'Serious?'

'Serious,' said Nollam. 'Can't even tell you. Lips stitched,
and all that. Maybe some day.'

'I'll take your word for it, Magister.'

'You do that, Scholar, you do that . . . How's Kwarive?'

'Fine,' said Darvin. 'She's been called up to . . . a different
part of the project.'

'And I shouldn't ask what, right?'

'Right.'

In fact Darvin didn't know either. That Kwarive had been
urged to bring the trudge kit along suggested it had something to do with the Sight's plans – whatever they were – for
the articulate members of that species.

Their walk had converged with that of other arrivals and resi-
dents, at one of the larger barracks blocks. All furniture had
been removed, except for a stage at the front with a table on
top, a telekinematographic recorder and projector to one side,
and a screen behind it. There was standing room only. As they
crowded in, Darvin was surprised to see Nollam push ahead
and walk up to the front, where he took a place beside
Markhan at the table. The crowd shuffled and settled. Looking
around, Darvin recognised Orro and Holder, and a few faces
from the earlier days of the project.

'You all know why we're here,' said Markhan. 'The new
arrival in the sky. What you may not know is that it has
already made contact with us.'

The effect was like a gust through trees. Markhan stared it
down.

'Nollam,' he said.

'It's a repeating message,' said Nollam. 'It definitely comes from the cone thing, it's on the same wavelength as the first message that got aborted, and it's definitely addressed to us. It's . . . startling. Let me play you a tape of it. Pull the curtains, somebody.'

The moments of confusion and shouted advice and complaint that followed gave him plenty of time to adjust the volume and focus.

'Right,' he said. He threw a switch.

The tape-deck whirred and the screen lit up.

The first image was of a white background with a flechette shape in the centre and a wavy, jagged line near the bottom. With a start and an intake of breath, Darvin recognised it as Kwarive's sketch-map, that had been originally projected to the aliens by the electric shittles. But only about a third of the crowd – those who'd been there then – so recognised it. The others gasped and nudged each other at the next image, which faded in as the first faded out. It showed a picture from above of the same coastline and interior of Seloh's Reach, immediately recognisable as such because it was superimposed for a few seconds on the black line on the map.

It pulled up, back and back, until the nearby facing coast of Gevork came into view, and the whole channel and the ocean, and then back farther to show the outline of the six great islands of the north. Cloud formations appeared as whorls of brilliant white. Farther and farther back, until the Southern continent filled the lower half of the screen, and then, almost unexpectedly, the image no longer filled the screen but became a circle, the whole globe of Ground, black and white and shades of grey against a background of solid black.

It was a view he had often imagined, but that no one had ever seen. For a moment Darvin thought it blurred, but then he blinked, and his vision cleared.

The process was reversed, as though the camera dropped again, hurtling down. The illusion of falling was so powerful that Darvin felt an atavistic urge to close his eyes and spread his wings. Noises in the crowd told him he was not alone in this; that others, indeed, had enacted the braking reflex.

The fall stopped. What now filled the screen was a view from above of the camp they stood in, as if seen from a not very high-flying airship. The very building they were in could be identified. Darvin braced himself against a surge to the windows. It came, just for a moment, and then everyone stood still and looked embarrassed. Somebody laughed. Even Markhan smiled.

The view changed: first to a similar but not identical camp or military base, and then to a rapid series of brief images of aircraft and rockets, familiar images that must have been recorded from Selohic and Gevorkian telekinematographic news displays, because fragments of voice-over in both languages boomed from the speakers.

Another familiar image appeared: the alien who had appeared on the first, cryptic communication. He stood facing the camera, which pulled in to show his face, dark and hairless with the characteristic scalp-tuft of the wingless.

'We – see – you – now,' he said. The movement of his lips had no relation to the sounds.

Darvin stood transfixed. The hairs over his spine stood up. Chills rushed down his cheeks and the sides of his neck. It was as if the alien's tiny eyes looked straight at him, and the words were literally true.

'We – say – not – hit – you – *grrr* – you.' A flash of aircraft and rockets again. 'We – say – no.'

'Open – door – trudge.' This was accompanied by a picture of, indeed, a stable door opening and a trudge shambling out. Darvin could only imagine that it was a view through the eyes of one of the trudges that gave off etheric transmissions.

'No – hit – trudge.' The picture was to the point.

'No – cut – trudge.' Again an illustration, a vivid one. A

collective wince shuddered through the crowd. Darvin felt a
stab of shame. He had speculated on this, but still it dismayed
him to see it verified, that the aliens had seized on this
accepted cruelty and thrown it back in humanity's face.

'We – see – you,' the alien said again. The view pulled back.
The alien walked over to a screen of its own and pointed. It was
a map of the land hemisphere of Ground. He pointed at three
places, locations marked with spots which the camera zoomed
in on and then drew back from. At a first guess, they were
Kraighor, Lassir, and the Great City of the Southern Rule.
Then a fourth: an island in the Equatorial Ocean.

The alien stepped aside. The map filled the screen. Black
lines crept from the three cities to converge on the island.

'We – meet – you – there.'

On the quay at Kraighor in the middle of the night under the
glint of the alien and artificial moon, Darvin felt around him
for the first time a tremor of the panic that he had once imagined. He could smell it. There was no reason for the crowd
to be there. Few would have friends or relatives among the
Project scientists and soldiery departing on the Southern ship.
There was no reason for people to take wing, every so often,
and wheel about like night-flitters above the dock. Yet he was
tempted to do so himself. One of the main streets away from
the dock opened on to a large square. Around that corner, out
of his line of sight, stood a high public screen. Its grey light
flickered on the sides of buildings and the faces of the crowds
watching it like a cold flame. Whatever words boomed from
its speakers were mangled by echoes and buried under the
susurrus of murmurs and wing-rustlings as if under snow.
Darvin knew what was being said, and wondered how this
new word from the Height would be taken.

Metal cables squealed on winches as supplies and apparatus

were craned on board. The ship had already been to New
Lassir. Gevorkian and Southern faces lined the rails. Darvin
recognised Lenoen, the astrologer, and Orro, but neither was
looking his way. The quay was too crowded for Darvin to leap
into the air. He shouldered his way towards the gangplank.

'Darvin!'

A tiny figure skittered over indignant heads, leapt to his
chest, grabbed the fur and nuzzled his collarbone.

'Oh! Hello, Handful.'

He looked around. 'Kwarive!'

She sidled through a gap towards him. He caught her neck
and stroked.

'It's great to see you! Thanks for coming all this way, you
shouldn't—'

'I'm not here to see you off,' said Kwarive.

'Then why—' He stopped, shocked and delighted. 'You're
coming on the expedition?'

'I most certainly am,' she said. 'Sight's orders.' She retrieved
Handful. 'I've been told it's very important to talk to him a
lot.'

'You'll have plenty of time for that,' said Darvin.

'Oh, it's not just me,' said Kwarive. 'All of us. Don't shirk
it.'

'What can I talk to him about? Astronomy?'

'Yes.'

'Astronomy!' said Handful. 'New moon!'

'You're off to a good start,' said Kwarive.

They had at last reached the gangplank.

'Cold bad meat,' said Handful, sniffing the air.

'No, that's salt,' said Kwarive. 'Salt water.'

'Salt water cold bad.'

'Yes,' said Darvin, looking down at the black gap beside his
feet. 'Keep that in mind.'

The deck was made of long planks of a soft, resilient wood,

like float-bark. The superstructure and fittings were of hard-wood and brass. Southern crewmen leapt and flitted in the rigging. The air smelled of tar and rock-oil derivatives. Selohics and Gevorkians mingled, eyeing each other, trying out phrases. Grenadiers and sabreurs debated tactics and con-trasted weapons in their martial creole. Scientists of the three powers quibbled in ungrammatical Orkan. Stewards and clerks stalked the deck, fussed over ladings and fastenings, fluttered frantic pages of lists on clipboards.

Chains rattled. Late arrivals and departures took wing to or from the ship. Sails snapped to the wind's attention. The deck began to vibrate. Water churned at the stern. The quay glided past. The town diminished. The western headland displayed its black muzzle and white teeth. The horizon became a line beneath the stars, that within two hours encircled the world.

After that it was just a sea voyage.

Black above the ocean rose the eroded volcanic sea-mount. White around the foot of its pleated basaltic cliffs boomed the surf. A cloud floated high above the island's plateau like a watercolour of ancient smoke. A hazy sun burned a line across the sea to the left. Through binoculars Darvin watched the soaring white specks of cliff-dwelling sea-flitters, and the broader and darker shapes of the island's dwellers, some already wing-beating their way out to meet the ship. The distance, though diminishing as the ship approached, looked terrifying.

'Fly over water bad,' said Handful, from Darvin's shoulder.

'Yes,' said Darvin, who had been impressing this on the kit for the past fortnight.

An unlikely-looking harbour, a black-sand beach at the bottom of a steep cove, became visible as the ship angled in. Locals descended on the deck, neck-bags and belt-baskets laden with lewd or cute carvings of pumice, or with unknown fruits of dubious hue. The island was a Southern possession, languidly disputed by Gevork; the inhabitants, for the most part, the descendants of Selohic mutineers and maroons. They spoke all three main languages, but at the same time.

'These people are going to be a problem,' said Kwarive. 'What if they're superstitious?'

'No "if" about it,' said Darvin. He inclined his head to the forward deck. Already the chief scientist and the ship's priest busied themselves with explanations and invocations.

'Fortunately there are only a few eights of them,' said Lenoen. 'A supply of stumblefruit has been set aside for their benefit.'

'Doesn't it grow on the island?'

'A sour vintage,' said Lenoen. 'The little carved idols are worth having, by the way. The prices drop on landfall.'

The originals of the carvings hove into view as the ship rounded into the harbour: on a slope that reached from the top of the cove to the lip of the plateau, gigantic statues, priapic or comic, leered down on the huddle of roosts around the tiny stone quay.

Sea-beasts, like flitters but the size of a man, plump and streamlined, swimming with webbed feet and short fleshy wings, escorted the ship in and leapt for scraps. Kwarive was almost as delighted with the sight as Handful.

'Water-wing! Water-wing!'

'Clever Handful,' Kwarive murmered. She grinned at Darvin. 'It's the same word as the scientific name: *aquopter*.'

Darvin looked down at the darting, splashing animals.

'They have big heads,' he said. 'Let's hope the aliens don't try to educate them.'

'Time to educate you,' said Kwarive. 'The cranial bulge contains oil, not brain.'

'Reputedly delicious,' said Lenoen, 'and it burns with a clear and smokeless flame.'

Kwarive pretended to cover Handful's ears.

'That's . . . horrible.'

'They swarm in the seas around the southern pole,' said Lenoen, sounding defensive.

The ship hove to, dwarfing the quay, the top deck overlooking the native roosts. The turbines reversed and fell silent. Ropes were flung and caught, and inexpertly wound around boulders. After some commotion the expedition disembarked.

'There will be no flying,' said Markhan, addressing the teams. 'The air currents and thermals around the cliffs are unpredictable and dangerous to all but the locals.'

Everyone gazed with envy at a brace of soaring natives, scouting high above for nests to rob.

'So how do we get up?' Darvin shouted.

Markhan pointed to a barely detectable zig-zag of steps hewn in the side of the cove. 'Climb.'

Two hours later they collapsed exhausted on the sharp grass of the clifftop. After a rest and a snack they made their way on, a long straggling line of four eights or so, mostly scientists, with here and there pairs of soldiers lugging etheric devices or sacks of supplies.

'We should have brought an aeroplane,' gasped Orro.

'And taken off from exactly where?' asked Darvin.

'A ramp built at the prow of the ship. Possibly assisted with . . . a catapult. Or rockets.'

Holder looked thoughtful.

'Big prick,' said Handful, touching a statue as they laboured past it.

'New word,' said Kwarive.

'Curiously,' said Lenoen, shaking sweat from his brows, 'the stone of the statues is not native to the island. Its nearest quarries are on our northern coast.'

'Hence your claim,' scoffed Holder. 'Despite the first historical sighting—'

'First in *whose* history?'

'Gentlemen,' said Kwarive. 'Do spare your breath.'

A call from Markhan brought the line to a welcome halt. Soldiers lowered their loads. Nollam cranked up a generator and sent a taped etheric message into the sky. He had kept this up day after day since leaving Kraighor, to no response from above. None came this time either.

'Onward!' shouted Markhan.

The slope was worse than the cliff. It seemed endless, without even risks and slips and panicked flapping and flying to break the monotony. Darvin's legs ached. Handful whined, demonstrating that he had learned a small vocabulary of complaint. Small lizzards and skitters scuttled through the grass and cringed from circling patrols of predatory flitters.

After another hour the plateau spread out before them, black and bare, littered with boulders, crusted with salt, spotted with semi-saline pools above which minute endemic insects buzzed in sinister clouds. Everyone slumped down. Water bottles were passed back and forth, dried fruit and meat munched. The Sun, now past noon, had dispersed the cloud and glared down from almost directly overhead in a deep blue sky. The heat was intense, the wind nugatory, every zephyr welcome. People stood and spread their wings, flapping slowly to cool their blood.

An etheric receiver buzzed. Nollam crouched before a tiny TK screen, shading it with his wings, then jumped up.

'They're coming!'

Yells of triumph and delight gave way to apprehension. Nobody knew how the aliens would arrive. Orro had talked about a gliding vehicle, Holder about a rocket descending on a pillar of fire. Soldiers, their movement sluggish in the heat and stumbling on the rough rock, spread banners across boulders: the golden lizard of the South, the claw of the Reach, the roundel of the Realm. People made their way behind large rocks, low pinnacles, and banks and little cliffs where the ground had slipped aeons ago. They stood or crouched in that notional shelter and scanned the sky. Binoculars were reluctantly lent and eagerly borrowed. Markhan circulated like an anxious teacher, warning against looking through the lenses at the Sun. The Sun slipped away from the zenith.

It was Orro who spotted the arrival first. He shouted and pointed straight up. Darvin swung his binoculars around and saw a black dot. Sunlight flashed on it, and it became a still-tiny shape, with a hint of rectangularity. With a great effort of goodwill he handed the binoculars to Kwarive.

'Wow,' she said. 'No rockets, no jets, no wings.'

'The wingless have mastered gravity,' said Darvin, restraining himself from grabbing back the glasses.

'They have not,' said Orro, with better eyesight or better binoculars. 'I see a rope above it. It is descending like a load on a crane.'

'Where might such a crane be mounted?' said Holder. 'On the moon?'

'On *a* moon,' said Kwarive. 'Remember how the alien moon appeared last night – directly overhead? That's what it's hanging from.'

Darvin stifled a laugh, embarrassed by his companion's ignorance of physics; Holder guffawed. Orro removed the glasses from his eyes to frown, and without thinking relinquished them to Darvin's grasp. This time he saw the now fast-descending thing as a tall box, and saw too the line stretching into the blue above it.

'She's right,' Orro was saying. 'Why should that be more absurd than a satellite staying above the same spot on the ground? Even you, Darvin, were wondering aloud not too long ago why it didn't fall down. Oh, and the binoculars, if you please, old chap.'

Darvin passed them back with as much grace as he could.

'It isn't *that*,' he said, trying not to let irritation infiltrate his voice. 'I'm not saying it's absurd, or impossible in principle. But in practice! The length of line that would be involved is simply inconceivable.'

'One wonders why the aliens bother coming here,' said Kwarive. 'You know so much about them already.'

The descending box was now visible without binoculars. It was obvious from the exclamations around him that most people still shared his first assumption, that the thing levitated. As it drew closer the line became apparent to the naked eye, and the marvel at the sight only increased. The box now looked in parts transparent. Wisps of vapour puffed from its sides every few seconds: course corrections, Darvin guessed. Its speed seemed to increase as it descended, but Darvin knew for certain that this was an illusion. After another couple of minutes and several more corrections, it came to rest on the rocky plain a few eights-of-eights of paces away from them.

No shouts of command could stop the civilians walking forward. The soldiers too, after an urgent argument, ran to keep pace. The order they obeyed was to keep their crossbows slung.

As though at an unseen barrier, everyone stopped at the same place. The box now looked much bigger than it had seemed before. The afternoon heat hung heavy. The lurid pools stank like ammonia. Creaking and cracking noises echoed across the rocky flats. A door opened in the side of the box. With one accord everyone took a couple of paces back.

A wingless giant stepped out. Its body was black with a dull gleam. Around its head was a glassy globe. The alien stopped, the globe moving this way and that. It seemed to see them. It raised both hands slowly from its sides, above its head, and walked forward.

The urge to flee almost possessed Darvin. Eight eights of steps – its steps – away, the alien stopped. It lifted the globe from around its head, and placed it in the crook of one arm. The other hand it kept upraised. Black-faced, fuzz-scalped, this was to all appearances the same alien who had spoken on the screen.

Someone remembered to take a photograph. Nollam, huddled over his apparatus, muttered curses to himself.

The alien reached to the round collar upon which the helmet had sat. It pulled something like a stiff cord to one of its small flat ears, and another to the front of its lips. Its lips moved.

'Good day,' it said.

Nobody moved or said anything. It struck Darvin that in all their planning for this encounter, no one had thought to establish that priority. He glanced sideways at Markhan. The chief scientist stood with knees trembling and wings furled tight. Darvin noticed that the same was true of himself. He tried, just as an experiment, to take a step forward. His foot would not move.

As he looked down he glimpsed a forward movement and heard a voice.

'I'm a biologist,' said Kwarive. 'This is a new species.'

She was on her way before he could stop her. She walked straight up to the giant. She stopped just beyond his reach and spread out her wings.

'Good day,' she said, her voice firm and loud. 'Welcome to Ground.'

'Welcome,' repeated the alien.

'You spoke of trudges,' said Kwarive. 'Here is a trudge kit.'

The alien reached forward and took the small shape in its huge hands.

'This is a trudge?' said the alien.

'I trudge, me,' came Handful's thin voice. 'You man smell bad.'

The alien's shoulders shook. Its voice made a deep repeated bark that might have been laughter. Darvin could see the kit flinch and squirm. The alien handed him back to Kwarive.

Handful immediately buried his nose in her shoulder, as Darvin could detect from Kwarive's movements. The alien was looking down at its hands.

'Shit,' said the alien.

For the past two eight-days, all over Seloh and Gevork, scientists and Sight agents and civil servants had been talking to trudges. They had been doing so in confined but comfortable spaces, none of which were barred with metal or surrounded with mesh. Some of the trudges had been old and angry, bitter at being made conscious at a time when they had nothing to look forward to but death, and nothing to look back on but a maimed and brutish life. There had been suicides. There had been attacks, some fatal. Others of the trudges had been young, some even younger than Handful, some older. A few had been mature, wary and wise. They had kept their understanding to themselves, and only their etheric emissions had betrayed them. Some of them could not be coaxed to speak. Others talked until they and their interlocutors dropped with exhaustion.

Signals beamed forth from cunning secret coils an alien alchemy had spun close to their spines. The ever-extended vocabulary of the trudges reached the sky.

Beside that etheric flood was another. Every TK transmitter in Seloh's Reach repeated the proclamation from the Height, and every one in Gevork the new decree from the Rock of Lassir. They repeated it until every citizen had heard that trudges were no longer to be mutilated, that any trudge who could speak was to be sold at a good price to the Reach or the Realm and then emancipated as a free worker, with compensation; that all trudges, articulate or not, were to be treated without violence. More to the point, they repeated it until even the aliens could not fail to understand it.

'I do not understand it,' said the alien to Markhan. The two stood at the focus of a silent semicircle. 'You are to let go the trudges?'

'Yes.'

'Like . . .' The alien threw out his hands.

'Yes.'

'With no kick or hit among you?'

'With some hurt,' said Markhan. The vocabulary the alien had learned was still restricted and concrete. 'But we must. The trudges speak. They too are men.'

The alien was silent for a while.

'Your fight men make ready,' he said. He pointed to the soldiers. He made zooming movements with his spread hands. 'Fight in the sky. Drop hurt on you and them roosts. We say no.'

'We make ready to fight men from the sky,' said Markhan. 'Ground is ours.'

The alien squatted down. His hands touched the ground. 'Ground is yours,' he said. 'We men from the sky will not fight you. Ground is yours.'

'Good,' said Markhan. 'Then we will not fight you men from the sky. But other men come from the sky. We make ready for them.'

The alien rotated his head from side to side. 'No, no,' he said. 'No other men come from sky. Only us men from sky.'

'We hear other voices from the sky,' said Markhan. 'Not only your voice.'

'*Ah!*' said the alien. He looked about for a moment, then pointed to the sky in the east. 'Green suns are our roost. You hear voices from green suns.'

'No,' said Markhan. He glanced over his shoulder and beckoned to Nollam, then pointed west and then north. 'We hear a voice from a white sun, and from a yellow sun.'

The alien rocked back on his heels. 'What?' he said.

INTERLUDE: WHITE AIR

Synchronic stood in the garden for the last time, and looked
out over a drab and depleted landscape. The only living thing
in sight was grass. The trees had been felled or dug up. The
lakes and rivers had been drained. The animals had been
slaughtered or herded indoors. The grass itself was torn or
stamped by the tracks and treads of the huge machines that
now stalked across the devasted scene like alien invaders.
Domes had replaced many buildings, or covered those of special significance. Other buildings had sprouted new
equipment: aerials and defence batteries, solar-power collectors, long tubular connecting corridors, closed-system
recycling plant. Windows had been sealed, roofs diamond-
plated, doors replaced by airlocks. The whole terrible process
followed a standard schematic, for preparing the habitat for an
almost unthinkable combination of drive failure and unavoid-
able collision. It had taken four months.

The warning sirens echoed through the now barren habitat
like a shout inside an empty drum. Synchronic sighed and
walked back to the house. The airlock closed behind her. She

entered one of the rooms where the children watched from behind the reinforced windows and moved to spread reassurance, picking up one child after another, touching heads and shoulders.

'It's going to be exciting,' she said. 'You'll never have seen it so dark. I'll keep the lights off in here, so we can see out. We'll see all the lights of the towns.'

'Why does the sunline have to go out?'

'We need the power plants to keep us warm and well,' said Synchronic. 'And to take us to our new homes. We'll have light and heat from the real sun there.'

'I'm scared.'

'There's nothing to be scared of. Here, let me hold you up so you can watch it all.'

The sirens sounded again. Outside nothing moved except the great machines and tiny space-suited figures.

The sunline went out. The children gasped. Some of them cried. Despite herself Synchronic shivered.

As their retinae adjusted, she and the children saw that the darkness of the cylinder was not complete. Clusters of light were sprinkled across its whole interior.

'Look at all the towns!' Synchronic said. 'Let's put the lights on, and everyone will be able to see us too, and they'll know we're all right.'

Weeks later she stood again, this time alone, before the window and watched the air fall like snow. As more and more molecules crystallised out their fall met less and less resistance, until the last specks hurtled down through vacuum. In time the entire internal atmosphere of the cylinder lay over everything like a thin layer of frost.

Across that chill scene the space-suited colonists swarmed in the tens of thousands, the machines in the hundreds. They still had much work to do.

Later: 'Look, we're all getting lighter.'

Later still: 'We're all floating! Isn't this fun! Oh, let me help you clean that up.'

Then: 'Look! The sun!'

The ends of the cylinder drifted away. The cylinder itself broke up into a thousand pieces, each an independent habitat, moving slowly apart. As their transfer orbit took them to the rich resources of the asteroids, the frozen air warmed up and streamed out behind them, to form the tails of a thousand comets, and the banners of a coming conquest.

TWENTY-ONE

But the Sky, My Lady! The Sky!

LEARNING THE WORLD

14 376:10:21 12.17

Is this thing *live*?

14 376:10:21 12.18

I see it is. How embarrassing. But I suppose it does none of us any harm to be reminded of our adolescent stumblings and fumblings. And I have to add, the person I was ten years ago got some things right. For the rest, well, my plea to the reader is to remember: people change. We grow up.

I don't think, though, that I'll add more entries to this long-neglected biolog. It seems fair to sum up, and to close it. I don't flatter myself that everybody who reads this will know what has become of me and the people I mentioned, or even, perhaps – for not everything is recorded, and not all who remember are willing to recount – the early history of our settlement around the Destiny Star. If you, dear reader, are looking at this across some great gulf of time and increase of knowledge, spare me your condescension. You too were young once, and ignorant once, and from a future standpoint – perhaps your own – you are young and ignorant still.

A case in point. Two years ago, the first instalment of a continuing stream of advice arrived from the Red Sun system. The burden of their frantic admonition was to avoid all contact with the indigenes, to stealth all our activities, to – as it were – act natural, in the hope that observers on the planet would mistake our arrival for some unusual but non-sentient phenomenon. The reason given, with frantic insistence, was that awareness of a vastly superior intelligence might cause the aliens' culture to collapse from a sheer sense of futility.

Ha ha ha. A few days before Red Sun's advice arrived, a clunky robot probe from Destiny II came snooping by.

The bat people want nothing from us. After they found that *they* had discovered two more radio sources, from hundreds of light-years away, that we had not so much as thought to look for, they held us not in awe. In their eyes we became, I suspect, merely the closest of the aliens that *they* had discovered. Our standing with them dropped even further when our own conflicts with each other became impossible to conceal. We assure them that the really violent episodes are few, and that only machines and resources are harmed and consumed in them, but they're understandably not impressed.

I still blame Synchronic, frankly. It was her idea to steal a march on us while we were preoccupied with the contact. The resentments from that will take a long time to cool. Writs, claims and counterclaims fly across the system to this day, and every so often some more tangible exchanges take place. It's all very embarrassing, like a fight in front of the children.

But then – who are the children here? We were so certain that the aliens were about to plunge into conflict, between their powers and with the trudges. Our arguments were over whether and how to step in and sort it out. Yet as soon as they became aware of us and thought we were a threat to them all, they united – grudgingly and with mutual suspicion, it's true – and as soon as they found rational beings emerging among the trudges, they treated them as equals. Well, perhaps not quite equals, but at least as rational beings like themselves.

In a sense, it's we who are learning from them. The genetic machinery for transmitters still functions along with that for speech, and we can enter the virtualities at any time. I used to do that a lot, though not for some time now. As the translation software came to have more and more to work on, as the emancipated trudges began to take a full part in society, so the translation became more colloquial and precise. It created a sense of familiarity with the bat people's institutions and ways that may be in part illusory. Are these teetering towers of logs and branches, mats and screens, within which alembics and astrolabes are plied, and little beasts cut up, and curious devices of glass and wire devised, really universities? Are these vast caverns of chirping, fluttering, sometimes brawling crowds really parliaments and councils of the realm? Or is that just another kind of translation, in which some subtlety – and indeed crudity – is lost? I know that when the verbal translation is off, I see things differently – what I'd seen as a nod or a smile becomes a twitch or a grimace; what had seemed a comfortable and well-appointed dwelling becomes a reeking hut on stilts; what had looked like an appetising meal a revolting carcass and a heap of rotting fruit.

But for all that, as I say, I hope we can learn from them. They are a more rational and kinder species. I have two theories to explain this. One is immediate and, as it were, specific. The other is more general, and one I must approach less directly, by way of some recent events.

The specific theory is this, and it's very simple: they never bore the yoke. Because they had the trudges, they never enslaved each other. Because they had vast herds of wild prey and forests of fruit trees, they never toiled in fields. They fought, yes, they had their lords and kingdoms, but the discontented always had the possibility of flight. To cripple a human like a trudge was unthinkable, for all but the worst crimes. Compared with us, they had in every sense an easier ascent.

I turn now to the recent events, and my provisional final theory, which is at the same time my solution to the problem that bothered me from the first discovery of the aliens: a problem now increased, at the latest discovery of an alien radio source, thirteen times over. A Galaxy we had thought was empty is lighting up with intelligence, and all at once. What is strangest in that baffling simultaneity is the singularity of our precedence; and this I think I have at last understood.

The ship, with the old cones now joined to a new and almost full cylinder, began not many days ago the long burn of its acceleration out of this system, and on to the next. In times past, Constantine once told me, it used to be hundreds of years after a ship arrived in a new system that it departed for another. Today the interval is down to a decade: turnaround time, no more or less. Every new departure selects, yet again, for the footloose.

People change. Some you wouldn't expect have left with the ship. I'd never have figured Grant for someone who wanted to be a founder, and to spend the next three hundred and seventy-two years turning that full tank into a spacious habitat. But there you go – he sold up his waterworld orbital resort business and bought his stake. Personally I put it down to the novel – after researching it he wanted to live the story, not write it.

Horrocks was a more painful loss in a way. As you might guess from my teenage rattlings, he and I did eventually hit it off, at a crew party shortly after the contact. So that distasteful little genetic bet that (I soon learned) had been made by Synchronic and Constantine paid off. Probably enough to buy them both a drink, anyway. Grant, Genome, Horrocks and I formed a complex mutual orbit for years.

And then Horrocks went off to the founder-controlled asteroids and shacked up with Synchronic. I still shake my head over that. It's not unheard of, but it seems almost indecent.

But it's Constantine, strangely enough, that I'll miss the most. He was never more than a gene-father when I was a child, except for that one wondrous incident when he took me to see the engine. But in the years since the contact I've seen more of him, and he's always been understanding and kind, if a little distant.

I called him up just as the ship was leaving. He wasn't as busy as I'd feared. We talked a little about what are, to me, old times, and new ideas.

'And what do you think now?' he asked me.

'I have a theory,' I said.

'You always do,' he said. 'Grant was right about you, back in the day. Your thinking is metaphysical.'

I laughed. 'You read that?'

'Oh yes.'

'Well,' I said, 'here's my latest metaphysical theory. You remember when you took me to see the engine?'

He nodded after a moment. The light-speed lag was only just becoming noticeable.

'You said then that you had named it. You never told me why, but that I would know some day. I once thought I knew, but now I'm not so sure. Anyway, this is my theory. The engine generates new universes all the time. These universes are similar but not identical to the one we live in, yes?'

'To the best of our knowledge, yes,' he said. 'Information is conserved.'

'Well then,' I said, 'what that means is that in some of these universes, there will be starships with cosmogonic engines of their own.'

His expression was inscrutable. 'That would seem to follow, yes.'

'So,' I went on, 'just as the birth of universes from black holes selects over cosmic time for universes with laws of physics such that black holes can be formed, hence universes with stars and galaxies, so the birth of universes from starship engines selects for more universes in which starships can exist. And what more likely universes to have many starships in than ones in which intelligence emerges all over the place at almost the same time?'

This time the pause was longer than the light-speed lag could account for.

'There may be something in what you say,' he said. 'What inference do you draw from it?'

I swallowed. 'That we're not the first,' I said. 'Not the original universe, by a long, long way. We're a long way down the line from the first universe in which somebody looked at a high-energy physics experiment and saw that it could fly to the stars.'

'That's a good inference,' said Constantine. 'It's one I once made myself, and—'

The screen went fuzzy. I adjusted the gain. The image came back.

'I'm losing you,' he said. 'It's time we said goodbye, just in case, and then we can carry on until we're too far apart.'

'Goodbye, Constantine,' I said. 'I just wanted to ask. You said information is conserved. How *much* information?'

'More than you might think,' said the Oldest Man.

The picture and sound became hopelessly indistinct. He may have said more after that, but I didn't catch it and could never retrieve it. The transmitters the bat people build back there on Destiny II are good, but not good enough to reach us now as we accelerate away.

But as I go about my work with the rest of the crew I'm haunted by two thoughts. One is of a man in the Moon Caves, looking at a high-energy physics experiment and looking up and saying, 'But the sky, my lady! The sky!'

For when I imagine that man, I see Constantine.

The other is more troubling. If cosmic evolution works on the scale that I outlined to Constantine, and that he seemed to find plausible, and if as he said information is conserved – then perhaps those like us who come first are changed the least, and are thus doomed always to find themselves in a universe in which they are in every sense primitive, and to encounter species wiser and kinder than they.

Long before the starships and the Moon Caves, these words were written:

> **We teach that the soul is immortal; we teach that there is a future life; we teach that there is a Heaven in the ages far away; but not for us . . .**

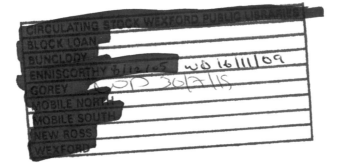
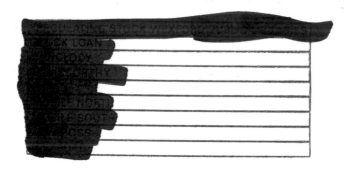